Madeleine always loved writing stories and this one had been in her head for many years. Now in her late 70s, she had a decision to make: write it or forget it, so she wrote it and hopes you enjoy it.

To my grandson, Ellis, who encouraged me enthusiastically to try to publish and who one day may actually read the story.

Madeleine Wilson

FROM WELLIES AND CHAPPED LEGS TO BROGUES

AUSTIN MACAULEY PUBLISHERS™

LONDON · CAMBRIDGE · NEW YORK · SHARJAH

A CIP catalogue record for this title is available from the British Library.

ISBN 9781528919104 (Paperback)
ISBN 9781528919111 (Kindle e-book)
ISBN 9781528962568 (ePub e-book)

www.austinmacauley.com

First Published (2019)
Austin Macauley Publishers Ltd
25 Canada Square
Canary Wharf
London
E14 5LQ

To my daughter, Rebecca, for reminding me I had started the story many years ago and encouraging me to continue; and to my friend Peter for his constant encouragement and patience due to my lack of computer skills.

Chapter 1

The five children looked down into the hole in the ground where they had laid the dead bird they had tried to save earlier in the day. Rebecca said a small prayer, filled in the hole with soil, stuck the cross made from lollipop sticks into the mound and placed a flower on top.

"Will the worms eat it up now?" asked Jack.

"Don't talk about it," said Sally, screwing up her face, unable to bear the thought of it. "Let's go and play."

They all ran down the hill to the playing area that was flat and had a large grass verge where they would congregate and play. Tom had gone off on his paper round and joined them on his return.

"Dog 'as dug up t'bird, and thi dad as put it int bin," Tom announced.

Rebecca gasped, her jaw dropped, and she covered her mouth with her hand, then burst into laughter. The others joined in, and there was a discussion as to whether the bird's spirit would have gone to heaven as soon as it died, or when it was buried, or would it be trapped in the bin because the lid was on?

No one but David had noticed the bus stop and his mother alight.

"I've got to go now," he said, and off he went, hands in pockets, head down.

Moments later, his mother staggered past the children, her head wobbling like a puppet's, and she blinked very hard and focused on the group of children watching her as she negotiated the pavement and said, "Hello," before she tottered off singing and swinging her handbag.

"You could see her tits," said Tom, who couldn't take his eyes off her blouse in disarray.

Rebecca couldn't take her eyes off the bright red lipstick and long red fingernails, and as she passed, felt there was something familiar about her although she didn't know who she was, as did none of the other children, because she was hardly around during the day where the children were.

Rebecca spotted her father waving at her from up the hill so she said cheerio to her friends and went home for tea. She ran down into the garden to look where the little grave had been, but her father had raked over the soil and there was no trace of it ever being there, not even the little cross. As she walked past the bin, eyes forward, she quickly lifted the lid and replaced it, just in case the spirit had been trapped.

She washed her hands at the sink and sat down at the table for tea. She loved Monday tea times, because they always had vegetables left over from Sunday lunch fried up in the pan, so it got burnt on the bottom and was crunchy, with cold meat, and if there was no cold meat, they had bacon.

"I've seen a drunk lady just now," said Rebecca. "She got off the bus and went onto Bury Street. Some of her fingers were brown, but she had long red fingernails and red lips."

Rebecca's parents knew who she was but were reluctant to continue the conversation, so the subject was changed.

"It's such a lovely evening, shall we take Barney for a walk on the wood top after tea?" said her father.

An hour later, they were sitting snuggling together on the wood top, whilst Barney snuffled around amongst the trees and finally settled at their feet. They looked across the valley at the patchwork of fields, some brown, some green, some yellow. There were horses peering over a wall where a farmer was watering his vegetable patch, and the only sound echoing through the valley was that of squawking geese from the distant farm yard.

The air chilled, and it was time to go home.

For as long as she could remember, they had gone collecting blackberries for pies—and if there was enough sugar, to make jam—and holly for the house at Christmas, but since her father had introduced her to the beauty and detail of what was around her, she was fascinated by it all and collected acorns and ash keys and rose hips and kept them in a bowl in her room.

"Why do you keep doing this?" asked her mother as she moved the bowl on the window ledge. "What's the point?"

"When they die, I know it's nearly winter, and the wood has gone to sleep," replied Rebecca.

On their way home, they met Hobo, the tramp who carried his belongings in a pram. He wandered in and out of the village, no one knew where he came from or where he went, but unless he needed to go to a shop, he avoided being around when the children were out playing for they would goad him and interfere with his belongings. Mr Brown would always acknowledge Hobo in a polite manner, and sometimes, if he passed his home, they would chat about the weather or garden, but nothing personal. Rebecca would stand and look at him for he was nothing like she imagined a tramp would be. His hair was long and white and clean, not matted, and his beard was white and neat too and didn't have any food trapped in it, and he didn't smell. He had kind eyes and spoke in a gentle manner, and Mr Brown often pondered what could have happened in this man's life to put him in this place.

The following day, Rebecca was expecting to go into town for new school shoes and a treat in a cafe, but there had been no mention of it, so at breakfast, Rebecca asked, "Are we going to town today?"

"Don't bother me now," snapped her mother. "We'll see."

Mr Brown peered at his wife over his glasses, said nothing, picked up his hat and sandwiches, pecked Rebecca on the cheek and left. Recently, her parents had been arguing, and she didn't like it at all and buried her head under the pillows if she could hear raised voices when she had gone to bed. This place was her sanctuary, her protection against things that hurt her or she was afraid of, and something was happening that she didn't understand. She would lie for a long time and remember how they used to go for picnics on weekends and play silly games on an evening when it was cold outside. She remembered going downstairs one evening for a drink, and her mother was sitting on her father's knee. He pretended to be so surprised he dropped her mother on the floor, and they all piled into a heap laughing, with Barney yapping round them, but remembering made her realise this was a long time ago; there were more arguments now than funny half-hours.

Rebecca had gone to her room not knowing whether she was going for new shoes or not. Her mother went to the bottom of the stairs and called her. "Go out and play," she shouted. "We'll go next weekend for your new shoes." Rebecca was disappointed but went out to play with the others after lunch, spending the rest of the morning in her room re-arranging her bits and pieces that she treasured.

Having played hide and seek for a while, the children were having a rest and sat in a line on the wall. Unusually, David had stayed with them all afternoon. The children tolerated him rather than made him welcome at first, but he could be quite funny, never said anything bad about anybody, and in time, he became part of the group. He had been given a pair of shoes which were slightly too big for him, and as they sat on the wall, one dropped off. He was wearing them because his wellies rubbed his calves and made a sore red ring round them. Tom jumped down, and as he picked up the shoe, a piece of cardboard fell out, and you could see daylight through a hole in the sole. Tom snatched the other shoe which was just the same.

"Are these so you can see where you are going?" sneered Tom, as he poked a finger through the hole and wiggled it before he tossed the shoes to the others who threw them around from one to the other.

"Give me back my shoes," said David.

"Come and get them," said Tom, a shoe in each hand, jumping from side to side, enjoying the moment.

"Wop 'im one, son" said a voice, and all the children turned and stared at the woman they had seen drunk some days earlier. They fell silent, realising that this was David's mother leaning on the arm of a man dressed in a soldier's uniform. Rebecca took the shoes off Tom and handed them to David.

"Sorry," she said and left to go home without saying a word to the others.

David couldn't look at her or the others and ran off in his bare feet, carrying his shoes. The man lunged at the group of children, and they scattered like flies and went home.

Rebecca had walked slowly up the hill feeling very sorry for David, for the shoe episode was bad enough, but now they all knew who his mother was, and that was bound to make his life more difficult. David thought his heart would burst and was dreading what lay ahead for him. He loved his mother deep down, and he knew she was different from other mothers, and although he felt guilty about it, he couldn't help feeling ashamed of her. Although he noticed how the other children lived, he accepted his life would never be like that, but it didn't stop him wishing things could change.

He wandered off and sat in one of the derelict houses whilst his mother took her soldier home. He stayed there crying and thinking until he heard the soldier say 'cheerio' to his mother and leave.

Tom caught Rebecca up. "Go away, you are wicked and unkind," she said.

"It was only a bit of fun," said Tom, "but just fancy that woman being his mum."

Rebecca didn't answer. She didn't talk to her parents about what had just happened, but it was ironic that her own school shoes became a bone of contention later that evening, after she had gone to bed.

Nobody actually mentioned shoes whilst Rebecca was there, but she could hear her father brushing for all he was worth to make the best of her scuffed school shoes which she wasn't sure would still fit her. If they didn't, she would have to wear her best shoes, she decided. She wasn't going to be laughed at or get blisters.

David knew that he would be the target of cruel remarks about his mother the next time the children saw him, and he didn't want it to be at school, but he only managed to join them for a game of cricket on the evening of the first day back at school. Only Tom tried to goad him, but David ignored him and carried on bowling until he bowled Tom out, who argued he was not ready, and the wicket had fallen over and he hadn't been bowled out, but the rest of the children shouted 'out, out' so he wielded the bat at David and threw it on the floor.

"Get 'im," said Tom and started chasing David, and the other boys joined in, perhaps thinking it was a game. David fled, ran across the main road towards the railway embankment and stood on the wall to look back to see if they were coming. They were; they started shouting when they saw him. He panicked and fell off the wall into the brambles and nettles, and unable to stem his fall, he rolled and rolled and thought he would never stop. Suddenly, he hit something hard and fell into a black hole with a thud.

His body was screaming at him, having been ripped by the brambles and stung with the nettles, and he could feel blood running down his neck and arms and legs. He heard a sound in the corner and someone lit a torch—it was Hobo!

"Shh!" Hobo said, putting a finger to his mouth. "Don't be afraid." He stood up and pushed the corrugated roof back into place and stood holding it until the boys had gone and all was quiet. It was well camouflaged, and in any case, the boys would not be crawling through the brambles; they had run down the path.

David was coiled up in the corner, shivering, in shock, smarting all over from nettle stings. His shirt had rolled up his back and not protected him at all.

"You are safe with me," said Hobo. "Let me help you. Take off your shirt and let me see. What is your name?"

"David, and I have to go home."

Hobo lit some candles, put a pan of water to heat on his primus stove and took a small bottle of antiseptic and some cotton wool from a tin with a red cross on it. He put some antiseptic in warm water to bathe and try and clean the bleeding wounds.

David pulled back, knowing it was going to hurt.

"It will hurt a little bit," said Hobo, "but I can tell you are a brave boy, and it's very important that these wounds are cleansed." He did what he could until he felt it was too much to expect the boy to stand anymore pain, so he made some tea and they sipped it in silence.

"I will take you home and make sure you are safe," said Hobo. "Can I ask you not to tell anyone that I am here?"

"I will never tell anyone; you can trust me," said David. He meant it and never did.

They walked up the hill with David carrying his blood-stained shirt for he couldn't bear to wear it. Some of the gashes were still bleeding, and he was a pitiful sight.

"My ma is at the pub, working," said David.

They walked towards the pub and Hobo went in. Heads turned as he walked towards the bar and quietly spoke to the barmaid.

"Are you David's mother?" he asked.

Defensively, she replied, "Yes, what about him?"

"He needs you," replied Hobo. "He's been in a harrowing situation and is outside waiting for you." He turned and went outside and waited for her with David.

Moments later, she came out of the pub with the landlady and stopped dead in her tracks at the sight of her son's little body, blotched, swollen and striped with bleeding gashes. She ran towards him instinctively to hug him, but he put his hands up and stepped back to stop her.

"What the hell happened here?" she asked Hobo.

"David will tell you, and you must take him to the doctor's tomorrow without fail," replied Hobo. He nodded, smiled at David and was gone.

The landlady had gone inside and returned with some old sheets for David's mum to use as bandages. "I've never seen anything as bad as that in my life," she said and shook her head.

David related the story to his mother as they walked home and told her how kind Hobo had been.

"Where did he come from?" asked his mother.

"I don't know," replied David, which was kind of true, "but I'm glad he was there to help me."

The night was horrendous for David. The house was cold, he couldn't bear anything to touch him so he couldn't wrap a cover round him, and to lay on his bed was an impossibility.

His mother's mind was festering in anger thinking about what could have happened if David hadn't stopped and a train had been coming, and she made up her mind that this was in no way over.

The morning came, and they had some toast and a cup of tea. This was only the second day back to school, and David was upset because he just couldn't face going. His mother gently slipped his other shirt on and looked down at his blood-stained trousers and socks. She wasn't going to do anything about them until she had done what she had to do.

"Come on," she said.

"Where to?" asked David.

"School," she said and grasped his hand and dragged him off, picking up the blood-stained shirt from the night before.

"No," said David, "I can't."

"Yes, you can," she said. "We're not staying, but we are going now."

David was dreading it and couldn't work out why they had to go at all, but nothing prepared him for what was about to happen.

The children were all gathered in the big hall for assembly, and the headmaster was just about to announce the hymn they should sing when the hall doors were flung open and David, dragged by his mother, marched to the stage down the centre aisle and up the steps. The children gasped, then fell silent, but some were secretly glad he was still alive. The headmaster and members of staff had expressions of pity and disbelief.

"What happened here?" asked the headmaster.

"You might well ask," said David's mother and took off his shirt and turned him around for all to see. She turned to face the children and stretched out her arm and pointed her nicotine-stained finger in an arch sweeping across the room.

"Some little buggers down there know," she said. "So when you sing hymns and pray, make sure they know the meaning. SOME NEED TO WORK ON IT."

The headmaster took David and his mother to his office.

13

"Whilst I am truly sorry for what happened to David, I have to point out that it happened out of school hours and has nothing to do with the school," said the headmaster.

"Yes, it does," retorted David's mother, "because they are all here receiving no guidance. Just singing hymns and reciting prayers without understanding the meaning behind them is not good. I know what my reputation is in the village. If there was another way to pay the bills and put food on the table, I would do it; nevertheless, I teach my son about kindness and tolerance, he's never in trouble for doing bad things, he avoids confrontation and you should know he does well at school."

"It's up to parents to teach their children the difference between right and wrong," said the headmaster, struggling to continue the conversation, he was so taken aback. He looked at David, who was crying and trying to put his shirt back on.

The headmaster's secretary came into the office with two shirts, a pair of trousers and a pair of socks.

"These were donated by pupils who left this year because they were having new uniforms. Please, will you accept them?" asked the secretary.

"Thank you very much," said David's mother. "That will be a big help. He doesn't have any more trousers, and the blood stain will not come out, thank you."

They left the school via the side door, avoiding any more contact with the children and headed for the doctor, who looked wide-eyed at David, almost as if he couldn't believe what he was seeing.

"What happened here, then?" he asked.

David's mother explained as the doctor pulled out thorns with a pair of tweezers and dressed the wounds.

"Come back tomorrow to have new dressings, and try not to get them wet. It's important that you come; you'll be in real trouble if they become infected."

David and his mother called at the library for a book for David and returned home. The stinging from the nettles had eased, and David was able to lie on his bed, and he was so exhausted, he did manage to sleep. His mother also slept in the chair, wrapped in a blanket, and when she awoke, she cooked a sausage each and some mashed potato. David was about to settle with his book.

"Not yet, David," said his mother. "It's not over yet, we have calls to make." She led him to Stuart's house and knocked on the door. Stuart's mother opened it.

"Please come in," she said. "I wanted to come and see you but don't know where you live. Stuart has been very upset and knows not to engage with any of Tom's pranks in the future." David's mother had removed his shirt so they could see the extent of his injuries, which made Stuart burst into tears.

"I'm very sorry, David, it was just supposed to be a game," Stuart gulped.

"Ok," said David and just wanted to be out of there.

They continued to a further three houses down the street to the homes of the other boys involved in the chase, and David wished he had never told his mother who they were. His shirt was off, on, off, on and he was really fed up and wanted to go home. The next house was Tom's.

"Oh no," said David, trying to break free from his mother's hand. "He'll just go for me again the first chance he gets, and he'll lie and say he wasn't there."

"He can't lie," said his mother. "All the others said he started it." She banged on the door.

Tom's father opened it, his stomach was hanging over his trousers, his vest was dirty, his chest was hairy and he needed a shave.

"I need you to see what your son caused last night, and I need you to deal with it," said David's mother. Off came the shirt again!

"Don't come here laying down the law," said Tom's father and was about to shut the door.

"If you don't, I shall tell your wife," said David's mother.

"She won't do owt about it," said Tom's father.

"She might do something if I tell her what and where your tattoo is," said David's mother. She peered at him, raised her eyebrows with a look that said, "Changed your mind, then?"

Tom's father opened the door, so they could enter and took off his belt.

"Tom, get down here," he said. Tom, unaware that David and his mother were in the house, ran down the stairs. He looked at his father, who just nodded at him. He bent over the chair and took the whipping, wincing but not crying out. David's mother was uneasy, sensing things that were going on between Tom and his father were not good for a child. David squirmed; he just didn't want to be there.

"That's enough," said David's mother. She looked at Tom and pushed David in front of him. "Look what you caused," she said. "Remember, Tom, if you are always causing trouble, no one will want to spend time with you. Just leave David alone, because if you don't, I'll be back." She slipped David's shirt back on, and as she left, she turned and winked at Tom's father. What did that mean? She left him wondering!

They returned home, and because there was no money for the electricity meter, David was left with a candle and his book whilst his mother went to work.

Every day, for the rest of the week, David went and had his wounds dressed, and on the last day, the doctor gave him some witch hazel in a bottle and some cotton wool for his mother to use on the wounds until they had healed properly.

"This will help soothe anything that is still hurting, just dab it on gently," said the doctor.

"Thank you," said David and left the surgery to walk home when he saw Hobo walking towards him.

"Now then, young man, how are you feeling?" asked Hobo.

"Much better now, thank you," replied David. "I think I would have stayed in the hole and died if you hadn't been there to take care of me."

Hobo smiled. "Keep the wounds clean," he said. "Are you still having them dressed?"

"Just been for the last time now," said David. "But the doctor has given me this stuff. I am going back to school on Monday."

"Glad to see you are doing well," said Hobo, and he turned and went towards the shops.

Over the next few weeks, David crept carefully and in secret to visit Hobo, making sure there was no risk of being spotted. They chatted, each glad of the company, and when they parted, Hobo knew so much more about David, and David knew nothing more about Hobo. The time came when Hobo told David he would be moving on as the cold weather approached, and he would not have the cover of the trees as they shed their leaves, but that he would be back late spring in the new year as usual and would look forward to seeing him then.

15

There was always a great buzz in the cloakroom and playground on the first day back at school after the summer break. Rebecca was pleased to see friends who didn't live near her, but there was just one girl who really irritated her and many of the others, Dorothy Wade, and sure enough, when Rebecca arrived at school, she could hear her from the other side of the cloakroom. Dorothy's voice boomed over the rest as she related how they had four wonderful weeks in their bungalow by the sea, many adventures, how expensive her daddy's brand-new car was and how lovely her new bathing costume was with a pleated frill round the bottom and how they had lots of fresh strawberries and cream and huge juicy peaches and the weather was absolutely perfect all of the time and who knows what else they may have had to add to the list had not the school bell rang.

This was the beginning of a new school year which meant a new classroom and teacher who was Miss Brook. The desks were in rows, in pairs, and Rebecca's place was to be next to David which would be the beginning of the next week. He was still needing to have his wounds dressed daily and was still recovering from his ordeal and not sleeping very well, because he was still very sore. Some of the other children would not have wanted David to sit with them, for sometimes he did need a wash, and his clothes were always shabby hand-me-downs, but Rebecca didn't mind that at all; she cared about him.

"Don't you ever clean your teeth?" Rebecca asked him one day.

"No, I don't have a brush, and ma says there's no point because she can't afford the paste," replied David.

Rebecca wished she had never asked but gave him half her orange, and the awkwardness passed. She always felt sorry for him. She knew he spent a lot of time on his own now, because the other children would make fun of him and say nasty things about his mother that would upset him, but whilst they were at school, she stuck up for him and shared her treats, not knowing that his school dinner was sometimes the only meal he would have in a day. He and Rebecca enjoyed their lessons and worked hard and showed promise. During this term and the spring term, the children were working towards taking their 11 plus exam to see who was good enough to go to Grammar School, and both Rebecca and David were good candidates, but David knew that even if he did pass, he would not be going. His mother was always pleased with his results and school report but had made it clear to him that the financial situation made it an impossibility.

Term passed quickly and soon they were practising carols for the service and nativity play which parents attended and getting excited about the Christmas party.

Dorothy Wade was the Virgin Mary and Rebecca was the Angel Gabriel. Rebecca didn't mind at all, because she had to stand on a stool at the back of Dorothy, and she kept nudging her in the back with her toe, disrupting her performance, until Miss Brook realised what was happening. She threatened Rebecca that she would lose her part unless she started behaving like an angel, so that put a stop to it.

The headmaster said all dress rehearsals were chaotic, so why was Miss Brook screaming at them and pacing the floor with her head in her hands? When one of the wise men sat on his crown, and Rebecca fell off her stool and bent a wing, she looked as if she was going to burst into tears, but the headmaster was right—everything went perfectly well for the real performance.

The huge hall was lit only by candles to enhance the atmosphere as they sang the carol 'While Shepherds Watched Their Flocks by Night', the black curtain keeping Rebecca from sight was raised, and she said her lines beautifully, to the delight of Miss Brook and her parents, and all the staff and children were worthy of praise for the effort they had put into it.

Rebecca felt uneasy when Dorothy Wade's father patted her on her head and said, "Well done," and when she was curled up on her father's knee drinking warm milk just before bed, she kept thinking about Mr Wade's thin moustache which looked like it had been drawn on his face with a thick pencil.

Walking home from school, the children were discussing the party and Christmas in general, but David said nothing.

The following day was a Saturday, and Rebecca was going into town with her father to do some Christmas shopping. They always went to the big store to see the grotto and to buy her mother's Christmas box and have tea and cake in a snack bar. Rebecca had already bought her father some socks and hidden them at home and had just bought her mother some chocolates, so she counted up the money she had left in her purse.

"What are you wanting to buy?" asked her father.

"A toothbrush for David if I have enough," Rebecca replied.

They went into the chemist and bought a toothbrush, and no more was said about the matter by either of them, although Mr Brown was quietly bemused.

They went home to a snug house and put up the Christmas tree, which stood on a small table in the corner of the room, and listened to the radio before going to bed. Rebecca noticed her mother was snappy and impatient and could hear her parents having an argument as she lay in bed, but then everything went quiet, and she fell asleep.

The following Monday and Tuesday, it was hard to get the children to concentrate, they were so excited anticipating the party on Wednesday. The children were allowed to go home at lunch time and change into their party clothes. Rebecca had a new red velvet dress with a white lacy collar that could be taken off and washed, some white socks and silver shoes, and for the party, she had her hair down instead of in plaits. There was great excitement when they all returned, that is, all but David. Rebecca felt really sad when she realised he wasn't there, and asked Miss Brook if she could have some party food to take for him. At home time, Miss Brook gave her a parcel made up of what was left over from the table.

When Rebecca got home, her mother was not there, so she went to Bertha's next door. "Mum isn't in," said Rebecca, taking off her coat to show Bertha her dress.

No, she won't be, thought Bertha, who had seen her go out all dressed up earlier but said nothing.

They chatted, and Rebecca explained to Bertha that she had some party food to take to David but actually didn't know where he lived. "Your father will know, and mind he goes with you," said Bertha.

Mr Brown arrived, and Rebecca explained that she had the party food for David and must take it straightaway, but she didn't know where he lived.

"I have a good idea," said her father. He put Barney on his lead and they set off to find where David lived. He knew the area, not a place many people went to because most of the buildings were derelict. There was a lot of rubble and rubbish about, a lot of the houses had windows boarded up although it was clear that some of them still had occupants, and all of them had outside toilets across a yard. An old lady was on her doorstep so they asked which house David lived in and she pointed

17

to the one on the corner. Mr Brown knocked, and moments later, the door was answered by David's mother. She still had red fingernails, red patterns on her legs and a cigarette dangling from the corner of her mouth and a tartan blanket over her shoulders.

"Is David in?" asked Rebecca.

"Yea," the woman replied. "What's he been up to?"

"I've brought him some party food from school because he didn't go," said Rebecca.

"Come here, David," shouted his mother. "Have you been telling these people you don't get anything to eat at home?" she screamed as she slapped him on the back of his head. "Don't you start telling tales to your charitable school friends!" Rebecca felt a lump in her throat and started to cry, because her good deed was getting David into trouble.

"Please don't hit him," she cried. "He didn't tell tales; he just didn't come to the party." The woman stopped shouting and looked first at David and then at Rebecca, who were both in tears.

"I'm sorry, child," she said. "I have not been well lately, and it makes me cross, but it was very kind of you to think of him."

David took the parcel off Rebecca, said a tearful, "Thank you," and went inside.

"We all have problems," said Mr Brown quietly, "but we shouldn't take it out on our children. Good evening to you."

"Gosh," said Rebecca, who had never experienced anything like that in all her life, "poor David." She fired questions at her father all the way home. "Why was she so dirty? Why had she horrible red patterns on her legs? Why didn't she comb her hair?"

The questions had to be answered as vaguely as possible for a 10 year old to understand, for you cannot tell a child that her friend's mother is an alcoholic who takes men home to make a living as well as working in the pub, and that his father is a petty criminal spending a lot of time in jail and rarely coming home. David believed his father was a sailor at sea. Mr Brown's answers were gentle and fair and told Rebecca nothing really, but he didn't want her putting her foot in it again, consciously or otherwise, and he certainly didn't want her asking why she took men home.

When they reached home, her mother was back and making tea. She listened as Rebecca related her story of the events in the past hour but only commented with the occasional, "Oh dear!"

When Rebecca went to bed, she gave her parents a big hug. "I'm glad you are my mum and dad; it would be terrible to have to live with David's mum. Night night." Off she went to bed but lay thinking for a long time about what she had seen, and would she be getting David into trouble if she gave him the toothbrush as a gift?

On the last day of term, Rebecca asked David what he wanted for Christmas.

"I don't know," he replied, "but I'll get something. Ma is working in the pub, so I might have to wait until she gets home. I might get some socks."

"Does that mean you will be alone all day, then?" asked Rebecca.

David just shrugged his shoulders and looked away.

Late afternoon on Christmas Eve, Rebecca and her father had been into town for some last-minute shopping when they bumped into David huddled in a doorway near the Christmas tree where the Salvation Army band were playing carols and quite a large crowd were singing. He had been around the market and collected some fruit and vegetables that had been discarded in boxes by the stall holders for the pig farmer to collect later as the market closed down. One stall holder had shouted at him and sent him away; another had helped him pick out the best and given him some chestnuts in a little bag. He'd been to the bakery and bought some bread and a bag of broken biscuits, and the assistant had slipped a raspberry bun in his bag and winked at him as she did so. He was feeling pretty happy with himself as he clung on to his bags of goodies.

"Want a lift home, David?" asked Mr Brown.

"Please," replied David. He would love a ride in a car and would save his bus fare.

They dropped him off at the end of the lane where he lived.

Merry Christmases were exchanged, but Rebecca's father stood for a moment, moved by the sight of the boy, alone, shivering, carrying his bags of scraps and so happy about it.

"I wonder what sort of Christmas David will have," he said.

Rebecca replied, "His mother is working at the pub, so he will have to wait until she gets home anyway."

"Who told you that?" asked her father.

"David did when we finished school," Rebecca replied.

It's unlikely he'll be getting a Christmas dinner, thought Mr Brown.

Home was cosy and warm and smelt good because the turkey was cooking in the oven. They were lucky to have a turkey as a gift from Mr Brown's best friend who was a farmer who reared them. Mr Brown would go and help pluck them and deliver some in his car for the customers, to help out. It had to be cooked on Christmas Eve because there wasn't room in the oven for anything else that needed to be cooked on Christmas day.

Tea on Christmas Eve was always pork pie, tomatoes and either pickled shallots or pickled beetroot that Rebecca's mother and Bertha had prepared in the autumn to be stacked in the cellar for Christmas.

After tea, when Rebecca had helped clear the table, she went to her room and wrapped the socks she had bought for her father and chocolates for her mother and took them downstairs and put them beneath the table that had the small Christmas tree on it.

Whilst she had been upstairs, her parents had been discussing David's situation and agreed to have him for Christmas dinner if he wanted to and if he was still going to be alone on Christmas day.

Rebecca was fidgeting. It was only 6 o'clock, and she wanted it to be bedtime, so Christmas morning would come quicker.

"Do you think David would like to come for Christmas dinner?" asked her father.

"Oh, yes!" replied Rebecca emphatically. "Bertha says he could do with a good meal or two down him, and I've forgotten to give him his toothbrush, so I can give it to him when he comes."

Mr Brown was thinking he would call at David's house on his own, considering how the previous visit had gone, but Rebecca already had her boots and coat on and was wrapping her scarf around her neck and standing by the door with her hat and gloves in her hand. Barney was put on his lead, and off they all went, crunching through the hoar frost, with the icy air numbing their faces. The bare branches of the trees and the bushes twinkled as if they were made of glass when the light from the gas lamp caught them. There was a brief conversation about Barney's paws freezing, but as they turned into the lane where David lived, Rebecca forgot about it and just wanted to get to the house, but when her father had knocked at the door, she held his hand and stood slightly behind him. No one answered, but they thought someone must be in, because the bare, dim light bulb was lit. They knocked again and stood in silence, waiting for someone to answer, but no one did. Still holding Rebecca's hand, her father opened the unlocked door and tentatively stood inside the passage.

"Hello," he called, "is anyone there?"

There was no answer, so they turned to leave when they heard a moan from the room. He pushed open the door slowly, and what confronted him filled him with awe. There were newspapers and empty beer bottles everywhere, the walls were brown, stained from nicotine, damp and neglect, the stench of stale smoke and vomiting made the air unbreathable, and there on the stone floor lay David's mother, her bleached hair making a stark contrast to the blood oozing from a deep gash in her head and a pale brown foam oozing from her mouth. "Must get an ambulance," said Mr Brown. He felt angry with himself that Rebecca had witnessed such a sight. Rebecca was numb, her heart lurched inside her and she could feel it throbbing as if it was fighting its way out. The stench from the room was choking her, making her feel sick, and every time she blinked, she saw red flashes. She didn't hear her father speak, but suddenly lifted her eyes away from the floor and glanced across to a gloomy corner of the room, for some tiny sound or movement had brought her back to reality. As her father turned to go to the telephone box to call an ambulance, David appeared from his huddled position behind a chair filled with discarded clothes and papers. He did not speak; he was trembling with fright. Mr Brown took a child in each hand and ran into the lane with them.

"Stay there. Do not go back inside," he said and ran to the telephone box. The children, holding hands, didn't even speak to each other. David was still crying and shivering when Mr Brown returned, but Rebecca was standing silent. He went back into the house, but didn't touch David's mother who was still on the floor in a very distressed manner.

"The ambulance is coming," he informed her.

"Get the two envelopes off the mantel piece," she said, "and keep them safe for David."

"I have them," said Mr Brown. "What happened here?"

"I got up to get ready to go out," said David's mother. "And I just fell over and caught my head on the table, and I've such a pain in my belly."

The ambulance and police arrived almost together, and it wasn't long before she was on her way to the hospital.

"I'm taking the boy home with me," Mr Brown told the policeman. "He needs to go in and get his coat and anything else he might need."

"Poor do for this kid at any time," said the policeman, "but especially at this time of year. I will need a statement from you. I'll give you a lift home with the children."

Rebecca's mother heard the car pull up outside and went to peep through the curtains to see who it was. She was seized with panic when she saw the children get out of a police car because Barney had come home on his own earlier, and she was worrying as to what could have happened. She stood in the doorway waiting for them, but knew it was not the right time to be asking questions when she saw the state the children were in.

Mr Brown spoke, "Take care of the children. David's mother has been taken to hospital."

"She's cut her head," said Rebecca, "and been very sick. David can't stay on his own, can he?"

"He must stay here until his mother is well," said her mother, who looked across at David who was standing near the fire, sobbing and looking very grubby and wondered what she was going to do with him.

It wasn't doing the children any good listening to Mr Brown and the policeman going over the events of the past hour, so Rebecca was asked to show David where everything was, and perhaps he would like to wash and freshen up before supper. He followed Rebecca upstairs like an obedient dog.

He had never been in a bathroom in his life, and he thought it was wonderful that the toilet was inside the house and that it flushed, and hot water came out of a tap.

"Make sure to rinse all the dirty soapy water off before drying, because mum gets really cross when the towels are dirty," said Rebecca.

She showed him all the toiletries, and they tested one or two, and when they went back downstairs, Rebecca's father just looked at her, shook his head and held his nose.

The policeman had gone, and there was porridge, a bun and a cup of cocoa waiting for them. It had been agreed with the policeman that David should stay there until it became apparent what condition his mother was in, so they put up the camp bed in Rebecca's room and gathered spare blankets.

There was a knock on the door; it was Bertha. "What's bin goin' on?" she asked.

Mr Brown explained briefly, and Bertha was gone.

An hour later, she returned. She knew the children had gone to bed because the light was on in Rebecca's room. She had a bundle of things she had collected from neighbours who had reacted to David's plight willingly. A jigsaw, books, knitted gloves, sweets, socks, a scarf and a pullover from a lady whose son had grown out of it but it still looked good. Now they had to wrap them and put them under the tree for him along with the other presents.

Whilst Bertha and Rebecca's mother set about wrapping the gifts, Mr Brown went upstairs to see the children. David didn't have pyjamas so Mr Brown gave him a shirt to wear in bed and was shocked when he saw the scars on the boys back.

Rebecca hugged her father and whispered, "Will David's mother get better?"

"We hope so," replied her father. "She's in good hands, and they will take good care of her in the hospital. I've promised the policeman I will take him to see her tomorrow if the hospital will allow it, but I will have to telephone them tomorrow."

David came back into the bedroom and looked at Mr Brown. "Thank you," he said, and he couldn't say anymore, he was choking trying not to cry. No one could know the pain and feeling of despair in the boy's heart. He wished his mother could be there where it was warm and things were nice and clean, and there was food to eat, and she was not in hospital, hurting.

He thought back to early evening when he had returned home with his bags of shopping. There was a man in the house and he and his mother were drunk, and he was taunting her and she was chasing him round the table to get the bottle he was waving in the air at her. They were laughing, and eventually, he let her have another drink. Her blouse was torn, and the man pushed his mother against the wall. Suddenly, she noticed David standing in the doorway.

"Hello, shon," she slurred and burped!

The man picked up his coat to leave, and it was then that his mother lunged to try and stop him that she fell and banged her head. The man left; he didn't even look back to see if she had hurt herself.

"Ma!" he'd shouted, and knelt and nudged her shoulder. She had opened her eyes and stared as if she didn't know him, and then she was violently sick and groaned and grasped her stomach. David had heard the knock on the door but panicked until he realised it was Mr Brown and Rebecca, and not the man coming back. He heard Mr Brown saying to the policeman she had just stood up to get ready to go out and collapsed, so David said nothing about what really happened so as not to disgrace his mother.

The police had only become involved because it was possible she had taken a beating from one of her male callers, as in the past, but Mr Brown's explanation of the events released them from their obligation.

Mr Brown left the children, opened a bottle of beer and sat in his chair, reeling from the evening's events. All the presents were wrapped and under the table, and his wife and Bertha were having a sherry.

Chapter 2

Bertha had brought round mince pies and a Christmas cake for Christmas day for she always came around for Christmas dinner. She sat and sipped her sherry, deep in thought about David. His short life had been so blighted, yet he had done nothing to cause it himself, and she thought about what could happen to him if his mother didn't make it.

"Some Christmas Eve this has turned out to be," she said. "It's a damn shame for the boy. The copper said there was nowt round at his house for Christmas for the lad that they could find, but they didn't stay in t'ouse long it is in such a state. They say she'd bin int Crown wi' a feller all afternoon, well that's up to 'er, she can please 'erself, but I can't bear to see a child suffer ever, let alone Christmas."

She finished her sherry in a gulp. "Peace on earth, goodwill to men," she said. "I'm away to mi bed, see you tomorrow." And she left.

Mr Brown was restless and uneasy, but he wasn't sure why. He regretted very much the fact that Rebecca had witnessed everything that had taken place. Mrs Brown had gone up to bed and he was sitting in his chair by the fire when Rebecca appeared, stood perfectly still in front of him, burst into tears and flung herself at him. He realised that's what had been troubling him, he hadn't seen Rebecca cry, but now she couldn't stop, and he was glad she would have the relief that tears bring. The focus had been very much on David, and it was only when she lay quiet in bed that things caught up with her. David, exhausted, cosy and warm, had gone off to sleep fairly quickly, but Rebecca couldn't; she just needed to have a cuddle with her father and a chat.

"What's going to happen?" she asked.

"Well," replied her father. "Tomorrow we will have a lovely Christmas day, and I promised that I would try and take David to see his mother later. Bertha will be coming as usual, there are presents and we will play games, and more than anything, you will have made sure David has a wonderful day. Just remember that if we hadn't have gone when we did, David would have been in a terrible situation. His mother would still have had her accident whether we were there or not, but because we were, he is in a good place, with us, safe." She thought for a moment and seemed to settle. She noticed the presents piled up but knew better than even to mention them, so she went back to bed quietly and finally went to sleep. Mr Brown went up to bed quietly, thinking his wife was fast asleep. She lay motionless but was wide awake and remained that way for another hour at least. She was deep in thought, searching for answers to a problem that only she could find, things which there seemed to be no reasonable answer to. Her sleep was shallow and she kept waking up, so she was relieved that the children had slept until 9 am. She heard them race downstairs and heard the excited chatter.

"Go on, David," Rebecca said. "Open them, they are all for you."

David flushed with excitement; he had never had so many presents in all of his life, let alone at one time. He didn't know quite what to do after he had opened one and stood looking at Rebecca beaming with pleasure as he hugged the pullover.

"I'll open one of mine now," she said. "We'll take it in turn."

Rebecca's mother appeared, looking very pretty in a new dress. "Go and get your father up," she said.

Rebecca ran upstairs and dived onto her father in bed. He groaned. "I was having a terrible dream," he said. "I dreamt an elephant had jumped on me." Rebecca laughed, nipped his neck playfully and ran off shouting, "Hurry up!"

Her mother sat with the children and waited for father to appear, and they opened their presents. Rebecca had managed to slip the toothbrush into the pile and was determined David would use it. There was a present left for Bertha, a box of lavender soaps, which they bought her every year because that is all she wanted. They gathered all the paper and rubbish and rolled it into a tight bundle for Mr Brown to burn later. He put on his coat and hat and took Barney for a walk and called at the telephone box to ring the hospital to enquire about David's mother and whether it would be in order to visit her later that day. They were quite reluctant to give him much information because he was not a relative, but when he explained about David, sister gave permission for a visit, but after 4 pm that day.

When he returned, the children were dressed and playing Ludo. His wife was busy in the kitchen and refused any help, so he joined the children until it was time to set the table. David watched it all happen with interest for he had never seen anything like it. The tablecloth was red, all the plates and dishes matched, having a pretty pattern of flowers around the edges, and the cutlery also was the same for them all. Bertha came around and chatted to the children about their presents and was thrilled she had managed to scrounge so much for David, seeing the pleasure it had given him.

Christmas dinner was wonderful. David didn't know what everything was in the dishes, but he tried a little bit of everything and cleaned his plate. "I've never had turkey before," he said. There was a pause. "In fact, I think I've only had mashed potatoes and peas before." Rebecca reminded him about his school dinners. "You can't always recognise what you are getting at school," he said, and they all burst out laughing. They took their time and appreciated the effort that had gone into preparing the meal and said a big thank you and toasted Rebecca's mother for a job well done. She was happy to sit back in her chair whilst Bertha and the children washed up. Whilst they were in the kitchen, Mr Brown told her quietly that he had arranged to take David to hospital to see his mother at 4 pm, and by the time the clearing up and washing up was finished, it was time to get ready and go. David had been restless since his meal, and they knew he wouldn't settle until he had been to see his mother. Bertha went home to see to her fire, and Rebecca, her mother and father and David got into the car and left for the hospital. It was a foreboding Victorian building and it had an eeriness about it as the Christmas chimes caught the draught from the open door. They walked down the corridor, and David noticed everywhere there were dark green tiles half way up the walls, and the rest of the walls were painted a sand colour. Suddenly, crepe shoes squeaked on the floor as a nurse came towards them.

"Can I help you?" she asked.

"Matron gave us permission this morning for David to see his mother in Ward 15," said Mr Brown.

"I will take you to the visitor's room," said the nurse, "and sister will come and see you."

"Why do we have to see her sister?" asked David. "I want to see my ma."

The young nurse explained what she meant and left, smiling.

Sister arrived briskly and in a flurry of dark blue and white. "You may go in and see your mother," she said to David, "and she is also asking to have a word with you, Mr Brown. Do you want a cup of tea?" she asked mother, but she declined and just sat down with Rebecca.

David trotted along with the nurse, pulling his new socks up and trying not to squash the mince pie he had brought for his mother.

"Are you awake?" the nurse asked quietly. "Your son is here."

David's heart lurched, his eyes grew wider, and he felt very cold. His mother lay very still, she had two black eyes, some of her hair had been shaved off, and the gash had been stitched.

"Do your stitches hurt?" he asked. "They look like flies."

"No, son," she replied. "It's my belly that hurts."

"I believe you have been taken care of at Rebecca's house, have you been good?" She looked across at Mr Brown. "Thank you so much," she said. "Did you pick up the envelopes? It's David's birth certificate and an insurance policy, just in case." She held out her hand to Mr Brown and squeezed it weakly.

"I will leave you now, so you can have a moment with David. I can tell you are very tired," said Mr Brown and left before David's mother could ask him to take care of David, because he knew he could not make that promise, and it would make it hard to refuse.

David chatted to his mother and told her about his day and his presents and his dinner, showed her his hat and scarf and pullover, and asked how she was feeling.

"I've got a burning pain in my belly just now," she said. "But they will fix it. I'm very proud of you, David, you are a good son, and I love you very much."

"I love you too," said David, not realising the significance of the conversation.

Sister came back and said it was time to leave. His mother blew him a kiss as he left the room and closed her eyes.

Sister had spoken to Mr Brown away from Rebecca and her mother, the prognosis was not good, it seems her liver function was failing due to her lifestyle, and he left hospital with a heavy heart, unable to discuss things with his wife until the children were in bed.

On the journey home, David was chatty, he went into detail about the stitches and his mother's black and swollen eyes, and how they had shaved some of her hair off, just so Rebecca didn't feel she had been left out, for she was certainly petulant when she realised she couldn't go to see his mother with him. She didn't want to listen to reason from her mother and sit in that room; she wanted to go and see for herself.

Bertha had returned and made turkey sandwiches for tea, and there was trifle and Christmas cake and cheese. Nobody was very hungry, but it was a nice relaxed tea at the end of a hectic day. They had a game of snakes and ladders, listened to the radio for a while, and then the children took their new books and went upstairs to bed. Half an hour later, Rebecca's mother peeped in and they were both sound asleep.

She removed the books from their beds, turned out the light and went and had a bath as the children had not run all the hot water off. She went back downstairs in her nightie and dressing gown and curled up in her chair. Mr Brown and Bertha were chatting about David's situation. They knew a welfare officer would be calling in the next few days with regard to David being taken to an orphanage either until his mother had recovered or a foster home could be found for him.

"Well, he can't stay here," said Rebecca's mother, in quite a sharp manner, which took her husband by surprise.

Bertha didn't say anything, just looked at her, for she knew what was going on in her mind, even though it had never been discussed.

Trying to hide her attitude, she pointed out that they would need a separate bedroom for a boy, it was not acceptable for teenage boys and girls to share, but perhaps it would be all right for him to come for a weekend sometimes.

Mr Brown was weary with it all. He had a beer and fell asleep in the chair whilst Bertha closed her eyes and listened to the radio for a few minutes, then she got up to leave.

"Am I still baby sitting on New Year's Eve?" she asked quietly. Rebecca's mother nodded 'yes', and Bertha was gone, miming the words, "Thank you for today."

As she walked the few yards to her door, she looked up into the night sky but could see no moon or stars.

I'll bet there are clouds up there, full of snow, she thought, and she was right, for during the night it had come down thick and fast.

Chapter 3

"Rebecca, Rebecca," whispered David and prodded her. "Come and look, it's been snowing."

Rebecca hugged her cover and snuggled down, not wanting to get up, but David persisted, so she put on her dressing gown and went to the window to look.

"Yippee," said Rebecca. "Let's see if dad will take us sledging." She ran down the stairs, knowing her father still had a day's holiday because it was boxing day, whatever that meant, because she had never understood it but was glad to have him at home all day. "Can we go sledging?" she asked her father.

He had anticipated this and was ready with his answer. "Yes, we can, but later, because there is no point in going when it is snowing as thick and fast as it is, and I need to clean up the sledge irons, so it will be this afternoon."

"Oh," said Rebecca, who wanted to go that minute.

"Don't moan," said her father and gave her a look which signified it was not up for discussion. "Find your wellies and see if they still fit."

David only had his wellies, but he had new socks, so they didn't rub his legs and make them sore and a new scarf and gloves, and he was very happy about that and was looking forward to sledging with all the others that would be gathering in the sloping field.

The children played games and read their books for a while, but it was hard for them to settle for long, and they kept looking out of the window to see if it had stopped snowing. Mr Brown had brought the sledge up from the cellar and was cleaning the runners on newspapers on the floor under the watchful eye of his wife. Earlier he had opened the door and cleared the snow from the path, so Barney could go out. He loved to romp and roll in it and came back in wet through and smelling of wet wool.

They had cheese on toast and were ready to go at last, once it had stopped snowing. Bertha used to knit pom-pom hats for something to do, and they had several in a drawer, so they all put one on and tapped at her window as they passed. Mr Brown threw a handful of snow at Bertha's window, so she shook her fist at him and they all laughed.

"Come with us," said Mr Brown, teasing. Bertha just shook her head from side to side and pointed to her head, noticing they were all wearing a hat she had knit, which pleased her greatly.

There were many families in the field when they arrived, all having a wonderful time. The farmer, who owned the field, was there with his own children and was happy to see everyone there. Some of the adults quietly asked how David's mother was, but Mr Brown was unable to tell them much, although he sensed a great sympathy from the people in the village. An hour later, very cold and very wet, they decided to return home.

"Let's go down by the stream," suggested Rebecca. "It might be frozen."

They all slid down the banking on foot because there was not enough room to sledge. Rebecca fell over and was laughing at her father who was trying to keep his balance, but in the end, the icy carpet won, and he ended up flat on his back at the side of her.

"Gosh dad, look," she said. She was looking into the sky which was a deepening pink and was mesmerised by the red sun sliding down the sky, turning the snow pink and making the silhouettes of the bare trees look like a black army of twisted, gnarled men bowing their heads humbly against the skyline.

"Look here," said David, pointing to a row of icicles under the bridge, but the frozen stream creaked beneath him when he tried to reach them, so he waited for Mr Brown to get to his feet, and he managed to break one off for each of them. They sucked at them, which made their lips numb, had a sword fight with them, and then smashed them against a tree. They shattered and fell to the ground and settled like pink gems as they picked up the light from the setting sun. It was time to go home.

They removed their wet clothes and put them on the clothes horse in front of the fire or on the hearth to dry and tucked into cold turkey and chips and warm mince pies. The children washed up, and Mr Brown took Barney for a walk and telephoned the hospital. He spoke to the sister who remembered who he was. "Things are not looking good," she said. "It's not a good idea to bring the boy to see his mother today, try tomorrow."

When Mr Brown returned home, David must have expected him to have telephoned the hospital because he asked straight away, "Am I going to see my mam today?"

"Not today, David," answered Mr Brown. "The snow is too deep to take the car out. I've spoken to the nurse and your mother is comfortable, so we will try again tomorrow because the snow ploughs will have been out and cleared the roads, especially to the hospital, because ambulances will need to get through." Mr Brown was wondering where that explanation came from but was glad it did, and David accepted it. "I have to go to work tomorrow, but when I get home, we will see what can be done. They are taking very good care of your mother, you know, and right now she needs it."

David sat curled in a chair, a lonely, quiet little boy, wanting to run and hug his mother and finding it really hard when he couldn't go to see her.

When the children went to bed, David disclosed his feelings to Rebecca. He had overheard the conversation between Mr Brown and the policeman and knew he couldn't stay at Rebecca's home, and that he was only able to because it was Christmas and they had offered to have him.

"I don't want to go to an orphanage, I want my mam to come home," he said. "If she can, will you help me to look after her?"

"I will," said Rebecca with great feeling. "She may only be in for a week."

"Then why can't I stay here?" asked David.

"I don't know," said Rebecca and was left wondering herself why he couldn't if it was only going to be for a short while.

The following morning, Rebecca lay listening for sounds downstairs and eventually went down to find it was later than she thought, because her father was almost ready to leave for work. "I'm a little bit early, but I need to shovel some snow away," said Mr Brown.

There was a knock at the door which he answered.

"Good morning," a lady said. "I'm Mrs Gee, I've come to see David."

"He's still asleep," said Mr Brown. "But please come in. I have to leave for work, but my wife will see to things."

Rebecca sat quietly; she didn't want to be sent out of the room. She listened as the lady explained that David's mother was much worse and should really be moved to another hospital, but whatever was decided about her, David had to go to an orphanage and maybe fostered with a family later, until such time as his mother returned home, if she recovered.

Golly, what if she dies? thought Rebecca. *What will happen then?*

Mrs Gee arranged to return at 10:30 am and asked that David be ready with all his belongings packed.

Rebecca's mother went upstairs to awaken David and sent him to the bathroom to get washed and dressed, and when he returned to the bedroom, he saw all his things in a pile on the bed ready to be packed into a brown paper bag.

"Am I going away?" he asked, huskily.

"Just for a little while," said Rebecca's mother, "until your mother is well. Mrs Gee, who is coming to collect you, will explain everything to you. Go and have some breakfast. Rebecca is downstairs waiting for you."

David went into the bathroom, collected his toothbrush and went downstairs. He had been pushed aside and into the background so many times in his life and accepted it, but now he had experienced the comfort of a proper home, he didn't want to leave.

Bertha popped in and was totally oblivious to what was going on and chatted away, wanting the children to go to the shop for her because she was afraid of falling in the snow. Suddenly, she picked up on the atmosphere in the room. "What?" she said and looked at them all in turn and noticed David was hugging his brown paper bag.

"David's going to an orphanage in a minute," blurted Rebecca, "and it's not fair."

"Who said owt about life bein' fair?" said Bertha. "David needs to be cared for and safe whilst 'is ma gets better. Tha'll see 'im at school next week, and 'is mam might be 'ome bi then."

Someone walked past the window and knocked at the door, so Bertha held Rebecca's hand.

Mrs Gee walked in with a man. "Hello, David," she said. "Are we ready?"

David stood up and walked towards the door, he turned and said, "Thank you," to Rebecca's mother, who nodded and smiled at him, then he looked across at Rebecca and quietly said, "Goodbye," turned and left. He was dazed, didn't know where he was going, whether he was going to be able to see his ma, and who were these people that were taking him away?

Rebecca ran to the window and saw David sitting in the back seat of the car, hugging his brown paper bag, facing forward, not even glancing at the window, and he was gone.

Rebecca stood for a while wondering where on earth he was going. "Flippin 'eck," she said, "I'm glad it's not me."

"Aye," said Bertha, "but it's a luxury for that lad to 'av someone to care for 'im. He's nivver known a 'ome like yours, tha knows. Anyway, what about New Year's Eve, what are you and me goin' to do whilst thi mam and dad are out?" Rebecca shrugged her shoulders and went up to her room for the rest of the morning. After lunch, she took Barney on a walk into the woods where some children were sledging, but she avoided them, just wanting to be alone with her thoughts.

When her father came home, she was sitting by the fire with a book, alone. Her mother had gone out, somewhere, she didn't know where, and Mr Brown was stunned when he heard that David had actually gone that morning. He had the envelopes that were David's property and hadn't a clue where to find him. He had thought Mrs Gee was coming for a chat, not to take him away there and then.

"Where has he gone?" he asked Rebecca.

"I don't know," she replied, "but he didn't want to go and was very sad."

"Didn't your mother ask where he was going, and where is she now?" asked her father.

"No, she didn't ask," replied Rebecca, "and she just got ready and said she wouldn't be long but didn't say where she was going."

Rebecca kept going over everything in her mind, she kept wondering where David was, but remembered what Bertha had said about him being cared for and safe, and that consoled her. She was looking forward to spending New Year's Eve with Bertha; that was always special for her. She enjoyed listening to stories of what it was like when Bertha was growing up and stories about her husband Sam, who worked at a brick works making red bricks for building houses, and when he died because the red brick dust closed his lungs, Rebecca had filled a gap in Bertha's life and eased the grieving process, so they were very close and caring about each other. Rebecca would stand on a stool at the kitchen sink and watch Bertha preparing vegetables, nibbling at a piece of raw carrot or watch her baking at the table, waiting patiently for a piece of pastry to roll herself. She would make a pastry man with currants for his eyes and nose, and if there were a few currants spare, she would make him have chicken pox, and best of all was scraping the bowl if Bertha had made buns.

People often called on Bertha in a crisis; she was reliable, honest and dealt with things in a practical manner and was respected in the village, and as Rebecca grew up, she was to rely on her more than ever.

On New Year's Eve, Bertha arrived with a tin of coloured sewing silks, a pillow case and a large white piece of cloth that she had drawn daisies on. She sat chatting until Rebecca's parents were ready to leave for the party, and once they had left, she asked Rebecca to choose a colour for a daisy.

"This is called embroidery," said Bertha, "and a few nice flowers on a pillow case or table cloth make all the difference."

"Yes," said Rebecca, "but why don't mine look like yours?"

"Because the stitches are too tight," replied Bertha. "But it will come wi' practice. I'll draw you some more daisies and leave you some silks and then you can practice some more tomorrow and show me what you have done. We 'ad better put a piece of coil ont doorstep for thi mother to let New Year in when thi come 'ome, afore we forget."

Rebecca went to the door with Bertha. The sky was clear, the moon shone down, and stars were like diamonds on a black cape. It was very cold, a hoar frost had settled, and they didn't linger long.

"What happens at New Year?" asked Rebecca.

"Nowt, really," answered Bertha. "Just sayin' goodbye to an old calendar and 'allo to a new un. Some years are good, and some aren't, but ivvery one matters, more at my age than it does at thine. People like to party and welcome the New Year at midnight, and in a few years' time you will be doing the same, but my partyin' days are over."

Bertha made cocoa, they snuggled on the sofa and chatted for a while, and then Rebecca went to bed, settled and went to sleep quickly, being more relaxed than she had been over the past few days.

Bertha wrapped herself in a blanket rather than put more coal on the fire and listened to the radio. By the time Big Ben was striking midnight, she was fast asleep and missed the whole celebrations and didn't wake up until Rebecca's parents returned home.

"Happy New Year," they greeted her as they entered with the piece of coal.

"Aye, same to you," replied Bertha.

They had a hug and a kiss, Bertha put on her coat, and Mr Brown saw her to her door safely.

She stood waiting for the kettle to heat water for her hot water bottle to take to bed, and wondered how many more New Year's she would see in. She blew a kiss at the photograph of Sam. "You were a good man," she said, "and I still miss you." And away she went to bed.

Chapter 4

New term started on a biting cold morning. As Rebecca arrived, Dorothy Wade was getting out of her father's car wearing a new coat made out of teddy-bear material. Rebecca would have loved it but decided in that moment she hated it. Dorothy didn't even notice Rebecca and ran straight into the school gates, but Mr Wade sat in his car and wound the window down.

"Hello," he said to Rebecca. "Have you had a nice Christmas?"

"Yes, thank you," she stammered and felt herself going pink. *I hope he couldn't tell what I was thinking*, she thought. She never forgot something Bertha had said, that Rebecca's thoughts were never far from the expression on her face.

"Goodbye," said Mr Wade and drove off, leaving Rebecca feeling uneasy and wondering why he even spoke to her.

The school bell rang and there was a great surge into the cloakroom. Rebecca could hear Dorothy speaking above all the chatter.

"If anyone needs to know the time, I have a new watch," she announced.

There were groans, a few squeals of interest, and to Rebecca's delight someone shouted, "It's ok, Dot, I've got one of my own."

"Oh!" said Dorothy, totally undaunted. "Well, for the rest of you, I mean!"

Once in the classroom, Rebecca realised David was absent. Her friends asked if she knew why but she couldn't give them an answer, and she didn't tell them that he had gone into an orphanage, because she didn't want to talk about it and be bombarded with more questions.

Her parents had not heard anything when she questioned them at tea time that evening, but her father promised to try and find something out the following day.

"I've been promoted," said her father, proudly.

"What does that mean?" asked Rebecca.

"I've been made a manager," said her father, "so I will earn more money."

"He's not got the car anymore," said her mother, scathingly. "Some promotion."

"The salesman needs it to do his job, like I did, and I will be in the office all day and will not need a car to do my job," responded Mr Brown to his wife.

"Will you have to go to work on the bus now?" asked Rebecca.

"I will," replied her father, "until I can save enough to buy my own car."

"Sometime, never!" commented his wife, looking out of the window, her back to both of them.

She put on her coat and flounced out of the house.

"Is she mad about the car, then?" asked Rebecca, giggling and nodding in the direction her mother had gone. "She will have gone to Bertha's house."

"Let's take Barney for his walk," said Mr Brown.

It was dark and cold, so they didn't go too far, and on the way home called at Lil's shop. Lil knew everything about everybody in the village, 'the font of all knowledge', Mr Brown called her privately. She had terrible brown and broken teeth, and he used to tell Rebecca if she didn't clean her teeth she would end up with a smile like Lil's, so that is why Rebecca had this routine where she hardly ever missed cleaning hers.

"Hello, you two," greeted Lil. "A Happy New Year."

"Thank you," said Mr Brown, "and the same to you. Two packets of crisps please." He passed the money over and was almost at the door when Lil said, "Shame about David's mother passin' on. Lord knows what will become of 'im now."

"We hadn't heard," said Mr Brown. "When did this happen?"

"Today, I heard," replied Lil, nodding her head in the familiar know-it-all manner she had. "She'd nowt on 'er to fight an illness, she spent all 'er brass on booze and precious little else, and she must 'av raked enough in from 'er fellers."

"Yes," replied Mr Brown, raising his eyebrows and glancing at Rebecca to stop any more information being voiced that he didn't want Rebecca to hear. "Thank you for letting us know."

Rebecca squeezed her father's hand tightly all the way home, but neither spoke, both deep in their own thoughts. When they arrived home, Rebecca's mother was not there so they went to Bertha's house. "Your mam isn't here," said Bertha. "I expect she'll be at Lil's."

"We've just come from there," said Mr Brown. "And it's over an hour since we left and I dropped the latch, so where can she be? She was in a mad hig when she left because I have had a promotion at work but will not have the car anymore."

Rebecca interrupted. "David's mother died today," she said.

"Poor lad," said Bertha. "D'ya think they will let 'is father out of jail for the funeral? I shall 'av to get mi black 'at out for an airin'."

"David's father is not in jail," said Rebecca. "He's a sailor away at sea."

Both adults realised they had said too much by letting Rebecca know David's father's whereabouts, but neither knew she didn't know. Obviously, David would be ashamed that his father was in jail and would try and hide the fact, but maybe he did believe he was at sea, and did it matter? The point was who would be there to comfort the boy? They didn't know where he was, and it was imperative now that Mr Brown found him, because in one of the envelopes in his safekeeping was a penny insurance policy that his mother had kept up to date, and his birth certificate was in the other envelope.

He discussed it with Bertha, and she advised him to go to the hospital or telephone them to find out which undertaker had collected the body, and he could find out when the funeral was to be. He could let the undertaker know about the policy which would cover a decent funeral, and she would go to the funeral and ensure that David was given his birth certificate.

They could hear Rebecca's mother raking the coals in the grate, so they left Bertha's and went home as it was way past Rebecca's bedtime. This was no time for a confrontation with his wife over her tantrum and where she had been, Mr Brown decided, so nothing was mentioned about it, but they did tell her about David's mother.

"Oh dear! That is very sad," she said sympathetically, and said no more about it because her thoughts were elsewhere.

Rebecca was unusually quiet and pensive before she went to bed.

"We'll leave her for a day or two," said Mr Brown. "She needs a bit of time, these past few weeks have been so disruptive and emotional for her, and at least nothing else can happen now."

"I'm going up with Rebecca," said his wife. "Can you see to things tonight? I'm very tired."

Mr Brown cleaned the shoes, made his sandwiches for the following day and went to bed, deep in thought about the change in his wife's personality, but he did fall asleep eventually, which was good.

Rebecca lay awake, unable to sleep. She thought it was raining at first, but then she heard a shuttering sound at her window, so she plucked up courage and had a peep out of the curtains, and there on the path below was David, clutching his brown paper bag.

Bloody hell! she thought, wincing as the words flashed through her mind. She crept downstairs and found Barney at the door, wagging his tail in greeting. Quietly, she opened the door and let David in.

"I've run away," David whispered. "I don't like it there, and I want to see my mam."

"When did you run away?" asked Rebecca, realising he didn't know his mother had died.

"Yesterday," he choked. "I went and hid in the loft at our house because I knew they would go there looking for me, and I've had to wait until there was no one about. I have not had anything to eat since yesterday."

Rebecca cut a slice of bread and put butter and jam on it, and gave him a drink of milk. She sat opposite him and licked the jam off her fingers.

"What are we going to do?" she whispered.

"Can I hide under your bed until tomorrow, and I'll sneak off when your mother goes out, and I can go and see my mam. They wouldn't let me at the orphanage, and she'll think I don't care about her," said David.

Rebecca's heart lurched, she knew his mother had died, but he must have run away before they could tell him, and she just couldn't. She made another jam sandwich and put it in a bag with an apple and two biscuits so he didn't die of starvation whilst he was under her bed. She cleared up the crumbs and put the jam and butter away whilst David slipped outside for a wee.

"Well," he said, blushing slightly, "I can't use the bathroom, your dad will hear me."

They crept upstairs, rolled a towel up for a pillow and used the only spare blanket they could find. David rolled himself up, tucked his bags into the corner and was soon asleep. Rebecca, however, had a restless night tossing and turning, and it was a wonder the twanging of the springs in her bed didn't keep David awake, but he slept on.

I think I'll have to run away tomorrow, she thought. *I'm sure to get found out, we'll never get away with it, and in any case, David's mum isn't at the hospital, who will tell him what has happened? It's all for nothing…* Finally, she fell asleep, but sleep was shallow, and she remained restless all night. When she woke up, she peered under her bed hoping she had been dreaming, but David was there fast asleep.

"Rebecca, it's time you were up," said her father, peering around the door.

She leapt out of bed and stood pale and dark eyed in the middle of the room for a moment and then went into the bathroom, washed and dressed ready for school. When she went back to her room, David was awake.

"Go to the bathroom now, they'll think it's me. Get some water in this cup if you need a drink," she instructed him, "and be quiet."

She went downstairs and sat at the table and wondered if anyone had noticed some bread had disappeared overnight, but to her relief, no one commented. She listened for any sound from upstairs, but none came, so she was just calming down when her father said, "Are you going shopping today?" to his wife.

"I don't think so," she replied. Rebecca's heart sank, she felt like a bag of grain with the corner cut, losing control gradually.

"Will we need some more bread?" asked Rebecca.

"You can fetch a loaf when you come home from school," replied her mother, so that was the end of that conversation.

Rebecca left for school and as she turned the corner, bumped into Bertha.

"Morning, Rebecca. Sleep all right, did you?" she asked.

"Yes," said Rebecca, lowering her eyes. "Did you?"

"Not really," said Bertha. "I was up wi' indigestion. Best get off to school, or you'll be late."

The cloakroom was full of chatter about David and his mum, and Dorothy Wade was voicing her opinion about the whole situation, and Rebecca would have given anything to put the record straight, but she knew she couldn't.

She was hoping David would succeed in getting away unseen, and she knew he would try not to get her into trouble, and probably there would be someone at the hospital waiting for him to be with him when he found out about his mother. If Bertha hadn't been up in the night, she would be less troubled, but she felt pretty sure Bertha had either seen or heard something to make her comment at all. She was dreading going home in case David was still under her bed, and surely her mother would find him when she made the beds, and what if Barney had gone up? He would surely give the game away, and maybe the police would call to search the house, and supposing…

"Rebecca, will you please go to the headmaster's office straight away?" said Miss Brook.

"Yes, miss," replied Rebecca, turning bright red, legs into jellies and heart pounding. She knocked at the door.

"Come in," said the headmaster.

As she did so, she saw her mother and a policeman sitting with the headmaster in the office. She stood facing them all with the most angelic demeanour she could muster, whilst she was reprimanded by all three for different reasons. At the end of it, all she was so relieved it was over, and she knew there would be punishment due when her mother said, "I'll deal with you later."

After Rebecca had returned to the classroom, the policeman said, "Wouldn't you want her in your corner? I know I would. Don't be too hard on her."

Rebecca went back to the class room and at playtime was swamped with questions as to why she had to go to the headmaster's office. She informed them that David had run away from the orphanage, and the police wanted to know if she knew where he was, which she didn't.

Her punishment was no pocket money, and in bed by 7pm for a week, and she knew no one would weaken because what she had done was irresponsible, even though she was helping her friend.

She sat at the table at tea time and was aware her mother's mouth was opening and closing, but Rebecca didn't hear any of the words, for she was deep in her own thoughts. *Where was David? How was he feeling now he knew his ma had died?* She would write a letter to him for Bertha to take to the funeral to give him, so she could explain that she hadn't told anyone where he was, and that it was Barney that had given him away.

"Are you listening to me?" yelled her mother.

"Yes," replied Rebecca, jolting back to the moment and hoping her mother didn't need an answer to a question she hadn't heard. "I need to go to the bathroom."

Mr Brown found the funeral director and they were able to contact the insurance company and procure the money due towards the funeral. Whatever David's mother may have done, she made sure there was enough money for the rent, and for her insurance policy, as if somehow she knew that one day he would need it.

Rebecca's mother and Bertha attended the funeral along with others from the village. David was distraught, standing there with people he didn't know, and he couldn't bear to look into the grave and turned his back on it, shouting, "I'm not throwing muck in there." He spotted Bertha and ran to her and hung on so tight, and sobbed. Mrs Gee ran after him.

"Give us a moment," said Bertha. She whispered to David, "I am squeezing into your pocket two envelopes, one is a letter from Rebecca, and t' other is very important, it's your birth certificate and you must never let anyone else 'av it. Hide it. Keep it safe. You will need it in the future. If anyone asks if ya 'av it, say NO." She gave him a hug and a kiss, and Rebecca's mother came and did the same, and then Mrs Gee took him away.

"God almighty," said Bertha, as they walked home. "Whatever next for that poor lad?"

When Rebecca returned from school, she went straight to Bertha's to find out if she had managed to give David her letter and was so pleased that she had. She fired questions at Bertha about the funeral, and the answer came in a typical Bertha take on the events.

"They buried his mother in a nice coffin, in a grave, and everyone said their goodbyes. Yes, David was upset and did cry, but everyone does at funerals." That was all Rebecca could glean out of Bertha.

As the weeks went by, Rebecca settled and was working hard at school. She so wanted to go to Grammar school, and the 11 plus exams were nearing. Her school work had suffered for a while, but Miss Brook knew her potential and worked with her, so by the time the exams were upon them, she had caught up and her enthusiasm had returned. When her name was announced in assembly as a pass student, she was bursting with pride and relief, and just wanted to go home to her parents with the letter.

The playground was buzzing with excitement and anticipation from the children who had passed, and acceptance and disappointment from those who had not, Dorothy Wade being one. When Rebecca saw her crying, she felt a pang of pity and walked towards her and would have tried to find some words of comfort. Dorothy saw her coming and spat out, "Go away," so Rebecca turned and re-joined the others.

At home time, Rebecca ran almost all the way home and burst through the door with her good news. She hadn't expected her father to be there, but he was sitting in his chair, lost in his thoughts, looking sad.

"Dad, I've passed for Grammar school," Rebecca announced excitedly. "Are you pleased with me?"

"Very much," he replied, stood up and hugged her and was unable to control his tears.

"What's wrong, Dad? Where's Mum?" asked a startled Rebecca, and in that moment, she wondered if her mother was dead to make dad cry.

Mr Brown had sat absorbing what had happened during the day and decided to be honest about things from the start with Rebecca.

He, in a shaky voice, replied, "She's gone, she's left us to live with someone else, and this will upset you, because it is Dorothy's father."

Rebecca screwed up her eyes and pursed her lips and so much pain and hatred swept through her she froze on the spot and felt sick.

"Is my mum going to look after Dorothy Wade instead of me?" she asked.

"No," replied her father. "Dorothy and her mother are going to live somewhere else."

"Where?" demanded Rebecca. "Why can't everyone stay where they are? Is it because he has a posh car?"

Now she understood why Mr Wade had been trying to be friendly.

There was a knock on the door so Rebecca ran upstairs out of the way. She went into the bathroom and saw that all her mother's things were gone, and as she passed her parent's bedroom, she saw that the wardrobe had been emptied. A numbing realisation, her mother had gone.

Bertha opened the door at the bottom of the stairs.

"Come on down," she said. "I've made some ginger bread, let's celebrate thi passin thi exam."

Rebecca sighed, ran downstairs and flung her arms round Bertha.

"What are we going to do?" she asked.

"Manage," said Bertha in her pragmatic manner. "You've got thi dad and me, what more do ya want?"

Bertha chatted about Rebecca's choice of school, who else had passed the exam and where they were going, what would her uniform be like and anything else she could think of to divert the conversation from her mother.

Rebecca produced a form to be signed so a parent or relative could accompany her to the new school once she had been accepted, to receive information regarding uniforms, expected discipline, the standards of the school and its targets in education.

"Put me down," said Bertha. "I'll bi thi granny, unless thi mother wants to go with you."

"I don't want her to," said Rebecca, and so the form was signed for Bertha to accompany her.

Mr Brown was bereft; he knew his wife had been snappy and not herself recently but never guessed the reason behind it, although he had tried to talk to her. Bertha had known for a long time, but it wasn't her place to say anything as they had both been good to her, and she was hoping it was just a passing fancy and that no one would get hurt.

The next few weeks were harrowing for Rebecca and her father, both trying hard for each other to hide their feelings, dealing with them alone, at night, in bed. They aimed for some kind of routine, they had cooking disasters, pink washing disasters, shrunken washing disasters and iron implants on shirt flaps, but in time, with Bertha's continual help, things became more orderly and settled. She looked after Barney during the day and was glad of his company, and Rebecca was glad of his welcome when she returned home from school.

On the very last day at junior school Rebecca took Miss Brook a thank you letter and a trinket box as a gift, and said, "Goodbye."

"I'll see you at the leaver's party this afternoon, won't I?" Miss Brook asked.

"I'm not coming," said Rebecca, fed up with all the questions about her mother and Mr Wade, just glad to be away from it all.

"I hope you will change your mind," said Miss Brook, "but if you don't, I wish you well."

"Thank you," said Rebecca, turned and was gone from the school wondering what lay ahead.

Under pressure from her father and Bertha, she was going with her mother as the time grew near to starting her new school for her new uniform and dreading it. Her father insisted it was the right thing to do and that she should see her mother from time to time because the problem was between her parents, nothing to do with her, and they both loved her.

Not enough, or she wouldn't have gone, thought Rebecca, but she didn't say it.

Rebecca caught the bus and met her mother in town.

"Where are we going first?" asked Rebecca, stepping back as her mother approached her for a hug.

They did the rounds and were loaded with packages.

"Let's have coffee and cake before we go home," said her mother and led the way into the cafe and waited to be served.

"I'm so sorry I spoilt your day when you got your news about passing your exam. I had no idea it would be the day I was leaving; I could have changed things if I'd known," said her mother.

"Why did you go, and to THAT man?" snarled Rebecca, "Dad is a good man, everyone says so, and people are not saying nice things about you. Is it because he has a car, and we don't?"

"Life is not as simple as that," replied her mother. "And I hope you are never in a position to find out."

They left the cafe and walked along the street to where Mr Wade was waiting for them in his car.

"I'm not going in THAT car with HIM," said Rebecca, emphatically.

"Get in the car and don't be silly," said her mother.

"If you don't give me my bus fare, I'll walk home, I'm not going with HIM," shouted Rebecca, loud enough to make heads turn.

Her mother gave her the bus fare; she dropped the parcels at her mother's feet and ran off.

When she arrived home, Bertha was there with the parcels her mother had left. She was still huffing and puffing with indignation, but Bertha got her to open her parcels to show what she had bought, and the tantrum passed.

"Thi father 'as paid for all these, ya know," said Bertha. "That's why he's been working longer to get the money together. He'll be mad I've told you, but in my book it's only right you should know."

Rebecca was glad to hear it.

Bertha decided to stay until Mr Brown came home, so she and Rebecca made a cheese and onion pasty, and the mood was relaxed. The three of them sat and enjoyed the pasty with some cabbage and for the first time for a while there was some laughter at the table when Mr Brown started rolling about, pretending he was suffering from food poisoning.

Mr Brown took Barney for his walk whilst Bertha and Rebecca washed up and cleared away, and on his return, they sat round the fire and had a cup of tea.

"I called at the shop for a loaf of bread," said Mr Brown, "and Lil was telling me Mrs Wade and Dorothy have returned to her family home somewhere down south."

"Good," said Rebecca. "Shan't be seeing her again, then."

"Just remember, Rebecca," said Mr Brown, "she will have been hurting like you. She has lost her father, so to speak, the comfort of the home she grew up in, and none of it would have been her fault, like you were not to blame. She has had to move away from her friends and all she has known all her life. You have not," he reminded her.

Rebecca sat quiet, thinking about what her father had just said, for she hadn't given Dorothy a second thought since their lives became splintered, and as Bertha pointed out, Mr Brown was right in his usual considerate, kind way.

Bertha stood up, took her door key out of her pocket and made for the door.

"Thank you for tea," she said. "The pasty was good, Rebecca, you're improving. Good night, God bless."

Mr Brown made his sandwiches for the following day and sat beside Rebecca on the sofa.

"A week to go," he said, "and you will be ready for your first day at your new school. Another stepping stone in your life."

They chatted about bus times, making new friends, she showed him the purse Bertha had bought for her dinner money and was enthusiastic about what lay ahead. Bertha had stitched all her name tapes into her new uniform, and everything was neat and tidy, ready to start another chapter in her life.

She kissed her father 'goodnight' and went up to bed feeling good and looking forward.

Chapter 5

David had made a big mistake running away from the orphanage, because when the authorities caught up with him, he was sent to a remand home, which was a more secure place with a harsh regime to survive in. He was put in a dormitory with 12 beds, each with a locker. He was sent to a room and given a grey shirt and a new pair of boots as he was still wearing wellies that were now too small for him and made him limp because his toes were sore.

Everyone was interested in a newcomer and what had happened in their lives, but David's history was uninteresting to most of the boys, who bragged about their misdemeanours, and very quickly he was just another boy.

Adam was older and much bigger than the other boys, and he was a trouble maker and a bully, with a following of many of the boys who dare not question him or refuse to do his bidding in case he turned on them. He had tried to provoke David, but he didn't rise to it, and even then, Adam put it down to the fact David was afraid of him.

One morning, Adam was trying to put new laces into his boots and making a real mess of it because he couldn't grasp how the master wanted the boys to do it. David spotted him hiding round a corner.

"How about if I do this one?" he said. "And you do that one. Undo what you have done and then we'll start again, together, and they will both end up the same." David was careful not to imply that Adam didn't know how to lace up his boots, but they sat together and ended up with a pair of boots with neat laces.

"Want to be in the gang, then?" asked Adam.

"No," said David, "don't do gangs, and I have to tell you that anything you say or do to me will make no difference because I've been through so much, nothing bothers me."

This wasn't true, of course, but speaking quietly and privately to Adam was far more effective than a full-blown confrontation in front of the others. David's heart was pounding, he couldn't believe he had been brave enough to speak to Adam that way, neither could Adam, because usually people shouted at him or criticised him, not that he didn't deserve criticism for his behaviour, but now for him and David there was an understanding and he left him alone.

There were lessons to attend, but so disruptive were the boys, that the teachers gave up and left the room. There was a library where David and a few of the other boys would go, but most of the books, and there were not many, had been defaced or had clumps of pages missing. There was a teacher who would go to the library and engage with the boys who were keen to learn, but he just had to talk things over with them because so many could neither read nor write. David thought this is what they should be being taught. There were boys who were good and skilful in the woodwork room, but there again there were those who just messed about and spoilt it for the rest.

Sometimes they were allowed supervised time outside, and it was supposed to be every day, for recreation, but that didn't happen, or just for work in the garden where they grew vegetables for the kitchen. David never said anything, but he did wonder what happened to the vegetables, for he saw very few on his plate.

Every evening, after the meal, a lady would wheel a trolley round and collect the roller towels from the wash rooms and hand and bath towels from the staff bathrooms. David saw her struggling and went to help and took it upon himself to help her each evening. As time passed he was doing it himself and taking the trolley down to the laundry. He was more than glad to do this to get away from the dining table before some of the masters arrived and chose some of the boys to go upstairs. He didn't like what he had heard about what happened up there, and he had heard screaming coming from one of the rooms as he was collecting the towels.

David had been hit and thumped by staff members and he never knew why and could only reason that it was because he was last in line on gardening duty, or couldn't keep up in PE. Some of the boys who reacted to this treatment were hit with a cane until their backs bled.

David, during his short life, had become an expert in blending into the background, so when something was happening to draw the attention of the staff, he would try to disappear out of sight, and usually he managed it, but he was fearful that his turn would come.

Kate was the lady he helped in the laundry, she knew his mother and knew what had happened to David, and had gentle thoughts for him and felt he shouldn't have been in that place at all. When she was on her own in the laundry, she sometimes had a treat for him, maybe a scone she had sneaked from the kitchen or a small piece of cake. David never saw any of these in their dining room, so he really enjoyed them. Kate's assistant didn't bond with David at all, so when she was there, he just left the laundry as soon as he had delivered the towels.

Kate had a cough and was arthritic from working in a damp atmosphere and was in a lot of pain most of the time, but as she explained to David, she needed the money and had to continue despite her doctor telling her to find another job in a drier atmosphere.

One morning, David spotted a roll of towel on the staircase that had dropped off the trolley the previous night, so he picked it up and took it down to the laundry. Kate was just taking in a parcel from the postman, and David noticed that when she locked the door she put the key back into a niche in the wall.

Kate's cough worsened over the weeks and David knew in his heart she would have to stop working in the laundry and then he wouldn't be able to escape there, and he would be vulnerable and was afraid. He started collecting things and hid them in the coal house adjacent to the laundry. An enamel mug, a knife, fork and spoon, two slices of carbolic soap, a pair of socks and a towel. He didn't like to think he was stealing, more that he had earned these things whilst he had been working in the laundry and garden. He took more notice of what happened at bedtime with the staff and what their routine was, who did what and when.

Kate had a few days off work, and when she returned she told David that she had managed to find a cleaning job in two houses, for the same family, so she would only be in the laundry another week whilst they found someone else. David knew the woman who didn't talk to him and watched him out of the corner of her eye all the time would be put in charge and that he wouldn't have his little job any more.

He went to bed that night thinking his escape through. The home was in the valley not too far from the village, and when he was in the van being taken to the home, he memorised the route, which was easy. It was springtime, and Hobo may be back in his den, but even if he wasn't, it was a place to go to and hide.

The following evening, he collected the towels and sat with Kate for a short while as she was alone.

"I hope you like your new job, at least you will not be in a dark, damp place all the time," he said.

"No," said Kate, "and I won't have to be up at the crack of dawn every day, either. Just three more days to go in this place, I can't believe it!"

David left the laundry and went straight up to the dormitory and put all his clothes on. He got into bed wearing two pair of socks, two shirts, one his own, one uniform, and two pullovers. In his brown bag in his cupboard, he had his hat that Bertha had made, his scarf and his gloves. His jacket was tucked under the bed next to his boots. Gradually, all the boys went to bed, and David lay there for a long time, almost falling asleep himself until the night watchman walked through to check all was well.

David lay there taking deep breaths, realising that if he was going to go it had to be NOW.

Blocking all thoughts of what might happen to him if he was caught, he slipped out of bed, put on his jacket, picked up his boots and quietly opened his cupboard to get his bag and carefully crept away. There was nobody about, anywhere, and he was very glad of that as he tiptoed down the stairs to the laundry. He crept through to the coal house for the things he had collected to take with him, and sat on the steps leading up to the door to put his boots on.

He opened the door with the key from the niche, went outside, closed it quietly and locked it. He put on his hat, stuffed everything into one bag, pushed the key through the letter box and was on his way. He crept around the building in the shadows, ducked down below a window where there was a light on in a room, ran for the wall, climbed it and set off running along the edges of the fields, heading for the road that would take him to the embankment. He bent down behind a wall when he heard the milk cart horse clomping down the road and the bottles jangling in the crates. They were about to deliver the milk churn for the home, so he had to be out of sight for when they returned. This was the risky part of the journey because he had to go on the road to get to the path leading to the embankment. He looked and listened, there was no sound, just an eeriness to the morning as the day was beginning to break. He ran for all he was worth until he reached the place to gain access to Hobo's den, and then he crept quietly, his heart pounding as he tapped on the panel.

"Hobo," he whispered and tapped again. "Hobo."

There was a stirring inside, and Hobo moved the panel and stepped outside, for he had recognised David's voice.

David flung himself at him and clung to him. "I've run away," he sobbed. "It's so bad living there, and no one ever comes to adopt boys from there because they're all bad, and I would be there forever."

He paused for breath, looked up at Hobo and wiped away his tears with the back of his hands.

"We'd better get inside," said Hobo.

"No one has seen me, or I wouldn't have come here," said David.

There was a fire lit in a square of bricks in the corner, and Hobo had salvaged two shelves from an oven discarded in a quarry which he had put over the bricks, so he could heat his kettle or pan.

"I'm making porridge," said Hobo. "Do you want some?"

"Please," said David, desperate for something to eat.

Hobo saved enough milk for cups of tea and used the rest with some water to make porridge. David had his out of his enamel mug because Hobo didn't have enough of anything for two in the way of crockery or cutlery, except an extra mug for tea.

David, now much calmer because the den was like a safety blanket round him, told Hobo what life was like in the home, how there were beatings with canes by the cruel staff, and how they had PE outside when it was pouring with rain, how they had to let their clothes dry on them, how the food was poor and very little of it, and he was terrified of having to go to the room upstairs.

Hobo listened and when David had finished, asked him, "How exactly are you planning to live, do you have any money?"

"No" said David. "I did have some from ma's policy after the funeral, but they took it off me. Bertha gave me a letter from Rebecca and my birth certificate and told me to keep them safe and give them to no one, so I pulled the stitching out of my jacket sleeve and hid them in there. I couldn't stitch it up so I used two safety pins, and they're still there. I never wore my jacket outside so they didn't get wet and spoil them. If you hadn't been here, I would have gone to Rebecca for some food."

"That's the first place they will go looking for you, I should imagine," said Hobo.

"Are you angry with me?" asked David.

"No! No!" said Hobo. "You shouldn't have your life wasted in such a terrible place where you shouldn't be. I just need to think about what to do next."

They washed their dishes in the remaining warm water. They couldn't talk because a train had stopped at the water station just down the line and it was very noisy. Hobo's den was a shelter dug into the hillside for the men when they were building the water station for the steam engines to replenish their water to continue their journeys, but the shelter was long forgotten and buried in thick undergrowth. Hobo had bought some lino to cover the floor, and a brush and dustpan to keep it clean, and he had organised it in such a way there was a place for everything, even his pram.

At daybreak, Hobo walked up to the water station, emptied his slop bucket, rinsed it and collected coal that had been left behind from the engine. He returned and filled another bucket with water, to be used for washing. He had two large lemonade bottles he would take up to the village and have filled with drinking water, usually by the butcher.

Whilst Hobo was doing that, David took off his extra clothes, folded them and put them in his brown bag so everything was together. He put the pieces of soap on the ledge by the bowl used for washing, and his mug and cutlery on the shelf by Hobo's.

"I've got to go up to the village," said Hobo, "and you need to sleep. You must not under any circumstances go out of here whilst I'm away. Right now, you are safe, and to stay that way you must do as I say, or we'll both be in serious trouble."

Hobo left, and David rolled up in a blanket and used the towel he had taken as a pillow. He lay thinking for a while about all that had happened in the past few hours and felt very lucky he had succeeded in what he set out to do. He hoped that Kate had found the key and managed to put it back in the niche. Kate was picked up each morning at 6am in the van, along with three other people from the village who worked at the home, so no one could implicate her if they found out how David had left. Like any other morning, she had heard the letter box clatter and went to pick up the post, and as everything fit through the letter box she didn't need to open the door. As she was walking away, she heard the key scrape on the step. "Oops," she said, picked it up and put it back in the niche and never thought any more about it until she was informed of David's escape, and then she realised what could have happened, but said nothing.

Good luck to the lad, she thought. *I hope he makes it.*

It was chaotic at the home, staff blaming each other, and the staff and the boys were wondering how David had managed it but for very different reasons.

David fell asleep until the next train came along, and then he was restless until Hobo came back.

The police had been informed and joined in the search, making Rebecca's home the first place to visit, before Mr Brown had left for work, and despite strong denials of knowledge as to David's whereabouts, they insisted on looking under Rebecca's bed as well as the rest of the house.

Where can he be now, thought Rebecca, and for the next few nights she had a peep through her bedroom curtains at bedtime.

Hobo had walked the two miles into the next village and bought two sausages, a pork pie and a tin of vegetable soup. He retraced his steps and went to his usual butcher and bought exactly the same, and had his bottles filled with water. He called at the bakery for a loaf of bread and called at the farmyard for milk. He didn't want to draw attention to the fact he was doubling up on his food purchases.

The village was buzzing with the news of David's escape from the home, for they knew the boy and his history, and most people were wondering what he had done to be taken there in the first place.

Hobo listened, but didn't engage in the conversations as he waited in the shops to be served, but that was normal for him and no one noticed.

The people from the home and the police had been scouring the village, the woods and the allotments from early morning until mid-day, to no avail, so they had given up and gone their separate ways.

When Hobo arrived back at his den, David was awake. He fired questions at Hobo who confirmed there had been a search in the village, but for the time being it seemed to be over.

For their meal, they shared a tin of soup and had a pork pie each. Hobo heated water and they washed the mugs, and then Hobo insisted on having a good wash before bedtime, as he would every night they were together.

He's not a bit like a tramp, David thought. *He's so tidy and clean. I thought they were supposed to be dirty and smell.*

Because there was always plenty of coal to collect from the spills from the engines, Hobo kept the fire going all the time. He'd collect it and lay it out in a corner to dry so that it didn't smoke when it was put on the fire and attract attention. The towel and sometimes socks were hung on a piece of band stretched across the ceiling, and that's why they always smelt of smoke.

Hobo went into his pram and brought out a small chess set.

"You need something to occupy your mind," said Hobo. "Have you played chess at all?"

"No," said David, "but I'd like to learn."

They settled down to play for a good hour, then a train travelled through, and when Hobo moved the panel, it was dark outside. He beckoned to David, gave him the slop bucket and a torch and took him to the water station to empty and rinse it. Hobo jiggled at the coals in the fire and removed the ash tray carefully.

"Come with me," he said. "I'll show you where to dispose of these."

Just a few yards away, there was a thick clump of brambles. Hobo lifted them up with a thick stick that was always there, and tipped the ashes that hissed and fizzed as they hit the ground. He went back to the den for the water they had used for washing earlier, and poured it over the ashes to prevent a fire breaking out. David wondered why they had saved the water; now he knew.

"This you must do every night," said Hobo, "after the 9:30pm train has gone. We don't want the bucket smelling all night, and it's a good time to get rid of the ashes or the fire would choke up and go out. Always remember: good hygiene is important however you choose to live." They had a drink of warm milk, washed the mugs and the pan, put more coal on the fire, rolled themselves up in blankets and settled down for the night.

Hobo lay thinking about what was to be done. He would never hand David over to the authorities, so the only thing he could think of was to somehow send him to his brother living on the south coast for a while. He spoke to his brother John by telephone once a week at a pre-arranged time so they could both be at a public telephone box to take the call. Hobo's real name was Jake, and he and his brother had lived in the family home together; neither had married and had children, so he didn't know how John would feel about taking in a boy. He could only ask, and if it was only temporary, he would probably be prepared to help Jake out. He was to make the call in two days' time, so he would have to ask him then.

The mail train thundered by in the middle of the night, and David, startled, sat bolt upright and wondered what was happening until he realised where he was.

"Mail train," said Hobo. "Go back to sleep."

He put more coal on the fire, rewrapped himself in his blanket and was soon asleep.

David took a little longer, but he was beginning to realise that a lot of what happened in the den and Hobo's life was governed by trains and listening.

The following morning, they had porridge again, and Hobo went to collect coals and water and then asked David to sit with him.

"I need to explain what will be happening over the next few days," said Hobo. "Today, I will go to the village for some supplies, and tomorrow, I will be going to town. I go every week to the Salvation Army hostel to have a bath and to do my washing, I stay overnight, and I will be telephoning my brother John as I do every week. I have other business to attend to so it will be late in the day when I return. I know it will seem a long time for you, but you must do it because this is the safest place for you right now." Hobo decided not to tell David of his plan in case John refused to help.

David nodded at Hobo. "I'll do whatever you tell me," he said, although he did feel a pang of nervousness at being on his own all that time, but he was determined not to take any risks that would result in him having to go back into the home, or even a place that was worse, and he didn't want to get Hobo into trouble.

"I'm going into the village now," said Hobo. "But I will not be too long today."

When Hobo returned, he brought candles, milk, jam, cheese, bread and two apples and had filled the empty water bottles. Also, to David's delight, he had been in the second-hand shop and bought a copy of Treasure Island and a Biggles book to keep David occupied whilst he was away.

They had another session at chess, a spelling test, some mental arithmetic, and then chatted until it was time to prepare the food. They had two sausages in a sandwich and a slice of bread and jam.

They followed the routine from the night before, and when everything was as it should be, Hobo sat David down and gave him his instructions for the following two days.

"There are matches to light the candles up on the shelf, remember to dry the coal out for the fire before you use it, and be careful when you are using hot water or the sharp knife to cut bread. Don't forget the slop bucket, or to fill the other one if you need to, the ash pan needs extra care, and you must remember to pour water over the ashes, do you understand how to do that?"

David nodded. "How do I know if it's the 9:30pm train?" he asked. "I don't have a watch."

"Not the mail train in the middle of the night, but after that, there are seven trains through during the day, count them off," said Hobo. "It will be dark."

In the morning, they had porridge again. Hobo collected what he needed to take with him in a brown canvas pouch that he wore over his shoulder and removed the panel to leave.

"You'll be all right, David, just remember what I have said, take your time with things, always listen before you do anything outside, and there's an apple each day for you," said Hobo.

He replaced the panel and was gone.

David washed up and put things back in their place, lit another candle and settled down to read his book.

Chapter 6

David did everything that was asked of him but just couldn't resist sitting outside for a while after he had seen to the ashes. The fresh air felt good after being inside all day. He listened to the rustling in the undergrowth, an owl hooting in the distance, and there were bats whizzing about. He stretched out his legs and leaned back on his elbows and gazed up at the huge moon for a while and then felt the cold and went back into the den to settle for the night. He built up the fire, went to sleep, the mail train woke him up, he built up the fire again and slept until morning. He'd so quickly become programmed to the routine.

He didn't feel confident enough to make porridge for breakfast, so he had bread and jam and was content with that. The previous day he had spent a lot of time reading Treasure Island, but as he put his book back on the shelf, noticed there were two books belonging to Hobo. He picked one up and started turning the pages and became fascinated by it. There were pictures of body parts and an explanation of how they worked and what they did. He noticed the word renal and remembered he had seen it when he visited his mother in hospital. He decided to have another look and spent the morning browsing through the pages.

He fell asleep for a while, until a train stopped at the water station, and although he was hoping Hobo wouldn't be long, he knew he wouldn't arrive until the train had gone. Eventually, he heard footsteps and a tap on the panel, Hobo was back and glad to be in the warmth of the den out of the rain. His canvas bag was bulging, and he had several packages too, which he stacked in the corner to open later. He had brought some eggs, flour and milk and they made pancakes and spread jam on.

"Ooh!" said David. "They were good."

Hobo smiled. "Yes," he said, "I thought you would enjoy them."

He was pleased by the way David was coping, sometimes overlooking the fact that he was only 11.

"What does renal mean?" asked David,

"That's a strange question," said Hobo.

"I've been looking at your books," said David. "Are they private?"

"Not at all," replied Hobo. "Anything you want to know, I'm sure we can find it, but not just now."

Once they had gone through the routine of the chores and were sitting wrapped in their blankets, Hobo decided to explain to David what he had planned.

"This is what is going to happen in a few days' time," he said. "I have arranged for you to go and stay with my brother, and when you are asked, you have to say he is your uncle and you have to stay with him because your mother has died. The journey will be long and will take time, but I am not going to tell you anything more about it, and then if we are picked up, you can't tell anyone anything because you will not know anything. There are kind people who are willing to help us on our way, but I wouldn't want to involve them by a slip of the tongue and cause trouble for them. I will be taking the pram for new tyre's fitting, so tomorrow we must empty it. I have many things to do over the next few days, but the sooner they are done, the sooner we can get on our way. We will have to travel through the night and rest up during the day. How do you feel about all that?"

"Ok," said David. "I just want to get away from here and not get you into trouble."

He didn't ask how far away he was going, how long it would take, how long he would be staying and what his brother was like. He wanted to ask and to know, but he understood why Hobo was not going to tell him, in case he blurted something out by accident and spoilt everything. They settled for the night, listening to the wind lashing the rain against the panel and appreciating being cosy, dry and safe.

The following days were hectic. The pram was emptied and taken for new tyres, and Hobo went into town shopping twice. One day, he returned with a new jacket and long waterproof for David who was thrilled when he tried them on and then burst into tears.

"Whatever is the matter?" asked Hobo, taken aback.

"I don't have any money, you are spending all yours on me, and I won't be earning for a long time yet to pay you back," said David, choking on the words.

"Well, you'll just have to pay me back when you are earning, then," said Hobo, touched by David's thoughtfulness. "Pass me the primus stove and the Tilley lamp, they both need paraffin."

Hobo collected the pram the following day and packed it with precision, and when they left two days later, the den was empty apart from the slop bucket and some coal and the brush and dust pan. The fire was out, the ash pan emptied and the lino swept for Hobo's return.

The pram was heavy fully loaded, but with a lot of huffing and puffing, one pulling, one pushing, they managed to get up the hill and on to the main road. It would have been easier to go downhill onto the low road, but this passed the remand home and that would have been too risky. It was easier pushing the pram on the pavement, but as soon as it was possible, they went into the country lanes. They heard foxes calling to each other, now and again they heard a dog bark as they neared a farm or houses, they saw a hedgehog scurrying down the gutter, and could hear an owl hooting, but to their relief, they saw no one.

They walked for six hours and eventually arrived at a huge abandoned building. Hobo knew exactly where they were heading because he had used it many times in the past. David didn't know where he was, or where he was going, but he was just glad to be well away from the village. The rotting wooden door scraped on the floor as it was pushed open and startled the pigeons which flew out of the broken windows into the nearby trees. Hobo pushed the pram into a corner, put the brake on and pointed to the floor.

"This is your accommodation for the night," he said, smiling at David who had just been standing there looking round. There were bits of metal and machinery scattered around in the vast space, and most of the lower windows were broken.

"What's that smell?" asked David.

"They used to scour wool here, before it was sent to another part of the mill to be dried," said Hobo. "Through the door near the pram is a washroom, and the last time I was here, there was still running water."

48

"I'm really tired," said David, wanting to divert Hobo's thoughts from washing, but that wasn't going to happen.

"Me too," said Hobo. "We will have something to eat, clear up and have a wash, and then we can have some sleep."

Hobo went to the washroom, turned on the tap and let the water run for several minutes before he filled the kettle. They had bread and cheese and an apple. By this time, the kettle was singing on the primus stove to make a drink of tea, and Hobo put the hot water that was left into their bowl and passed David a piece of carbolic soap and towelling rag.

"Take off your boots," he said to David, "and clean your feet. Let me see them."

David wiggled his toes in the fresh air and Hobo inspected them.

"Your boots are not rubbing then?" he asked.

"No," said David. "The only good thing about the home was a pair of new boots." He cleaned his feet with the soapy rag, dried them and put his socks back on.

"My feet were clean," said David.

"Your feet would have a lot of bacteria on them," said Hobo.

"What's bacteria?" said David, taking his socks back off to have a look.

"Germs which can cause infections," said Hobo, "but you can't see them."

David was hoping there wouldn't be too much of the washing during their travels, but Hobo found a way every single stop they made. He was fastidious about cleanliness and he was trying to educate David to become the same. This seemed so strange to David, he didn't understand at that time what it was all about, but whatever it was, he always did what Hobo asked.

When it was time to settle and sleep, everything but the blankets were put back in the pram in case they had to move on quickly for some reason. There were some hessian bags hanging from a rail that Hobo had used before. He put them on the stone floor to lie on, and before long, both of them were cocooned in their blankets and fast asleep.

They had a busy day before they left the den, they had walked six hours, there were no trains to wake them up and so they slept a solid eight hours. Hobo was awake first and lay planning the night ahead and hoping the rain would stop.

The washroom door creaked. David woke up, sat up and shivered, for he felt really cold. Hobo put his blanket around him and put the kettle on to make a warm drink.

"I think we will get rid of the eggs and have pancakes again," said Hobo.

David sipped his tea and hugged the warm mug and watched Hobo mixing and cooking the pancakes.

"Can you toss them?" asked David.

"Not going to risk it," replied Hobo. "They could end up stuck to the ceiling or on the floor."

He cut an orange in half and squeezed some of the juice onto the pancakes and gave David what was left to eat.

When they had cleared up, David had wanted to explore, so they ventured into other parts of the mill, and Hobo thought it was a good idea to pass another hour or so on because they couldn't leave until it was dark. They came across a very long room with looms that still had partly-made cloth in them.

"Why is it like this?" asked David.

"I don't know what happened here," replied Hobo, "but it's a great shame. I hope someday it will be up and running again. So many people would have worked here, I can't imagine what would have happened to them."

The light was fading in the mill so they made their way back to the pram whilst they could still see where they were going.

Hobo peeled two carrots for them to munch on during their next trek, they put on their waterproofs, opened the door and set off into the wet, blustery night. The cloud covered the moon, so it was much darker than the previous night, and it would have been easy to go back to the mill, but there had been a time worked out by Hobo and his friends, and they had to continue.

The journey to the next resting place was horrendous, with wind and rain blowing against them all night and in some places the lanes resembling streams. Hobo had secured a waterproof cover over the pram, with the blankets folded under the hood and covered in newspapers.

He knew the next day would be difficult because they were to stay in a recess in a disused quarry, the space was limited, but for him alone it had always been adequate, but there was nowhere else for them to go at this stage of the journey that he knew of.

Fortunately, the wind and rain were blowing on the back of the recess, so at least it was dry inside. Hobo unfastened the waterproof covering on the pram and let the water run off into the small bucket which he then left outside to fill with more water.

I'm not washing my feet today, thought David as he watched the bucket filling with water, but he did, as did Hobo, after they had vegetable soup, bread and cheese.

"David," said Hobo, "you did well, I'm proud of you. Do you know how long we walked?"

"No idea," replied David. "It just felt like forever. I'm really tired."

"We walked for eight hours," said Hobo. "It wouldn't have taken so long if we hadn't had to battle against the wind."

The blankets were dry except for some damp on one edge, so they wrapped them around themselves and put their waterproofs on over the top for an extra layer and settled down to try and get some sleep.

The morning, despite the daylight, was dank, the wind moaned as it blew into the quarry, and David found it hard to sleep. Finally, he did fall asleep, but it was a shallow sleep, he was restless, got tangled in his blanket and waterproof, kicked the pram wheel and woke Hobo up, and for six hours, it was just one thing after another so they decided not to try and sleep any longer and had a cup of tea to warm themselves up.

They sat gazing out into the quarry, and Hobo pointed out to David the ruts that the carts had made as the men pushed them up out of the quarry full of heavy stone.

"It was a very hard labour job," said Hobo, "and I guess that most of the village properties down the road were built with stone from this quarry. It made sense not to have to transport it too far after they had got it out of the ground."

"How did they do that?" asked David.

"Blast it out with dynamite," replied Hobo, "and then they would chip away at it with picks to make it manageable to move. There were special men called masons who were skilled at cutting stone into regular shapes with a chisel and a hammer. A lot of men lost fingers that had been trapped, and there were many broken joints caused by falling stone."

"There was a quarry in the village at home," said David, "and a boy went swimming in the water at the bottom and he drowned."

"Yes," said Hobo, "there is no way of telling how deep the water is, and it is far too cold to swim in; never be tempted on a hot day. We need some more milk and drinking water, will you be all right if I walk down to the village?"

"I'll be ok. Will you be long?" said David.

"No," replied Hobo, "I'll be as quick as I can." He took the empty bottles from the pram, passed David his book and set off up the rutted path and disappeared.

David heard something clattering on the shale on the path, and a dog appeared and barked. David held out his hand and the dog went towards him wagging his tale.

"Good dog," said David quietly, and patted its head and tickled under its chin. *What if someone comes looking for it, what do I say?* he thought, panicking.

"Timmy," someone shouted, and the dog was gone.

David sat listening in case the dog decided to come back, but it didn't.

Phew! That was close, he thought.

When Hobo returned, he told him what had just happened.

"I've just seen them along the road," said Hobo. "They were just like me, wet through."

He took off his waterproof, shook it, hung it over the pram handle and lit the primus stove to make something to eat. He cooked sausages and then poured a tin of baked beans over them to heat up.

"A feast," said David, whose eyes had lit up when Hobo passed him his plate of food. He gobbled the food down and wiped his plate clean with a piece of bread. Hobo shook his head.

"It's not good to eat so quickly," he said. "Take your time and make it last, enjoy every mouthful."

"I did enjoy it," said David, not understanding what all the fuss was about.

"What I am trying to get across to you is that it is not acceptable to eat like that when you are sat at a table in company, and you do have to learn to use your knife and fork correctly," said Hobo. "Just remember that I am trying to help you so that you will fit in to your new surroundings."

"I do know," said David, emphatically. "They showed us at school."

"Then try and remember, and don't use your fork like a shovel," said Hobo.

There was a silence between them until they started to wash up and pack up, but Hobo was quietly pleased that David did have a spark in him.

The rain had stopped, and the wind had calmed, but the sky was still grey and darkness fell earlier than expected, so they were able to set off sooner.

They walked through the village, David walking close behind Hobo. They passed the pub, the only place where there were any signs of life. David had a flashback to his mother when he heard the chatter and laughter and could smell the beer, remembering how it was when he would sometimes sit on the wall and wait for her.

Into the country lanes they trundled along. Sometimes, at crossroads there were signposts, but these meant nothing to David, he just trusted Hobo knew where he was going, which of course he did.

As dawn was breaking, they turned into a lane that led off to a farm house.

"What if they see us?" asked David in a panic, for he'd seen the two border collies racing towards them.

51

The dogs fussed around and ran back to the house when they heard a lady call them. David stayed behind Hobo as the lady came towards him and gave him a hug.

"Glad to see you, what kind of journey have you had?"

"Not the best," replied Hobo. "We are glad to be here. This is David, and this lady is Dora."

Dora took hold of David's cold hand and led him into the house, into the warm kitchen with a blazing fire recently lit.

"Where's Hobo?" David asked.

"Is that what you call him?" Dora said. "It's a good name for him right enough. He will have gone to seek out my husband Bill, but they will be here soon for breakfast. Come with me and help me collect the eggs." She gave David a basket and they walked around the farmyard and into the barn and collected eggs, some still warm.

"They don't get any fresher than that, do they?" she said looking down at David.

Soon they were all sitting round the table enjoying bacon and egg and toast, when Bill, through the window, noticed a car coming up the lane and realised it was the local policeman. He took David's plate and emptied what remained on it onto his own plate and put the empty plate, knife and fork into the sink, whilst Dora hustled David upstairs and told him to be quiet.

The policeman knocked, and Dora opened the door.

"Any eggs to spare?" asked the policeman.

"Yes, there will be," said Dora. "Are you having a cup of tea?" She always asked him, and sometimes he did and sometimes he didn't, but today he did.

"It's a bit early in the year for your visit, isn't it Jake?" the policeman remarked. Jake's elusiveness irritated him.

"I don't have a timetable, I come and go as I please. I'll be back for the harvest," replied Jake.

Chat continued for a while, until Bill got up from the table and said he would have to get on, so he and the policeman left the house together.

As soon as Dora saw the car leave the lane, she went upstairs for David, who hadn't moved an inch since she left him.

"Bill ate the rest of your breakfast," she said. "Do you want some toast?"

"I'm tired," said David. "I've been walking all night."

"I'd forgotten about that," said Dora. "Do you want to go to bed?"

"Where's Hobo?" David asked.

"He'll be in the barn, that's where he normally sleeps," replied Dora.

"I want to sleep there too," said David.

"He won't leave you," said Dora.

"I know," said David, "but he's my friend and he might be lonely."

They walked over to the barn, and there was Hobo washing his feet.

"Oh, no!" groaned David and sat down and took off his boots.

"I offered him the bed," said Dora, "but he wanted to be with you."

"Wake us up after three hours," said Hobo. "We need to adjust to normal time."

David loved the next few days at the farm. Dora was like a mother hen, loving every moment because she missed her own son who was hardly ever at home. Hobo worked with Bill on the farm and they enjoyed each other's company, always. In the past, Hobo had just turned up to fill his water bottles and see if there were eggs or milk to buy, when he overheard a conversation that Bill was struggling to find labour to get his crop in before the weather turned. Hobo offered to stay and help, and they had remained friends ever since. Hobo made sure he was always there to help with the harvest. Every week, as with his brother John, Hobo would call Bill at a certain time at the public telephone box in the village, and that is how they kept in touch.

Dora did the washing and made really good meals for them all for the end of the day. She involved David with the chores, and he spent time with the dogs, and he wanted to go up into the fields with them to see the sheep, but he could have been seen from the village up there, so that wasn't allowed.

Hobo had mentioned to Dora that David had not mentioned his mother at all and felt that was not a good thing, so one afternoon she asked him about his mother and he blurted everything out and cried uncontrollably. He only saw her once in hospital when Mr Brown had taken him on Christmas day, and they, whoever made the rules, wouldn't let him go again, and he didn't want her to think he didn't care about her.

"I think," said Dora, "that when she was so poorly, so she didn't have any pain, they would have given her something that would make her sleep, and the last thing she would remember was you visiting her."

David wiped his eyes. "Would she?" he said. "Is that what she would remember?"

"Was she able to talk to you when you visited her?" Dora asked.

"Yes," said David, "she said I was a good son and she was proud of me and loved me, and I said I loved her."

"Well," said Dora, tears streaming down her cheeks, "I think that was a wonderful conversation for a mother and son to have. I think she knew how ill she was and it was important for her to tell you how she felt, and she had that chance, and to hear you tell her you loved her was all she needed."

"She didn't die then," said David. "She waved and smiled as I left her room."

"She was proud of you then, make sure she still is as you grow up, she may be watching over you from on high, you'll feel her closeness sometimes."

At that time, Dora's remark was more than he could understand, but later in his life, he understood.

Dora related the conversation she had with David to Hobo.

"I hope it helped," she said. "But who can tell how an 11 year old can cope with all that has been thrown at him. I don't know how you came to be involved with him, but I thank God you did."

"That's a story for another time," said Hobo, "but I will tell you one day."

Dora had noticed how skinny David was when she finally persuaded him to change his shirt to be washed, and it was her mission to beef him up a little bit before he moved on. She noticed the scars on his back and arms and thought he'd been whipped.

She made roast beef, Yorkshire puddings, roast potatoes and cabbage one day, ham, eggs and chips another day, and they were having stew and dumplings that day, and it had been cooking slowly in the oven all afternoon and smelt tempting. There was always plenty of apple pie or custard tart to finish off.

David had remembered what Hobo had said about using his knife and fork correctly and eating slowly, and most of the time, he remembered. Hobo didn't say anything, but he gave David a sly nod to let him know he had noticed.

The following morning, they were having breakfast when Hobo said, "Try and have a few hours' sleep this afternoon, David, we are leaving tonight."

David was stunned, his expression said it all, he was happier than he had ever been in his life and he didn't want to leave. He ran out of the house and into the barn, followed closely by Dora, who thought he might run off. She sat at the side of him and put her arm around his shoulder.

"It isn't possible for you to stay because sooner or later, the policeman would see you and start asking questions," she said, "and you know what would happen then. I've made you some currant buns and ginger biscuits to take with you, and a jar of my blackberry jam, and see if you can find any eggs. Maybe in time you will be able to come back and see us, and you will always be welcome here. I'd be happy to receive a letter from you now and again. Jake writes to us sometimes."

David was glum, he just rolled himself up in his blanket and shut his eyes. Dora went back to the house, but it wasn't long before she saw David with the basket collecting eggs. He sat with the dogs and stroked them for a while, and then he went and sat on the wall opposite the barn and watched Hobo loading up the pram. He walked into the barn to check Hobo had packed the buns and biscuits in the nick of time, because the policeman turned into the lane and made his way to the farm house.

"Quick," said Hobo, "go up to the loft and be still." He gave David his blanket, and as soon as he had scurried up the ladder, Hobo removed it and laid it propped against the barn wall on the floor. Bill called the dogs and fastened them up on their chains because he didn't want them giving the game away, and he had no idea where David was.

"No need to fasten them up, they know me well enough," said the policeman.

"They're getting in my way," said Bill. "I need to know where they are when I'm using the truck."

"Any spare eggs?" asked the policeman.

"Not today," Dora said, "laying has dropped off a bit. Are you having a cup of tea?"

"Need to be getting on with the job," the policeman replied.

He got in his car and drove slowly down the lane, stopping at the barn when he saw Hobo. He wound his window down. "Still here then?" he commented.

"Yes," replied Hobo, thinking what a silly question. "I'm thinking of moving on for a while now; Bill doesn't really need me until the harvest."

"Where will you go?" asked the policeman.

"I don't even know whether I will turn right or left when I get to the end of the lane," replied Hobo. "That's the joy of my freedom."

The policeman had always been intrigued by Hobo and wondered if he was running away from some crime, but he had never been able to glean any information from Hobo, and Bill and Dora only knew he was a man of the road, hardworking and reliable, so they were unable to tell him anything when he had tried to quiz them in the past.

"Must get on," said the policeman and drove away.

Hobo watched until he saw the car disappear, and then he put the ladder back for David to come down from the loft.

"Now do you understand why we have to move on?" said Hobo.

"Yes," said David quietly. The point had been made and it couldn't have worked out better if it had been planned. He spent most of the rest of the day in the house with Dora and managed a couple of hours' sleep before tea. There was cold ham, baked potatoes with crunchy skins and butter, and carrots. There wasn't a lot of chatter, but suddenly David said, "Is this like the last supper then?" They all laughed.

"I hope not," said Bill. "I've a lot to do tomorrow."

Dora kept David busy helping her to wash up and stack the dishes, but eventually it was time to get ready to go. David stood by the truck whilst they used two planks to make a ramp to get the pram up, he gave Dora a hug and climbed into the truck so they could hide him behind some bales of hay. David was crying, Dora was crying, the truck doors slammed shut and they set off down the lane. Dora watched them disappear and walked back into the house. She didn't like the emptiness and silence, so she let the dogs in and talked to them.

Chapter 7

Bill dropped them off at the crossroads, shook hands with Hobo, and went on his way to deliver the bales of straw to another farmer.

Hobo didn't expect David to be too chatty on the journey, but he'd loved his time at the farm and had much to say about it.

They didn't seem to have been walking long compared to previous nights, when Hobo stopped at a big gate. Behind the wall was a recently furrowed field which they had to cross to reach the thick copse which grew where four fields merged. It was a struggle to get the pram across in the long grass at the edge of the field in the dark, but they managed it eventually and sat down for a breather. Hobo shone his torch and found a suitable place for them to rest up. He placed the waterproof cover from the pram onto the ground for them to sit on and made a drink of tea.

They rolled up in their blankets and waterproofs and tried to sleep. They could hear things scurrying about and David really didn't like being there, but he was so tired because of lack of sleep from the previous day that eventually, he did fall asleep.

Hobo woke him up, and it was daylight.

"I need to go into the town," he said. "I'm leaving you here, you will be all right, the work has been done in the fields, so no one will be working them, and I am leaving the pram which will make it easier. Read your book or go back to sleep. I had to wake you up to let you know what I was doing."

David, still bleary eyed, rested his chin on his bent knees, and watched Hobo disappearing through the mist hovering over the field, his presence sending rabbits scurrying for their burrows.

There was a flash of russet against the wall, and a fox ambled along, sniffed the air and used the style to get into the next field.

All went quiet, very quiet. He was beginning to feel very anxious when a robin appeared and bobbed from branch to branch quite near him. It had started to rain, not heavily, but the sort of rain that was very fine and wet you through. He pulled the pram further into the copse where the bushes and trees gave better cover and replaced the waterproof cover. He propped himself against a tree trunk and wiggled until he was comfortable, and as he sat quiet, he noticed the robin was still close by.

He started thinking about all that had happened since he ran away from the home, and wondered what had happened there since. He hoped Kate liked her new job and was feeling better now she wasn't working in the damp.

Hobo had shown him such kindness from the moment he fell through the roof of his den and whatever happened in his life, he was determined to repay him in every way he could. He knew that soon he would be leaving Hobo to live with his brother John, and that troubled him, but he knew he had to go and try and make the most of it and be thankful that John had agreed to give him a chance.

He was glad to see Hobo, hood up, head down, walking towards him.

"Have you been all right?" he asked David.

"It seemed a long time," said David, "but there's been a robin flitting around here all the time you have been away, and I saw the rabbits and a fox."

"Shall we have something to eat now?" asked Hobo. "We can move on in a couple of hours."

"In the daylight?" asked David. "Will it be safe?"

"Yes, it will," replied Hobo. "We go that way."

He pointed through the copse, indicating they would not be retracing their steps back onto the lane they had come from.

They had bread and a slice of ham from Dora and ginger biscuits. No washing up, no water warming to wash their feet, not even a mention of it, and David certainly wasn't going to in case Hobo had forgotten, but he did wonder what was going on.

Hobo looked at his watch several times.

"That's us away," he said. "Come along, I'll need some help with the pram."

They struggled through the copse and along the edge of another ploughed field, through a gate, along a path and onto the canal towpath.

"This is a canal," said Hobo. "Do you know anything about them?"

"I know they are like a water road," said David, "but I've never seen one before."

David leaned against the wall and watched the longest boat he could imagine coming towards him. He'd never actually seen a boat at all, but he'd seen pictures of boats, but nothing like this one.

The man at the very back of the boat doffed his cap at Hobo.

"Good day, Jake," he said. "They were next in line at the lock so they shouldn't be long."

"Is that your lad, then?" said a gruff voice from one of the children leaning over the side.

"Are they prisoners?" asked David.

"They're children that live on the boat," said Hobo. "What made you ask that?"

"They were strapped in," said David.

"Yes," said Hobo, "that's so they can't fall in when they are on the move."

"Are we going to go on one of these boats?" asked David.

"We are," replied Hobo, "for a few weeks until John is ready for you. I think it's time you started calling me Jake."

David stood still, thinking, not knowing what would happen next. This was an adventure, something he would never had imagined in his wildest dreams, of which there were many. His head was full of questions, but he just waited to see what would happen next.

Another boat came slowly towards them and stopped alongside the towpath. A man got off the boat, walked along the towpath and turned a corner of the tarpaulin back and pulled off two planks so they could get the pram on and stood talking to Jake.

A lady came out of the cabin and beckoned to David.

"Come on, lad," she said. "We'll be moving soon."

Jake helped him on, because David wasn't going anywhere without him, still unsure of what was happening.

"This is Betty," said Jake, "and her husband is Jed."

Jake looked at David with a look and a nod that said 'remember your manners'.

"I'm David," he said. "Pleased to meet you."

Jake's brother was a stickler for good manners, so Jake had been trying to educate David quite gently and subtly, in small ways, to help him fit in better for what lay ahead when he moved to John's. He would have to go to school and mix with new people and be able to present himself favourably because no one would know about his past and make allowances for him.

"Come down into the cabin," said Betty. "See where you will be living. This is the kitchen, living room and bedroom," she said, spreading out her arms with the palms of her hands up, indicating that this small space was all there was. It was very clean and tidy, which was a necessity considering everything that took place in that small space.

"Where do we sleep?" asked David.

Betty explained that they folded down the cupboard door to fill the gap between the cupboard and the side bench, and this served as a bed which you could sleep on or under. She showed him a cupboard with a large number of shelves for stowing things like bedding and clothes, crockery and cooking utensils and the top of the cupboard folded down to make a table under which was a drawer for cutlery. Opposite was a solid bench used for more storage, for sleeping on if you were a small person and for seating space during the day.

Everywhere David looked, there were paintings of flowers and castles, both inside and outside the boat, and even the chimney stack had flowers painted on it and three polished brass rings around it.

There were plates displayed with flowers on them and lattice holes round the rims which had ribbon threaded through them.

"Don't you ever live in a house?" asked David.

"This is our home," said Betty, "although one day we will probably live in a house and it will seem very strange. Neither Jed nor I have lived anywhere else but on the boats. We've had more room than many because sadly we have no children. We have visited people in houses, but the space does not draw us to them or the permanent closeness of other people. Do you like our home?"

David looked up at her and beamed. "It's magic," he said and couldn't put into words how he felt. "Can I go outside?"

"Don't touch the chimney stack," said Betty.

He leaned over the side and kept calling for Jake to look at things he was pointing at, things that he had never seen before, like a heron and ducks in the wild. He had only seen ducks hanging in the butcher's shop with no feathers on. He was very excited and enthusiastic and kept darting from one side of the boat to the other, not wanting to miss anything. Jake was reassured that he had made a good decision in giving David this opportunity with the willingness of Betty and Jed to help. He wanted David's confidence to grow, and living with the boat people would help. Moving on from there to John's would be another matter, but he would deal with that when the time came.

A boat came towards them from the opposite direction. There were greetings passed across from the adults, and one of the children shouted across to David, "What's your name, then?"

"David, what's yours?"

"Dougy," the boy replied. "Might see you later."

"I'm wanting to get through the lock before supper," said Jed. "Then we can have an early start tomorrow."

Betty took over the boat whilst Jed set off on a bicycle on the tow path to check if anyone else was waiting.

"What's a lock?" whispered David to Jake.

"Wait and see, you'll be going through one soon," said Jake, thinking the experience would be far better than an explanation from him, and of course it was.

David was mesmerised by the size of the huge oak gates and the surge of rising water. He looked startled when the boat juddered and everything in the cabin rattled, but finally, the huge lock gates closed, and they moved along and moored behind another boat to spend the night.

Jake took a large triangular water can decorated with pictures of castles and filled it with drinking water from a tap near the lock house and also his own water bottles.

Must be going to wash our feet again, thought David, and he turned out to be right.

"Remind me to fill up the can again in the morning before we leave," said Jake. "We'll use all this tonight."

As soon as the children from the other boat saw David, they came running for him to play, and apart from asking his name, it was as if he had been with them forever.

"I hope he is careful and doesn't fall in," said Betty.

"So do I," said Jake. "He can't swim."

The children played, laughing and screaming so loud that when supper was ready, Betty had to walk down the towpath to them to be heard. She chatted with them all for a little while and then returned to her boat with David.

There was a pot of rabbit stew in the middle of the table, four enamel plates, spoons and forks, and a plate of bread cut to dip into the stew and mop the gravy up off the plate. Jake had brought the currant buns down that Dora had made; they ate two each and they were all gone but very much enjoyed.

Jake and David washed up, Jed smoked his pipe and Betty put things back in the cupboard and brought out blankets and pillows.

The cargo was wood, so Jake rolled the tarpaulin back and he and David retired with some hot water for washing and settled down in the cargo to sleep. Jake liked to sleep that way, the boat sides sheltering from draughts and able to breathe fresh air. If it rained or the cargo was not suitable for sleeping on, then they would have to sleep inside but he didn't care for the smoke or smell from the bituminous coal. The fire always died down after the meal was cooked, but the stove was still hot enough to heat the water required.

David lay flat on his back and looked up at the clear sky, after Jake had turned the Tilley lamp off. It was black, the moon a golden crest, and the stars were glinting and twinkling, and he thought of his mother.

I wonder if she can see me? he thought. *Is it all heaven?*

He felt as if someone had just stroked his cheek as he fell asleep.

Chapter 8

It was still dark, but David could hear voices and thought he hadn't actually been to sleep. He lit his torch and looked at Jake's watch and screwed his eyes up, thinking he wasn't focusing properly, but yes, he was, it was 4:30 in the morning. He looked at Jake, who was still asleep, and walked round to the cabin in a daze. Jed was about to start up the engine, not bothering to light the fire because the range was to be cleaned later.

"Good morning, lad," he said. "Betty will make breakfast soon."

David just stood there like a statue for a few moments, wondering if this was really happening, or was he dreaming? He gave Jed a watery smile, turned around without saying anything, went back to Jake, wrapped himself in his blanket and went to sleep.

He was aware of the movement of the boat and the chugging of the engine, but somehow, he slept until 7am, when Jake made him get up and wash. Jake had moved the pram off the cargo of wood, so it wasn't there when they arrived at the off-loading bay, and he walked there, but before he set off with David, he helped Jed roll back the tarpaulins, so the hoists could have access to the wood.

"Don't get in the way," he said to David. "Come with me."

They set off together and arrived before Jed, who was second in line for off-loading. Betty had wrapped two slices of bread and jam for David, because breakfast was long over, and Betty was doing the washing in the cabin. It was a good time to do it whilst they were waiting to be off loaded. She had a large galvanised bucket with a lip on the bottom to secure it to a huge primus stove to heat the water, and because they were not reloading until the following day, Jed strung a line between the masts to hang the washing on to dry.

When all the cargo had been hoisted from the boat into the timber yard, Jed moved further down the canal, glad of a space without having to encounter a lock to re-load his cargo the following morning.

They collected several buckets of water from the tap just off the towpath for Betty to rinse the washing, and then she pegged it out on the line to dry and freshen in the wind.

In the afternoon, David went with Betty into the village to buy food, and on their return, was expecting to see if any of the other children were about, but after they had a drink of tea, Betty produced a basket of cleaning materials. The range was polished shiny black, and the brass rail around three sides of the stack was polished until it gleamed. The ornate painted jugs from the shelf at the back of the range had to be washed and put back clean.

David was exhausted and relieved to hear they would only have to do it twice a week. His arms ached, his knees were sore from kneeling, and apart from being black, his fingers ached. He could see how spick and span the cabin was, but there was never a lot of cleaning done when he was at home so he had no idea how much effort went into it. When the time came to leave, he certainly knew just how very hard the boat people worked, not just carrying cargo up and down the canals in all weather, and all that entailed, but the effort and pride they took to maintain their boats, both inside and out.

Betty cooked tea for them on the primus stove; there was no point in lighting the fire now. The weather was clement, and the washing was dry.

"Do you like eggy bread?" she asked David.

"I don't know," he replied. "What is it?"

Betty explained that she soaked bread into beaten eggs and fried it until it was crisp and brown on both sides.

"Sounds good to me," said David and tucked into it with gusto when it was served to him with fried tomatoes and a few green runner beans that had been left in a box by a farmer for the boat people to help themselves to.

Every now and again, churches in the villages would have a social evening where they welcomed the boat people to join them, always charging an entrance fee for the adults so as not to appear patronising. There were singers, a jumble stall, games for children and a pea and pie supper and buns made by the ladies of the church. It was usual for someone from the boat people to perform a song or a clog dance, and the villagers always appreciated this.

Some of the men stayed with the boats because always there was an element of people who would cause trouble if they could.

"Are you worrying about David being spotted as a new child?" asked Betty.

"Yes," replied Jake. "I recognised the man that was here the other day from the authorities, trying to find out which child belonged to who. He always attends these gatherings, and if you watch him, you will see he stands in corners and makes notes, because children will naturally return to their parents from time to time. It's futile, but he is paid to do a job. If he singles David out as a strange face, I've told him to say he is on holiday with his granddad, and he doesn't know his address because he is going to live with an uncle he has never met, because his mother died. Not good to lie, but we will not be hurting anyone. I would be very surprised if the man came to me for clarification. He's seen me before and he knows I come and go. I just had to make David aware."

There was nothing to concern Jake. David was never still long enough for anyone to have any conversation with him. He joined in all the games, musical chairs, team games, sucking dried peas on a straw for which he won a bar of chocolate, and bobbing apples, but he gave up on that, not liking the water up his nose.

At 9 pm, there was a hymn and a prayer and a vote of thanks from a spokesman for the boatpeople, and it was time to leave.

David returned to Betty. "Here's your bun," she said. "Are you going to eat it now?"

"No," he replied, "it's for Jed."

In that quick moment, Betty's heart melted, and tears welled in her eyes.

This little boy is someone special, she thought. *Despite all he's gone through, he's considerate, never greedy and willing to help when needed.* Now she could see why Jake had taken it upon himself to make sure David had a better life that was not wasted.

61

The following day was Sunday, a rest day regarding the movement of cargo boats, but a day when the range and everything round it was polished and cleaned, maybe some paintwork touched up, and some of the men would go for a beer if they were near a place that was specifically for them.

When the chores were done, they went into the village to visit Jed's sister. She and her husband had been boat people, but when her husband had become ill, they sold their boat and bought a small cottage in the village, but he died from pneumonia shortly after moving, so Jed's sister had lived there alone for several years, never happy but nowhere else to go. Now she was very frail, and the need to be cared for was very obvious. There was room for Betty and Jed because the cottage had two bedrooms, they had no furniture and just a few belongings to take so the situation was perfect, but Betty left the decision to Jed, although she did make it clear she was happy to care for his sister.

They would only need to buy a bed, bedding, a wardrobe, chest of drawers and a rug, and they would have the funds from the sale of the boat.

Jed had always maintained his boat well and it was often admired, and recently one of the bosses from the wood mill depot said he would be interested in buying it to convert it into a pleasure boat for his family. He was in a good position to do so, having all the wood needed for a conversion and a workforce to call on to do it.

A few weeks earlier, Jed had called at the canal side pub to cash a cheque, where there was a letter waiting for him from Jake, asking if he and David could visit for a few weeks. The landlord read the letter to Jed and wrote a reply to Jake at the Salvation Army hostel and another letter and a telephone call, and everything was in place and had worked out. Jed was so pleased to see Jake and be able to talk things over with him regarding selling his boat, for he valued his opinion and knowledge of the world outside the insular life on the canals. They spent a few hours at his sister's, Betty cleaning and washing, Jake and Jed talking and planning, and David sat and read a comic for a while. He had tried chatting to Jed's sister, but she didn't want him there he realised when she shut her eyes and pointed to the door, so he had a wander around the neighbourhood.

Jake had pointed out to Jed that he should sell his boat now rather than wait until there were more coming up for sale, because buyers would be in control and sellers would have to take what was offered. Jed understood what Jake was saying, but it was with a heavy heart he finally made up his mind to sell.

On their return, Jake spent a good two hours with David doing sums, times tables, spelling and copying a page from Treasure Island to improve his writing. He had explained to David that he would have to take a test, and do well to be accepted in the school John had in mind for him, and he had missed so much schooling this revision was very necessary.

"Couldn't I just stay here?" asked David one day.

Jake explained that very soon Betty and Jed would not be working on the canals, and this would probably be their last year. There was less work for everyone still running a canal boat for a living, because companies were using the road and rail networks because they were quicker. Betty and Jed were finding it harder to cope, especially in the winter months and because of their age.

Whilst Betty and David were in the cabin playing cards, Jake and Jed were talking quietly out of earshot. Jake was to be away for two days to ascertain train times and dates with John. Jed had his week planned out and was able to say where he would be for Jake to re-join them by bus, and a plan was set in place, so they would be where they should be for David to catch his train to John's the following week.

David wasn't worried at all to be left with Betty and Jed; he was loving the lifestyle, the calmness of the journeys, the ever-changing countryside and the people. He had become good friends with Dougy, and when their paths crossed, they spent as much time together as they could, and David taught him how to write his name and copy the letters of the alphabet, for he had never been to school and was keen to learn to read so he could have books. David had learned how to ride a bicycle, because these were often used for people to ride ahead on the towpath to prepare the lock, and he and Dougy would ride up and down, and those watching were amazed that one or both hadn't fallen in.

Because Jake was away, it was decided David would sleep in the cabin. He had settled down and gone to sleep, but was woken up by someone he thought was felling a tree outside. It was dark. *What time is it*, he thought, then he realised no one was felling a tree, it was Jed snoring. It continued for ages, David tossed and turned and buried his head under his cover, and finally the snoring stopped. *Thank goodness*, he thought, but the snoring had only stopped because Jed was up lighting the fire. David just picked up his blanket and pillow and disappeared to the cargo hold. He felt the vibration from the engine, but he was used to that, and was soon asleep. It was almost 10 am when he heard Betty calling him.

"David," she called, "it's time you were up. You need to wash and do your schoolin'."

Clearly, Jake has left his instructions, David thought as he walked bleary eyed to the cabin.

Betty made David some tea, and put the rest of the hot water from the kettle into a bowl so he could have a wash. She looked at him. "Would you ever have a wash if we didn't make you?" she asked.

He looked up at her. "Probably not," he replied playfully, "or maybe once a week."

Over the two days Jake was away, Jed spent more time with David, explaining how the canal system worked and how it had changed over the years and what the traditions of the boat people were. Both he and Betty had been born on a canal boat and had known no other way of life. They had met at a social evening, and both families had worked in tandem when they could so that he and Betty could spend time together, and soon they were married. In time, they sold their parents' boats and had enough money to buy their own and had lived in it for over 30 years.

Jed had loaded with bags of flour, which took longer than loading timber because he had to be sure the load didn't shift in transit, or they could capsize. He and David had walked over the bags to tread them even, and the boat was ready for leaving when Jake appeared, so they moved on and passed through the lock before they stopped for the night. A boat carrying coal was moored further along, so Jed went to fill his coal bucket, as was the custom, and chatted to the boat owner for a while. Jed was very quiet during supper.

"Is anything the matter?" Betty asked.

"I've just been talking to Harry," said Jed. "He's heard the National Coal Board are trying out rail and road transport for deliveries. He's already taken a cut in pay to ensure some business and can't take another, so he's thinking this might be his last trip."

Harry's boat had carried coal for years and was not in good condition, and although Jed knew his boat was in good condition, he realised there were others better than his, so he should accept the offer made by MrButterworth, who owned the wood mill, and do the deal as soon as possible. Because Jed's sister lived in a two-bedroom cottage and had become ill and needed caring for, he and Betty had somewhere to live, but Harry, his wife and four children had no idea what would happen to them. Jake suggested they should decide where they wanted to be, apply for a council house, and if it was near a pit, Harry could find work there, and the children would have proper schooling. The idea lifted Harry's spirits, and he went back to his boat to discuss it with his wife.

"Come and sit with me," said Jake to David. "It's time to have a serious chat."

They rolled the tarpaulin back and sat on the sacks of flour. David knew what Jake was going to tell him, but he didn't want to hear it.

In 5 days' time, he was to be put on a train to travel a whole day alone, to be met by John and to start another chapter in his life.

David couldn't speak, tears burnt his cheeks and dropped off his chin. Jake put his arm around him and gave him a piece of cloth to wipe his nose.

"I don't want to leave, can't I stay with you?" pleaded David.

"You know that's not possible," replied Jake. "And although it will be strange at first, you will have a good life with John. He's going to have to get used to having a boy around the house, and I think you will be good for each other; just remember what I told you about good manners. Let's go and have a drink of tea with Betty. I'm going to ask her to take you shopping for some new clothes and shoes and a bag to carry everything in. I can't send you to John with nothing to wear."

They returned to the cabin where Dougy was sitting with Betty.

"He's going to be staying on our boat for a few days," said Betty. "We thought you might like the company."

"Come on," said Dougy, "let's go on the bikes." And off they went.

Having Dougy on the boat proved to be a brilliant idea, such a good diversion for David. Dougy was a ball of energy, rolling from one idea to another for things to do, imaginative, sometimes reckless and so happy to have someone his own age to spend time with. For them both, it was a first experience of a true friendship bond.

David had taken time to help Dougy with his reading and writing, they had a little session each day when they could, because David could tell Dougy really wanted to learn.

Jake had given Betty money to take David shopping for his new clothes and shoes, so she took him and Dougy on the bus into town. The first thing she bought was a holdall for carrying his belongings in, then they went to the shoe shop. It was the first time in his life he had a new pair of shoes, and he couldn't hide his excitement. The salesman sensed this was a special occasion for David, and he let him try a pair of black patent dance shoes on just for fun.

"I don't think so," said Betty, raising her eyebrows and laughing at David pretending to waltz. The boots he had from the home were still going strong, but these shoes were very special, they had no laces, were called slip-ons. The salesman had got caught up in the excitement and gave David a tin of polish so he could look after his new shoes properly.

"That is kind of you," said Betty, "much appreciated."

"I see so many obnoxious, ungrateful children, it's wonderful to come across a child who appreciates things," said the salesman.

David thanked him, said "goodbye," and headed for the department store.

They bought three vests, three underpants, two pairs of pyjamas, two shirts, a pair of long trousers, socks and two long-sleeved jumpers. The jacket Jake had bought him before they left the den still fit him and had hardly been worn, so that was everything on the list taken care of.

Betty saw David watching her as she paid for everything and could tell he was anxious about it, so when there was a moment when Dougy was looking around she whispered, "Don't be worrying about paying for these things, Jake has paid, and he says he has an arrangement with you to pay him back one day." She winked at him, put a finger to her lips, "Shh!"

Neither David nor Dougy had ever been in a big store before, and they were mesmerised.

They looked at the plastic models dressed in fancy clothes, with bright red lips and long eyelashes, and stood for a long time gazing at pictures on the walls of ladies in underwear until Betty realised and dragged them away.

The boys' giggled and whispered on their way to the barber's shop for haircuts, but Dougy resisted and waited outside.

"Come on," said Betty. "I'm going to treat you both now."

She took them down a narrow passage to a shop that only sold men's hats and caps, and bought them a flat cap each, which they wore straight away.

"Just need a toothbrush and toothpaste, and then we're done," said Betty.

"I've got a toothbrush," said David.

"Yes," said Betty, "but Jake says it is well used and needed replacing, and if you were to protest, I had to remind you of Lil at the corner shop."

An image appeared in David's memory of Lil and her broken, brown teeth, and he smiled. He would keep his old toothbrush, he often thought about Rebecca when he used it and wondered what she was doing in her life.

They went into a snack bar where Betty had tea, and a first again for the boys, they had a strawberry milkshake and a ham sandwich, and then they sat in a little park for a while until it was time to catch the bus back to the village. The walk from the bus stop to the canal wasn't far, but they were all tired and glad to be back.

The day before David was due to leave, Dougy had to re-join his family, and that was going to be a wrench for both of them.

"I'll sit hi agen," said Dougy, doffing his new cap.

"I hope so," said David, wondering how that could be, but really hoping it could happen. "Keep trying with the reading and writing."

Jed was touching up the paintwork on the chimney stack and the outside of the boat, and Betty got out the polish and rags to do the range and brass work and called for David to help her.

"It's changes all round," Betty said. "It's probably the last time I will be doing this. Tomorrow, after you have left, we are going to the wood mill with Jake to off load for the last time. We are hoping MrButterworth hasn't changed his mind about having our boat, but he and Jed have always had a good relationship, and we think his offer was genuine. We will have to live on it for a few more days until the legal side is dealt with, but Jake is helping us with that. A spit and a handshake is not appropriate in a transaction like this, he told us. The landlord from the pub will move our belongings to the cottage, and you will be in your new home, and so will we."

"Where will you go?" David asked Jake, who was packing up his pram for moving on.

"Back to the farm to see Bill and Dora. I will be there for a few weeks, and then maybe back to the village where we started from, who knows?" replied Jake. "I will write to you and speak to you on the telephone when I speak to John."

David was comforted by that, for at least it wasn't going to be 'goodbye forever'. "You can write to us," said Betty. "We can get someone to read it to us and write one back for us with our news. Jake can write our address down for you."

Once the cleaning was done, Jed lit the fire and Betty prepared a stew for supper, and as a special treat. They had mandarin oranges set in jelly, which Betty had prepared the day before and left in a cupboard to set.

The food was good, and everyone was trying to be normal, but the mood was sombre. Jed felt his life was reeling out of control, forced to be taking a step he wasn't really prepared for or wanted, and Betty sensed her husband's anxiety and she, too, was nervous about what lay ahead for them and how they would settle, and she was going to miss David more than she could ever have anticipated.

David lay, trying to sleep. He didn't even know where he was going, even at this late stage, and what if this man he didn't know but was going to live with, didn't like him? And what if he didn't like living with this man?

The questions were in his head, but he didn't voice them, he knew he had to go, and in 24 hours he would have met John and be in his new home.

Chapter 9

No one slept very well that night, and it was an early start in the morning. David just had a small piece of toast and a cup of tea, washed and put on his new clothes to travel in. Jake had cleaned David's boots, wrapped them in paper and put them at the bottom of the holdall.

"Come here, David," said Jake. "I need to show you something."

Jake had put David's envelope with his birth certificate, his letter from Rebecca, a piece of paper with Jed's new address on it and an envelope for John underneath the boots. "I'll put everything else on top, but don't forget to give John his envelope and your birth certificate," said Jake.

David shook hands with Jed and said, "Thank you, I hope you like your new home."

He hugged Betty tight.

She looked into his eyes. "Off you go," she said. "Make the most of your life."

David climbed off the boat and joined Jake on the towpath and walked towards the pub landlord's truck for a lift to the station, but he didn't look back.

The train was in the station, the engine hissing steam. Jake had a word with the guard and explained that David was travelling alone, and could he please make sure he got off at the right station. The guard had just helped two elderly ladies into a carriage and thought it would be a good idea for David to travel with them.

Jake slipped a piece of paper into David's hand. "This is where you are going," he said. "Don't lose it."

He handed David his holdall. "You will be all right," said Jake. "You really will." He stood watching, hoping he had made the right decision.

There was no handshake or hug, David couldn't bear it. He climbed onto the train and followed the guard down the corridor to the carriage where the two ladies were.

"I've brought the boy along, he's travelling alone, and I thought it would be nice for him to have some company," said the guard who promptly turned and left, looking at his watch. Moments later, the whistle blew, and the train lurched forward as the engine released its power.

David ran to the corridor window to wave goodbye to Jake who stood on the platform until the train disappeared, and then went back to the carriage window to see the sights that were familiar to him, having passed them in the boats. He saw the mill but couldn't hear the clatter of the looms, but the ladies in their wrap overalls and headscarves were out on the fire escape smoking and having a break in the fresh air.

Down on the towpath, he could see the children racing the train, as he had done, and then he saw the boats lined up at the lock. He stood and pressed his face and the palms of his hands against the window. Jed was waving his cap, Betty a white cloth, and by the lock, Dougy was waving his cap and jumping up and down in danger of falling in the canal. Then they were gone.

David was choking trying to hold back the tears, but in the end, he slumped down into his seat, covered his face with his hands, and sobbed.

"There, there," said the gentle voice of one of the ladies as she patted David's shoulder. "There's nothing good about goodbyes, I don't know why we say it, but 'hello' can be good and prove to be very interesting."

David took a deep breath and wiped his eyes and blew his nose on his new handkerchief. His eyes were sore, he was tired and he was wondering why every time something good happened to him it was taken away.

"Have a humbug," said the lady. "I'm Cissie, and my sister is Jenny."

"I'm pleased to meet you, and thank you," said David, remembering the lecture from Jake about good manners.

Cissie could see David was tired. "Why don't you have a little nap?" she suggested. "We can put paper on the seat where your feet are." He used his holdall for a pillow and was glad to close his eyes and shut out the world for a while. When he was asleep, Cissie covered him with a shawl and he slept for over two hours, awakened by the buffers hitting the carriages after a water stop.

The ladies were looking out of the corridor window, admiring the most beautiful floral display.

"Come and look," said Jenny. "Someone spends a lot of time planning and planting to achieve was has been done here. Do you like gardening, David?

"Never had a garden," said David. "Don't know much about flowers."

"We have some in our garden," said Jenny, "but we grow mostly vegetables and herbs, something we continued after the war, and it saves us money and earns us a bit."

"Have you something to eat?" asked Cissie, opening a picnic basket.

"Yes, thank you," replied David and opened the parcel Betty had prepared for him. There were warm cheese sandwiches because he had been laid on them, a hard-boiled egg and an apple which he kept for later.

"At the next water stop you can buy an ice cream," said Cissie. "The ice-cream cart is usually there."

David was looking forward to that, he really liked ice cream, and had change in his pocket to buy one.

"Can we get off the train, then?" he asked.

"Oh, yes," replied Cissy, "it usually takes around half an hour. It's good to get off and stretch your legs in the fresh air. The guard always blows his whistle and gives you time to get back on."

Cissie settled into knitting small squares to sew together for a blanket.

"Are you making lace?" David asked Jenny and went to sit beside her to have a better look.

"No," she said, "it's called tatting. It is sort of a fine lace. I'm making mats to sell at the church bazaar."

David went back to his seat and gazed out of the window at the scenery that was totally different to anything he had seen before. The patchwork of fields stretched out of sight, there were sheep or cows in some fields, crops growing in others, and for a short distance, the train ran alongside a canal, and the boat people waved.

It seemed such a long time to the next water stop when he knew he could buy an ice cream, but eventually the train slowed down and stopped at another station with anticipated, beautiful floral arrangements and the ice cream cart. People stood in line to be served, others just wandered about to stretch their legs and admire the flowers, and a little boy with his hands in his pockets stood back and looked at the ice cream cart. A lady approached the little boy and spoke to him gently and took his hand.

"Sorry, Ben," she said. "Mummy doesn't have money for an ice cream."

Ben didn't have a tantrum or cry, he just looked sad and turned to walk away with his mummy, but David had heard what she said and ran after them and squeezed a three penny bit into the boy's hand from the money Jed had given him from time to time, which he had saved and was in his pocket.

"That is so kind of you," said the lady, and was about to say to Ben, "Say thank you," but he was gone, standing at the end of the line, smiling.

When they were back on the train, Cissie said, "That was a lovely thing you did for that little boy, David."

David smiled and shrugged his shoulders, but he did feel good inside, remembering how he used to feel when the ice cream cart was in the village and he was the only one who didn't have any money to buy one.

"How much longer?" David sighed.

Cissie looked at her watch. "After the next stop, 1 hour," she said.

"How do you know that?" David asked.

"We make the journey four times a year," said Jenny. "Our sister lives in the north of England."

David realised then how they came to know about the water stops and the stations and why the station masters greeted them fondly and how they knew that the flowers growing now would be replaced by crocuses, snowdrops and daffodils in the spring.

The hour after the stop seemed to drag until the guard came looking for him.

"Ten minutes, young man, and then we'll be there, you'd better come with me." The ladies stood up and hugged him.

"It's been lovely to spend time with you," said Cissie. "Take good care of yourself."

"Thank you," said David. "Goodbye."

Chapter 10

He felt tense, kept taking deep breaths, and his stomach was churning.

He got off the train with other passengers who quickly left the station, and he stood alone and watched the train disappear into the tunnel in a haze of steam.

He heard a gate squeak open and slam shut, and saw a man walking towards him and for a fleeting moment thought it was Jake, so like him was John.

The man spoke. "David?" he asked.

"Yes, sir," David replied and held out his hand. They shook hands.

John smiled, but didn't let David see, but he just knew Jake would have been training David in the ways of becoming a presentable young man, and of course, he agreed manners were important, but he didn't want David being afraid of him.

"No need to call me sir," said John. "I am Uncle John."

They walked down the platform and through the gate, and there in the lane was a white pony and trap to take them to his new home.

"Don't go near the pony," John said. "She's feisty, and don't ever stand at the back of her." He took hold of the reins, "Walk on."

He flicked the reins and the pony was off, clearly not understanding the word "WALK." They clip clopped through the village on the road.

"Hold tight," said John, and suddenly the pony turned right down a cart track, not slowing down at all, and David felt as if all the bones in his body were rattling .Suddenly he felt and heard a thudding at the side of him, and there, over the wall, was the biggest most magnificent horse he had ever seen, running alongside them. John didn't say a word, the pony just stopped at a big gate where the shire horse was waiting. John got down from the trap and handed David his bag.

"Stay here," said John. "I need to put the trap undercover." He took the reins off the pony, put a bucketful of feed into a trough, pushed the trap under cover and closed the gate. By this time, the two horses were having a frolic together round the field.

"Blimey," said David, "I've never seen a horse that big before, how big is he?"

"Actually, it's a she, a mare, 16 hands," said John. "Her name is Bibby, and the pony is Trot."

"That's a good name for the pony," David said. "Is it deaf?"

"Why deaf?" asked John.

"Because when you said 'walk on', it set off at one hell of a pace," said David.

"No," said John, "not deaf, just wilful."

They walked down the lane and came to a cottage where an elderly man was sitting in the garden.

"Getting cool, Wilfred," said John. "Do you need helping inside?"

"No, I can manage," came the reply.

"Annie won't be long," said John.

As they came upon the cottage, David was expecting that this was to be his new home, but they walked straight past, took a right turn, and the most imposing building was silhouetted against a darkening sky.

"Here we are, "said John. "Come in and meet Annie."

"Hello, David," said Annie. "I expect you are hungry; supper is ready. I need to take you upstairs and show you your room first, and then I can get off home."

David picked up his bag and followed Annie into a hall and up a large staircase, along a landing and into a room. "This is yours," she said and took his bag off him and dropped it on the floor in the doorway. They turned and walked back along the landing. Annie stuck her left arm out and pointed to another door, "That's the bathroom," she said. "Clean towels are in the cupboard, and the dirty washing goes in the basket."

They were back in the kitchen in minutes.

"Supper is on the table," Annie said. She took her coat off the hook at the back of the door and said, "See you in the morning," as she left.

David stood in the kitchen, alone. He had no idea where John was, so he decided to sit at the table and eat the sandwiches and drink the milk that had been left for him. His eyes moved around the kitchen. There was a bunch of sage and a bunch of mint hanging from hooks, which smelt really nice, there was a wooden tray with onions in rows and a big bunch of carrots still covered in dirt. The huge dresser was stacked with blue and white crockery, and there was a row of pans and strainers hanging from a metal bar against the wall. A creel was hanging from the ceiling near the fireplace with towels hanging on it to dry. On another wall were two shelves stacked with empty jam jars waiting for the next crop of blackberries and apples for jam and chutneys. He could see that this was a room where a lot of things happened. He sat still for a while but could hear nothing, so eventually he left the kitchen and walked into the hall when he noticed a light coming from a room. He walked across tentatively, knocked and pushed the door open gently.

"Come in," said John, who was sitting at a desk. "You need to know this is my study, and you are not allowed in here. It's usually locked, but if it isn't, you must never be in here unless I am here, do you understand?"

David nodded and looked around the room at the bookshelves on two walls from floor to ceiling, crammed with books.

"Have you read them all?" asked David.

"They are reference books," said John, "not novels. Was there anything else?"

"I can't remember where my room is," said David. "Annie rushed me around and dropped my bag in one of the rooms.

"Come along," said John. "I think we can take an oil lamp up and some matches, do you know how to use one safely?"

"Yes," replied David, "we had them on the boat."

"We have a lot of power cuts here," explained John, "so this lamp is here when you need it."

As they walked past the bathroom, John pushed open the door so David could find it when he needed it, and then he switched on the light in David's room.

"Are you going to be all right now?" asked John.

"Yes," answered David, "can you wait a minute, I have a letter for you from Jake and my birth certificate. He rummaged to the bottom of his bag, found the envelopes and gave them to John, just keeping the one from Rebecca.

"You must be very tired," said John. "Get ready for bed now. I'll see you tomorrow."

David undressed and put on his new pyjamas, the very first pair he ever had, and went to the bathroom where he saw the biggest bath he had ever seen, and then he returned to the biggest bed in the biggest room he had ever slept in with the biggest windows he had ever seen, except in the church, and the longest and widest curtains he had ever seen. He clambered into the bed with soft white sheets and pillows and snuggled down. Everything appeared enormous because he had been living in small cramped places for months, but he did feel very small in the big bed in the dark room. He wondered what Jake and Betty and Jed were doing. He could hear a sort of rumbling outside, must be the wind, he thought and soon fell asleep.

David slept soundly, a good catch-up sleep he desperately needed, and when he woke up the room was still dark, but he did see a chink of light through a gap in the curtain, so he knew it was daytime. He yawned, stretched, sat up and then walked across to the window and pulled the curtain back. He stood with his eyes and mouth wide open. The noise he thought was the wind was, in fact, the ocean, and whilst he knew what an ocean was, he had never seen one, so much water, as far as the eye could see, as if it would topple over the horizon like a waterfall.

He was sitting on the window seat hugging his knees and watching birds diving into the sea when Annie called him from the doorway.

"Come on," she said, "time to get washed and dressed. I'll make you some porridge; Jake said you liked it."

David sat eating his porridge and enjoying it very much because Annie had put a dollop of jam on it, and he had stirred it up until it was all pink, and he made it last.

"Where's John?" asked David.

"He's working," said Annie. "He'll be home around midday."

"What's his job?" asked David.

"He's the village doctor, a GP," replied Annie. "Didn't you know that?"

"No," said David, "Jake never told me that."

"Did Jake tell you he was a surgeon?" asked Annie.

"No, he didn't," said David, but thoughts then flooded into his mind. *That explains a lot*, he thought. *That's how he knew about bacteria and why he was so quickly able to attend to my wounds.*

Annie sent him to make his bed, which he had to run around to tidy the covers, and then he was allowed to go out, but not to the beach.

Chapter 11

He put on his boots and set off up the lane towards the field where the horses were but came across Wilfred sitting outside his cottage. David waved, Wilfred waved back, and thus began another friendship.

"Do you sit here all day?" asked David, remembering that Wilfred was sitting outside when he had arrived the previous night.

"As much as I can, before it becomes too cold," replied Wilfred. "I potter in the garden when I can; it was my hobby until my breathing got bad."

They chatted for a while, and then David left and continued up the lane to find the horses.

"Bibby," he called as he stood on a slat in the gate so he would be tall enough to stroke the horse walking towards him nodding her head and swishing her tail, and trotting at her side was the pony, but she stood well back from David. He twisted his apple until it broke in half, offering one piece to Bibby who took it straight away, but Trot just curled up her lip and showed her teeth.

What does that mean? wondered David. *Was it a smile, or I'll bite your fingers off if you come near me warning?* He gave the rest of the apple to Bibby, stroked her soft nose and neck and talked to her gently. Eventually, the horses returned to their grazing in the field, and David was sitting on the wall watching them when John came by in his car.

"Get in," said John. "We'll have some lunch, and then I'll take you along the coast."

They returned to the house where Annie had soup and a thick slice of bread and butter ready for them.

After lunch, John went into his office for a while, and David stayed in the kitchen and chatted to Annie as he cleared the dishes from the table and washed up.

"Goodness me!" said Annie. "How well trained are you? Thank you very much."

David smiled and felt proud, remembering Betty had made him help, explaining that chores had to be shared, and it had become second nature to him.

John reappeared and sent David for his jacket and waterproof, and they set off for their walk along the coast, down the stone steps from the garden at the back of the house, along a rough, uneven path edged with tall grasses and orange flowers, and the vista opened onto a stretch of almost white sand and a gently lapping sea.

David had never been to the coast, so for him this moment was spellbinding, and he just stood and looked and listened, and bent down and picked up a shell and looked at John. "Can I keep this?" he asked.

John nodded and explained to David about the tide and how it came in very fast, so it was always advisable to keep on the path. Further along the path, they stopped at a point where they could look down and see the sea thrashing against the rocks, booming like thunder, spraying the air, and David realised the full might of the ocean. "Gosh!" he said, "what a lot of water."

"Yes," said John, "and very powerful, and always to be respected. Can you swim?"

"No," replied David, "never learnt."

They retraced their steps and by the time they reached the sandy beach the tide was flowing in, devouring the sand, so David was able to understand what John had said to him previously.

They climbed up the steps to the house.

"Lick your lips," said John.

David did. "They're salty," he said. "Why?"

"Salty air from the salty sea," replied John.

Oh, yes, thought David. He did know the oceans were salt water.

They returned to the warmth of the kitchen and the smell of food cooking.

David took his waterproof up to his room and stood gazing out of the window for a while, reflecting on how much he had done and seen since he arrived less than 24 hours ago.

Annie shouted, "Tea is out."

David dashed to the bathroom, washed his hands and returned to the kitchen where Annie had set a place for him opposite John. Jake's voice was in his head, "Don't use your fork like a shovel."

He tucked into his chicken dinner and apple pie and once again, helped Annie with the dishes, which meant she could leave a little earlier.

John needed her, she had run the house for him for many years, even when Jake lived there, but he understood her plight since Wilfred was unable to work and was relaxed about the way she adjusted her time and her work. The days were long and lonely for Wilfred, but he knew Annie had to work, so he never complained but was always pleased to have some extra time with her. David took to visiting him for a chat from time to time until he didn't want visitors as his health became worse.

She took her coat from the back of the kitchen door, put two slices of apple pie in a dish, said, "Goodnight, see you in the morning," and was gone.

"Right," said John, "homework. We have two weeks before your admission exam for the school I have selected for you, so we have to work hard so you achieve a pass."

John was a governor at the school and knew the headmaster very well, so a place had been reserved for David, providing he could pass the entrance exam, because the standard of education was high. If he failed, it would mean he would have to go to another school in the next village.

For the next two weeks, David worked hard with John from books loaned by the school, so he would know what was expected. He walked along the coastal path reciting his times tables and spellings which he had written down on a piece of paper. He would sit in a little cranny he had found that hugged him like a cocoon, and tried to remember capital cities, body parts and plant parts. This was a place he visited as often as he could, because, despite the thundering boom of the waves, he found it peaceful. He thought about his mother and what she would make of it all, and he missed Jake and was looking forward to speaking to him on the telephone when he had the result of the exam, hopefully with good news. David, still a young boy, knew and would never forget how Jake had taken care of him and taken risks so he could have a better life, and for that reason alone, he had to do well and pass his exam. He would so like to have written to Rebecca to let her know that he was all right and to learn what had happened in the village, but he knew he could not.

The day before the exam, he was taken for a haircut, and he and John walked to the school, so he would know in the future just how to get there.

The following morning, David couldn't eat much breakfast, but John insisted he had a small amount of porridge and a cup of tea. He dressed in his best clothes. Annie had shined his shoes for him and gave him a big hug as he left, and shouted "Good luck," as they drove past.

The headmaster was waiting at the door when they arrived.

"Good morning, Doctor," he said, addressing John. Then he turned and looked at David, "And you must be David."

"Yes, sir," replied David and held out his hand which the headmaster shook.

John nodded at David in a reassuring manner. "I'll be back to collect you," he said and left.

"Follow me," said the headmaster. "I'll take you to your classroom."

The school smelt of polish, there were lots of wooden panels on the walls in the corridor with gold writing on and cabinets with cups and shields. David followed the headmaster on tiptoe, so he didn't slap his feet on the floor and make too much noise. The headmaster, very aware of what David was doing, said, "We wear crepe-soled shoes as part of our uniform here, but no need to worry today."

David was shown to a desk in a classroom where he was met and introduced to a teacher and governor to ensure the exam was done in the appropriate manner. The exam commenced with a spelling test followed by two question papers on maths and general knowledge, and there was a break for lunch. The papers were taken away to be marked, and a lady came in with a cheese sandwich, a banana and a glass of milk. When he had finished eating, the teacher asked, "Would you like to take a look around the school and stretch your legs?"

"Yes, thank you," said David, "I would."

He saw several more classrooms, the chemistry laboratory, the gymnasium with lots of unfamiliar apparatus and ropes hanging from the ceiling, washrooms and showers, a library, and the dining room, and then they went through a courtyard into an annexe.

"This is the dormitory where the boarders sleep," said the teacher.

The bedding and the curtains were clean and pretty, and there was a wooden locker at the side of each bed, and a wooden box at the bottom, but David didn't like it in there at all.

"Why do boarders sleep here?" asked David.

"Boys come from a long way off to this school because of its reputation and couldn't possibly go home each day. Some go home for weekends, some of the boy's parents live abroad because they are in the armed forces and only go home for the summer holidays, like now, when the school is closed for six weeks," explained the teacher.

They returned to the classroom, David commenced the afternoon with a mental arithmetic test and two more written papers, one on English grammar, one on English appreciation. As each test was completed, the papers were taken away to be marked, so by the time he had finished there was not long to wait before he was summoned to the headmaster's office. The teacher had stayed with him and chatted, but David was very careful not to reveal too much about his past, just that his mother had died, and he was living with his Uncle John.

The governor tapped on the classroom door and beckoned for them to follow him to the headmaster's office where John was also waiting. The headmaster looked over his glasses at David. "Well done," he said. "Indeed, very well done. I am pleased to tell you that we are able to offer you a place in our school. How do you feel about that?"

"So relieved and happy," replied David, sighing the words out.

"We must thank you all for taking time out of your holiday for us today, it's very much appreciated," said John.

"Oh! Yes!" said David. "Thank you," realising that was what had happened.

John and David walked down the corridor together.

"It smells of polish, everywhere," said David.

"I think polish is holding it together in some places," said John, "it's a very old school with a brilliant academic reputation, and you will do well here if you work hard, and you will have to, but at the same time, they try and make education enjoyable."

They drove along to the village and sat outside the telephone box until it was time for Jake to ring. David told John about the tests, and that he knew he would not have been successful without his help. He was glowing with pride and fizzing with excitement when he spoke to Jake, who was equally pleased that things had worked out as he had hoped. They chatted for a while, and he was pleased to learn Betty and Jed had sold their boat and moved to the cottage to take care of Jed's sister. Jake knew how hard they were finding it to settle but didn't mention this to David.

"Sit in the car, David, I need to speak to Jake," said John.

When John had finished his private conversation, they set off for home, stopping to put feed into the trough for the horses. Biddy came to the gate and David stroked her soft nose and told her his news, and Trot stood and curled her lip at him.

"How old is Biddy?" asked David.

"We think about 17 or 18," replied John. "She was at the plough for the farm in the next village for years, but when the son took over, he bought a tractor, so I took her on. Someone just came in the night and left Trot and the trap in the field, and that was three years ago, so I doubt they will be coming back to collect her now, but she's been good company for Biddy. If I pull the trap out, she comes straight away, she seems to really enjoy it, and that's why I try and take her out once a week."

When they arrived home, David dashed into the house to tell Annie his news who squealed with delight and gave him a huge hug.

"It's only two weeks to the beginning of the school year, so we need to go into town and get your school uniform," said John.

David stopped in his tracks and looked at John. "I didn't know I had to have a uniform," he said. "I thought I just had to have some shoes with crepe soles."

Jake had explained to John that David was sensitive and became anxious when things were bought for him, so straight away to avoid this, John said, "I know you have an arrangement with Jake over money, so have the same arrangement with me, and I'll keep all the receipts for the future."

David nodded, and there was no doubt in his mind that he would repay them one day, but it was a long way off.

76

Chapter 12

Two days later, after the surgery, John and David went into town for David's uniform, with a very long list. There were other boys in the shop being served and it took a long time because some things had to be tried on to make sure of the fit. David was overwhelmed by the way the shop assistant was dealing with him, not realising the respect there was for the school, or the value of the sale, and he was glad John was there with him taking it all in his stride. Finally, when they had ticked everything off the list, they took the parcels back to the car.

"Right," said John, "we need to get you an alarm clock."

"Do I need one?" asked David.

"You will when I go up to London, which is usually once a month and for 3 days. Annie turns up later when I'm away, and I don't want to change anything there, so you will be responsible for getting yourself to school on those days, and it will mean setting off sooner because you will have to walk all the way. I suggest you do this one day to time yourself before school begins."

They went into a shop which sold clocks and watches and bought an alarm clock with two huge bells on the top, and after a demonstration, David was confident as to how to set it and intended to try it that night.

"Right," said John, "we need to get something to eat. I told Annie not to bother today."

If anyone had told John a few week earlier that he would be sitting on a bench at the side of the river, eating fish and chips out of a paper bag, with vinegar dripping though his fingers, he would just have given them the most withering look which conveyed 'don't be ridiculous', but there he was, on a bench at the side of the river, eating fish and chips out of a paper bag, with vinegar dripping through his fingers. David looked at him and beamed a smile. "Good, this, isn't it?" he said.

"Well, it's certainly different," said John, hoping no one he knew would see them but quite enjoying the experience.

They could smell vinegar all the way home, and even Annie could smell it when they arrived carrying all the parcels into the house.

"Hello," Annie said. "Had a good day? It looks like it. David, take your shirts out of the packets and be sure to remove all the pins so I can wash and iron them ready for school."

"Why?" asked David. "They're new."

"Do you want to go to school with all the creases in them just as they have come out of the packet?" Annie said, raising her voice impatiently. "And hang things up in your wardrobe."

David looked at her as he picked up his parcels to take to his room. "I've never had a shirt in a packet before," he said and left her, wishing she had not been so brittle with him.

David did as she asked, and by the time he returned to the kitchen, she had gone.

John was about to go into his office when David produced his tie. "I don't know how to tie it," he said.

"Not tonight," said John, "I have work to do. Go and have your bath."

"Ok," said David, "and then can I have a look at one of your books?"

David loved having a bath, feeling the comfort of the warm water round him, and he always took a long time wallowing and thinking. This was sheer luxury for him considering he had never had a bath in his life until he was at Rebecca's house at Christmas, and now he could have at least two a week. He cleaned the bath as Annie had showed him and returned to the kitchen where John had left him a book on anatomy. He curled up in a chair near the fire and flicked through the pages for he still had the word 'renal' in his mind.

Feeling tired, he passed John's office, tapped on the door and shouted, "Goodnight."

He went to his room and sat on the window seat behind the curtains. He had a moment every evening before he went to bed to look out of his window. No two nights were the same, sometimes the tide was in, sometimes out, sometimes there was a heavy swell if the wind was up, sometimes the sea was calm, and if there was a full moon, it seemed to bounce on the waves and it was magical. If there was a sea fret, it seemed the house was wrapped in an eerie, damp grey haze, and on those nights he could hear the haunting sound of the fog horn somewhere along the coast in the distance. All these things fascinated him.

He set his alarm clock for 7 am, but the constant tick tock was annoying him so much he couldn't get to sleep, so he put the clock at the back of the curtains on the window seat and hoped for the best. He lay for a while reflecting on the day, and the past few weeks, and he would have loved to have the children who had been so cruel to him in the past see him now and how lucky he had been. He fell asleep, warm, comfortable and happy.

The alarm clock woke him up, and he leapt out of bed and ran to the window to stop it ringing. Still in a daze, he got back into his warm bed and lay wondering what he was going to do all day. When he did go downstairs, John was already having breakfast.

"What are your plans for today?" asked John.

"Not sure," said David. "Might go on the coastal walk. I like it there."

"Perhaps it would be a good idea to run along, instead of walking," said John. "Build up your stamina so you can cope with the cross-country runs when you start school."

"What's stamina?" asked David.

John went into his office and returned with a dictionary. "Look it up," he said.

John explained about the cross-country runs, and that it was important not to race off at the beginning and burn up energy quickly, but just to maintain a steady jog and also that they had to do the runs in all weathers and usually once a week.

David didn't think he was joking, he just hoped he was.

"Have a nice day," said John and left for the surgery with a wry smile on his face.

David flicked through the pages of the dictionary until he found STAMINA: resistance to fatigue, hardship, endurance, it read. Then he looked up ENDURANCE; ability to last, stand pain, it read.

"You can't go running today, you need proper shoes," said Annie, so David spent the day helping Annie move furniture about, so she could clean, and in the afternoon, he put his alarm clock in a paper bag and timed his walk to school as John had suggested.

When John returned home, Annie was on her hands and knees drawing around David's feet on a piece of paper.

"What's happening here?" asked John.

"David needs some running shoes, and I've just found out his Wellington boots don't fit him anymore, so I thought I'd get some in town tomorrow, if that's all right," said Annie.

David was cutting round the lines in the shape of his foot that Annie had drawn.

John looked at him. "Had you not thought to look at the size on your new shoes?" he asked. "And why is the clock in a paper bag on the table?"

"I needed to time my journey to school, and it was too big to put on my wrist and I didn't have a strap," answered David mischievously.

Annie burst out laughing and almost toppled over as she stood up. John just shook his head, went into his office and closed the door.

Once David had his running pumps, he ran along the coastal path almost every day until school term began and enjoyed it. On his return one very warm, still day, he found John sitting outside reading. He beckoned to David. "Let me have a listen," he said, using his stethoscope, then he let David listen to his squelching, beating heart, which he found to be a very strange sensation. "Go and freshen up, Annie has gone but left us corned beef salad, and I thought we could have it out here for a change."

When David returned, the food was on the table outside and he thought it was wonderful to be sitting in the sunshine having tea. He was quieter than usual and kept looking at John, so eventually John asked him, "Is there something you want to say, David?"

David blushed and paused. "Well, I just wondered why Jake didn't want to live in such a lovely place. I'm here and he is not. Didn't he like it here?"

John pondered for a moment and made the decision to explain to David what had taken place to make Jake leave.

"There is a family in the village by the name of Brody, and at one time, there was a father, mother and five sons. Apart from the mother, who struggled with the stress of trying to cope with them all, they were trouble. The father and one of the sons worked at the abattoir, the rest did odd jobs here and there, but they were always in the pub drinking heavily, every night. They would fight, pull down people's fences and chop them up so they could have a fire in their home, steal vegetables from gardens, girls became pregnant and they denied any knowledge of it, leaving the girls and their families to cope without any help. All the shopkeepers were intimidated by them, and the landlord from the Crown pub dare not ban them, because when the landlord from the White Swan tried, they wrecked his pub. They were toxic, and completely ignored any intervention that was tried by the police.

"The father had an accident at work and broke his hip and leg very badly. When he was taken to hospital, he couldn't actually feel his legs at all. Jake operated on him, but couldn't save him, he died under the anaesthetic, which meant the family had lost their main bread winner. It was only a few weeks later Mrs Brody died from a massive heart attack, and the boys decided Jake was to blame for not saving their father.

"The butcher overhead their conversation in the pub threatening to come to the house to 'sort out Jake and smash his hands, then he wouldn't be able to work anymore' so he got on his bike and cycled here to warn us.

"We closed the shutters, all around the house, and sat in the dark, hoping they wouldn't come and that it had all been beer talk, but they did come, shouting threats, banging on the door and shutters and smashing whatever they could find outside. The butcher stayed with us, and we kept his bike in the house, for they surely would have wrecked it, and it would have meant trouble for him in the future if they realised he had alerted us.

"We heard one of them say they were going 'round the back of the house, but it was all part of the melee, and no one bothered to go and look. Eventually, they left, cursing, laughing, threatening, and I have to be honest, David, we were all frightened.

"It was a good hour later before the butcher left us, he didn't see anyone and got home safely, thankfully.

"Jake and I locked ourselves in my office, and we slept in chairs with a blanket, and waited for morning before we checked on the damage which was mostly smashed plant pots, and the fence had been pulled out of the ground and broken up.

"Annie arrived early, for she and Wilfred had heard the racket and knew there would be a mess to clear up. We decided to leave the shutters as they were for a few days, to be safe, in case they decided to return, but no one went round to the back of the house until Annie wanted parsley. She opened the back door and went out, moments later she was screaming and pointing into the garden. When we went to look, we found what turned out to be the youngest brother, laid dead, his head in a pool of blood. He had fallen over, smashed a cloche and severed his jugular vein, so then, of course, we had to involve the police. The other brothers were so hung over when the police called with the news, that they hadn't realised he was missing.

"The county police were involved, and the Brody's were told to stay away from us or they would end up in court, but they were always hanging about in a sinister manner, and of course when they had been drinking there was always a risk with them, so Jake decided to take time out, away from here, and that was four years ago, and he feels he can't return until the Brody's are gone. We sneaked him to the station with two bags of belongings, and he caught the first train that came and at some point, ended up in the village where you lived, and you probably know more about how he lives his life now than I do. We grew up here with our father caring for us after our mother died when we were only 7 and 9, we went to the school you are going to and built our careers in such a way we could still live here, and there you have it, David, that's all there is to know, but if you ever come across them in the village, stay well away."

"Gosh!" said David and just sat thinking about what John had told him. He felt very angry with the Brody's but realised that if all that hadn't happened, he wouldn't be sitting there now, and he felt pangs of guilt that he had the comfort and care he was getting and that Jake was living in the den or pushing his pram through the countryside in the wind and rain. "It's so sad," he said.

"He will come home one day, I'm sure," said John. "There's no work here for the Brody's, no one will employ them and if they can't pay the rent and the landlord evicts them, they will have to move on, and perhaps go back to Ireland. They come into the surgery sometimes, and I try to get my partner to deal with them, which I'm sure they prefer, but if I have to see them, I behave as if they have no history, and we get through the awkwardness."

David shivered. Although the air was still warm, the wind was picking up and the sky was darkening.

"Let's get the things inside," said John. "There is a storm coming."

Whilst David was washing up, he saw a lightening flash way out at sea and heard a distant rumble of thunder.

"Come on," said John. "We'll go up to the top of the house and watch."

The lightning flashed in straight lines and forks and lit up the whole sky, the thunder cracked and shook the house as it came nearer, the rain poured and they could see the huge waves pounding in and it was the most exhilarating half hour. They were in the turret room at the very top of the house, where David had never been before because the door at the bottom of the stairs was usually locked. "All these things up here are Jake's," said John. "Well, apart from the box of Christmas decorations, that has been here for years."

They returned to the kitchen. "Do you want some cocoa?" said David.

"Do you know how to do it?" asked John.

"Of course I do," replied David. "Jake taught me. We had a lot of cocoa and porridge. He said we had to have porridge in the morning to get our engine running, and we had a lot of soup so we got our vegetables, and I think he had proper dinners when he went to the Salvation Army hostel for his bath. Until he was taking care of me, he would stay there three nights, so he probably will be doing it again now." John struggled with this information but didn't let it show and enjoyed the cocoa.

"I need to work now, David. I'll see you in the morning," said John and went to his office.

David went up to his room and sat on the window seat and watched the ocean for a while, then he wandered into the bathroom to clean his teeth and had a moment when he wondered what Rebecca might be doing. He went to bed, but his mind was full of the story of what had happened to Jake, he missed him so much and wanted him to come home.

Chapter 13

David was restless on the last few days before starting his new school, so Annie asked him to accompany her to the village to help carry the shopping. They called at the butcher's shop first.

"Hello, Annie," said the butcher. "What can I get for you today?"

"Here's my list," she said. "I'll call on my way back."

"Is this the doctor's nephew, then?" asked the butcher, nodding across at David who was looking at all the meat displayed in the window.

"It is," said Annie, "and he's fed up with himself now, ready to start school."

"Can you ride a bike?" the butcher asked David.

"Yes, I can," replied David, who had learned on the tow paths between the locks.

"Do you want a job delivering orders for me, so I don't have to keep shutting the shop?" the butcher asked. "I'll pay you."

"That would be good," said David, "but I'll have to ask Uncle John."

"Go to the surgery now," said Annie. "You'll probably have to wait for a while, but at least you will be able to let the butcher know whether you are able to help or not. Just go straight in and there will be a lady at a desk who will help you. Call at the greengrocers and collect my order. If you forget, you'll be coming back for it. I'll see you at home."

David opened the surgery door and went in for the very first time. He walked up to the lady sitting at the desk. "I'm David," he said. "I need to speak to my uncle, John."

"Take a seat," the lady said. "I'll let him know you are here as soon as I can, but he's with a patient at the moment, and I can't disturb him."

There were four other people sitting in line, waiting to see a doctor and David pondered as to what might be wrong with them, thinking definitely the man with the rasping cough had pneumonia and should be in hospital.

Suddenly, a telephone rang and startled him, the lady answered it and wrote down some details, and David was left wondering why they used the telephone in the street to talk to Jake when there was one in the surgery.

Eventually, he spoke to John who thought it was a splendid idea for David to help the butcher, so David ran straight past the greengrocers back to the butcher's shop to confirm he could do the deliveries and arranged to go Fridays after school and Saturday mornings. He had a ride around on the bike in case the saddle needed adjusting and was just about to hurry home with the news for Annie when the butcher said, "Do you need to be taking something home for Annie?"

David had been so excited at the thought of actually having some money of his own, he had forgotten all about collecting the bag from the greengrocers. He grinned at the butcher. "Thank you," said David, looking rather sheepish, and left to collect the bag from the greengrocers.

On his way home, he took out a carrot from the bag and stood on the gate rung waiting for Biddy to come. She seemed to be limping, but he wasn't sure. He told her his news, stroked her soft nose and left to go home to tell Annie he had got the job.

The first day of term finally arrived, and David could only manage a piece of toast and a cup of tea at breakfast.

"Let's have a photograph so we can send it to Jake, and he can see how splendid you look in your uniform," said John, taking his camera outside.

David stood and smiled, feeling very proud, and not looking at all like the little boy Jake had rescued.

"We will send it to the Salvation Army along with his other mail," said John.

David picked up his new briefcase and sat in the car waiting for his lift to the top of the lane, where John dropped him off, leaving him to walk the rest of the way. Most of the boys were being dropped off by parents with cars nearer to the school, but on this day, they were all first-year students, as it was the tradition of the school to welcome the new students on the first morning of term, and the boarders arrived in the afternoon with the rest of the students.

There was a meet and greet half hour in the hall, names were called for class allocation, and then the boys were taken to their classrooms to meet their form teachers, who wore the traditional black gowns all the time. They were told before they left the hall that they must always stand when a teacher entered a room. After lunch in the huge dining hall, they returned to their classrooms and were given books and had to write down the timetable to follow for each week. School rules were explained to them, and they were informed that each week they would go by bus to the town swimming baths for lessons, and that there were many after school clubs for sport and music. The last words from the teacher before they left at the end of the day were, "Tomorrow we begin." All day students in white shirts, instead of the usual grey, were around ushering the boys, these were sixth form students and it was explained that they were there to help at all times if possible.

David hurried home, just stopping to stroke Biddy briefly. John and Annie were waiting for him, eager to hear about his first day.

David delved into his brief case and produced his timetable and a key for his locker.

"Uniform off first thing every day," said John, "and I have a chain for your locker key to attach to your brief case, or belt, whichever you want, but if you lose your key, you have to pay for another to be provided, and it will come out of your earnings. After tea, I would like you to do another copy of your timetable, so we have one here."

"Why?" asked David.

"Then you are not likely to forget your PE kit or swimming trunks and towel when you need them. It will be your responsibility, but I think it will be a 100 lines penalty if you do forget them."

David settled into school life, and although he was enjoying it very much, he quickly realised he had to keep up and work hard. He did what he had always done, stood back and observed on the social side of school, but here he had no history and was included in group activities. There was always going to be a swaggering know all amongst a large group of boys, but David was strong enough mentally to ignore him, and the boy must have sensed it, because he never bothered him.

Homework had to be done either just before or after tea, John always checked it had been done and was always ready to help if David needed it.

John was reassured on parents' evening that David was doing well and there were no problems, so he was happy to let Jake know that his instinct for David's potential had been right.

There was to be the traditional carol service at the school for parents and villagers, and John and Annie were there as they always were, but this year it was special because David did a reading of the poem "Christmas Landscape" by Laurie Lee.

"Let us pray," said the vicar, and everyone closed their eyes and bowed their heads, but David didn't hear a word he said for his mind had drifted back to the previous Christmas. He wondered what Rebecca would be doing and her parents and Bertha, who had all been so kind to him, and wished he could have sent them a Christmas card. Suddenly there was an 'Amen' and everyone stood up to sing 'Come, All Ye Faithful', as the boys in the choir walked through the hall carrying candles.

There was much chatter and laughter after the service, and it took a while to get away because John was so well known, and everyone wanted to wish him Merry Christmas.

They dropped Annie off on the way home, and as David walked her up the path, he asked her to get the trimmings box down from the top room.

"Don't know about that," she said. "John doesn't trim up, and we don't have a tree."

"Please!" said David. "We'll manage something."

The following day was the last Saturday before Christmas, so David did his deliveries for the butcher and then caught the bus into town with his earnings that he had saved from the past few weeks plus some Christmas box tips he had been given that morning which delighted him. He bought a packet of three handkerchiefs for Jake to send to him, a tin of shortbread for Annie and Wilfred, a bar of chocolate for the butcher, and a ballpoint pen in a box for John because he was always running out of ink and two sheets of paper with a holly pattern to wrap them in.

When he arrived home, he went straight to his room and hid his purchases in the bottom of his wardrobe. He went looking for Annie to see if she had brought the trimmings down, which she had, and then he went to the shed where he had painted a huge twig white, along with most of the shed floor. He dragged it into the house and secured it in a bucket of stones so it didn't topple over when he put the baubles on. By the time John returned from wherever he had been, the twig was finished, standing in the corner of the lounge heralding Christmas, and David was up in his room wrapping his presents and securing them with wool from the sewing box.

Annie opened the lounge anxiously to let John see what David had done. Both John and Jake were at university when their father had died, and even though they both came home for Christmas, they never bothered to decorate the house. Annie, much younger then, of course, looked after them when they were at home, kept the house in order when they were not, and Wilfred looked after the gardens, so things were in fairly good order when they both returned to live there permanently. The last time the decorations had been used was the last Christmas John and Jake had with their father, so Annie was not sure how John would react.

"Gosh!" said John. "Those baubles have not been out of the box since father died, it's a wonder they have survived. The twig looks good actually, let's light the fire in here on Christmas Eve and bring Wilfred down. I'm sure we can manage it between us." Annie was so relieved John had taken it so well and happy they could all be together on Christmas Eve.

In the past, Christmas Eve had been a quiet affair for John. Annie usually prepared some food for him in the afternoon and returned home to be with Wilfred and sometimes their daughter, if she had travelled from Ireland to spend a few days over Christmas with her parents. He would settle in the evening with a book or listen to the radio, or play records on his gramophone, and he was content with this and a nice glass of port.

However, he was very aware that this Christmas Eve was going to be anything but peaceful, and he found himself looking forward to it.

David was at the butcher's shop at 7:30 am. He looked at the row of turkeys hanging from hooks and felt sorry for them. "Poor things," he said.

"Food chain," said the butcher and hitched a heavy rucksack onto David's back and filled the basket on the bicycle. "This is your furthest delivery, and we'll work back from that so that you are nearer home when you finish."

It was 3 pm when David wheeled the bicycle into the back of the shop, his calves and back aching and his face stinging from the wind, and he was really tired and hungry.

"You've been a Godsend to me today, David," said the butcher. "This is for you." He gave him a 10/- note.

"Gosh, thank you," said David. "I've never had one of these before." And he remembered the bar of chocolate he had bought for the butcher and presented him with it, "And this is for you Merry Christmas." He was hoping it hadn't melted in his pocket, but it was cold outside and should be all right.

It was getting dark as David walked down the lane, but he still stopped to have a few moments with the horses and counted the money he had been given as tips during the day, so totally unexpected and very much appreciated.

When he arrived home, Wilfred was already there, John having collected him earlier whilst it was still light. The table was set on a white tablecloth with plates and cutlery he hadn't seen before. There was a ham, a pork pie, tomatoes, chutney, beetroot, and Annie had boiled some potatoes to slice and fry with some herbs when they were ready to eat and mince pies to finish off with.

The meal was enjoyable and the atmosphere relaxed, with David entertaining them with stories about his deliveries that day, and Wilfred related what it was like at Christmas when he was a boy. He was one of eight children, so they each had an orange, an apple and a toffee bar, and a game that they could all play and share. As they grew older and some of the siblings were working, things got better, but whilst only father was earning and mother had a small cleaning job, things were a struggle on a weekly basis. They knew they were poor, but so was everyone else where they lived, and the community helped each other out when they could. David thought back and could understand very well what Wilfred was saying, and although he made no comment, he thought, *no one helped my ma.*

After the meal, Annie and David cleared away, washed up and joined the men in the lounge. There were parcels by the twig, so David went and brought his down and placed them with the rest.

"I think we should open them tonight," said John, "whilst we are all together."

There were lovely moments opening presents. Annie had given David a compendium of games, so they played snakes and ladders and Ludo. There was some cheating, groaning and laughing, but by 9 pm, Wilfred's eyes were shutting, David was yawning, and it was time to take Wilfred home. David led the way up Wilfred's path with a torch so no one stumbled, and Annie and John supported Wilfred until they were safe in their own home, and although everyone was tired, the frosty air had livened them up, and it was apparent they had all enjoyed the evening.

"Merry Christmas," shouted John and David as they left to return home. They sat in front of the fire, sipping cocoa.

"I wonder where Jake is," said David. "I hope he's not out in the cold."

"No," said John. "Sorry, I have forgotten to tell you, he's at the farm with Dora and Bill, helping out for a while because Bill had to go into hospital for a procedure and cannot do heavy work for a while. He would have done had Jake not been there to keep an eye on him and help."

"What are we doing tomorrow?" asked David, suddenly realising Christmas Eve and Christmas Day had been rolled into one.

"We are going to church," replied John, "and then on to the vet's house to spend the day with the Gray family, as I have been doing since Jake left."

"Am I invited?" asked David.

"Indeed, you are," replied John. "I was told you are most welcome. They have three boys, two of which go to your school, and a girl, so they will be good company for you. Bedtime, I think. The service is at 10 am so we do not need an early start, but Annie doesn't come on Christmas Day, so set your alarm for 8 am."

Just then, there was a frantic banging on the door, and when John opened it, a young man almost fell into the house, panting out the words, "Dad's gone really queer and he can't stand or speak."

"Wait by the car," said John, "I'll just get my bag." He looked at David, "Lock the door and take the key out when I've gone. I'll not be long."

The house was very cold upstairs, so David didn't linger long looking out of the window as he put the alarm clock on the sill behind the curtains. He wasn't troubled being in the house alone as he had already experienced it in the past when John had been up to London, although Annie was there in the mornings when he went down, making sure he didn't leave without breakfast.

He hadn't noticed during the evening, but Annie had put a hot water bottle into his bed, and although it had cooled, it was still warm enough to snuggle up to, and he was soon fast asleep and slept through until the alarm rang. He ran across to the window to turn it off and tried to look out through the lacy patterns the frost had made on the window. He pressed his hand on the window to melt a space, and although the sky was clear and blue, all the plants and bushes were white.

He wrapped his rug around him, put on his new slippers and went downstairs.

John was already up. "Toast?" he said.

"Yes, please," said David, and sat down at the table, where he noticed John had set a place with several pieces of cutlery lined up.

"I'll explain after breakfast," said John when he saw David looking at the place setting.

Also on the table was a black box which David had assumed was from John's medical bag, but when breakfast was over, John slid it towards him.

"Now, David," he said, "it came to my notice recently that we had missed your birthday, so Jake and I have bought you this because you need it."

"Oh, yes!" said David. "I didn't even remember my birthday, fancy forgetting that."

He licked honey off his fingers and opened the box tentatively to find a watch. He gasped, ran to John and gave him a huge hug.

"You've been so kind to me, both of you, sometimes it's hard to believe how lucky I am," said David, becoming emotional.

"That's enough of that," said John. "Neither of us have been married, and we're both enjoying having someone to care for, and I'm sure a wife would have been a lot more expensive." He smiled and winked at David. "Go and get washed and dressed, put your check shirt and new jacket on, and then I'll explain about the cutlery."

David was shown how to use the cutlery from the outside in, for each course, and to leave the cutlery on the plate to be taken away. "And," said John, "what does Jake say?"

David answered, "Don't use your fork like a shovel."

"It doesn't matter how the other children behave at the table," said John, "you know what is expected. It's their home, their parents will guide them, and you may think good manners and table manners are not important, but as you become an adult you will realise they are. Learn now and you will be able to go into any restaurant, to any function or people's homes without worrying about how to behave."

David remembered Jake had told him John was a stickler for good manners, and if he hadn't noticed it before, he certainly did now.

They left for church, and in the silent moments, David's thoughts were back at Rebecca's home a year ago, and how his life had changed so much from the chaos of that time.

Mr Gray and his wife and children were also at the church so they all left together for the Grays' home after the service.

David had wondered why John had taken their slippers with them, but on arrival at the house, he understood, for everywhere was covered in carpet, and everyone had to wear slippers or soft shoes. David was introduced to the family, and he did recognise the two boys who went to his school, one was in the sixth form, and one the year ahead of him, and the eldest boy was at university, home for the holidays. The little girl was at nursery school and very keen that David should meet her new doll. She had obviously overheard a conversation between her father and brothers when they had been instructed not to mention David's mother passing away, so she looked David straight into the eyes and asked, "Was your mother very sick when she died?"

"Very," replied David, hoping that would be the end of the conversation, but the girl persisted, "Did she have an injection then? That's what father does when a dog dies."

A lady entered the room wearing a black dress and white apron.

"Come along children, dinner is ready," she said, so the conversation between the girl and David discontinued.

The dining room was amazing, there was a basket at the door with fancy hats to wear, and a cracker on each place setting, red serviettes, red wine glasses for the adults, red tumblers for the children, and the table was groaning with food. David made sure he sat next to John, and he had a wonderful time, as did everyone. They pulled the crackers and read the jokes and enjoyed the meal. At 3 pm, still sitting at the table, they listened to the Queen's first Christmas speech prior to her coronation, and when she had finished, the radio was turned off, and the lady in the black dress and white apron appeared with a Christmas pudding in flames. Everyone cheered, so David realised the lady had not set it on fire by accident. Mr Gray served it with rum sauce for the adults and custard for the children. Two ladies arrived with a trolley with cups and saucers on, a coffee pot and cream and milk jug.

"I think we need to thank the ladies for a splendid meal," said Mr Gray. "As usual, it was delicious and very much appreciated,"

"It certainly was," said David, enthusiastically, and clapped. The ladies laughed as the others joined in clapping too, and they left looking very pleased.

David tried coffee for the first time in his life and liked it, but he couldn't manage a mince pie, he was so full.

"Can we leave the table now, Dad?" asked one of the boys.

"Off you go," said Mr Gray, "and remember you've just eaten, don't start larking about."

John saw David looking at the table and just knew he was about to start clearing it, so he just quietly said, "Leave it, go and join the others."

Everyone went back to the lounge so the ladies could clear away and get back to their families. They were paid well and happy to work on Christmas day, and any other time when Mrs Gray was entertaining; otherwise, she prepared the meals for her family.

David was in a corner playing with a Meccano, helping to build a crane when John came looking for him.

"Time to go," he said, "before I fall asleep."

They put on their coats and shoes, thanked the Gray's for their hospitality and kindness, shook hands with Mr Gray and left.

As they drove home, David was playing with the small car he had in his cracker, and when he arrived home, he took it up to his room and put it in his memory box with the toothbrush from Rebecca, the first shell he had picked up on the beach, a broach he had picked up off the floor when his mother had fallen over and a photograph Jed had given him of his boat.

On Boxing Day, John was busy in his office for a while, so David walked up to see the horses and called to see Annie and Wilfred who were cosy beside the fire listening to the radio. When he returned home, John had packed up some pie and ham sandwiches and a thermos flask of tea, and they set off along the coastal path, walking much further than David had been before. The sea was calm, almost whispering at the shore as it rolled in and out, there was no wind, but the icy air tightened the skin and numbed the lips.

David started to tell John about the previous Christmas and what had happened to him and his mother. John never pressed David for information; it had to be his choice when he felt ready to talk about it. He spoke about Rebecca and her parents who had taken him in and about the people who took him to the orphanage and wouldn't listen to him when he wanted to visit his mother in hospital, how much it troubled him that she would think he didn't care about her, and how they had taken the money from him that the undertaker had given him that was left from the cost of the funeral.

"Did you never visit her in hospital?" asked John.

"Oh, yes, just once," said David.

"And how was she then?" asked John.

"Well," replied David, "she had some of her hair shaven off and had stitches that looked like flies on her head, and she said she had a fire in her belly and that she loved me."

"I think she did, very much," said John, "and I'm sure she would know how much you loved her. It's possible that she asked that you didn't visit her again because she knew how ill she was and didn't want you to have that memory of her. Think about that, David, perhaps the people at the orphanage were doing as she asked."

David went quiet for a while, thinking about what John had said. "Do you think that's what happened?" he said.

"I think there's a strong possibility that's what happened," said John. "People do this all the time because they don't want loved ones to see them suffering, especially where children are concerned."

David did consider what John had said to him but all his life felt the people at the orphanage were cruel.

They stopped in a sheltered hollow and had their picnic, and set off back home before the light faded. Now the tide was coming in, announcing its arrival as it thrashed against the rocks and rumbled across the bay as they neared the steps to the house.

John had laid the fire in the lounge before they left, but on their return, it was burning brightly and the room was warm. Annie had been and had lit the fire.

After tea, John asked David, "Have you done your homework?" knowing full well he hadn't. "Maybe now is a good time to do it."

"I'd forgotten about it," said David. "I'll do it in the morning when you are at the surgery, promise."

The following morning, he did his homework as promised and then went to meet John after surgery with the intention of opening a bank account at the post office for David with some of the money he had earned over Christmas, and it was agreed that half his earnings each week from the butcher would go into the bank.

On the way home, John stopped to put some feed out for the horses and noticed Bibby's limp was getting worse, so he tried to see if there was anything obvious as he walked round the horse, stroking and patting her. Trot was feisty and turned round and kicked out with her hind legs, but John knew what was coming and kept out of her way, but it frightened David.

"What's matter with her?" he said.

"Oh! She'll be wanting to go out with the trap, but she goes too fast for these slippery roads and we could end up in someone's garden or even a shop window if she skids and loses control," said John.

David did his New Year's Eve deliveries for the butcher and went home and read for a while and listened to a play on the radio and was in bed before the New Year celebrations were being broadcast. New Year's day was just another day to him, and he was glad to be going back to school the following day.

Chapter 14

New term started with the usual meet and greet half an hour for the boys to chat about the holidays before they went to the classrooms for lessons to begin. David noticed a boy at the edge of a group, not engaging with the boys, just listening, so he went to him.

"Are you ok?" he asked. "Have you had a good Christmas? I'm, David, by the way."

They shook hands.

"I'm Ted," said the boy.

Ted was a boarder and had been in school over Christmas, with a few other boys, because his father was in the RAF in Cyprus, and it saddened him listening to the boys who had been at home with their families.

If only I had known, thought David, *we could have spent time together*.

David really enjoyed school apart from the cross-country runs in the cold and the rain, but he had been warned, and the runs along the coastal path had improved his stamina as John intended when he suggested he did them. Always, John oversaw his homework, particularly the Latin and sciences, guiding David to the answers rather than giving them outright. He had learned to swim, he played hockey which was unusual at a boys' school, but he really enjoyed it, and intended to learn to play tennis in the summer.

One morning, as John was driving up the lane, he noticed Biddy lying down in the top corner of the field. Sometimes, he stopped to put some feed out, but he carried on and David didn't notice because he was searching for something in his brief case.

John telephoned the vet and met him in the field after surgery.

"It's not good, John," said Mr Gray. "I've been trying to improve things over the past few weeks for the mare, but this really is the end of the road, the fibrosis of the distal limbs is so bad she can't even stand and is in great pain trying.

"Do what is necessary," said John. "I want her out of the way before David comes home."

The vet went to his car to prepare the strong sedative required to put Biddy to sleep. Some owners had their horses shot, but Mr Gray wanted to spare John witnessing that.

John bent down and spoke to Biddy. She raised her head as he stroked her. "Sorry, old girl," he said, "it's time to go."

The vet injected her, muscles in her body rippled, stopped, and she was gone.

John stayed with Biddy whilst the vet returned to his office and telephoned the abattoir to have the horse removed, and everything that could go wrong after that, did.

John was concerned Trot may become a nuisance, but she stayed diagonally across the field from him and never moved, just stood watching.

A hoist arrived, and the driver realised there would be too much weight for him to handle on his own, so they had to send for another to assist. When the flat wagon arrived to take Biddy away, it couldn't get in the field, getting bogged down on the soft ground, so John had to get the farmer from the next village with his tractor to pull the wagon into the field. The second hoist arrived late from a previous job, but finally, everything was in place, Biddy was secured in chains between the two hoists working in tandem, towards the flat wagon, silhouetted against the darkening skyline. The machines were noisy, but John heard the screams from the bottom of the field and saw David running towards them with his arms outstretched.

"Stop, stop!" he screamed. "What's happening? Is she dead? Don't take her away."

"Stay where you are," shouted John and walked towards David.

David sank to his knees and beat the ground with his fists. It was more than he could bear, seeing his beloved horse dangling between the hoists, dead, and when Biddy slammed onto the wagon, he was sick. John went to comfort him but he shrugged away and stood in the middle of the field, dazed, and watched the hoists leave, the wagon driver cover up Biddy and rope up his wagon, the tractor pull the wagon out of the field, the driver close the gate, and they were gone. David was bawling and pacing up and down, so John left him and went home, picking up the briefcase David had dropped in the lane.

"Has something happened?" asked Annie, "I have not seen you all day."

"I had to have Biddy put down, and the whole process of getting her to the abattoir was so problematic, it was still going on and David saw her go, unfortunately. He's very distressed, and he will need a bath, perhaps you could run one for him."

"Where is he?" asked Annie.

"I left him in the field to have a few moments," replied John. "I'm not his favourite person at the moment. I will go back for him in a while if he doesn't come home."

David remained in the field, pacing up and down, until it started to rain heavily, and he was just turning to leave when he became aware of Trot walking slowly up the field to where Biddy had been, then she walked across to the gate where they had all left from, and she just kept doing it over and over again. He called her, but there was no response, she didn't even turn to look, so he shut the bottom gate and headed home.

He kicked off his shoes in the porch, opened the kitchen door and stood there dripping, face puffy and covered in blotches from crying, muddy streaks running down his face and off his chin. His waterproof looked as if it had been streaked in charcoal, and the drips were making a grey pool on the floor, so Annie sent him back outside to stand in the rain and rinse some more dirt off.

John went to call him. "Come in," he said, "take your clothes off there. Annie is running a bath for you."

David felt soothed by the warm water, but his mind was still in turmoil from what he had just witnessed.

Annie knocked on the door and popped her head around. "Leave the water in the bath," she said. "I'm going to rinse your waterproof. Are you calming down?"

"I don't know what I am," said David. "I feel numb and sick."

"I've brought your blanket and pyjamas for you. Come down and have some soup when you are finished here," Annie said.

David went down to the kitchen and sat in the chair by the stove, where Annie was stuffing his wet shoes with newspaper. She pulled up a stool beside him and held his hand.

"Now, David," she said, "we've never taken time to explain to you the ways of country folk and how things are done.

"Understand that it's the same for animals as it is for humans, and once they are dead, they don't know what's happening to them. Biddy worked hard at the plough for many years, so imagine how hard her legs had to work hauling a plough to turn the soil, plus carrying her own weight. When she came here, John looked after her very well, and I'm sure she would have been glad to have known you, she must have liked you or she wouldn't have bothered with you. If she's gone to heaven perhaps your ma will take care of her, did she like horses?"

"Oh, yes!" said David emphatically. "She liked horses a lot. There was a man at the pub who had race horses, and she used to give him money for them."

"Oh! Right," said Annie, sucking her cheeks in so she didn't smile.

David joined John at the table but only had some soup and bread, and they ate in silence.

"I'm going to bed now," said David, left the table and walked towards the door and suddenly turned, "Oh! Hell," he said, "I left my briefcase on the wall."

"It's here," said John. "I brought it home and it's fine. You can't go to school tomorrow, Annie can't clean your clothes in time, and you've had a terrible shock, you need the day to recover, but you can do your homework in the morning."

"Goodnight," said David and went up to bed in a very sombre mood.

Annie put his clothes on the creel to dry out, and put more fuel in the stove to prolong the heat through the night.

"Hopefully," she said, "when they are dry, the dirt will brush out, it looked like he was rolling about in the mud."

"He was," said John. "I've never seen anything like it, such raw emotion and desperation, such a shock for him. I just wish things had gone to plan and he hadn't seen any of it." John paused in his thoughts for a moment. "Whatever we say to him, he'll never forget what he saw, and even though the rawness of the pain he is feeling now will fade, the memory of this afternoon is bound to stay with him for a long time, he's to go past the field every day."

Annie went home and John went to speak to David, who was curled up in his blanket, hugging his knees on his window seat, and he just couldn't stop crying.

"I will miss her so much," he sobbed. "She was such a wonderful horse."

"I know," said John, sympathetically. "If you remember, she has been limping for a while. Heavy horses like shires that have worked hard for a long time, and weigh so much, suffer from fibrosis of the distal limbs, the leg joints, and if it's left, the horse suffers great pain. The vet had tried to deal with it, but today Biddy couldn't stand up, so we had to help her. If we had left her, she would just have starved and died in the field. Come along, into bed now, I'll telephone the school in the morning and explain your absence."

He left David and went and sat in his chair by the stove and had a glass of port. Here he was, sharing the boy's pain, desperate to help but unable to provide much comfort to the shocked, grieving boy. This was the day John realised how much

David had come to mean to him, and any doubts he had about taking him in had gone, and he understood why Jake had taken risks to get him to a safe place and give him a chance in life. He felt he was part of the family now, and it was never in doubt again.

The following morning, David did his homework and watched Annie frantically brushing the dried mud out of his trousers and blazer sleeves. His shoes had been stuffed with newspaper near the stove and had dried out, so she passed them to David to polish. He had a moment remembering how Mr Brown used to clean shoes over a piece of newspaper on the floor, and he wondered what Rebecca would be doing, and would she even remember him now?

"Can I go out?" he asked Annie.

"No," she replied, "John wants you here when he's finished surgery. Can you clean the bath please, it's full of grit, looks as if it's been pebble dashed."

On any other day, David would have laughed at Annie's comment, but today, he just went and cleaned the bath.

After lunch, John told David to put on his wellies and coat.

"Why?" asked David, thinking he wasn't allowed out because he should have been at school.

"We are going to check on Trot," said John, who had noticed both on his way to and from the surgery that she was rooted to the spot at the top of the field where Biddy had died. He felt it was important that David should see her and was involved in any decision made for her. She was there, megalith-still, at the top of the field, no swish of the tail or toss of the head, and as they walked towards her, she kicked out her back legs and ran off to the gate that Biddy had gone through when they took her away. John pulled the trap out of the shelter to see if that would interest her, but there was no response, she just stood with her back to them.

"She's fretting for Biddy," said John. "I'm going to leave her for a few days to see if she comes 'round."

"What if she doesn't?" asked David, hesitating to ask the question.

"Well!" said John. "The farmer has two boys who each have a pony, and we thought we could try her with them. If she has company and is in a different place, she could settle."

The following two days, as David went to and from school, Trot was in the same place, head hanging low, the feed hadn't been touched, the nights has been bitterly cold, but they couldn't catch her to put her blanket on, and there was nothing there of the spirited horse she had once been, so it was decided that on the weekend, the farmer would come and collect her.

What should have taken quarter of an hour took well over an hour to catch her and get her into the horse box. She was distressed and weak but still managed to give them a real run around, kick out and evade capture, so in the end, the vet managed to sedate her, so they were able to get her into the horsebox with a wonky gait, and as she passed David, she still managed to curl her lip at him.

David never spoke of her or Biddy again, although he remembered them every time he passed the field for a long time. He never knew if Trot had settled at the farm or not, he hoped she had, but never asked in case the outcome was different.

Life settled down for David into a calmer routine. He was enjoying school and the sporting opportunities that were available and also a social side with invitations for tea or outings with other students. He continued working for the butcher and would sometimes meet Ted when he had finished his deliveries on a Saturday and take him home for lunch or pick up a packed lunch to take to the beach if the weather and tide were suitable. They would swim if the sea was calm or walk along the coastal path, and sometimes, John would drop them off at the cinema in town for a matinee and collect them in time for Ted to be back at school for the evening meal. The boys amused John with their chatter and joking, and he felt it was a shame that Ted's parents were missing so much.

When David was 13, he celebrated with a picnic on the beach with ten of his friends from school. Annie had prepared sandwiches, cheese and onion pasty, sausages, fruit and cakes for the boys to collect and carry down to the beach along with a box of crockery and bottles of lemonade and dandelion and burdock. John was not prepared to leave them unsupervised, so he tucked himself into a corner and sat reading and writing, and at one point took photographs of them behind a fort they had built in the sand, soon to be dissolved in the incoming tide, which signalled it was time to leave. John ran the two boarders back up to the school, whilst parents arrived to collect the other boys, all leaving expressing their thanks and agreeing they had a wonderful time.

On his way home, John called in to see Wilfred and Annie. He had noticed how Annie had become far too stretched between her duties at his home and caring for a much more needy Wilfred, who had taken to his bed, wouldn't get dressed or even washed if he could get away with it, which was totally uncharacteristic. John had a chat with Wilfred and then asked Annie to sit with him. "I've organised some help for you," he said.

"Why?" snapped Annie.

"Because you need it," said John. "There is a lady in the village who has recently been widowed, with four children, and I've asked her to come and help out three days a week under your supervision. Once you have explained what is expected of her, you will have three full days here with Wilfred. She will not work Saturdays or Sundays, and has made that clear at the outset, because she feels it is important to be with her children at the weekends, and I respect that and have agreed to it. David and I are around at the weekends, and would only ask that you prepare our evening meal for us, so even on those days you would have more time for yourself. The lady's name is Fay, and she is coming to meet you on Monday, I'm bringing her down with me after surgery. She is young and strong, so consider this and where she could help you the most."

Annie sat quiet for a moment, knowing full well she was stressed and tired with the situation, and feeling her age, which she never disclosed, but John knew she was in her 70s from her medical records.

"What about my wages?" she asked in a worried tone.

"Nothing will change there," said John. "Not after all the years of service you have given us, it's the least I can do. See you tomorrow."

He stood up and left, but as he reached the gate, he realised he had left his hat, so he retraced his steps to the door. He could hear Annie crying, so he left the hat and went home.

David had washed up and stacked the crockery in the box for Annie, because he didn't know where it had come from.

"You've been a long time," he said to John.

"Yes," replied John, and related what had just taken place with Annie. "Just be aware of her state of mind if she's snappy, she has a lot to think about at the moment.

"How is Wilfred?" asked David.

"Poorly," replied John. "In a lot of pain from his arthritis, and inactivity could bring on pneumonia, and although I've explained all this to him, I doubt very much he's taking the pills I've prescribed for him. Anyway, shaking off the gloom, did you have a nice day?"

"Fantastic," replied David. "My first ever birthday party, and I've got twelve birthday cards. I only used to get one from my ma. Everyone enjoyed themselves. Thank you so much." He gave John a hug.

"I've just remembered," said John, and went to fetch an envelope hidden behind the jug on the sideboard, "this came from Jake a few days ago."

David opened it and a £5 note fell out. "I wish he could have been here today."

"We can telephone him later in the week, and perhaps we will get to see him in a few weeks' time. I have to get his signature on some forms, but there's no point in going until I've got them all to deal with in one visit. Now what is there to eat?"

They made a chicken salad and chatted about the picnic, and John asked David to make tea and take it to the lounge. He carried the tray in and placed it on the table and as he turned to close the door, he saw a television. David ran round it and touched it and beamed at John. "When did this come?" he asked.

"Today, whilst we were on the beach, but it will not be set up until Monday afternoon. I felt we should have one to watch the coronation, but homework must be done before it is switched on. I'm bringing Fay down to meet Annie after surgery, and the technician will be coming in the afternoon to set up the television.

Annie arrived as usual on Monday morning, made breakfast and busied herself. "What time is SHE coming, then?" she asked.

John answered, "If you mean Fay, I'm bringing her home with me after surgery, so it will be late morning, perhaps lunch time. She's a pleasant, gentle lady, so I don't want any petulance, thank you." He peered at Annie over his spectacles with a stern look.

"You don't need to speak to me like I'm a five-year-old," she retorted.

"Well, I won't," said John, "as long as you don't behave like one."

Annie clattered the dishes in the sink, and John left, dreading the afternoon, relying on Fay's calmness to ease things along.

When Fay arrived, she had been told that Annie wasn't ready to accept help and might be tetchy, but when she left, she had managed to reassure Annie that she would only do what was asked of her and was glad to be able to help. She had asked about Wilfred and lightened the mood by talking about her children, a boy 11, a girl 9, a boy 4 and a girl 2.

"I hope we can get along," said Fay. "I have to come, I need the money to get by. Think about when you want me to come, and what you want me to do, and I'll come tomorrow and you can explain everything to me."

Fay was as tactful as she could be, and she and Annie were able to work things out and get along fine for which John was truly grateful.

Three weeks later, Annie arrived later than usual one morning and just stood in the doorway and looked at John.

"Are you all right?" he asked.

"He's gone," she said. "He died in the night, and he's in a bit of a mess. He was choking on all this stuff he was bringing up, and I couldn't help him." She slumped into a chair and buried her head in her hands.

"Why on earth didn't you come for me?" asked John.

"He didn't want it," said Annie. "He just wanted it to be over. It was a terrible time for him."

"Off you go to school, David, I need to deal with this," said John, and David was glad to leave the house.

After the funeral, Annie's daughter Bridie managed to have a quiet chat with John. She had suggested that her mother returned home with her to Ireland to live, but Annie wouldn't even discuss it.

"Too soon," said John. "She needs a few months to find out for herself whether it's a good idea to remain here or to be with you. I'll keep in touch with you, and we'll take care of her as much as we are able. She needs time to re-adjust."

Chapter 15

The evenings were staying lighter for longer, and it had been a lovely day, so John and David had walked up to the surgery to speak to Jake on the telephone. David looked forward to speaking to Jake, and this time he had a chat with Betty also, because Jake was staying with them for a few days.

On the way back, they came across Annie, in the garden, in her nightie and slippers.

"What are you up to?" asked John.

"Oh! Just doing a spot of weeding," she said.

She was pulling up everything, bulbs that were dying off, shoots that were just coming through, all ending up in a pile in the corner.

"I think you've probably done enough now," said John. "Perhaps you should go in, it's getting cool out here."

Annie stopped what she was doing, looked at John but didn't speak, she just turned, wiped her dirty hands on her nightie, went indoors and locked the door.

David giggled, he'd no idea what was happening to Annie, but John had noticed a change in her for a while. He had overheard a conversation between Annie and Fay a few days earlier. Annie had brought the washing in off the line and was putting it back in the washing machine, and Fay was trying to explain to her that it was ready for ironing. John intervened, but it seemed that Annie, momentarily, wasn't sure who John was.

John briefly explained to David that Annie may be in the first stages of something called Alzheimer's disease, and that they must look out for her to make sure she wasn't careless and hurt herself and never to draw her attention to any silly things she may have done, because it's possible she wouldn't remember, and it would upset and confuse her more, and that he'd asked Fay to try to ignore things but to keep him informed.

Annie turned up for work the following morning and had an indignant outburst because someone had pulled up all her plants during the night, and Wilfred was going to be very annoyed when he came home. David turned and looked at John but said nothing, he just gathered his things and left for school, puzzled and troubled, so that evening, he asked John if he had a book he could read to learn about what was happening to Annie. After David had done his homework, John sat with him and explained about Alzheimer's in terms appropriate for David to understand, rather than the medical terms in a book.

"Let's watch television," said John, diverting the conversation because he didn't want David dwelling too much on what they had discussed.

Sadly, Annie's decline was rapid, and when the butcher took a note to the surgery to be passed to John informing him that she had been to buy three sausages three times that morning for her and Wilfred, John realised he had to contact her daughter,

Bridie. He telephoned her that evening, and she agreed she needed to visit her mother and make a decision about what needed to be done. Two weeks later, Bridie, her husband and another man turned up in a hire van, totally unexpected by everyone. John felt they may have had the courtesy to inform him, and although it was obvious what the plan was, he wondered about the outcome. He was so taken aback, he asked Bridie into his office to have a private word.

"When I telephoned you," said John, "I didn't mean come and take her away, but that you just needed to know what was happening to Annie, to know how things were with her."

"We didn't think that at all," said Bridie. "We know how good you have been to Mum and Dad, but Ireland is too far away for me to travel every time there is a crisis, she is my responsibility, so we decided that whilst Graham was here, we should come and collect her. Graham is my brother from Australia."

They went back into the kitchen, and John walked across to Graham, shook his hand and said, "I'm pleased to meet you, I never knew Annie had a son."

"Mum never forgave me for leaving," said Graham. "She has never met my wife or her two grandchildren, but we have a good life over there, and I've never regretted going."

"So explain to me what the plan is," asked John.

"I'm going to sleep with Mum tonight," said Bridie, "and the men are going to sleep in the van, and then if you would be kind enough to give us a lift to the station for the early train, Mum and I will travel by train to the ferry, and the men will return by road, obviously, with her furniture and bits and pieces. We want her to have her own familiar things so we emptied a room before we left and Graham and his family are in a B&B for their last week before returning home.

"How do you think Annie is going to feel about all this?" asked John.

"We're not telling her everything," said Bridie, "just that she's going on a trip with me, then hopefully she will be spared the wrench of leaving the home she has lived in all her married life. Don't forget, both Graham and I were born there, and it will be emotional for me when I leave in the morning knowing I'll never be back."

John looked at his watch. "I just need to catch David," he said and went outside to wait for him, pondering on the chaos that ensued.

David smiled at John as he walked towards him and wondered why he was outside waiting for him.

"There's a big van up the lane," he said.

"Yes," said John, "and Bridie and her husband and brother are inside, they have come to take Annie to Ireland." He could see David was going to ask questions, so he put his finger to his lips, "Shh! Just listen. Don't ask any questions about anything, do your homework in my study, and get up and go to school on your own in the morning because I'm taking Annie and Bridie for the early train."

They walked back into the house, just as Annie appeared from upstairs with a bundle of washing.

"Bridie," she said, "what are you doing here? Did you say you were coming?"

"No," said Bridie, "it's a surprise. I was thinking you needed a little break, so I've come to take you on a trip tomorrow."

"Oh! I can't do that," said Annie. "I'm needed here, and who will look after Wilfred?"

"I'm going for fish and chips," said John. "Put the plates to warm, please, Annie."

Annie glowered at John. "Who do you think you are telling me what to do?" she snapped.

Bridie laughed. "I'll deal with it," she said, so John and David left for the village fish shop. When they returned, everyone was sitting round the table chatting.

Annie looked at David. "I'm going on a trip tomorrow," she said. "Shall I bring you a stick of rock back?"

"No, thank you," said David. "I'm not allowed rock, it spoils your teeth."

"Well, he's a dentist," said Annie, nodding towards John. "Tell him to sort them out for you."

David helped Bridie to clear the table and wash up. "I'll really miss your ma," he said. "She has been really kind to me, and we have had lots of fun."

"I know she has enjoyed having you around," said Bridie, "but now she is becoming confused and unwell, I have to take her home and look after her."

David went to John's study and settled down to do his homework, followed closely by John who poured himself a glass of port and slumped uncharacteristically into his chair.

"Have they gone?" asked David.

"No," said John. "It's really weird in there. They are sitting watching television, and I think Annie is pretending she doesn't know who Graham is. She wouldn't know at first, of course, she hasn't seen him for many years, but he made himself known to her, and Bridie has told her twice since who he is, but she is still blanking him, and honestly, he doesn't seem to care. They haven't been in each other's company for so long, it will be hard to rekindle a relationship with so much distance between them. Now and again, she is asking where she is going on her trip, and I'm convinced she thinks it is only for a day, and I also think Bridie's husband is beginning to realise how life-changing it is going to be to have Annie in his home."

David went into the lounge to say 'Goodnight' and went up to his room, and shortly afterwards, Annie and Bridie left for the cottage. The men hung back, used the bathroom, and then walked quietly past the cottage to sleep in the van.

As arranged, John picked Annie and Bridie up at 7 am and dropped them off at the station. He was feeling at odds with the situation and felt emotional because Annie and Wilfred had been in his and Jake's life since they were boys. He wanted to hug her, thank her and wish her well, but he just sat in the car and said, "Cheerio, have a nice time." He nodded at Bridie and lip-mimed, "I'll call you in a few days." She nodded back and they parted company.

He was just about to drive off to the surgery when Fay tapped on the window of the car.

"Is everything all right? Have I just seen Annie going for the train?" she asked.

"Get in," said John. "I'll run you down." He related the whole story to a stunned Fay who asked, "Did she know she was going to live in Ireland with her daughter?"

"No," replied John, "she doesn't know now, and I doubt she will realise it until her furniture and belongings arrive."

When they passed the van, it was partly loaded, so John stopped the car and walked into the cottage. "You must take that chair," he said. "I see you've got the bed and chest of drawers in, where are her pictures and vases?"

"We just need to get the wardrobe in on its side," said Bridie's husband, and then all the crockery and pictures and vases can be rolled in the bedding and will be secure for the journey wedged in the wardrobe."

Graham came into the room from the van. "I'm glad we had the chance to meet," said John, "and I hope by the time you return home, your mother has made peace with you."

"That will not happen," said Graham. "I'm here to help Bridie. I'm sure my mother means more to you than she does to me, you've certainly seen more of her."

John ignored the terseness of Graham's comment.

"It saddens me that it's possible neither of us will see her again. She's your mother, bear that in mind. Leave the key on the window sill, please. Safe journey."

When he returned to the car, Fay had gone and made her own way to the house, bumping into David on his way to school. He had seen John's car as he passed the cottage but carried on his way, noticing the van was almost loaded and thinking Annie would already be on the train.

During the next few days, even though Fay was around some of the time, they felt an emptiness which surprised them. They missed the clattering and bustle Annie brought to the kitchen, the hub of the home and the cursing on the landing when the carpet sweeper misbehaved with the runner and her singing when she was upstairs working, always the same song, 'We'll Gather Lilacs in the Spring Again'.

John waited until Graham had returned to Australia before he telephoned Bridie. "How was your journey?" he asked.

"Well, I did know it wouldn't all be plain sailing, and it was such a long journey, but honestly, John, I was exhausted when we arrived," said Bridie. "Every time the train stopped, Mum wanted to get off, she insisted on walking the length of the train over and over again, and I had to follow her. She had a nap for about an hour, but I couldn't risk it in case she woke up and took off again, and the people in the carriage were really fed up with us, so the first chance they got to move, they did, and it did make it easier when we were on our own. At the ferry, she panicked when she saw cars and lorries being loaded on the lower decks. There was no way she was getting on that ferry, she was convinced it would sink, and of course, to see a ferry boat for the first time, so huge, with many tiers and bright lights, must have been very daunting for her. In the end, a nun came to help me, and she calmed Mum and we got her on board and found some seats. The crossing was the roughest I've ever experienced, she was sick and wanted to get off, and I've never been so glad to see my friend who collected us from the ferry port to bring us home. I took all our clothes off, and threw them into the bath, had some tea and toast and went to bed. She did ask where she was, and I told her she was in my home in Ireland where I could look after her."

"How did she respond to that?" asked John.

"She just went to sleep," said Bridie, "and the following morning said nothing. Fortunately, I'd taken a change of clothes for her so she could get dressed and sit outside where I could keep my eye on her until I could peg the washing out and sit with her. I think seeing her clothes on the washing line triggered something off, because she had been calm and enjoying the garden, when she suddenly flared up, called me a bitch, said I'd kidnapped her, and said she was going to the police. Fortunately, my friend arrived so Mum told her what a bad person I was and what I'd done. My friend asked Mum if she really wanted to go on the ferry and train again so soon, and Mum just shut up as if someone had turned her switch off, and she chatted normally. The following day, the van arrived, and since she has had her things around her, she has been better, but she keeps trying to move the chest of drawers and look behind them, but I'm not sure what all that is about because we've moved them to different places in the room and she still does it. Anyway, all is calm at the moment, but who knows when the lid will fly off again."

"It will not be easy for you, Bridie," said John, "I'm sure you are realising that already, and I do respect and admire you for wanting to take care of your mother. We do miss her, there's no one to tell us what to do anymore."

Bridie laughed, "Yes," she said, "she's always been good at that."

"I'll keep in touch," said John. "I don't know if it's a good idea to tell her I've telephoned, it might stir things up in her mind again, but you do know we are thinking about you, and if you need any help, don't hesitate to contact me. If Annie mentions us and thinks we don't care about her, then that might be a good time to say we called."

The following Saturday, after David had done his deliveries for the butcher, and because it was pouring down, he decided to go to the cottage and tidy up and see what had been left. There was a well-cared for drop leaf table and four chairs, Wilfred's old arm-chair, a three-drawer chest and a bookcase Wilfred had made. Annie was house proud, so the cottage wasn't grubby at all, but David wanted to be there, so he found things to do. He took the hard bristle brush to sweep the floor and caught the head on a protruding stone, and when he tried to push it back into the wall it moved, so he pulled it out and found a tin hidden behind it. He didn't open the tin, but it rattled, indicating there could be some money in it, so he took it straight home to John, and they sat at the kitchen table and opened it. Yes, there was money inside, and Annie and Wilfred's birth and marriage certificates.

"We must send them on," said John. "I'll bank the money and buy a postal order, and I bet this is what she has been trying to find behind her chest of drawers at Bridie's."

"If we sell the furniture that's left behind, we can send even more money," said David. "I can put a 'for sale' notice in the post office."

"If you want to do that, go ahead," said John. "It's your responsibility, I'll keep the tin safe until you have tried."

John suggested prices and David wrote his note to put on the 'for sale' board in the post office, and took it in after school on the Monday, and by the following weekend, everything had been sold apart from a spoon he had found at the back of a drawer, and that he kept for his memory tin. He felt very proud that his enterprise had been successful, and John was impressed but didn't tell him in case he started looking around his house for things to sell.

"Is Fay going to live in the cottage now?" David asked John one day.

"No," said John, "I'm not letting it again at the moment, and in any case, it is too small for Fay and four children, she's better off where she is now, near her mother, but I was thinking that she may want to bring her eldest two down to watch the coronation on television, and Ted, if you wish. What's the situation at school?"

"I know we have the day off, but I'm not sure what the plan is for boarders. I know there is a television in the staff quarters, but all the boarders will not fit in there. I'll ask the question," said David.

Chapter 16

The day before the coronation, Fay had been busy making buns with red, white and blue icing, and jellies were in the fridge. Fay decided there was no point in making anything else as they were going up to the village to the street party after the ceremony. David had put up bunting and arranged chairs round the television in the lounge and put cushions on the floor for the morning when Fay arrived with her two older children, and Ted, who they had met at the top of the lane. The youngsters were giddy, so John suggested they went down to the beach until the interesting part of the coronation programme for them was due. They had a game of cricket and then just sat in the sand and chatted until John called them. The television only had a small screen, and the picture was in black and white, but once Princess Elizabeth had arrived at the Abbey, they were absorbed by the proceedings. They were surprised to see it was raining in London, but it didn't stop the crowds from gathering, some had been there all night, the commentator said. David was fascinated by the buildings, especially Westminster Abbey, and was dumbfounded by the number of people there.

"Who are all those people, where do they live?" David asked John.

"There will be people in the crowds from all over the world," John replied. "This is a very momentous day."

"Just look at those beautiful gowns," said Fay. "How much work has gone into those? And look at the pageboys, what an honour for them."

"They've got frills on their shirts and buckles on their shoes," commented her eldest child. "They'll soon mess those up playing out."

"They are special costumes for the occasion," said Fay, and nodded to end the conversation before it became silly and distracting, as so many conversations with her children did.

As soon as the queen left the Abbey, the children raced up to the village for the street party. The main street had tables down the centre of the road with benches and chairs collected from the junior school and Sunday school, and from anyone who was willing to risk having their furniture outside and even crates with cushions on. Probably every house and business had contributed in some way to the celebrations organised by the Women's Institute. There were egg sandwiches, jelly, blancmange, buns and ice creams for the children, and pork pies, pickled onions and ham sandwiches for the adults. There was music being played on record players from open windows, and the pubs at each end of the street were full of adults enjoying a glass of beer and good jokes.

"There will be a few headaches in the morning," mused John quietly to David as they passed.

Around 4 pm, as requested, John went to the platform with the microphone and thanked the ladies of the Women's Institute, and all the volunteers who had worked so hard and been so generous with their efforts to make the party such a great success. He suggested a quick clear up as the rain clouds were gathering, so there was a manic rush to bag the rubbish and return the tables and chairs to their rightful places.

Ted had to return to school with some other students who had attended the celebrations, so David used it as an excuse to escape from a group of giggling girls and went home without saying anything to John. He was sitting at the table doing his homework, luckily for him, when John arrived home, none too pleased that David had disappeared when the clearing up was to be done, and soaking from the downpour.

"Why didn't you do your homework last night?" asked John.

"I was helping Fay set up for today, wasn't I?" replied David and didn't admit he had almost forgotten to do it.

John went for a bath, and then joined David for a sandwich and a cup of tea.

"Fay isn't in tomorrow, she is working on Saturday morning for me, as I will be having business visitors for lunch. She wasn't happy to be asked, but I promised her an electric iron and a day off in lieu, so she accepted the bribe," said John, smiling wryly.

"What do you want me to do on Saturday?" asked David.

"You don't need to do anything different," said John. "Just don't disturb us in my office. Also, half term week, I have something planned for us, so don't make any arrangements for that week, but you don't need to say anything to the butcher, we will be back by Friday for sure."

"Back from where, what have you planned for us?" asked David eagerly.

"It will not be a surprise if I tell you now," said John, "and I'm not going to."

David knew he wouldn't, so he didn't even try to persuade him.

He sat on his window seat at bed time listening to the rain driving at the window, staring into the greyness outside, thinking over the day's events when John made him jump. "Set your alarm," he said, "remember Fay isn't in tomorrow."

The following day at first break time at school, a very excited Ted went to find David to tell him he had received a letter from his grandparents inviting him and David to spend half term with them.

"I don't know if I can," said David, remembering what John had said to him the previous night, "but I'll ask the question tonight."

David waited until after tea before he mentioned the invitation to John.

"You know you can't risk it," said John, "not for a full week. Remember you are using your own name because I had to produce your birth certificate at school, and a slip of the tongue is all it could take to stimulate someone's interest into asking more questions about your past, and another thing, and much more important, Jake would be very disappointed if I didn't take you with me."

David was feeling crestfallen, he'd almost forgotten he still had to be wary and careful in new company, especially away from the school and the village. He suddenly realised what John had just said to him about seeing Jake and leapt to his feet.

"Did you say we are going to see Jake?" asked David, hoping he hadn't misheard. "When are we going?"

John peered at David over his glasses and smiled; he had enjoyed giving David the news, knowing how much it meant to him.

"On Monday for three days, if the meeting goes well on Saturday," said John. "He is staying with Jed and Betty, so you will see them as well. You'll need to pack your holdall on Sunday as we will be going for the early train Monday morning and take a book with you and some money."

John had really not wanted to tell David about the trip too soon because he knew how excited he would be, but it could not be helped, and now he was bombarded with questions about the trip.

"Let's get the meeting over on Saturday," said John. "Then I can tell you, because at the moment I don't know the outcome."

"But what is it about, the meeting?" asked David.

"I'll tell you on Saturday," replied John. "No more questions, please."

David settled down at school, but at home he was restless, packed and unpacked his holdall several times, gathered his school reports for Jake to read, and hunted for the cap Betty had bought him.

When he returned home from the butcher's shop on Saturday, there were four cars outside the house that he didn't recognise. Fay had found a white tablecloth and had laid the table for lunch using the best crockery and cutlery. She had cooked a ham and sliced it, buttered bread, made cheese sandwiches from white and brown bread and cut them into triangles and put slices of tomato around the edge of the plate and homemade chutney in a dish. The china cups and saucers were on a tray ready to be served, and Fay had made a Victoria sponge cake to be served with the tea. David was about to help himself to a sandwich, but Fay slapped his hand.

"Your plate is over there," she said. "Take it to your room. I'll try and make sure you have a piece of cake."

"Who are these people?" asked David.

"Don't know," replied Fay, "but I think they are important, they are all wearing very smart suits and carry briefcases, but I don't think they are all doctors."

John opened his office door. "Is everything ready?" he asked and glanced towards the table.

"Yes, Doctor," replied Fay and put the kettle on to boil to make the tea. David smiled at John and pointed upwards to indicate he was on his way up to his room.

"I'll come and join you if that's all right," said Fay. "Just need to make the tea."

They sat on the window seat and had their lunch and chatted. Fay was easy to be with, she was good fun and relaxed, and although her life had become a struggle since her husband died, she just got on with things as best she could. Since Annie had left, she worked more hours for John and was able to give up her job in the pub one evening a week, which gave her more time with her children, and that meant so much to her and them, and of course to her mother who helped out so much but was glad of some time to herself.

They heard the men moving back into the study, waited a few minutes to be sure, and went back into the kitchen.

"I will not see you until after your trip; I hope you enjoy it. I never met Jake, but maybe one day he will come home," said Fay.

"I'm going out for a walk," said David, pinching a slice of cake. Fay laughed and shook her fist at him as he passed. He walked along the coastal road and sat in his favourite place and read his book for a while until the tide was coming in and it became chilly. Brown froth from the waves was being whipped up into the air by the breeze and would leave rotting strands of algae in stripes on the beach, like ribbons, once the tide had ebbed.

David suddenly remembered that once the meeting was over John was going to tell him what the secret was, so he hurried home hoping everyone had left the house. John was on the doorstep saying, "Goodbye," and shaking hands with the last man to leave. David walked towards them, wondering whether he ought to, but John introduced him to the man. "This is my nephew, David," he said, "and this is Mr Smyth."

"I'm very pleased to meet you, sir," said David and held out his hand for the man to shake.

"Hope all goes well with Jake," said Mr Smyth. "It would be nice to see him again. I hope you find him well, give him my good wishes."

David and John stood outside until Mr Smyth had driven away, and then John took off his tie, unbuttoned his shirt, kicked his shoes off and gave a huge sigh as he sank into his chair with a glass of port. He sighed and closed his eyes, and David sat in the opposite chair not knowing what to make of it, so he just sat quietly, waiting.

John opened his eyes. "We've sold our land to a developer. We are going to see Jake to get his signature on all the paperwork."

"What do you mean by a developer?" asked David.

"They are going to build houses on my land. We will have gas laid to the house which will eliminate the nuisance of power cuts, and almost as soon as they commence work, we will have a telephone installed here," said John.

"Will we still be living here?" asked David.

"Nothing is changing here apart from the gas installation and telephone, and eventually there will be a road with a pavement the length of the lane, which will be good, but that will be the last thing they do when all the houses have been built, which will take a few years probably," said John.

"What about the cottage?" asked David.

"That will be pulled down, and they will use the good stone for a rebuild. It will take time for all this to happen, and you must not discuss it with anyone, not even Fay, do you understand?" said John.

"Yes," replied David, his thoughts reeling. He didn't want to have to tell anyone, he didn't want it to be happening really.

"I've had a promise from the developer that he will give work to the men in the village where he can," said John. "This project can bring prosperity to the village and it tidies up our affairs for later in life. Now," he said, "what about something to eat? I didn't have much lunch, but I think the sandwiches will have curled up."

"Let's have fish and chips," said David. "We have to make our own dinner tomorrow because Fay isn't coming, so let's be lazy today. We can eat up the ham tomorrow."

"You'll make someone a lovely wife," said John, teasing. They went to collect the fish and chips in the car, taking their time in the lane, looking across the fields, neither saying anything but both probably thinking the same thing.

"Let's sit outside and have them out of the paper, with salt and vinegar," said David, on their return, but John declined on the grounds that they went cold too quickly.

They had just finished eating and cleared the table when they heard a child screaming and a banging on the door. David was nearest and opened it to be confronted by a man carrying a girl, a huge gash in her leg, blood dripping everywhere.

"Put her in a chair outside," said John. "I'll get my bag, get some of the boiled water from the kettle in a basin, please, David."

He cleaned up the wound, a long deep gash, and realised it needed stitches. He called David to one side and asked him to distract the girl if he could, whilst he did the necessary, but it wasn't easy, and to make it worse, when John produced the needle to inject to numb the gash for stitching, the girl's father fainted.

David was spinning like a top wondering what to do.

"Just leave him where he is," said John, as the girl screamed louder than ever. "Let's get this over with, hold her still."

Eventually, he managed the stitches and bandaged her leg. Her father had come around and was propped up against the wall when John enquired if he was all right, because his clothes were soaked in blood from carrying the girl, and he couldn't tell whether the man had hurt himself in the faint or not.

"Thank you, Doctor. Yes, I'm fine," said the man. "I'm so sorry for disturbing you, I had to come."

"Indeed, you did," said John. "Make sure she keeps it clean and dry and take her to the surgery in three days to have a clean dressing. How did you get here?"

"I carried her," said the man.

"Get in the car," said John. "We can't have you carrying her all the way back." He put a cover on the seat for the girl who had gone very quiet and asked the man to take his blood-stained shirt off before he got in the car and drove them back home.

When he returned home, David had hosed the blood away, wrapped the swabs in newspaper and left them for John to dispose of.

"What are we doing tomorrow?" asked David, when they were sitting having a cup of cocoa before bed.

"Absolutely nothing," said John, "apart from getting ready to go and see Jake. I need to tidy all the papers on my desk and make sure I have everything needed for Jake to sign to proceed with the sale of the land." He was mentally jaded with the business of getting the deal he wanted, he just needed to unwind, and was looking forward to a few days away to visit Jake.

"Goodnight," said David. "Can't wait until Monday." He shrugged his shoulders, smiled and went up to his room, but he sat for a long time wrapped in his blanket on his window seat, his mind too busy for him to settle and sleep.

The following morning, they both slept in, because they had found it difficult to get to sleep and had a restless night. After breakfast, John busied himself in his study, making sure all the documents he needed for Jake to sign were in order in his brief case, and David decided to do the homework that had been set for the half-term holiday.

John was amused at the way David took over when Fay was not there, but he let him get on with it, glad he had developed some 'life skills'.

"Are we having the ham for lunch?" John asked.

"Not for lunch," said David. "Is there an orange in the bowl?"

"Yes," said John and tossed it across to David.

"Right," said David, "we'll have pancakes for lunch, with orange juice."

"Pancakes for Sunday lunch," said John with a look of despair. "Whatever next, are you sure you know how to make them?"

"Certainly do," replied David. "Jake and I had them all the time."

John opened the door of their new fridge looking for something else to have but found himself passing eggs and milk to David and taking a share in beating the batter. He stood back as David prepared to toss a pancake, which he did successfully, and looked very pleased with himself. When the next one was ready, he handed the pan to John. "Go on," he said, "it's easy, do it over the draining board."

John knew it wouldn't end well, but he tried anyway, tossed the pancake in the air, caught half of it in the pan, the other half fell on to the draining board, spattered against the window and slid down the cupboard door. David laughed and continued to cook the half that had landed in the pan. "This is yours," he said, mischievously.

"Yes, and this is yours," John said and handed David the cloth to clean up the mess.

The rest of the pancakes were turned with the spatula, David cut them in to ¼'s and served them with half an orange. They both enjoyed them despite John's misgivings, and he was actually very impressed and said so, leaving David feeling quite proud.

Normally on a Sunday, John would have returned from church, had a traditional Sunday lunch prepared by Annie, and not seen or spoken to anyone until surgery the following morning. He was content in his own space; having no wife or children, he had not known any different, but surprisingly was enjoying the wacky world of David and his friends, the involvement with school from a different aspect to being a governor and was touched the way David turned to him with problems without any hesitation and chatted like they were old friends.

They had a walk on the coastal path in the afternoon, watched the television for a while, had the ham for tea, watched some more television and had an early night in preparation for the early start and the long day ahead.

Chapter 17

The following morning, David and John were up early. They had breakfast, made a sandwich for the journey, left the car outside the surgery and made their way to the station in good time for the train. The journey was pleasant, but time seemed to pass much quicker than it had done when David had left Jake and was travelling into the unknown. The stations were familiar, and David remembered what the ladies had told him about the plants and he felt quite proud of himself passing this information on to John.

Reaching their destination, David leapt from the train and ran up the platform to Jake, flung himself at him so hard they almost fell over. John just shook Jake's hand and patted him on the shoulder. "Good to see you," he said, few words, but a depth of feeling.

David felt a hand on his shoulder, turned and saw Betty smiling at him. "Look at you," she said, "how you have grown." He gave her a hug and asked after Jed.

"He's at home waiting for us," she said.

Jake introduced John to her, and they set off for the B&B to leave their holdalls, and then on to Jed and Betty's home, David staying close to Jake, chatting all the way.

"How are things with you, then, David?" asked Jake.

"Things are good," replied David. "I just wish you would come home. I don't like it when it's cold and wet outside, and I'm in your home wondering where you are. I know we speak on the telephone, but I don't really know where you are."

"I'm more and more in the Salvation Army hostel, or at the farm or here at Jed's," said Jake, "and if I am out and about, it's because I choose to be."

David started asking about the village and Rebecca.

"Rebecca goes to grammar school," said Jake, who had spoken over time to Mr Brown. "There is just Rebecca and her father at home now."

"Did her mother die?" asked David, concerned.

"No," said Jake, "she just left them to live with someone else, but Rebecca is fine, and the lady next door is good to them."

Jed was waiting at the gate for them, handshakes only, no hugs, but he did pat David on the head.

The cottage was small, so Jed had put the table in the centre of the room so they could all squeeze round to eat together. John was amused at the way David was busying himself with Betty and how much fun they were having together laying the table The meal was ready, fresh-baked bread rolls and a huge pot of stew in the centre of the table with a ladle for serving. There was a knock at the door.

"Get that for me, David," said Betty.

David opened the door but there was nobody there, then a stick appeared with a cap dangling on it, and Dougy leapt into the doorway, followed by an explosion of delight from the boys. David hadn't noticed the table was set for six, but Betty had planned it all and was delighted 'her boys' could spend some time together. There was chatter and laughter throughout the meal, and when it was over Betty sent the boys into the bedroom so they could have a catch up on their own.

"What's all this then?" asked David, tugging at the strap of Dougy's bag.

"I'm schoolin' now, learnin' to read and write," said Dougy, "I've brought my books to show you, and we live in a house now with three bedrooms and a proper kitchen, dad and Jack work at the timber yard, ma cleans at the big house, and my other brothers and sisters go to school as well." David had never realised they were a family of seven and couldn't imagine how they had all managed to live on one boat, but they did.

David looked with interest at Dougy's school books and praised him for his efforts, and although he noticed how much more advanced his own lessons were, he said nothing to deflate Dougy's pride, for he had only been going to school for a year and had a lot of catching up to do. They lay side by side on the bed reminiscing about the time they spent on the canals, and it was clear how much joy they had from this time together. Betty popped her head round the door to say it was time for Dougy to go for his bus, so David walked to the bus stop with him.

"I'm so glad you came today," said David. "Now you can write, we can keep in touch, get my address from Jake, and give him yours."

When he arrived back at the cottage John was waiting for him to return to the B&B.

"Goodnight," said Betty. "When Jake and John are sorting their affairs out tomorrow, we thought you might like to take a walk along the canal banking."

"I'd really love to do that," said David, excited by the idea. "See you in the morning."

The following day, after breakfast, they returned to the cottage, and within half an hour, Jed, Betty and David were on the bus to take them to the lane that led to the canal. The building on the corner that had always been buzzing with life, the boatmen having a drink, joking, arguing, doing business, but always busy and noisy, was silent and derelict, the windows were boarded up and brambles and ivy were growing over the doorway and up the walls.

"What happened here?" asked David.

"Not enough trade," said Jed. "The landlord had to move on to make a living. Most of the trade for the boats has gone to road transport, and the boats that are still working are mostly the ones owned by companies. They are still shifting coal and grain, but how long for is anyone's guess."

They walked past the cloth mill and could still hear the clatter of the looms, and there were still ladies outside on the fire escape having a breath of fresh air or a cigarette.

Although they could still hear the whining and buzzing from the saws in the timber yard, the loading bay doors were shedding paint like dead skin, and the hoist chains were hanging like rusty tears against the wall.

Jed sped up and went ahead to see who was in the lock whilst Betty and David sat on a stump.

"Is Jed sad?" asked David.

"He is, David," Betty replied in a sigh. "Both he and I were born on a boat, and for our whole lives, we have moved along the canals and enjoyed the countryside and all it brings with the changing seasons. So many friends along the way, reliable people always there to help.

"Some winters were so severe, the canals froze over, but we never thought of giving up, we just stayed cosy and waited for the thaw. Our bones are beginning to rattle now, and I do like the extra space in the cottage, and the washing machine, and of course, we are so glad we took Jake's advice regarding when to sell our boat. People selling now are having to accept poor offers, some can't sell at all and have had to move into houses with just what they could carry from their boats. One of Jed's friends says it's torture living in a council house, but at least he has a job. Employers are ready to take on the boat people because they have a history of being hard workers."

"I loved it here," said David. "I didn't want to leave, but it's very different now."

"You seem very happy now," said Betty, "are you?"

"I'm fine," replied David. "I live near the sea, I can see it from my bedroom window, school is good, and I like living with John, I just wish Jake would come home."

"Maybe one day he will," said Betty, who knew he had mentioned it recently, but it was not her place to say anything to David.

Jed came towards them, smiling. "I might have a run next week," he said. "William will pick me up from here on Monday, I'll go up to the depot with him and do a run of grain for the company he works for. He says there are boats loaded, and they can't get the right boatmen to take them."

"No wonder he's smiling," said Betty.

"I expect you to come too," said Jed, winking at her, "I need a cook and something to cuddle at night, the boats are fitted out, we'll just need bedding, towels and food."

"I wish I was staying longer, then I could come too," said David.

"He'll be looking forward to the trip," said Betty, "but I'm not altogether sure it's a good thing; these odd trips unsettle him."

They made their way back to the bus stop, David holding a bunch of bell heather he had picked for Betty, which they always had in the cabin on their boat.

When they returned to the cottage, Jed showed David his garden. He had planted potatoes, onions, carrots and beetroot. Every single day on the boat, they had beetroot in some form or other so David was not surprised at all to see some growing, for Jed believed it kept them healthy, and for sure something did, for they were never ill.

"It's fine preparing the soil and planting out," said Jed, "but it's a long time then before anything starts to happen."

Jake and John returned, and they had a jolly afternoon before they went out for tea in a local cafe, as a treat and thank you to Jed and Betty. As they returned to the cottage, Jed took David on one side.

"I want you to choose one of my watering cans and take it back with you,"

David was thrilled, he had been fascinated by the artwork on the boats, and spent a lot of time with Jed as he maintained the paintwork and artwork not only on the boat, but on the buckets and jugs also. He chose the one on the window sill with the traditional flowers and castle as decoration.

"Thank you so much," said David. "I'll keep it forever."

It was time to leave and go back to the B&B. John shook hands, but they were all going to get a hug from David, and he whispered in Jake's ear, "Come home."

Before they turned the corner at the end of the street, David turned round one more time to see Jed and Betty still standing at their gate, and he waved vigorously at them, little knowing that would be the lasting image he would have of them.

The train journey home the following day dragged. Rain poured, the windows steamed up and blotted out the view. John read his newspaper and passed it on to David, but tussling with the pages, and not really being interested, he just folded it up and put it on the seat.

"Are you bored, David?" asked John.

"Yes, I am," replied David, so John decided to explain to him the outcome of his meeting with Jake, and that the sale of the land could now go ahead.

"What happens next, then?" asked David.

"The developer is responsible for everything that happens next, once the cheque has cleared in my bank account," said John. "The companies that will cover the essential services will be first on the scene because building cannot commence until most of that work is done."

"What are essential services?" asked David.

"Water supply, sewage, drainage, electricity, gas and telephone," said John.

"Crikey," said David, "that's a lot of things to do."

"As far as I know, apart from the telephone system, everything else goes underground, so now perhaps you can understand why I wouldn't allow Biddy to be buried in the field."

They ran from the train to the car they had left at the surgery, and were glad of it, for it was still pouring with rain, gurgling down the gutters into the drains and huge puddles everywhere.

Fay had been and lit the stove and prepared soup, so the kitchen was warm and the tea was quickly prepared.

There was a note to say Mr Smyth had called, and would call at the surgery tomorrow, and that Ted had been for David.

After tea, David tried his jug on every flat surface he could find, over and over again to see where it looked best.

"Upstairs, on your window sill is the best place for that," said John, peering over his glasses and raising his eyebrows, and a few minutes later, that is exactly where it was.

David had a bath, and sat wrapped in his blanket on the window seat for a while. The rain had stopped, there was a clear sky and a full moon casting its reflection on a black sea like a silver ball bouncing in the swell. He went downstairs for cocoa and to say 'Goodnight' to John.

"Did you enjoy your days away?" asked John.

"I did," said David, emphatically, "it was just so good to see everyone. Did you enjoy it?"

"Yes," replied John. "It was good to see Jake after four years or so, and to meet his friends, who I believe were very good to you, and I know they are to Jake. Very kind people indeed."

David went to bed and didn't appear in the kitchen the following morning until turned 8:00 am and was surprised to find Ted there having a piece of toast and a cup of tea with John.

"What are you doing here? I thought you were going to your grandparents," said David.

"I did," said Ted, "it didn't work out."

"What happened?" asked David.

Ted explained that he had waited an hour at the school gate for them to collect him, there was hardly any conversation on the journey to their house, and when they arrived, he was shown to his room and told not to touch anything. In the afternoon, his grandparents sat in the garden and read their newspapers, whilst a lady called Molly was in the kitchen preparing food for their guests in the evening. "She was nice and talked to me, and I had my tea in the kitchen with her, and then offered to help Gran put up tables for her guests to play bridge in the evening, but she said she could manage and sent me to my room. There was nothing there for me, not a comic, a book or a game and I was really bored and fed up so I decided to go for a walk. I pushed the room door open where they were playing cards just to let them know I was going out. Grandad said it was ok and not to get lost, and I heard a lady say, 'How lovely to have your grandson to stay.' I heard Gran tell them I was sullen, moody and difficult, and she didn't know why they had to have me at all. I was angry, and I knew before I did it that I shouldn't, but I went back into the room and asked her how she thought she had the right to say those things about me, when she didn't know me, or speak to me, and that she had never taken any interest in me, and that I certainly didn't want to be there. I didn't shout at all, and as I left the room, I looked at her and said, 'It's very unkind of you, Gran, to say those things about me.' I think I might have ruined her evening, I hoped I had, and knew full well I'd be made to regret it. I went up to my room and realised they had invited you, so they wouldn't have to bother with me. I counted the flowers on the wallpaper until I fell asleep, but by 7am the following morning I was in the car being driven back. Grandad said I should never have spoken to Gran the way I did, so I asked him if he thought it was all right for Gran to say what she did about me. He didn't answer, of course, he just said I was my parents' responsibility, that they shouldn't palm me off, and that I wouldn't be welcome at his house again. I felt like saying YIPEE, but I didn't fancy walking the rest of the way home, so I said nothing."

"Their loss," said John. "You are at a good school which will give you a good foundation for the rest of your life if you work hard. You will make good friends along the way, and they are always better than awkward relatives."

John left for the surgery, David went to get washed and dressed, and Fay put up pork pie, tomatoes and apples for a picnic or lunch for the boys, depending on what they decided to do.

Fay had been in the kitchen listening to Ted and just couldn't understand why grandparents wouldn't love being involved with their grandchildren.

"What does your father do?" Fay asked Ted.

"He's in the RAF in Cyprus, at the moment, but he may be moving somewhere else quite soon," replied Ted.

"What would you like to do when you finish your studies?" Fay asked.

"I really don't know," said Ted. "I need to discuss things with my father if I ever get to see him."

David appeared ready to go out.

"Are you going to the beach?" Fay asked. "There's a bag there with food if you want to take it with you."

David gave Ted the picnic bag to carry and he picked up two rackets and a shuttlecock, and off they went.

It was mid-afternoon before they were thinking of going home. They had sat on the beach and had their picnic and talked over Ted's family situation. Ted thought it was very strange that David didn't have any grandparents. Actually, David didn't know whether he had or not, but he had certainly never met or even heard of them, but that was his past which he didn't talk about.

A fisherman pulled his boat on to the beach and walked over to the boys with two fish. "For the doctor," he said, "from Jacob, good day to you." And he went back to his boat and sailed away.

There was some line through the mouth of each fish so they could carry them. "I think they are looking at us," said Ted, teasing. David swung his fish round and slapped Ted on the leg and set off running home. When they arrived, Fay was not in the kitchen, so they propped the fish in the sink with their heads peering over the top and waited for her.

"Hello, boys," she said, as she walked back into the kitchen from the lounge. "Had a nice day?"

She saw the fish, but didn't react the way the boys expected, she slyly picked up a wooden spoon, sped across the kitchen and chased them round the table, slapping them gently when she could reach them. There were screams and shouting and laughter, and suddenly John's voice boomed out above the noise, "It's bedlam in here, what's going on?"

"Fay's beating us with a wood spoon," said David, playfully.

"And I wonder why that could be?" said John, noticing the fish peering out of the sink. "Did Jacob send them?"

David nodded yes.

"Can you deal with them?" John asked Fay.

"Certainly," she said, "take a seat boys, no not over there, here at this table."

She washed one of the fishes under the tap, scraped some of the scales off and chopped off its head. That was enough for Ted. "I think I will have to be going now," he said and left very quickly.

David was fascinated by all the bits and pieces that were falling out of the fish as she gutted it, and John noticed how he wasn't fazed by the blood or afraid to touch and poke.

"I'm afraid I don't know anything about the anatomy of fish," said John, as David looked at him and pointed to a stringy bit.

"The butcher has explained to me about how different parts of animals are used in cooking, like liver and kidneys, and pig's cheeks" said David, "but there doesn't seem to be much in a fish you could use."

"Take the other fish home for the family," said John to Fay, "although it will not go very far for five."

"Yes, it will," Fay said. "I'll make a fish pie. Thank you so much."

"I'll keep ours in the fridge and you can make a fish pie for us tomorrow, I'd like to try one," said John.

Chapter 18

The last term of the school year was busy, intense studying for exams, the anxious wait for the results, sports day, speech day when students were awarded prizes for excellence in studies or sports, and finally the last assembly of the school year on the last day of term. There was the bustle of parents collecting the boarders, others were struggling to the station with their luggage, and the day students left as they normally did each day.

By 5 pm, the school was empty and eerily silent apart from the squeaky footsteps of the caretaker, and the clunking of his keys, as if the school had gone to sleep.

As David sauntered down the lane carrying his brief case and holdall bulging with school books, and his hockey stick and tennis racket balanced on top, John caught him up and stopped to give him a lift home.

"Can't believe I've been here almost a year," said David. "My life has changed so much."

"So has mine," said John, "but I'm getting used to the chaos."

He stopped the car, got out and stood looking across the field where men were surveying the land and felt an unwelcome pang in his heart.

The developer saw him and walked across the field to greet him.

"Can't turn the clock back now, can I?" said John.

"I know it's a big moment for you, John," said the man, "but it will all be done sympathetically as we agreed, and hopefully, when it is finished, you will approve of what has been done."

John shook the man's hand and nodded.

"Come on, David," he said, "let's go home."

Fay had put a cheese and onion flan and jacket potatoes in the oven and was making a pot of tea for them all. John was in and out of the kitchen and his study sorting things out, but David sat at the table with Fay and chatted.

"What are you going to be up to during the next six weeks?" she asked David.

David looked at her, wide eyed, thought for a moment, and answered, "I've no idea." He had been very interested to hear about what his school friends were doing but hadn't considered what he might be doing with his time during the holidays.

"Has John told you he will be away for three nights next week?" Fay asked.

"No," replied David, "will you be coming?"

"I will," replied Fay, "and I would be glad of your help if you've nothing better to do. John has asked me to clean and tidy the unused bedroom as it hasn't been done for years. How do you feel about that?"

"Fine," said David, pleased that she was going to be around, and he would actually have something to do.

John joined them at the table to have a cup of tea.

"Where's Ted going to be these holidays?" he asked.

"With his family, I guess," said David. "I never asked him, and I didn't see him at all today, but yesterday he gave me a bag to bring home with his school uniform in, and an envelope with money his parents had sent him to replace anything he needed for his uniform."

"That's very strange," said John. "Why send him the money if they are going to see him? Why not give it to him when he leaves them to return to school?" There was something that made him feel uneasy, but he let it go. "You need to take your bags up to your room, empty them, get rid of all the rubbish, and put your books back tidily, and put your sports kit into the wash and don't have it growing penicillin until it's two days before you go back to school."

Fay followed David to his room and took his sports kit out of his holdall.

"I think we should check Ted's bag," she said, "he may have put his sports kit in."

She pulled out screwed up soiled shirts, sports kit and underwear and added them to the bundle from David's bag and hung the crumpled blazer in the wardrobe.

"This lot would have been a stinking mess if we had left them," said Fay. "It's a good job you mentioned you had the bag. Where is the money he left? I think you should give it to John to keep safe."

The following morning, the garden looked like the school laundry when Fay had done the washing and hung it on the line to dry, and once again, John was left wondering why they had to have Ted's uniform.

David sorted his books out and put them away in his holdall, and then went to the butcher's to do his deliveries as usual and waited for John to finish at the surgery.

After tea, John sat and explained to David that he would be away for three nights at the beginning of the new week, but that Fay would still be coming. The chimney sweep was coming first thing Monday morning, and John suggested he might like to help Fay clear and clean the spare bedroom.

"Fay has already asked me," said David, "and I will be helping her."

The weekend passed, John had gone to London, the chimney sweep had been and gone, and David and Fay worked tirelessly for two days cleaning the spare room. They had left the window wide open all the time, even through the night to rid the room of the smell of dampness and neglect, wiped the walls down with dusters fastened to brooms with long handles, washed the skirting boards and floor, and dragged the flock mattress so it hung over the bedstead near the window. David sat on the tab rugs and Fay pulled him along the landing until they rolled them down the stairs to take outside to freshen up.

Fay left earlier than usual, a chance to relieve her mother who was spending the days at her house so that the children were able to play with their friends during the school holidays but feeling sorry that she was leaving David on his own.

"Are you going to be all right?" she asked him.

"I'll be fine," he said, "and yes, I'll shut the bedroom window if it rains."

Fay smiled. "Got it," she said, wagging her finger. "See you in the morning."

David sat outside and read his book for a while, wandered up the lane and watched the men in the field for a while, made cheese on toast, watched television for a while, had a bath, made sure the doors were locked, made some cocoa, sat on his window seat for a while and went to bed.

The following day, he worked with Fay and everything was put back to where it should be in the bedroom, and the furniture was polished and the windows cleaned.

Fortunately for David, it had remained fine during the night because he had left the rugs outside. They were slightly damp when Fay arrived but dried out in the sun. "I'm not leaving the bed with just the mattress on, I'm going to make it up so it looks nice," Fay said and went to the linen cupboard for bedding. By lunch time, they were finished and feeling pretty pleased with the result.

"Are you ready for something to eat?" Fay asked David as they went downstairs.

"No, thank you," he said, "I think I'm going for a run first." He had decided to keep up with his running as he found it did help with his stamina for sport, but he was never going to like a cross-country run in the rain. They agreed a place to hide the door key in case Fay was gone when he returned, and off he went along the coastal road on his usual route. On his return, he had a quick splash in the bath to freshen up and tucked into the chicken salad Fay had prepared for him.

The following day, Fay arrived and picked up on her normal duties, so David decided to visit the Gray's house to see if the boys were about. When he arrived, he came across a man working in the garden. "What is it you want?" he asked.

"I came to see if the boys were about," replied David.

"They're away up in the Yorkshire Dales," said the man. "Gone for two weeks."

"Oh!" said David, and would quite liked to have had a chat, but the man turned his back on him and continued clipping at the bushes, so David left to return home.

Well, that was a waste of time, he thought. *What can I do now?*

He called in home and had some lunch, picked up his book and went to his favourite place along the coastal path to read. He had an old waterproof there which he left rolled up so he had something dry to sit on if the ground was wet, and he settled down, read his book and ate an apple and was quite content until he felt the coolness of the breeze and saw the sky darkening in the distance.

As he walked quickly home, he noticed the sea was grumbling as it rolled in across the sand churning up the pebbles, and then the sky grumbled, and he knew there was a storm brewing. He couldn't open the door, so he knew Fay had gone and left the key for him and he just hoped she would make it home before the storm set in. David gathered his shoes and some plants from outside and left them in the porch, and sure enough, the rain came, a few heavy drops like warning shots, followed by the torrent that accompanies storms. David dashed up to the room they had cleaned to make sure the window was shut, and wrapped himself in his blanket and sat on his window seat to watch. The lightning was out at sea against the horizon to begin with, and the rumble of thunder was almost gentle but quite soon hit the coastline, and a cracking fork lightning just in front of the house sent David dashing to his bed and burying himself under the covers. Moments later, the thunder bellowed and seemed to shake the house, and he was very afraid and laid still, listening, waiting. He knew it had lightened again because it lit up the room momentarily, he heard the thunder followed by a weird creaking sound and an almighty crash. When things had quietened down, he ventured downstairs and went outside, and although it had stopped raining, water was still gurgling down the path and cascading down the steps from the garden onto the coastal pathway. He could hear voices shouting excitedly, so he went around the corner and looked up the lane and was totally shocked to see the massive oak tree that grew behind the cottage had crashed through its roof and almost demolished it. The tree was steaming with only half its roots ripped out of the ground, as if it was trying to hang on to mother earth. The men who had been working in the field had been inside the cottage sheltering when they realised the tree had been struck and had managed to get out to safety before it creaked and groaned and fell to the ground.

David stood looking at the tree, he couldn't stop the tears, he felt very sad, but was glad Annie and Wilfred were not there for they would have been killed for sure.

"Are you all right, boy?" asked one of the men.

"Yes, thank you," David replied and turned to go back home.

Later in the day, when everyone had gone home, he went back and clambered amongst the branches and collected a few leaves to press in a book to keep. He remembered Wilfred telling him that the oak tree was a sapling when he and Annie had moved in, and they had been there over 40 years which seemed a very long time to a 13-year-old boy, but the tree was majestic to David, and he didn't like seeing it on the ground as if it had died.

When John returned the following day, he was shocked to see what had happened and over the following few days, observed how upset David was, especially when a man came with a saw that whined and cut through the branches that were protruding into the lane and just threw them back into the foliage. David dragged a log and put it at the bottom of the garden where he could see it from his bedroom window. John had a word with the carpenter in the village, and unknown to David, he collected a branch to be made into a stool as a surprise for Christmas. John also asked the developer if it was possible to have the tree disposed of whilst he and David were away the following week, and this was agreed. David was missing Ted to spend time with, and John was working every day, so David became restless and bored being on his own so much, so he took himself off to the cinema one afternoon and came across some boys from his school, but they were smoking and had some beer in bottles so he made an excuse for not staying and returned home. He dared not spend time in that company and suffer the wrath of John, who had told him what the consequences would be if he ever caught him 'up to no good'.

On Friday morning, at breakfast, John told David to let the butcher know that he would not be able to work the following week, because he would be away.

"Where will I be?" asked David.

"London, with me," replied John, bracing himself for the surge of excitement and questions.

"When are we going?" asked David.

"I thought we would go on Monday and return the following Monday. I will need to go into the hospital for a couple of mornings, but you can stay with Mrs Fry until I'm free. She is very nice," explained John. "I have stayed at her guest house for many years."

"Can't I go to the hospital with you?" asked David, not because he was anxious about having to stay with Mrs Fry, but because he was curious and wanted to see in the hospital.

"Not sure about that," replied John. "I'll have to see. You will need to draw some money from the bank for spending money, which I suggest you do today, and ask Fay to pack your holdall for you."

David very excitedly explained to the butcher that he was going to London and wouldn't be able to do his deliveries as usual but pleaded with him not to give his job to someone else.

"I'll do my own deliveries next weekend," said the butcher, "just like I always did before you came along. I just shut the shop early and can surely manage for one weekend."

John had informed Fay of his plans and told her to make sure they retrieved some logs if she could manage it, so on the day the tree was sawn up, she took a pram and her two eldest children with her for the day, and they filled the pram for home, and put a good pile in John's shed for winter. Fay had taken the man sawing the logs a bowl of soup and some bread at lunch time, and he kindly sawed her logs to fireplace size which she was very grateful for. People in the village saw her pushing the pram home, word got round, and within 24 hours, all the logs had gone that could be lifted, and that was just as John had wanted.

Chapter 19

David was very excited about going to London, remembering what he had seen when he watched the coronation on television, but he was not prepared for the noise and volume of traffic and people as he left the station, holdall in one hand, clinging on to John's coat belt with the other. As they stood in line waiting for a bus, he found himself staring at a very large man with almost black skin, tight curly hair, bright white teeth and a very deep voice when he spoke or laughed.

He must be from Africa, thought David. *What's he doing here?*

During the next few days, he saw people from many cultures, dressed in very different clothes from what he was used to, and there was always a question to John as to where these people were from. If John didn't know the answer, he quickly learnt to make something up to avoid the long list of possibilities that David suggested.

The bus arrived that would take them to Lambeth to Mrs Fry's guest house. John had stayed there for many years on his visits to London as it was near St Thomas's Hospital where he lectured from time to time. They climbed the steps to the front door and rang the bell and were greeted by a lady with snow-white hair tied in a bun, rosy cheeks and a lovely smile.

"Come in, Doctor John," she said, "your room is ready." She turned, "You must be David."

"Yes," said David and just stood looking at her.

John burst out laughing and patted David on the head. "He's totally bamboozled by the throb of London. He's only lived in village environments all his life, so to absorb London for the first time, I feel, is quite daunting for him," said John.

"Everything is so BIG and noisy," said David.

"You'll get used to it," said Mrs Fry. "There is so much for you to see and do, and I'm sure you'll enjoy it."

They climbed the three flights of stairs to their room, unpacked and stayed there until it was time for dinner. John read a book, and David stood by the window, enthralled by the hustle and bustle of the streets below and the height and closeness of the buildings.

After dinner, they had a walk around the area, sat and had a chat in the lounge with Mrs Fry and her daughter and returned to their room. John sent David along to the shared bathroom to wash and clean his teeth, and by this time, he knew to wash his feet. To have a bath, you had to put money in the meter to heat the water, which they had not done.

Before they drew the curtains, they looked out of the window at London by night, a myriad of lights, coloured, flashing, moving like a glowing ribbon as far as the eye could see.

"Wow!" said David, looking up at John, "that's some electric bill."

John smiled; he knew just where that comment was coming from, because he was always reminding David to switch off the lights and save electricity.

The following morning, John took David to the hospital with him and after speaking to the sister in charge, left David on the children's ward, where he would be less conspicuous. He was like a breath of fresh air on the ward, he engaged with the children playing Ludo and snakes and ladders and hangman with the children who were not confined to bed and chatted and read stories to the ones who were. He was conscious of the children being ill, so if they became grizzly or awkward, he just ignored it and showed great patience and understanding for a boy so young. Perhaps talking to John had instilled this quality in him.

When the children were having treatment from the nurses, he watched from a distance, and wanted to know what was happening, and why, hoping the nurse would tell him. The information was vague, and he didn't understand, but he just wanted to know. The children knew about their illnesses and talked to David about them, each trying to be much worse than the last, which amused the nurses, and there was laughter in the ward which was good for everyone.

In a corner near the nurses' desk was a curtained cubicle which was opened when the orange juice and biscuits came around, and in a bed was a very pretty girl with her eyes shut.

"Come on, Angie," said the nurse, "have a drink. Juice or water?"

The girl opened her eyes and saw David standing at the bottom of her bed. He smiled, gave a little wave and said "Hello," quietly.

She smiled back and wiggled her fingers at him.

"Can I stay and talk to her?" he asked the nurse.

"If Angie wants you to, you can," replied the nurse, "but don't pester her, she's very poorly."

David sat on the chair at the side of her bed. "What's wrong with you?" she asked him.

"I'm not ill," David replied, "my uncle works here. I'm just waiting for him to finish and then we are going to Westminster Abbey to have a look. Why are you here?"

"My kidneys don't work properly," Angie replied. "That's why my skin and eyeballs are yellow."

David had noticed, would never have commented, but as Angie had mentioned it, he remarked, "Well, dandelions and daffodils are yellow, it's a very popular colour."

They both burst out laughing, Angie thinking she would never forget that comment, and David thinking what a stupid thing to say.

They chatted away and David was saddened to learn that Angie had been ill all of her life that she could remember, she couldn't play with friends often and had missed so much schooling, having spent more time in hospital than at home.

John arrived, and it was time to leave. "Has he been all right?" he asked sister.

"He's been fine, it's been a pleasure to have him," she replied, "and Angie has certainly perked up having someone her own age to talk to."

"I have a further two lectures tomorrow, so will it be all right for me to bring David again?" John asked.

David looked up at her with 'please' written all over his face.

"Certainly," replied sister, so David went straight over to Angie and said, "See you tomorrow."

John put his briefcase in a locker and produced an exercise book and pencil for David to record his visit to London, and they set off for the Abbey, crossing Westminster Bridge. David stopped and tried to absorb the vastness of the river Thames, much wider and busier than he could have imagined, and then John drew his attention to the Houses of Parliament, and they stood and listened for Big Ben to strike 1 pm before they finally arrived at the Abbey. They spent the next two hours there, firstly being shown round by a guide, and then on their own, David being fascinated by the Tomb of the Unknown Warrior, poet's corner and the stained-glass windows. As they left, John bought a book about the history of the Abbey up to the time of the coronation, and over the next few years, David read from it often.

On the way back to Mrs Fry's, they called in a shop for a newspaper for John, and David noticed a tin displayed with pretty beads inside for making bracelets.

"I want to buy one of those for Angie," he said. "Please, will you lend me the money until we get back to the house?"

John was a regular visitor to the shop on his visits to London, so he chatted for a few moments to the owner, and when he went outside, David was laid on his back on the pavement, arms and legs spread.

"What on earth are you doing?" asked John.

"Looking up," said David. "Have you seen all those windows? They are all different shapes."

"Get up," said John. "Someone will be sending for an ambulance if they see you lying on the pavement." But he realised how little notice he had taken of his surroundings over the years, and now he was appreciating things through the eyes of a 13 year old.

During the evening, David had shown Mrs Fry what he had bought for Angie, and she found some paper with printed flowers on it to wrap the tin in and some ribbon to tie round.

The following morning, John and David returned to the hospital as arranged, and the children were pleased. They played games as they had done the previous day, and he read a story, but he wanted to see Angie who was enclosed in her cubicle by the curtain. When the orange juice and biscuits arrived, her curtain was pulled back and she waved at David straightaway.

He pulled up a chair to the side of her bed. "Hello," he said, "I've brought you this, I hope you like it." He took the parcel from his pocket and handed it to her.

"Aah!" she gasped. "How pretty."

Of course, the packet rattled, there were beads inside a tin, but she had no idea what it could be and was thrilled when she opened it. "I'll make a bracelet and show you it tomorrow," she said.

"I'm not coming again," said David, "but perhaps I could try before we go home. I can write to you if you like, write me your address down in my book."

"It doesn't matter," said Angie, "but thank you so much." She put her head back on the pillow and closed her eyes, so the nurse patted David on his shoulder and asked him to move so she could pull the curtain around the bed.

"I'll get you Angie's address," said the nurse, quietly. "Shouldn't be giving it to you really, but she can't read or write very well, and she would have been embarrassed. I think she would be very glad to hear from you, she has a very lonely

121

life, and her mother can only visit her on Saturdays because she has two jobs, so a letter or postcard would really cheer her up."

John arrived and thanked the sister and nurses, and David poked his head through the curtain, but Angie was still laid with her eyes shut.

"I'm going now," he whispered. "I hope you are soon feeling better. Goodbye."

She had heard him, and tears smarted in her eyes and rolled down her cheeks as he called out "Goodbye, and thank you," to the nurses as he left.

During the following days, they visited the British Museum, the Tower of London to see the crown jewels where John took a photograph of David with a Beefeater, and they were lucky enough to see the Tower Bridge parting to let a ship through. They walked along the Thames embankment many times and sat and watched the world go by as they ate sandwiches. David chatted and asked questions about everything he saw, wanting to know where the boats had come from, where they were going, until in the end, John had to say, "I don't live in London, I don't know why everything happens here, you would need to talk to the people who work on the river to answer your questions."

On Saturday, John had decided to travel by the underground and go to the London Zoo for the day. David had no idea where he was going when they started going down the moving staircase and felt a little anxious when he heard the rumbling of the trains. He didn't know anything about the trains that ran a service under the ground, and he wasn't sure if he liked it or not, but very quickly they reached their destination and were out in the fresh air again at Regent's Park.

"We're going to the zoo today, David," said John. "What do you think about that?"

"Terrific," David said, "where is it?"

They walked through the entrance gates and picked up a sheet with a route map on it, which guided them around the zoo in a way to see everything, and apart from spiders, David had never seen anything else in his life before. They spent the whole day there and were late back for dinner, exhausted. After dinner, David related to Mrs Fry all he had seen during the day from the list in his book, camels, lions, tigers, monkeys, chimpanzees, giraffes, snakes and lots of different birds. "We had an ice cream and there was a parrot that talked and said, 'Hello, darling,' on a perch near the cafe."

John had gone up to their room making ready to have a bath, having asked Mrs Fry to heat the water for them before they left in the morning. They would have to share, David going first, but it didn't matter as long as they had a bath.

"I forgot to ask you, did the young girl like her present?" Mrs Fry asked David.

"Yes, she did, very much," replied David. "I think she will have made her bracelet by now, and maybe we will have chance to call in and see her before we go home so I can see it. I think I had better go now, I've got to have a bath."

The following day was Sunday, the day before returning home, and London seemed quieter. They went to the hospital for John to collect his belongings from his locker, and David asked to go to the children's ward to see Angie, but she wasn't there. John looked at sister, who discreetly shook her head from side to side.

"Where is she now?" asked David.

"It's possible she has gone home, which is good," said John, "and it's time for us to get ready to do the same."

They left and went to Waterloo station so David could buy little gifts for Fay's children, had a ride on a sightseeing bus and went back to Mrs Fry's early enough to pack their bags before dinner, because they had an early start in the morning to catch their train home. David emptied his purse and put the money on John's bed. "This is what I have left, I want you to have it. This has been the best time of my life, thank you so much."

"Thank you," said John, and took the money and put it with his own, because he needed David to realise the importance of paying his way, "and let me tell you something, it's been the best time in my life too, but I'm going to need a holiday to recover, I'm exhausted."

John normally came and went between Mrs Fry's and the hospital, and apart from the odd visit to the theatre or ballet he didn't venture far, so this trip had been as interesting for him as it had been for David, who appreciated everything and showed it.

They had a table on their return journey home, so David was able to write in his journal for a while, then he looked out of the window and fell asleep to wake up an hour later with a stiff neck.

"Are we nearly home?" he asked John.

John looked at his watch. "An hour yet," he replied. "Read your book about the Abbey."

Another hour of sighing and squirming, and they finally arrived in the village. Walking down the lane towards home, David noticed the oak tree had all but gone, but he was too tired to even mention it, he just wanted to be home and go to bed.

"I need to go to bed," said David. "I'm really tired."

"So am I," said John. "I will not be far behind you."

Once ready for bed, David looked out of his window, and although it was very dark, he could hear the gentle sea just breaking the total silence. *Yes*, he thought, *this is much better than the drone and tooting and sirens of the London traffic, but I would like to go again.*

The following morning, he appeared bleary eyed for breakfast, long after John had left for the surgery. Fay made him scrambled egg and toast and sat with him at the table and had a cup of tea whilst he enthused about his holiday. He went to get dressed and appeared with his dirty washing and the gifts for Fay's children and took his book along the coastal path to his favourite place and languished in the sun.

Chapter 20

David missed lunch altogether, because on his way back home, he met up with some children playing on the beach. He sat and watched them for a while until they invited him to join in, and they had a game of rounders, children against adults, and had great fun. When the tide was coming in, he warned them it came in quickly, so everyone dispersed, and David made his way home.

Fay was ready to leave as he arrived. "Dr John wants you in his study," she said, looking serious.

"Am I in trouble?" David asked.

"No," Fay said, reassuringly, "he just needs to talk to you. I'll see you tomorrow."

David went to the study and pushed the door open gently.

"There you are," said John. "Come in and sit down, I have some distressing news."

David's heart pounded, his stomach knotted, and he could feel his face burning. "Has something happened to Jake?" he asked in a very weak voice.

"No," said John, "Jake is fine. There was a message for me at the surgery this morning from Jake to say that Betty had passed away whilst we were in London. The funeral will have taken place today, and Jake will be staying with Jed for a while. He is going to telephone the surgery tomorrow evening, so you may like to come up with me and talk to him."

David was numbed with mixed feelings, glad that Jake was all right but deeply saddened to hear about Betty. "Why did she die?" he asked.

"I don't have any details, Jake will be able to tell us what happened when we talk to him tomorrow," replied John. "Everyone will die, it's all about how happy and fulfilling our lives have been, and Betty was very happy, and you brought some joy into her life, so you should be pleased about that."

David didn't speak, he just left the study and went to his room, laid on his bed and cried. He loved Betty, she had shown him great kindness, and he remembered waving 'goodbye' to her as she stood at the garden gate beside Jed when they visited them earlier in the year, and she looked well and happy.

The following evening, when they spoke to Jake, he and John spoke in medical terms, but then Jake spoke to David. He told him Jed and Betty had enjoyed a lovely walk along the canal bank in the afternoon and sat in the garden in the evening chatting to passers-by, and Betty had said she felt tired and took herself off to bed. She was stirring when Jed went to bed later, but sometime during the night, her heart stopped. If she had been in trouble or pain, she would have woken Jed, but she didn't, she just died peacefully. The funeral had taken place in the local chapel attended by many boat people, and Jake was going to stay with Jed for a while. David just said "Oh!" handed the telephone back to John and wandered outside and sat on the wall until John had finished speaking to Jake. The London trip was not mentioned at all, and he had been so looking forward to telling Jake all about it.

For a few days, David was listless. John gave him a new exercise book and told him to re-write his London journal neatly, thinking it would divert his thoughts away from Betty, and then he could keep it until he saw Jake, or send it to him to read. John read the original one, added little bits and corrected spellings before David started, and then he inspected the new one and was very impressed.

The next time they were at the surgery to speak to Jake, Jed was there also to have a word with David.

"I don't know what to say to you," said David. "I feel very sad."

"I'm sad too," said Jed, "but I just have to remember my life with Betty and be grateful for it. Jake has been a great support, we are hopeless at domesticity, it took us a full day to work out how the washing machine worked because we couldn't find the instruction book, and we've had a few burnt offerings for tea, but we seem to be getting better."

Jed wanted David to think he was going to be fine, but he had recoiled into a grieving depression and Jake had confided in John that he couldn't think of leaving him. Jed wanted his estate to be shared between David and Dougy, so Jake had to explain the circumstances around David, and that neither he nor John were his legal guardians, and they didn't want to draw attention to this fact, so it was decided Jed would make his will out for Jake to be the beneficiary, and he would be responsible for the boys getting their inheritance. Jake accompanied him to the solicitor's office and then insisted they went to the doctors for some medication to help Jed. He was prescribed tablets which he insisted he was taking, and although Jake wasn't convinced, there was only so much discussion Jed would have about the matter before he became angry or upset.

Jake was right, because two months later, Jed took all the tablets in one go and ended his life. He'd fooled Jake into thinking he was all right to be left for a few days, and whilst he was away, Jed went to the pub, had a steak and two pints, went home, sat in his chair in front of the fire and swallowed the tablets he had collected. He left a brief note for Jake, because he had never really learnt to read or write, but over the weeks, without Dougy noticing, he had asked how to spell different words, and Dougy had written them down for him, feeling quite proud that he could do this.

Sorry, old friend, I need to be with Betty, the pain is too much to bear.
Thank you and bless you. Jed.

When Jake returned, he was shocked to learn what had happened from the neighbours who had agreed to keep an eye on Jed whilst Jake was away. He was distraught, for although he had doubts Jed was taking his tablets, he felt he should have been more assertive and insisted on giving them to him each day, but Jed had been good at manipulating Jake, and had clearly planned it all along.

Within a week, Jed was laid to rest with his beloved Betty, almost like closing a good book after the last chapter, and after the initial shock, David accepted this and felt it was right for them to be together.

"Will Jake be staying in Jed's home?" he asked John.

"He will until the cottage and furniture are sold, and it will take some time."

"Will he come home, then?" asked David.

"Well, we always hope he will," replied John, "but that really is up to him what he does and where he goes."

The following Saturday, they attended a garden party at the Gray's house, which turned out to be a farewell to all their local friends, because Mr Gray had taken up a position at a veterinary practice in North Yorkshire, preferring the rural environment to domestic pets. He had managed to get his two sons registered in a good school as boarders, and his young daughter would attend the local village school, and they were all set to move the following week. The boys played games in the garden, and when it was time for John and David to leave, Mrs Gray gave John a huge bundle of school uniform for David to wear as he grew. Mr Gray and John had been good friends for many years and intended to remain so, despite the distance between them.

"All the best to you," said John, as they shook hands. "Ring me at the surgery and let me know how things have gone. We will have our own telephone in the house soon, and that will make it easier to keep in touch."

"Who will be living in their house, now? asked David. "Will it be another vet?"

"I never asked," said John. "We will have to wait and see."

The summer break was drawing to a close, David was in his room looking through his bag with his school books in, thinking he wouldn't forget this break in a hurry, when the door opened slowly, and Ted appeared. They greeted each other as friends do, and then Ted asked David if he thought John would let him stay until they went back to school after the weekend.

"Stay for tea, and we'll ask him then," said David, "and he'll give you your money back. I need some new shoes, so we can go into town tomorrow and get what we need for school." He showed Ted his clean uniform in the wardrobe and told him to thank Fay for looking after it.

The boys went along the coastal path, and David was enthralled with Ted's stories of his holiday, and thought he might like to go to Cyprus one day.

They sat and had tea with John, and then David chose to ask him about Ted staying.

"That all depends," said John, looking sternly at Ted. "I want to know where you have been during the holidays?"

David was about to answer, but John held his hand up to stop him and fixed his gaze on Ted.

There was a silence, but Ted didn't know what John knew, so he owned up. He had received a letter from his father just three days before school broke up, and he thought it would contain his travel tickets, but instead it said they couldn't accommodate him because they were moving from Cyprus, so he would have to stay with his grandparents, but they had sent him spending money and money to replenish his uniform. "It would have been torture for six days, let alone six weeks," said Ted, "so I took myself off to a holiday camp, lied about my age and worked in the restaurant, so I can afford to pay for my lodgings if I can stay."

"Did you let your grandparents know what you were doing?" asked John.

"Yes," said Ted. "I sent a postcard saying, 'NOT COMING'."

David giggled. "What did you do at this holiday camp?" he asked, eager to know.

"Never mind that for now," said John, "and don't you think about doing it," he said to David, "and don't you think about asking him to," he said to Ted.

Over the weekend, Ted told David what it was like working in the holiday camp. He had been given a job in the kitchen at first, but his good manners had stood out, and he was very quickly moved into the dining room, serving at tables and helping out generally, and he was told he could re-apply any time, they would be pleased to have him. "We didn't have a lot of spare time, and we were glad to get to bed because we were up at 6 am to get the dining room ready for breakfast," said Ted, "but we did get a day off each week and had a party before we left for home. We played spinning the bottle and some girls kissed me, and I had some beer and a banging head the following morning, but I was lucky enough to get a lift rather than catching the train, so I saved some money there."

"Why did you lie to me about going to Cyprus?" asked David.

"I was testing my story out," said Ted, "and if you didn't know about what I had actually done, you could honestly say you didn't know if it became an issue."

When David had done his deliveries on Saturday, John ran them into town and took David for new shoes whilst Ted went to the uniform shop and purchased what he needed. They bought vegetables and fruit from the market for Fay, had coffee and cake in a little cafe and were back home mid-afternoon.

The wind had picked up and the tide was coming in, so the boys decided to go along the coastal path and watch as the sea crashed against the rocks.

"Just watch what you are doing on there," said John. "Don't be larking about near the edge, the sea can take you by surprise."

The boys sat away from the path edge and watched the sea hurled into the air and dissolve into a salty spray as it grumbled and roared against the rocks, and the ground beneath them seemed to bellow a response.

"You wouldn't stand a chance in that lot," said Ted. "I wonder what it's really like right out at sea in a boat in a great big swell."

"Don't fancy it at all," said David, "but you could ask the fisherman with the little boat to take you out one day."

When they returned, they were wet from the spray, so they hung up their clothes on the creel and put their pyjamas on.

"You are not sitting at the table in pyjamas," said John. "Go and get dressed."

They scurried off and dressed in dry clothes, sat and had their evening meal and watched television for a while before going to bed. David gave Ted his journal on London to read, and they chatted for a long time about all the things he had seen and done.

"My father has never taken me anywhere exciting," said Ted. "Your uncle is very kind to you; you are very lucky."

"Yes, I know," said David, and he truly did.

Chapter 21

John gave the boys a lift to school on their first day back, and this time for David it was exciting to meet up with his friends. Ted was a boarder, and in a year higher than David, so he didn't see too much of him at school. There was the usual buzz during the meet and greet in the hall, and David remembered how he felt as a new boy the previous year. The six-week holiday had so many highs and lows, he was glad to be back at school with a more familiar routine, lessons, homework, butcher deliveries and varied weekends with trips to the cinema or long walks with John. He was invited to celebrate birthdays with some of the boys who had been to his 13th birthday celebrations, and half term seemed to come around quickly. The boarders who couldn't get to see their families during this week stayed at school, so David spent time with Ted on Saturday afternoon, and the full day on Tuesday, and of course, there were other boarders so Ted wouldn't be lonely, David thought, although he had noticed him being less exuberant and quieter and more thoughtful than usual, but he said he was ok when David asked him if he was all right. They had been sitting on the wall overlooking the fields where trenches were being dug for drainage and sewage before any building could commence. The boys were fascinated by the mechanical diggers that were churning up the land, but they made their way home when it started to rain, had a sandwich for lunch and played chess for a while.

"Will you be going to your father's place at Christmas?" asked Fay. "It must be nice to be in the sunshine when it is cold here."

"I've no idea," replied Ted, despondently. "They said they were moving in the summer, but I had a letter last week to say they were still in Cyprus and could be coming back to England. I write to them every week, and I've only had two letters since Christmas from father. My mother has written, but that's our secret."

"Doesn't your father know she writes to you?" asked David, thinking it was very strange.

Fay butted in, uncomfortable with the way the conversation was going, "Sons and mothers have their secrets, don't they, Ted?"

"Yes," Ted replied, "and it's a good job, or I wouldn't know anything about my family at all. Father just tells me to work hard at school, and he will hopefully get to see me in the near future. I'm not sure what that means to him because I have not seen any of them for two years. My other grandparents on my mother's side write to me all the time, but they are both old and unwell, so I can't go and stay with them. They seem to think father is already in England, but he has not let me know if they are. They are supposed to let school know if there is a change of address, but it's awkward, should I have to go and ask in the office at school where my parents are? I think they might expect my parents to let me know. Father is a stickler for detail, always has been, so if he hasn't let me know, it's because he doesn't want to, and didn't want me to visit them at half term."

David walked up the lane with Ted when it was time for him to be back at school for the evening meal and tried very hard to lift his spirits, but Ted was just feeling glum, dug his hands in his trouser pockets and sloped off to school, turning once to wave at David, who was standing watching him and wondering what he could do to cheer him up.

When John arrived home, Fay spoke to him about the conversation she and David had with Ted, it troubled her so much. She couldn't understand why his parents would not make every effort to see their son.

"The structure of their lifestyle is so different to ours," said John. "Once they are in England, it should make it easier to have contact. We hope so, don't we?"

"But why would it have to be a secret that Ted's mother sent him letters?" asked Fay.

"It's best to remain a secret," said John. "There could be many reasons, and there's no point in speculating. Now, I'm just letting you know I will be away in London for three days next week as usual, so if you could plan your work around that and make sure you are here for David in the morning, I would appreciate it."

When John told David he was going up to London, David screwed up his face. "Couldn't you have gone this week? I could have gone with you."

John spent most of Sunday morning in his study whilst David did his homework and gathered his sports kit together for his return to school. In the afternoon, they enjoyed a long walk through the village and fields beyond, for a change. They stopped on the way back and leaned over the wall to see what had been happening on the land John had sold. There were rows of trenches and a stack of pipes to lay in them, and a row of telegraph poles had been erected.

"I don't think it will be long before we have the telephone installed in the house by the look of things," said John.

"That will be good," said David. "We will be able to talk to Jake without going up to the surgery, especially in the winter."

They returned home, had their meal, and when David had cleared away and washed up, he sat with John and asked about something he had been reading about in one of John's books. They had been discussing the digestive system at school, but John's book had a lot more information which David wanted clarification on, especially as he couldn't even read some of the words and, therefore, couldn't understand the explanations.

John was always prepared to go through whatever David wanted to know about his studies and helped him if he could, and he was pleased when he showed an interest in his medical books, but a career choice was way down the line, and he could only encourage David subtly as time moved on, and of course David had to make the grade and he was not going to put any pressure on him.

The following morning, John had gone when David walked into the kitchen, but Fay was there to make his breakfast, and she was there when he returned from school to make sure he had a proper meal before she left for home. She was slightly anxious about leaving him on his own, David seemed fine about it, but Fay didn't know his background and how he had lived as a young boy, and that he was stronger because of it.

First day back at the surgery, John dropped David off at school because it was raining heavily.

"I'll be late tonight," said John. "I'm doing morning and evening surgeries for the rest of the week. Cheerio for now." They parted company, so David was shocked to find John in the headmaster's office when he was taken there by a prefect from his PE lesson.

"What's it about?" David had asked the prefect on the way, but he couldn't tell him anything.

David was startled when he entered the room. John was there, the headmaster, the policeman in uniform from the village and another man who turned out to be a detective and the housekeeper for the boarders.

"When was the last time you saw Ted?" the headmaster asked.

"On the Tuesday of half term," replied David, wondering what Ted had been up to.

The housekeeper confirmed that Ted had returned that day, having spent the day with David. "We always ask the boarders where they are going when they leave the school and where they have been on their return, and this is recorded in case parents want to check on their children."

John could see David was stressing, and took it upon himself to explain. "I'm here as a governor of this school because one of our students is missing, and we need you to tell us if you know where Ted is. Has he confided in you? Do you know of his plans?"

David shook his head to indicate 'no'.

The detective asked David which holiday camp Ted had worked at in the summer, but David didn't know, Ted always referred to it as the camp and never said where it was, and he never thought to ask, he was just interested in the stories of what it was like.

"I know nothing," said David. "All I know is that he was sad. Fay will tell you." He looked at John, not knowing that she had already spoken to him about the conversation they had before Ted left for school on the Tuesday afternoon.

"Please do not speak of this when you return to class," asked the policeman, as he opened the door for David to leave.

"Can you fetch me the door key? I've forgotten mine," said John and nodded at David. "I'll wait in the corridor."

David returned with the key, not understanding why John would want it anyway as Fay would be there.

"Now if you are asked why you were taken out of class, you can say I needed my door key," said John. "Off you go."

Of course it was difficult for David to settle into his lessons, he was bombarded with questions at break time, and he couldn't wait to get home. Fay was waiting for him with a cup of tea and a hug. The police had been and questioned her during the day, so she too had been wondering what on earth Ted was up to and hoping he was all right.

When John came home, David ran to ask, "Have they found him?"

"No," said John, "but his family are at RAF Bentwaters in Suffolk and have been there almost a month."

"Does that mean Ted could have gone to see them at half term?" asked Fay.

"You would have thought so," said John, "but where is the boy now? That's the important question, all his clothes and personal belongings are still at school, even his wallet and money. It's all very strange." He turned to David, "Was he seeing someone in the village?"

"Not that I know of," said David, "and I think he would have told me."

"He didn't tell you he was going to the holiday camp," said John.

"No, he didn't," said David, defensively, "because he felt embarrassed about not seeing his father."

The following day, in assembly at school, it was announced that Ted was missing, and the children were asked to speak to members of staff if they had any information that would be helpful, but all that came up was that Ted was feeling worthless because his family never wanted him but no clues as to his whereabouts. The pity of it all was that he had spoken to some of the children about his feelings, but not to a member of staff or there would have been some help for him. The staff were usually very good at detecting problems with the teenage boys, but Ted had clearly slipped through the protective net, and they regretted it deeply.

At the beginning of all the disturbance, David was very unsettled, his sleeping pattern was erratic and he was not eating as he should, fretting over Ted, but eventually things settled down, and just now and again the subject came up. John had asked Fay to let him have any post that arrived for David but none did, and no one else had heard anything over the five weeks since Ted had disappeared until one morning a police car arrived at school, and within a few hours, the boys were told that the remains of a body in school uniform had been washed up on to the rocks further down the coast. The clothes on the body had his name tape stitched on to them, so there was no doubt it was Ted, and otherwise, identification would have been difficult.

John made a point of being at home for when David arrived, knowing how this could affect him, expecting an explosion of emotion, but it didn't happen. He just said to John, "Have you heard they found Ted dead in the sea?" John confirmed he had, and that was the end of the conversation that evening and for days afterwards, despite John asking on several occasions if he wanted to talk about it. The answer was always 'no'.

A windy Sunday afternoon, the tide was roaring in, so John and David had a walk along the coastal path and watched the waves hurling themselves against the rocks below. No matter how many times they watched, it was always compelling. They stopped at David's favourite place, where he hadn't been for quite a while, and John took apples from his pocket, so David pulled the waterproof from between the rocks to sit on and heard a clatter on the ground. It was an unfamiliar tin, and John could tell by David's reaction that he didn't know anything about it. David picked it up and shook it before he opened it to find a note inside, which he read to John.

You have been my good and best friend and I thank you and your uncle for being so kind to me. Nothing I do can make my father want to see me. He's cruel mentally, like he is to my mother, and I hope he pays. Thanks for the good times. TED.

David handed the note to John, sat with his head in his hands and bawled, all the compressed emotion that had built up over the weeks spilled out of him, and he was gasping for breath as he tried to speak. He had told himself it was an accident when they found Ted's body, but now he knew he had taken his life in despair.

John sat with his arm around him and let him cry out.

"He must have jumped from the rocks back there," said David. "How could he do that?"

"We don't know that for certain, but wherever it was, he would see it as an end to his pain, his turmoil," said John. "Now we must let the police see this letter, but you will get it back eventually if you want it."

On the way back home, David stood and looked down on the rocks for a long time, imagining what it must have been like to stand there and jump on purpose, convinced Ted had left the note just before he jumped.

Back home, John sent David for a bath whilst he warmed up the pie Fay had left for them and cooked the vegetables.

"You must come and have something to eat, David," shouted John, "and don't come down in your pyjamas." John wanted to keep things as normal as possible, and dining in pyjamas was not normal, as far as he was concerned.

David appeared in slacks and a jumper and a face puffed and like marble from crying. "When are we taking the letter to the police?" he asked.

"Tomorrow will be fine," said John. "Keeping it overnight isn't going to change anything. How do you feel about going to school tomorrow?"

John was thinking David probably wouldn't settle and sleep very well, so he was agreeable if he wanted to stay at home with Fay, but the decision was David's to be made in the morning.

"Don't I have to go to the police?" asked David.

"No," replied John, "I'll deal with that, and at least we have the answers now as to why and what happened to Ted. Such an unnecessary tragedy, and I'm just so sorry he didn't feel he could talk to me."

David went up to his room, wrapped himself in his blanket and sat on his window seat listening to the wind moaning, as if it was sharing his sadness. The clouds hid the moon so he couldn't see the sea, but he could hear it and wondered what other secrets it held. He had never thought he would not see Ted again, he was expecting him to turn up one day having had a wonderful adventure, probably getting into serious trouble, but being around as his friend forever, and was struggling with the fact that Ted had actually planned to kill himself because he was so unhappy.

Two weeks later, there was a memorial service held at the school for Ted which his family attended. The students stood in silence in the main hall, the staff and governors were on the stage, the headmaster and the vicar from the village church led Ted's family in to sit at the front of the rows of seats. John was watching Ted's father, an imposing figure in his uniform, and wondered who the girl was that was clinging on to him like a limpet and working out that the lady next to her who was crying must be Ted's mother. *How sad there are no grandparents here*, thought John. The choir sang 'All in the April Evening', with surprising tenderness from an all-boy choir, the headmaster spoke of Ted and his contribution to school life and drew attention to the cups and certificates he had won that were displayed on a table, the vicar led the prayers, everyone sang the 23rd psalm and said the Lord's prayer, and the service was over, the students returned to their classrooms, whilst the family and some of the staff gathered in the dining room for refreshments.

John approached Ted's mother, who was very distressed. He didn't introduce himself, but he just asked if she would like to take a look at the cups and certificates that Ted had won.

"In a little while," she said quietly, "before we leave."

Ted's father was approaching John, still with the girl hanging on to his arm.

John kept his cup and saucer in his right hand and a biscuit in his left hand because he didn't feel inclined to shake hands with this man, who had shown no emotion at all through the service.

"I gather you are the doctor who allowed my son to visit?" said Ted's father.

"Yes, he spent some time at my house, it was a pleasure to have him, there was always a lot of laughter in the house when he was around and he was a good friend to my nephew David," said John. "It's a pity he didn't see you at half term, all this could have been avoided, and we do know that you were at Bentwaters during that time. Your son was a boy to be proud of, you should know that."

Shouldn't have said that, thought John, *but glad I did.*

"We had only just moved back, and there was such a lot to do," replied Ted's father

"You had to find a school for me, didn't you, Daddy?" said the clingy girl, "and now you only have me to take care of."

"Are you Ted's sister?" asked John.

"I am," she said, in a manner of self-importance. "I'm Elaine."

"Well, I never," said John. "Ted never mentioned he had a sister, EVER, that is a surprise."

John decided he should leave, quickly, before he said even more than he should and said, "Please excuse me, I must be getting back to the surgery."

Ted's mother, still emotional, walked across and thanked John for being kind to Ted.

Ted's father looked at her, "I think you've done enough blubbering now, pull yourself together, woman."

"I'm not crying, Mummy, you have to be brave, isn't that right, Daddy?" said Elaine.

John turned to Ted's mother, "Do you want to see the cups and certificates? I'll walk you down to the hall on my way out," he said.

They walked down the corridor together so John told her that it had meant so much to Ted to receive her letters.

"It's very difficult for me," she said, "as you've probably noticed, but what can I do?"

"Go and look after your parents and live with them," said John, surprised he'd actually said what he was thinking.

Elaine yelled down the corridor, "Mummy, for goodness' sake, hurry up, Daddy is wanting to leave."

John stepped outside and took several deep breaths to compose himself, then walked towards the driver in uniform waiting for Ted's parents. "They shouldn't be long," he said.

"Thank you, sir," said the young man. "Still preening his feathers then?"

John wasn't sure what he meant, but he knew it wasn't complimentary by the sneering tone in his voice.

As he walked back to the surgery, he couldn't believe he had been so forthright in his opinion because his career relied a great deal on him being tactful, but the loss of a young life in such a way had affected him deeply because he had known Ted, and he'd looked for some sign of sorrow from Ted's father and he saw none. He may have had to advocate a stiff upper lip in his role in the RAF, but he knew his son had

133

killed himself. He had been shown the letter Ted had written to David, and yet there was no emotion shown at all. The only time there was any glimmer of reaction was when John confronted him about the half-term holiday, and it was clear he didn't like it.

Chapter 22

David had finished his deliveries for the butcher on the Saturday morning, and was walking home, remembering at the top of the lane that Ted used to wait for him there. He would sit on the flat stone on the wall by the gate post, and that was always remembered as Ted's place, but David's thoughts had calmed and he had accepted he would never see Ted again. He had not walked or had a run along the coastal path since he was with John and found the tin with Ted's message in, despite several attempts by John to persuade him.

David was sauntering down the lane, wondering how he was going to spend the weekend when he heard a vehicle approaching from behind, tooting its horn. He stood back against the wall and waited for it to pass and couldn't believe his eyes: Dougy was driving, Jake was sitting at the side of him, and they were both laughing and waving. The van didn't stop until it reached the house, where they sat and waited for David to catch them up. John, who knew they were coming, had said nothing to David, hoping the surprise would lift his spirits, and he was right. John went out to greet them and they waited for David to skid round the corner out of breath.

"Did you know they were coming and not tell me?" he panted at John.

"Maybe!" replied John, in a teasing manner. "Does it matter?"

David ran and hugged Jake, "Are you really coming home to stay?" he asked.

"I believe my room is ready for me now," replied Jake, and then everything clicked into place in David's mind. John and Fay had known for a while, that's why the room was cleaned and the bed made up.

"Come in and have some tea," said John. "We can bring your things in later."

"Bloody hell!" said Dougy. "What a massive house, the kitchen is bigger than our whole house. Oops! Sorry for swearing."

They sat and had tea and biscuits, and then emptied the van before it turned dark. All Jake's pans and enamel plates and cups, cutlery, torch, primus stove and container for paraffin were packed into a box which David was about to remove.

"These are Dougy's now, I don't need them anymore," said Jake, feeling good about being home.

After their evening meal, when the kitchen was tidy, they went through to the lounge and chatted away.

"How long are you staying?" David asked Dougy.

"Well," Dougy replied, "I have a week's holiday, I have to be back at work a week on Monday, but it took us two days to get here, so I think I had better leave on Friday. We kept getting lost, and I probably will be going back home. We ended up in the same town twice, so when we eventually got out and onto the road we needed to be on, we parked up and slept in the van."

"I didn't know you could drive," said David.

"My brother took the test and said he was me," said Dougy, laughing, "so I lend him my van when he needs it."

"Is it your own van?" David asked.

"Sure," said Dougy, "I need it for my work. I'm doing an apprenticeship to be a plumber, as well as going to night classes for my City and Guilds. I do odd jobs to earn a bit, and you need so much tackle when you are plumbing, I can't carry it around in a bag."

John sighed and thought, *I'll pretend I didn't hear that.*

Jake went into his shoulder bag and produced an envelope and asked David to sit with him, and he explained about Jed leaving his estate to be shared between Dougy and him.

"What does that mean?" David asked.

"The money from the sale of Jed's cottage and furniture and savings from his bank, less the solicitor's fees, was to be split between you and Dougy, which means we need to go to a bank in town and open an account for you," explained Jake. "I let Dougy's family have the furniture they wanted, and I've brought you the small chest of drawers and Jed's tall water jug to match the small one you brought home. That's why Dougy could afford to buy a van."

"Take Dougy up to your room," said John, "and I think an early night might be in order." He knew the boys would be chattering long after they had gone up to bed, so the sooner they went up the better. He looked in on them to check they'd had a wash and cleaned their teeth. "Not yet," said David.

"The ground rules are still the same," said John. "Explain what they are to Dougy, and don't be too late settling down. Goodnight."

"It's like living in a castle" said Dougy. "Everything is so big, even the bed, but it feels very comfy." He lay talking about clearing Jed's house until his words slurred into silence and he was fast asleep. It took David longer, because now he was quiet, he realised the full impact of having Jake at home all the time. He loved and respected both the brothers, it was like having two fathers, and even after all this time, he still wondered what his life would have been like without them. He felt happy as he fell asleep.

The following morning, after breakfast, they all went to church. So many people in the congregation made their way to greet and speak to Jake, which was very reassuring for him, for he had wondered how the villagers would react on his return, but people were very welcoming and glad to see him.

During lunch, Dougy said, "I want to go and see the sea. I've never seen it. I want to swim in it."

"It's too cold for that," said John, "but we can go for a walk, and the tide will be out so we can walk along the sands."

"That sounds wonderful," said Jake. "I've missed it so much."

John was expecting some excuse from David for not going, but it didn't come. They set off with Jake by David's side, and Dougy in front with John, running forwards and backwards like a pet dog, until he saw the almost white sandy beach, and the ocean beyond, and he stopped, put his hands on his hips. "PHEW," he said and charged across the sand, whipping it with a piece of seaweed he had picked up.

David was laughing at him and went to join in and showed him how to look for shells at the water's edge.

They crossed the beach and climbed the steps back on to the coastal road with John watching David carefully.

"Are you going to be all right?" he asked David.

"I'm going to," David replied. "I have to, don't I?"

"You don't have to, but it's time you did, and better if you do," replied John.

"What are you on about?" asked Dougy, looking puzzled.

"We will show you," said John, "further along the path."

When they reached the place where it was thought Ted had jumped from, John said, "It's very dangerous here, you have to be very careful. David's friend fell into the sea and drowned."

"I run on here to keep fit for our cross-country runs at school," said David, moving the conversation on before Dougy started asking questions about his friend drowning. Of course, the questions followed then about cross-country runs, but that was soon dealt with.

They walked quite a long way along the path before they turned back, and by the time they reached the beach, the tide was on its way in.

"If you come along here on your own whilst David is at school, you must not be reckless, you can't afford to be complacent, the sea is very powerful," said John.

When they were out of earshot from John, Dougy said to David, "What does complacent mean? He uses big words, your uncle."

"He's a proper doctor, they all use big words, you should see some of the words in his books," said David.

They had sausage, mash, cabbage and onion gravy for their meal, with blackberry and apple pie to finish, a lovely relaxed meal with funny stories and laughter round the table. When Jake and John were living there with their father, they were not allowed to speak at the table, and this is how John had expected it to be when David arrived because he was used to dining alone, in silence, or with Annie clattering the washing up in the background, but all that had changed, he looked forward to the chatter and enjoyed it.

The boys cleared up and went up to David's room for a while and talked about what they might do during the week, but of course, David had to go to school. Dougy was going to look at the disused outside toilet to see if it could be fixed, so it wasn't necessary to trail through the house and go upstairs all the time, and Jake would be around, so he was feeling fine about everything.

"I can't believe how well it went this afternoon along by the rocks," said John to Jake. "I just hope he will continue to feel he can go along there in the future."

"Let's see what happens this week whilst Dougy is here," said Jake, "although it's getting dark by the time David gets home. I'll take Dougy during the day if he wants to go, it's better to have someone with him, and when he has gone home, we can take the walk again with David, if he feels inclined to do it."

"Good idea," said John. "I want Dougy to enjoy his stay, but he is going to make the outside toilet functional again, I believe. I obtained everything you put on the list that he would need. It's handy having the contractors in the field, they have access to everything and were more than willing to help me out. I had to force the toilet door and it fell off, so that needs to be replaced. Are you sure Dougy is up to this job?"

"He'll be fine," said Jake. "He did quite a lot of work in Jed's house whilst I was living there, and it made a difference when we came to sell. He stayed there some of the time, but he was always up and working by 8. I left him to it and went off for a few days, visiting people and places I may not see again. I'm sure he's got the skill to fit a new water closet and toilet, just let's hope the sewage pipe under the ground has not been damaged."

The following morning, Fay met Dougy and Jake for the first time.

"Goodness me," she said, shaking Jake's hand, "are you John's twin? What would you like me to call you?"

Jake gave her a warm smile, "No, we are not twins, though many people ask the same question, and Jake will be fine."

John was away to the surgery, dropping David off at the top of the lane, and Dougy and Jake were investigating the outside toilet situation. It was Dougy's opinion that the toilet could be put into the recess between the porch and the kitchen, with access from just inside the house and much more convenient. Jake agreed, but it was far too big a job for Dougy on his own in the time he had, so they went along the lane and talked to one of the foremen in the field who was able to contact a plumber waiting for work once they had started to build the houses. He brought his son with him, and in two days, the three of them had installed an inside toilet that just needed a door fitting. The plumber was surprised when he saw how young Dougy was, but he quickly realised how willing he was to work and learn, and the job went smoothly. Jake paid the plumber and asked for his address in case they should need him again, and once he had gone, asked Dougy if he wanted to go along the coast for a walk.

The wind was strong and the tide was coming in so Jake knew it would be a dramatic scene for Dougy to see. They stood on the path and watched the sea surging across the sand.

"Now do you understand what John was explaining to you about the power of the sea?" asked Jake.

"Gosh!" said Dougy and just stood watching in silence for a while, until Jake moved to carry along the path to where the sea was thundering and booming against the rocks and spraying the air. The wind spiralled the spray high into the air, and Dougy held up his hands to catch it as it fell, hence he was wet through by the time they reached home.

"Get changed," said Jake, "and we'll walk up the lane to meet David from school."

Fay was ironing but made Jake a cup of tea and asked how the walk had gone.

"It's something I had never given any thought to," said Jake, "but we live on an island, and there will be so many people who have never been to the coast. Dougy was mesmerised, in fact, he was speechless for once."

"I heard that," said Dougy, as he walked through the kitchen and pulled the new toilet chain. He picked up a piece of tape from the packaging and stuck it into the wall at either side of the toilet doorway. "When John and David come home, we will have an opening ceremony, and I shall do it," said Dougy.

"Fine," said Jake, "is there anything I should know about tea?" he asked Fay.

"Tonight you are having fish and chips, and John has that in hand, so it's likely I will not be here when you return today," said Fay, "but you could ask David to take the dry clothes off the creel and exchange them with the wet ones still in the basket."

Jake and Dougy walked to the school and waited for David.

"John and I used to go to school here," said Jake. "It's a very old school, established in the 1600's, with a good educational record and traditions."

"That's over 300 years," said Dougy. "I'm surprised it hasn't fallen down."

Jake laughed. "If a job is done right in the first place, things last and you will do well to remember that."

"There's no chance that toilet will still be standing in 300 years," said Dougy.

"No," replied Jake," but we will not be here to worry about that."

The huge doors burst open to a flood of highly charged boys in school uniform, and somewhere from the middle of them, David immerged.

"Good afternoon, Doctor John," said one of the boys, thinking Jake was his brother.

"Good afternoon," replied Jake, making the boy none the wiser, he left that for David to do later.

"It's a bit posh," said Dougy, quietly. "You didn't tell me you went to a posh school."

"It's the only school in the village," said David, sensing maybe Dougy felt a little insecure amongst the boys, but they had all gone, and Jake broke the silence.

"Are you going home now?" he asked David.

"Yes, I'd better, I've got homework," David replied, "but John says I can use his study, so I will not be in the way of anything you want to do."

"We're going on to the surgery now, to wait for John," said Jake. "Apparently, he's in charge of fish and chips for tea tonight, Fay has informed us."

Jake enjoyed his walk through the village, not a lot had changed, but the cottage where the Brody's had lived had been demolished because by the time they left, it had been trashed. Word from their neighbours told that they had even pulled up floor boards to have a fire, and when the landlord told them to leave, they wrecked the place, smashed windows, pulled the wiring from the walls, chipped plaster from the walls and smashed the sink and toilet. The landlord despaired, but the contractors on the new build had offered him a price for the stone, and he gladly accepted this and was just glad that the rest of his tenants in the row of cottages took pride in their homes and looked after his properties.

David heard them return home with the fish and chips and joined them for tea.

"We've got some bits on them, whatever that means," said John.

"They're crunchy bits of batter that you sprinkle on your chips," said Dougy. "Have you never had them before?"

"No," said John. "Apparently, we have not lived until we've tried these, Jake."

"Better had, then," said Jake, pinching some and crunching them loudly.

After tea, David left to finish his homework, and Dougy washed up, and when David reappeared, Dougy had them all standing in front of the new toilet. He cut the tape, flushed it and said, "I name this toilet Looby Loo." They all clapped, John looked at Jake, shook his head, and shrugged his shoulders as Dougy said, "Every time you have a pee, you'll think of me."

That evening, they looked at the photographs from the London trip that John had collected that afternoon, and the boys were very excited to see them.

"You can stick these in your journal if you wish," he said to David. "That's why I took them really."

"Thank you," said David. "It will be something for me to do when Dougy has gone home."

The following day, Jake took Dougy into town and they went to the swimming baths and spent a pleasant hour before going into a cafe for coffee and cake.

They had travelled into town in the van, so Jake could have it filled with petrol for the journey home.

"Is there anything else you need for your journey?" asked Jake. "Fay will pack you some food, that has been taken care of."

"I'm fine," said Dougy, "but it's going to feel really strange back at home, crammed into the small house, and now we've got the furniture, there's less space than ever. Do you know it's the first time Ma and Pa have slept in a proper bed? Pa said he couldn't find Ma the first night they slept in it."

"Shall we make our way back and meet David from school?" suggested Jake.

"No, just let's go back to the house," said Dougy, who had seen all the big cars outside the school. He was proud of his little van, but outside that school, amongst those expensive cars, was not where he wanted to be.

"Will you come again?" David asked when they were packing Dougy's things together.

"I will if you want me to," said Dougy.

"Of course I do," replied David. "It's been great having you here, and I'm really impressed that you are studying for your career. You have to let me know how you go on with your exams, I can give you the surgery telephone number to call, and you can leave a message with the receptionist."

They talked about plans they had for their futures, and Dougy had certainly got a good idea as to what he wanted from life, to have a good job, a nice home for his wife and children, and to be able to take them to the seaside.

David hadn't a clue, he was just happy to be where he was, considering where he had come from, but he wouldn't discuss that, even with Dougy.

The following morning, after breakfast, David had a lift up the lane in the van as Dougy left for home. Jake had written down a route for him to follow, Fay had packed him a supply of food, he shook hands with John and Jake and thanked them and was on his way. As David got out of the van, he said, "Ring the surgery, and leave a message so we know you are home safe. See you soon, be careful."

"Will do, and remember me when you have a pee," shouted Dougy in a rhythmic manner, laughing. He waved and was on his way home.

Chapter 23

Before returning home, Jake had re-visited the village where he had spent most of his time away, by the railway track. Having spent a long time with Betty and Jed, it was over a year since he was last there, and much had changed. The den had gone, the water station demolished because now there were diesel engines pulling the carriages instead of steam engines, and the brambles had been burnt away. He did recognise a discarded piece of lino amongst the pile of rubble, and wondered what the workmen had thought when they came across his tidy den.

He walked around the village and up the hill where Rebecca lived. Mr Brown was in the garden lifting a few weeds. "Hello there," he said to Jake, "it's a while since you were in these parts."

"Yes," replied Jake, "but it's nice to come back."

"Would you like to come in and have a cup of tea? asked Mr Brown.

They chatted for a good hour, and in that time, Jake spoke of David vaguely. "Did you ever hear what happened to the boy who escaped from the remand home?

"Not a thing," replied Mr Brown, "he disappeared from the face of the earth. He should never have been in the remand home in the first place, and he must have been desperate to risk escaping. It was never explained to me what exactly was happening as far as he was concerned, or I would have dealt with things differently. Rebecca and I often speak of him, especially at Christmas. The home is closed now and not before time."

Jake sensed it still troubled Mr Brown. "How is your daughter?" he asked, changing the subject.

"Rebecca does very well. It was very difficult for her at first when my wife left us, but now she copes very well running the home and doing well at school. Bertha, our neighbour, has been amazing, and now she's feeling her age, Rebecca is looking after her too. We have a good youth club in the village so she has a good social life with people her own age, and I'm pleased about that."

"I must be on my way," said Jake. "Thank you for tea." He stood and shook Mr Brown's hand and just said quietly, "The boy is safe." He knew Mr Brown would have questions, he took a risk telling him, but he also felt he could trust him because he wouldn't want to cause the boy harm. Hopefully, now, Mr Brown wouldn't agonise about David.

"You do realise a slip of the tongue could prove very dangerous?" said Jake.

"I do," said Mr Brown, who knew there was no point in asking any of the questions that were flooding his thoughts. "No need to worry on that score."

After Jake had left, Mr Brown sat thinking and realised he had not learnt a single thing about Jake, this quietly spoken man, who Rebecca used to call the clean tramp. Where had he come from? Where was he going? Why was he on the road living rough with his belongings in a pram?

As Jake walked down the hill to the bus stop, he met a young girl carrying two bags of shopping.

"Hello," she said, as if greeting an old friend.

"Good afternoon," said Jake, smiling and nodding to her. *That must be Rebecca,* he thought.

Rebecca walked into her kitchen and put the bags down. "I've just seen Hobo," she said. "Haven't seen him around for ages, and he didn't have his pram with him."

"He's been here for a while, came in for a cup of tea. He's a very educated man, I sense, but he doesn't give anything away about himself," said Mr Brown, and that was all he said.

Two days later, Jake caught the train back to join Dougy at Jed's cottage, which is where he stayed until it was sold and time to travel home with Dougy in his van, an experience he wasn't likely to forget in a hurry.

Although he was happy to be home and settled, he did like to sit outside on an evening, in the dark, when the sky was clear, and the sound of the sea and a cool breeze soothed him.

Following an evening meal, John and Jake explained to David about his inheritance. Jed's sister and her husband owned their cottage, and when she passed away, it became Jed's, and he had made a will for the proceeds from the sale of the cottage and his savings to be split between David and Dougy, and this amounted to almost £2,000.00 between them.

"A £1,000 each," asked David. "Where is it? I've never seen £1,000."

"At the moment, your share is in my bank account, and when we go into town, we will have to open a new account in my name, at a different bank to mine, so you have a true record of your own money," said Jake. "And when you need some, I will have to draw it out until you are 21."

"Can't I just put it in the post office with my other money?" asked David.

"A large sum of money would draw attention to you," said Jake. "We have to avoid that."

David hadn't realised, but of course he couldn't draw any money out without Jake knowing about it, and he would be able to guide him and teach him about not being foolish or rash and spending wisely.

"I want to give some to you both for all you have done for me," said David. "I promised I would, and now I can."

"We'll discuss that later," said John, and he and Jake agreed that if the subject cropped up again, they would accept a small amount from David and keep it on one side for something special, because they had no intention of keeping it for themselves.

"If, one day, you go to university, you will need some funding behind you," said John, "so bear that in mind."

Their lives settled, John continuing as the village GP. Jake returned to hospital first to familiarise himself with the new practices that had come into place in his absence and then back into surgery, and David worked hard at school. They had trips to London and visited the Gray's in North Yorkshire during one of the summer breaks, which David enjoyed very much. Mr Gray took David and John with him on call outs and made their visit so interesting. They attended the difficult birth of a foal, walked around stables with the most magnificent horses, visited a pig farm where they saw many sows with their litters of piglets. David couldn't resist and had to pick one up for a cuddle, and the piglet couldn't resist having a pee, so David smelt wonderful for the rest of the day!

"Fancy being a vet?" asked Mr Gray.

"No, I don't think so," replied David. "I don't think I'd be very good at going up to my elbow in an animal's bum. I'm hoping to go to Cambridge to study natural sciences, but I need to do well with my 'A' levels."

"Which subjects have you chosen?" asked Mr Gray.

"Biology, chemistry, physics, maths, English and French," replied David.

"Quite a task, but he certainly enjoys his sciences, which is a big help," said John, "and he did very well with his 'O' levels. He's sent his application form in, we are waiting for information regarding his interview, and if he's given a place, he knows exactly what is required to be able to take it up."

"Our middle son, Joel, has just finished his first year at Cambridge, but he is doing medieval history," said Mr Gray. "You should keep in touch, and then if you do get in next year, you will have someone to connect with."

"It seems a long way off," said David, "but we've already been told the serious work begins when we return to school after these holidays."

John and David were made very welcome at the Gray's home which was a beautiful one-level stone house with a duck pond, hens clucking and strutting about, geese in a field until evening time when they were moved in front of the house as guards, and two border collies he had rescued and were his pets. There was another building which was Mr Gray's veterinary clinic for when people brought their animals for treatment.

"You didn't escape all the kittens and puppies, then?" said John, smiling.

Mr Gray looked at John and grinned, remembering he had said he preferred the bigger beasties in a rural setting when John had asked him why he was moving.

The week passed far too quickly, but was memorable, and as they journeyed home, there was much to chat about. On the way up to the Gray's home, they had diverted their route to drop Jake off to visit Bill and Dora at the farm where he used to stay and were on their way to collect him. John had not met these people, but as soon as the car had stopped in the farm yard, David was out and running to the house to greet Dora. He banged on the door, but when it opened, a man was standing there he had never seen before.

"We've come to collect Jake," said David, "and I'd like to see Dora and Bill before we leave."

"They're down at the inn," said the man abruptly and shut the door.

John had noticed the inn before they turned into the lane up to the farmhouse because the window boxes were full of flowers, so they returned, parked up the car and went inside to find Jake, Dora and Bill sitting at a table tucked into a corner. David gave Dora a huge hug whilst Jake introduced John to Bill.

"Just look at you, David, my, how you've grown up," Dora said.

"Who is the man at your house?" David asked. "He was very rude; he shut the door on me."

"That is my son," said Bill, with a saddened tone. "Out of the army, with a pregnant wife, running my farm into ruin and treating Dora like a servant. His wife does nothing to help, and mark my words, as soon as she's had the baby, she will be off, and I doubt she intends taking the baby with her." His voice quivered. "Sorry, folks," he said, "I shouldn't burden you with my problems, and I'm sure Jake is sick of it. He's had to stay here, they wouldn't make room for him at the farm, and they could have."

John had never met these people before so he just sat in silence, but he couldn't help but notice how jaded and unhappy they were.

"I think we have to make a move," said John, "but I'm pleased to have met you, and I do hope things work out for you."

Leaving them was gut-wrenching for Jake as he shook Bill's hand, Dora and David were crying as they hugged, and as they drove away, the couple looked bereft and forlorn, arms linked in the middle of the car park.

Jake was very quiet for a long time. Finally, he spoke. "That couple have been so kind to me in the past, and I cannot think of a way to help them," he said.

"I can," said John. "If he owns the farm, he wants to sell it and find themselves a home as far away from his son as they can. There's nothing his son could do about that. They don't need to tell the son what they are doing if they're clever enough to have the viewings when his son and wife are not there."

"That shouldn't be difficult," said Jake. "They spend a lot of time out drinking and socialising."

"He needs to get an agreement with the agent not to let local people know the farm is up for sale, and then his son doesn't get wind of it and make their lives any worse than they seem to be now," said John.

"That's brilliant," said David. "Are you going to write to Bill and tell him?"

"No," said Jake, "I'll keep telephoning the inn to see if he is there, I'm bound to catch him sooner or later, and it's better to have the conversation than put it in a letter that may get into the wrong hands."

They had intended having a meal en route, but apart from stopping for petrol and buying chocolate, they continued their journey, Jake taking over the driving and arrived home at 2 am.

They had cocoa and toast, and within the hour, were in bed and fast asleep, and unusually, David was first up the following morning and it was 10 am, so church was out of the question. He made a drink of tea and sat outside in the sunshine, and thought of Dora and Bill until Jake joined him and they chatted about David and John's holiday with the Gray's, which was a far happier story.

"Two more weeks, and it's back to school for your last year," said Jake. "Do you need white shirts this time?"

"Not sure," said David. "Mrs Gray sent a bundle of school uniforms when they moved. I had better check with Fay, she sorted it out. I know there were three blazers, different sizes, I haven't needed a new one since we bought the first one, which was rather good I thought."

Whilst David was adjusting to being a prefect in his last year at school, a network of John, Jake, Mr Gray and Bill were contriving to find somewhere for Bill to live and work, away from his son. When Jake had discussed the possibility with Bill, he didn't hesitate. The farm had been in the family for three generations, but his son had no interest and it was becoming run down because he didn't help Bill and would probably sell it as soon as it became his. Mr Gray was able to arrange for Bill to attend an interview at a farm where he looked after the cattle and sheep, and Jake accompanied him, for Bill had never been far from his home all his life. The owner shook Bill's hand and spent almost an hour talking 'farming', and then took him and Jake to look at the cottage that would be available in a month's time.

"Are you interested?" the owner, Mr Priestley, asked.

"Indeed, sir, I am," said Bill, "and would be glad of the work you suggested."

"Rent is collected weekly," said Mr Priestley. "We all help each other out, and I will expect it of you. Are we shaking on it?"

Bill felt emotional as they shook hands, and Mr Priestley sensed it.

"I think you'll fit the bill perfectly. A handshake as strong and rough as yours indicates hard work. I'll leave you to look 'round the cottage, you may need to measure, and I'll expect you in around a month's time," said Mr Priestley and waved as he drove off in his Land rover.

Bill and Jake measured the rooms and windows, hoping the curtains from home would fit. He had an offer on the farm, less than he was hoping for, but he had to accept it; he couldn't afford to lose this opportunity.

A month later, having survived several close calls regarding his son finding out what he was up to and several panic attacks, secret visits to the solicitors and the bank, he and Dora were sitting in a lay-by having sandwiches and tea, on their way to their new home. His truck was piled high with as much of their belongings as he could carry. Two chests of drawers, their sewing machine, the family clock, crockery, cutlery, pots and pans, bowls and basins, Dora's cooking utensils, bedding, curtains, two rugs, a drop leaf table and four chairs, clothes, a collection of Bill's tools, two oil lamps and a canister of spare oil, candles, a roll of chicken wire, four chickens and two border collies and their dishes and rugs. All was covered with tarpaulin apart from where the dogs were, and they rattled along at a steady pace, Bill realising they were overloaded, just praying they made it without an incident. They had left his son's and girlfriend's belongings packed in boxes in the barn.

The family that had bought the farm were moving in that day, and Bill had made them aware of his son who was away on one of his jaunts and warned them he would not like the situation when he returned. The family understood and didn't seem unduly perturbed. Only Jake, John and his solicitor knew where he was going, but he knew the information was secure with them, even Dora hadn't a clue, but she knew it was a long way, having bounced for hours on the hard seat of the truck. They had to leave the big kitchen table, and as Dora put some jars of her chutney and jam out as a gift for the new family, she stroked it. "So many stories," she whispered, "so many people have sat by you and told their stories resting on their elbows, I'll miss you." As they drove away quietly from their home for the last time, they both shed a tear, but now in the lay-by, watching the dogs have a run in the field, they were happy and perhaps a little daunted about what lay ahead but ready to make a go of it.

"Here's to new beginnings," said Dora. "Wherever they may be," she added, pointedly.

It was early evening when they arrived, the cottage was unlocked with the key in the lock inside, and as they entered, Bill knew someone had been in and cleaned and tidied from when he saw it before. He let the dogs have a run around the yard and then tied them up whilst he and Dora started to unload the truck.

Mr Priestley arrived in his land rover. "Good evening," he said. "Did you have a good journey?"

"Yes, thank you, sir," replied Bill and went to shake his hand. "This is my wife Dora."

"Hello," she said. "I'm very pleased to meet you, and want to thank you for giving us this opportunity."

"I hope you settle. I think you will need a few days to sort yourselves out, so I will come on Monday at 7 am and take you to meet the men you will be working with. The kitchen table and wardrobe go with the property, we couldn't get them out. If you have any problems or queries, they are to be discussed with me, not the workmen; festering problems are not productive. My housekeeper has sent this basket of provisions for you. I'll see you Monday," said Mr Priestley and was gone.

They unpacked, had something to eat from the gifted basket and from home, backed the truck into the barn, snuggled up in their bedding and slept on the truck, having decided it was going to be more comfortable than on the stone floor.

During the following few days, they had been into the nearest town and bought a new bed and a sofa and done the round of the shops in the village, the butcher's, the bakery and the green grocers. They went to the telephone and called the surgery to leave a message for Jake to let him know all was well, and Bill bought seeds to plant to start a garden if he had chance. Dora had arranged things in the cottage, and Bill had chopped some wood for the fire and stove and was ready to meet the other men and go to work and start his new life not being responsible for everything.

Bill could tell Dora was fretting about their son, so he talked to her about it.

"I just think it's so sad he won't even know where his parents are," she said.

"And you think that will bother him?" asked Bill. "What will bother him is that the farm is no longer his, that he can't sell it and squander the money, and where do you think either of us would end up when one of us has gone? We should have a good life here, now, the whole point of all this is to be happy in our later years and stress free."

The dogs were curled up on their mats, the logs in the stove were hissing and crackling, and Bill and Dora sat in the lamp light on their new sofa. Bliss!

"When I've sorted the money out at the bank, you can have a new dresser," said Bill, knowing that would please Dora.

"Did you say dresser or dress?" asked Dora, grinning at him.

"Both, if you like," said Bill, "but don't start taking advantage, or I'll have to send you out to work, labouring!"

Within a month, Bill had fit very well into the 'team', enjoying the company of the men, doing what was asked of him, helped willingly by the younger men if necessary and invited to join them for a pint after work. The wives had called on Dora, been invited to visit them, and joined the local WI.

All was well, and who would have thought it would all turn out this way from a comment from John just over a year ago, and so much kindness shown by Jake and Mr Gray, and everyone was happy, there was a contented feeling of 'mission accomplished'.

Bill telephoned Jake at home every week after the telephone was installed, and had the opportunity to speak to David and John, and despite his new life, it was very important to him to keep in contact with his old friends, and one day hope to see them again.

Chapter 24

Exam time soon came round, but having taken his 'O' levels, the actual experience was not as daunting for David, and he knew he had done all he could with his studies and revision, so if he didn't do well, he knew he was not up to going to Cambridge, and he would have to have a re-think. John and Jake had kept their eye on him regarding his revision time, but there was no pressure from them, just help when it was requested.

Jake had accompanied David to Cambridge for his interview for St John's. He had no idea whether it went well or not, but gathered it was hard to get a place there, but he may be accepted at Kings, favouring Natural Sciences Tripos.

At some schools, students finished when the 'A' level exams were over, but at David's school, they were expected to continue attending until the results were in. During this time, they were prepared for life at university or college.

Some of the students were from privileged families and had never had to do anything for themselves, and probably hadn't even considered that they would have to feed themselves and do their own laundry, so although it amused David to be having talks on these matters, he couldn't help but notice the look of awe and realisation on the faces of some of the boys. Thanks to Betty, Dora, Annie and Fay, he was well prepared for taking care of himself.

There was an opportunity for the students taking French to go on a visit to France, and David was really excited and keen to do this and pay for the trip himself, but once again, his situation caught up with him, he didn't have a passport, and because he was a minor the application had to be made by a parent or legal guardian, providing the documentation to back them up, which neither Jake or John had.

"When you are 21, you will be able to sort things out in your own right," said John, "but whilst the boys are away in France, I'll take you up to London with me."

David was downhearted, he hadn't thought it through, the Eiffel Tower, Notre Dame and croissants were more on his mind than a passport, but there was no point in having a moan, because he understood what John had said and looked forward to going to London again. The forms of acceptance or not were handed in to the office at school, and no questions were ever asked as to why students declined anything, all decisions by the parents were accepted, and that was the end of it, so David didn't have to offer any explanation as to why he wasn't going to France.

On the visit to London with John, he visited St Thomas's hospital, but this time instead of going to the children's ward, he went to speak to a man in administration to learn about the procedure moving on from university to a teaching hospital. David had not actually said that was what he wanted to do, but John thought he may as well have the fuller picture and know how long it would take him to achieve certain goals. Because they were only there for three days, John decided to take David to Covent Garden and have an evening meal as a special treat. He was overwhelmed by the

147

vibrant atmosphere, loved watching the hoofers and musicians and jugglers, and it was 11 pm when they arrived back at Mrs Fry's B&B. As they were getting ready for bed, John asked David about his chat at the hospital with the administrator, and whether he was considering going into the medical profession.

"Oh, no!" said David, mischievously. "I want to be a tour guide in London. I want to ride round on one of the buses without a roof all day and tell people all about what they can see."

"Oh!" said John. "Well, that's a different career, and I don't think you will need to go to university for that, but you may have less of a chance because you were not born in London."

When they returned home, there was a letter waiting for David defining what results he would need for acceptance to both of the colleges, where to telephone with his results when he would be told if he had been accepted as a student and in which college. Now all he had to do was wait for the results.

The weeks' leading up to results day were teeth gritting for John, Jake and Fay, who were really glad that David still had to go to school, because when he was at home, he was so restless, and they were running out of ideas to keep him occupied. Fay taught him how to iron his shirts, and how to be careful not to have the water too hot or mix colours when washing his clothes, because apparently there was a laundry for the students to use if they chose to be clean. Once he actually knew he was going to Cambridge, definitely she was to go to the market and buy Terylene cotton to make sheets and pillow cases for a single bed, and he needed new clothes unless he was staying on at school for re-takes if he didn't get the grades he needed, so everything was on hold.

At the weekends he had been swimming, to the cinema, to a party at a school friend's house, and the village fete, but it was the time when he was alone, he was squirming and sighing and deep in thought. Sometimes he would go for a run, and he still went to his favourite place to curl up and read for a while, but he was restless and just longed to know what lay ahead for him at the start of the academic year.

John and Jake had noticed that he didn't start up a friendship like he had with Ted, but there could have been many reasons for that, so they didn't mention it and just welcomed anyone he brought home, noticing that they were all boarders who didn't go home at weekends to their families.

Finally, results day came, and David was at school very early, standing in line to collect his envelope.

The master handed it to him and smiled. "Are you going to open it?" he asked.

"I don't know," said David. "Well, yes, I am, of course I am, but do you mean now?"

"I do mean now," replied the master. "We would like to know how you have done, and then we know if we have done our job well."

David stood for a moment, ripped the envelope open, read the results, handed the form to the master to read and had to bite his lip so he didn't burst into tears. "Thank you so much," he said as he took the envelope back, and once he was outside the building, ran all the way home.

He burst through the door and gave the envelope to Jake and hugged him. "I've done it, I've done it," shouted David. "I'm going to Cambridge. I need to telephone them, and tell them I've done ok." He tried for a long time to get through, the line was so busy, then he started panicking that all the places would have gone, but finally he did get through and was offered a place at St John's college.

"You have done extremely well to get in there," said Jake. "You must have interviewed well, and I'm very proud of you. Ring the surgery and leave a message for John if he isn't free to take the call."

"I'll walk up," said David. "I want to tell him myself."

John was thrilled with the news. After every patient he had seen, he stuck his head round the corner of the door. "Any message?" he asked the receptionist, so he was pleased to see David sitting there waiting, looking very happy with himself. David went back into school and joined the students who had been waiting for their results and were milling around discussing them, and a credit to the standard maintained at the school, there were very few poor grades. The following morning, there was a special assembly for the school leavers, who then enjoyed coffee and biscuits and bid each other farewell, exchanging addresses and telephone numbers. David sat for a moment, quietly, in a corner, watching and wondering whether he would ever see any of these people again, they had all grown into adults together, over the past six years, in one place, and now they were spreading out like shattered glass, and for some reason, the poem 'The Road Not Taken' by Robert Frost came into mind.

The headmaster approached him. "Very well done, David. Had it not been for Dr John, you would not have been given a place at this school, and you have justified his faith in you, and it has taught me that background isn't everything, and before you leave, I wanted you to know that we are considering offering a bursary to two promising students from under-privileged backgrounds, each year, for boys who show promise and are worthy of the education this school offers, and this is a result of what you have shown us can be done. I congratulate you and wish you well, and we will be able to follow your progress through Dr John, which will be good, because despite all we do here, some boys, once they have left, never contact us again."

"I'll call in if my breaks coincide," said David, mischievously. "Maybe I'll be able to watch a cross-country run in the rain, under an umbrella."

"Good luck to you," said the headmaster as he walked away, smiling.

The boys joined the rest of the school for lunch, and then were free to leave, but no one seemed in that much of a hurry to go. David walked out of the school gate and felt a pang of something in his stomach, and half-way along the road he turned and looked back at the school, punched the air with two fists and shouted, "Thank you," and hoped nobody had seen him.

The weeks before David was to go to Cambridge were hectic but enjoyable. He spent time in North Yorkshire visiting the Gray family with John. Now the children were older, the time they spent together was different but always good fun, and he had time to speak to Joel about what life was like at Cambridge. Mr Gray was happy to take David with him on call out if he wished to go, and on this visit, he was able to see Bill and Dora. He only saw Bill briefly because he had to leave for work but spent a whole day with Dora. He could tell they were happy the way she related how their lives had changed since they sold their farm and moved to their new home and a different way of life for them.

"Life is so much better for us here," she explained. "Bill doesn't have to get up at 4 am every day, he works when he's asked, which isn't everyday, so he's had chance to establish his garden and grow vegetables. In the winter, he hardly works at all, just the odd day, never refuses, but feels he should leave the work for the younger farm hands who need the wages to pay the rent, put food on their tables and bring up their young families. No one knows our circumstances, but Bill feels that because we have money in the bank from the sale of the farm, he should not take work opportunities away from those who need it. Mr Priestley is a good landlord and employer and treats his tenants very well, and because he does, he gets the best out of them, loyalty and a willingness to work hard. We all have a week each year rent free and a week off to visit relatives if we wish."

"That's great," said David. "You could visit us next year. Come down on the train."

They wandered down the country lanes, taking in the most stunning views and smelling the different changing aromas from the meadows and hedgerows. The border collies were still enthusiastic about being out and about, but now they were older, they trotted along at heel and just had the odd surge of enthusiasm if they saw a rabbit.

"You should see what it's like up here in winter," said Dora, "I've never seen anything like it. The farmers seemed to know the bad weather was on its way, and the cattle were brought into the barns, but the snow came whilst sheep were still out on the hills, so Bill and the dogs were out there helping to rescue them. The snow came in the night and was so deep, when we opened the door in the morning to let the dogs out, they disappeared. They spent the whole day battling through the deep snow and were exhausted, as was Bill when they returned, but with the job done. I think we need two pups to work with them and learn, because really, they are too old for that kind of work now."

They walked back to the cottage and sat outside to have lunch—home-grown tomato, cheese and fresh-baked bread, and a slice of rhubarb tart with cream and a cup of tea.

"This is so good," said David, "and you can do this every day if you want to."

"Well, not quite," replied Dora, smiling. "There is housework to do, and I go to the WI or other functions in the village hall, which usually means baking something, but compared to the farm, my life is much easier."

"What's the WI?" asked David, so Dora explained, and he was pleased she had things to do with friends that were interesting and new.

Mr Gray and John arrived to collect David. Dora hugged him tight, her eyes filling with tears. "Come again," she said, "and bring Jake with you, and don't forget all about us when you go to university."

She gave him a bag with some jars of chutney, jam, and a cabbage, solid and as large as a football from Bill's garden.

David wound the car window down and blew her a kiss. "Think about coming down to visit us next year," he shouted as the car moved away. "Tell Bill I was sorry not to see much of him today."

Dora stood waving until the car disappeared, and then she went into the house and talked to the dogs.

Chapter 25

There was much to chat about on the journey back home, and David was very enthusiastic about Dora and Bill visiting them the following summer.

"They have never been on a train or seen the ocean," David informed Jake and John.

"Neither had you, just a few years ago," retorted Jake, smiling.

"Yes, I know," replied David, "but they are a lot older than me."

"Point taken," said John, "but in the meantime, let's get you off to Cambridge, and that will be another first for you."

The next few weeks were hectic. They shopped for new clothes, for David had mainly had a school uniform and in any case, had grown so much he needed just about everything. Fay and her mother had knitted him a grey cable knit zip-up cardigan which he wore most of his student life until it was bursting at the seams and had huge holes on the elbows. John and Jake had bought him an iron and ironing board, which he wasn't too keen on taking, but Jake explained to him that if, in the future, he wanted to transfer to a teaching hospital, a clean and tidy student would be a preferable candidate, and if he kept his room tidy, he would always know where things were when needed.

John turned up with a box from the joiner in the village, with a built-in lock and two keys.

"What's that for?" asked David.

"To keep any food in that doesn't need to be in the communal fridge," explained John, "because unless things have changed a lot, and I gather they have not, anything edible, even if it has your name on it, disappears. I'm not suggesting you shouldn't share, but you do need to control things. I'm assuming you will use the student restaurant to get a square meal, but there will be times when it's not convenient, and you will need something to hand in your room."

Gradually, David began to realise that going to Cambridge was not simply to further his education, but that he was to be responsible totally for his wellbeing on a daily basis, and he found the thought quite daunting. There would be no Fay to make his breakfast and tea or do his washing and ironing, and John and Jake would not be there to help with his studies if he was struggling, although he knew he could telephone them.

The day before he left for Cambridge, he had walked into the village to buy extra ink and call in and see the butcher and say 'farewell'. As he walked back home, he stopped at the top of the lane at 'Ted's place' and leaned on the wall and wondered what Ted would have been doing had he lived.

John was to borrow his colleague's estate car to take David to Cambridge, and they were to load it up that afternoon, so David took himself off along the coastal path and propped himself up on a mound of sand and sat with his eyes shut and just listened to the ocean and seemed calmer for being there.

The following morning, they were away early, John and Jake in the front seats, David in the back surrounded with luggage and boxes. For some unexplained reason, Jake said, "I wonder what Rebecca will be doing today, do you ever think about her, David?"

"Yes, I do," David replied, "especially at Christmas. Maybe she is working already if she didn't stay on for her 'A' levels. She did well at school. Did Mr Brown say anything when you spoke to him?"

"Not really," said Jake, "he just said she was doing well at school as well as running the home and looking after her next-door neighbour. I think she would be doing her 'A' levels if she was still at school when I spoke to him."

"I really liked Rebecca," said David. "She was always kind to me and stuck up for me when the rest of them were just cruel."

No one would have guessed, at that moment in time, that their paths would cross again.

Cambridge was busy, bustling in excitement and awe, clattering and banging as cases and boxes were dragged along corridors and upstairs, mother's crying and fussing, fathers just wanting to get away, and students already settled in were wandering about, assisting or sending people deliberately in the wrong direction.

David's belongings were taken to his room and left, so they could move the car and find a tea room for a snack away from the bedlam of the university.

"Right," said John, "time to make tracks. Can you find your way back to your room?"

John and Jake shook David's hand and got in the car.

"You'll be fine," said Jake, reassuringly, "and you can always telephone us if you have a problem."

David stood on the pavement, quite stunned that they had left him, waved until the car disappeared and turned and made his way back to his accommodation.

John laughed out loud. "He'll wonder what has hit him during these next few days, but he's a man now, independent, and will have to learn to survive on his own."

"He'll do it all right," said Jake. "He survived much worse at a very young age," remembering how David was a lonely boy surviving a harsh situation, with nothing but the clothes on his back and no friends apart from Rebecca when he had met him at first.

David had stood by the door of his room and looked around at all the boxes, bags and suitcases and finally made a start at unpacking, realising that somewhere there should be some bedding, and until he found it, he couldn't make up the bed for sleeping in. He hid the ironing board and iron inside the wardrobe with his clothes, and everything else was stowed away neatly, and his bed was made up within the hour. Fay had sent some cheese and onion pasty and tomatoes, a loaf of bread, butter, jam, biscuits, tea and a carton of milk, so he didn't have to go looking for something to eat on his first day. He pushed the wooden box containing tinned food under his bed out of sight, put the key on a little ledge, and went looking for the communal kitchen and showers.

From his window, he could see there were lots of students about, so he decided to go for a walk and look at a notice board he had seen earlier, and on his return, he couldn't help himself and had to telephone home.

"Hello," said Jake.

"Hello," said David, "just wanted to check you had got back ok. I've unpacked and made up my bed and had a wander around, and I'm just on my way back to have something to eat. Please thank Fay for the food."

"Thank you for calling," said Jake. "You'll be fine. Keep up with your studies, but get involved with other things too, university isn't just about passing exams, and it's fine to join groups and have fun. When you come home for Christmas, you will have changed so much. What have you done with the ironing board?"

"It fits in the wardrobe," replied David, laughing, "otherwise it would have gone under the bed."

"We thought so," said Jake, "but nevertheless, it will be useful, eventually. Take care. God bless."

The money ran out. David felt comforted having spoken to Jake, and went back to his room and had something to eat before trying out the showers and getting ready for bed. He read for a while and then lay in his bed missing the swish and rush of the ocean, finally falling asleep, opening another new chapter in his life.

The following few days were taken up finding his way about the college, what his timetable was for lectures and where he needed to be and visiting a hall where students seemed to gather and learn about what was available other than studies. He quite liked the idea of becoming a member of a choir, but as he stood in line to register, he overheard a conversation which prevented him making a fool of himself; he couldn't read music! He had considered the drama group but didn't know how much time he would have spare to learn lines, so in the end he decided to just go to debates and any extra lectures that attracted his attention until he knew he was free to make himself reliable.

When his lectures started for real, he was with a mixed group of students all the time, who blended together socially and had a lot of fun. David had not had a lot of contact with girls in the past but he was comfortable with them, and they liked him because he was considerate and polite with them. Needless to say, some of the boys ribbed him about this, but he just took it as a joke and suggested they might do well to take a leaf out of his book.

A month in, and he was settled into a routine and enjoying his lectures and felt he had chosen his course very well. He had become friends with Monique, who had called on him to return a book she had borrowed and found him ironing his shirts. He blushed and laughed nervously, having invited her in, but she didn't react at all in the way he had expected.

"I'll finish that," she said. "Any coffee going?"

Before she left she had negotiated using the iron once a week in exchange for free French conversation lessons. David was happy to accept and this arrangement continued for two years.

Monique came from a family living in France, and she and her boyfriend Jean were studying with a view to returning home to work in the family pharmaceutical business, so it seemed their future was mapped out for them, but David at this time had no dedicated medical curriculum planned.

A group of friends had called on David to join them at a music night at the pub, so although he had been avoiding these nights out if he could, he went along, put his money in the kitty and kept drinking the glasses of cider that appeared until he felt the need for fresh air.

There was a quacking and a splashing, and David woke up, having been laid on a bench, somewhere. He sat up slowly, shivering with cold, the pattern of the bench slats embossed in his cheek, and a film of dew dampening his cardigan, shining like seed pearls, head pounding, eye lids heavy.

Where on earth am I? he thought. *What time is it?*

He managed to focus on the time from his watch, it was almost 4 am, so he waited until a clock struck 4, and stood to head in that direction, but as he turned, the world spun, and he was violently sick. "Phew," he said, several times, as he walked unsteadily on the path. He stopped and leaned against a tree and was sick again and felt so utterly wretched.

Finally, he reached his room, and was pleased no one had seen him. He had a shower to warm up and washed the splashes off his trousers and shoes and sat wrapped in a blanket sipping a cup of boiled water and nibbling at a thick slice of plain bread, before he took two aspirins and went to bed.

He had seen his ma in a drunken state so many times, and couldn't understand why she, and so many others, would do it, and was now aware of what had happened to her organs at the end of her life.

At least she always found her way home, thought David, smiling, as he snuggled into his covers and went to sleep. Nine hours later, he woke up, still feeling fragile, still with a headache, but not feeling sick anymore. Fortunately, it was a Saturday, so there were no lectures, he had made no plans, the time was his own to have a bowl of porridge and go for a walk. He tried to recollect the evening before and could not remember how he got to where he ended up.

"What happened to you last night?" asked one of the boys walking towards him who had been in the group in the pub.

"Just had enough," replied David. "Needed some fresh air."

"Are you up for tonight, then?" asked the boy. "The group are on again."

"Thanks, but not tonight, have some work to catch up on," replied David politely, but that was not what he was thinking.

Monique and Jean had invited David to go home with them for Christmas, but he declined. He had adjusted very well to university life, but deep in his heart, he was homesick and wanted to go and be with Jake and John for Christmas, and there was still the matter of obtaining a passport.

One of the students did knitting to make some extra money, so she had gone with David to buy the wool of his chosen colours, and had cable knit a jumper for John and Jake for their Christmas presents. When they were finished, he was thrilled with them and paid the girl more than she had asked. She sat and had a cup of tea with him and explained she had been very foolish with a boy and had a baby who was being looked after by her mother, and that anything she earned, she sent towards his keep. Her parents had insisted she attended university, having obtained a place, so she had to do well to secure a good future for her and her child.

"No one knows, here," she said. "Please don't tell anyone."

"Don't worry," said David, "I can't remember what you just told me."

"Thank you," she said, smiled and left.

As a result of that conversation, David ended up with quite a few jumpers and pullovers over the next two years and a pair of thick multi-coloured striped socks for Fay to wear with her boots made from wool left over.

It was dark when Jake met David off the train, and there was a biting wind, so it was such a pleasurable moment to step into the kitchen, feel the warmth and smell Fay's stew. She ran and hugged him, still with dumpling dough on her fingers. "I've missed you," she said, "but I was pleased to hear you had settled. Is that bag full of washing?" she asked.

"More or less," replied David, "but I'm really good at ironing now."

"That's wonderful news, I'll test you," said Fay and winked at Jake.

David went up to his room with his bag of presents, put them in his wardrobe and went and sat on his window seat and looked out, but there was no moon, so it was pitch black, and the tide must have been out because he couldn't even hear the ocean. The room seemed so big compared to his room at university, and his thoughts went back to the very first time he slept in the huge bed in fresh white sheets and huge bouncy pillows.

The stew and dumplings were welcome, and after tea, when the washing up was done, David sat with Jake and John in the lounge, in front of a glowing fire, and chatted until almost midnight without any one realising it was so late.

David was saddened to hear that Annie had died. Jake had decided not to tell David at the time because he didn't think it necessary, and they sent flowers and a letter to the family and included David in their messages. Annie had become more confused and took to going out in the middle of the night in her nightie and slippers and eventually caught pneumonia and didn't recover. She could be brittle sometimes, but she loved David and took care of him in her own way, and he knew this and relied on her so much when he moved to John's home. When he went to bed, he took the spoon from his memory box that he had saved from the cottage and slept with it under his pillow.

The following morning, straight after breakfast, he put on his boots, winter coat, scarf and cap and set off along the coastal road. He took deep breaths of the salty air and closed his eyes and felt the dampness on his face as the waves crashed against the rocks. He felt a chill thinking of Ted as he walked to the place he had spent so much time in the past, but he couldn't curl up and be sheltered anymore, because he had grown so much.

He was feeling the cold when he returned to the house, so he made some tea and sat and had a chat with Fay.

"You are going to have to find another twig if you want to trim one up for Christmas," she said.

"What happened to it?" asked David.

"I knocked the pile of logs onto it, and it smashed, so I burnt it," she replied hurriedly, glad to get it off her chest.

David laughed, "I'll find another. Have you been worrying about telling me?"

"Well, a little bit," replied Fay. "I knew it was special to you."

"That was when I was a child," said David. "Now I'm a man, or so John keeps telling me, so I'd better behave like one."

"John has booked for you all to go to the hotel for Christmas dinner, he just didn't see the point of all the work involved making it, I'm having four days off, so I'm cooking a beef joint and a ham for you to have, and you can shop and get the trimmings to have with it," said Fay.

David asked about the children, who were all doing well, her eldest son now had a job on the building site, so an extra wage made life much easier for her, and her eldest daughter helped care for the two younger ones which helped Fay's mother and gave her some spare time.

After lunch, David set off for the village and was amazed at the progress in the fields. The previous night, as he had travelled home with Jake, it was dark, and the workmen had long gone, so he never noticed or even thought about the new buildings. The houses were almost complete on the outside and were very impressive. He couldn't believe the progress made since he had left for Cambridge, but the developer had kept his promise to John, and it was going to be a fine group of houses made from dressed quarry stone.

He called to see the butcher and promptly got the job of deliveries for Christmas, as Fay's son was not able to do them because he was now working, and the butcher had been closing the shop and doing them himself, as he had done before David came along.

"Just the Christmas deliveries and New Year," said the butcher.

"I hope you've got a bigger bike," said David. "I'm too big for the old one."

"I'll sort that out," replied the butcher. "Come up on the 23rd."

David accompanied John to the carol service at his old school and was pleased to see some of the masters who had taught him and were interested in how he was doing at university. There was the familiar smell of polish and sweaty teenage boys, but he loved being there, it was like his starting block to a new life, and he had enjoyed his time there.

Christmas Day was different, they opened their presents and took a long walk along the coast and through the fields to the hotel for Christmas dinner. The dining room was full and everyone seemed to know John and Jake, but the atmosphere was jovial and relaxed, the food good, and by the time they left, it was getting dark.

They lit the fire in the lounge and watched television during the evening, feeling very lazy. David leaned back in his chair and closed his eyes.

"Are you all right?" asked John.

David nodded. "Just thinking about my ma, she was in hospital, very ill, on Christmas day when I saw her for the last time, it's seven years ago now, and she would never believe what has happened to me since."

"If she hadn't died, your life would have taken a completely different path," said Jake, "and you would have known nothing of this life."

"Yes, I know," said David emotionally, "and I have so much to thank you both for."

"You don't have to consider that all the time," said Jake. "I'm just glad we were able to help."

John took out his handkerchief and pretended to sob, wipe his eyes and blow his nose. "I could do with a cup of cocoa to calm me," he said.

John broke the mood and David made the cocoa, and because it was Christmas, they had a splash of brandy in it.

On Boxing Day, John had two call outs, there was a telephone call from Dora and Bill who had walked up to the telephone box in their village. It had been snowing where they lived, not much, but the sky was threatening. They had had a quiet Christmas but were quite content and enjoyed the chat with David.

"Better get back," said Bill. "The snow is falling again, thick and fast. Happy New Year to you all."

David spent a lot of time walking along the coastal road during his break, alone or with Jake, because John was busy working. He liked it because every day was different, the light over the ocean, its power or gentleness, the gentle ripples of a tide, or the pounding and crashing of an angry sea against the rocks.

In conversation about David's lectures and subjects, Jake asked if he knew where his studies were taking him, but he didn't know at that time, and Jake knew he had to let him find his own way into something he would enjoy, rather than being pressured into something he didn't really want to do.

David knew there would be good advice from Jake and John whenever he needed it, but he wasn't ready to make a decision yet, maybe the end of his first academic year and results of his exams would guide him.

They watched the New Year in on television. Jake had pointed out to David there was a dance in the village hall, but David declined. "Can't dance," he said. "I'd look a bit stupid, don't you think?"

"Better ask Fay to give you some lessons for next year," said John. "You're young, you should be out there having fun."

"I have fun in Cambridge," said David, "I'm going back in two days, so I'm happy here right now."

Chapter 26

David returned to Cambridge by train after the Christmas break. His holdall contained his clean clothes, a new blanket, the transistor radio and two hot water bottles and a pair of slippers he had been given at Christmas and a case containing his bedding and towels and a bag with butter, cheese, bread, jam and chutney. He struggled from the station to his room through the unusually quiet, frost-bitten streets.

His room was cold, smelt foisty and was unwelcoming, so he lit the fire and sat wrapped in his blanket until the room had warmed. He made up his bed and put the hot water bottles in, hung up his clothes, went to the kitchen to warm up a can of soup, which he enjoyed with the cheese and bread, and then sat listening to his radio, the most wonderful present he had received from John and Jake at Christmas.

He looked down at his slippers, shook his head and smiled. *I'm sat here like an old man*, he thought. *Just need a pipe.*

The following morning, he was awake early and after his porridge decided to take a walk along the banks of the river Cam. He crunched his way along the hoar-frosted pavement towards the bridge, breaking the unusual silence of the college grounds. *It's like being in a negative*, he thought. *Everything is grey, black and white, and how is it the ducks don't get frost bite in their feet?* He continued until he came to some sheds and a huge greenhouse and was just about to turn back and retrace his steps when someone said, "What are you doing here?"

"Just having a walk," replied David, recognising the gardener responsible for the beautiful college grounds during the spring and summer. "Not much you can do this weather, is there?"

"Come inside and have a look," said the gardener. "You'll be surprised."

He was a strange man, small, with a spine curvature and gnarled fingers, but his creativity in the gardens was wonderful. He just did what he had to do in the grounds, as early as possible in the summer light and tried to avoid contact with the students, some of who could be very cruel and vocal about him. He showed David his drawings which set out his plans for the flower beds for the summer and where some were already showing signs of growth, in rows of little pots.

"I don't have to worry too much about spring," explained the gardener. "Tulips and daffodils follow the snowdrops every year, but everything needs to be ready to go in when they have died off."

"My home is by the sea," said David. "Not a lot grows in the salty air, but we do have a bright orange flower that grows in the hedgerows each year, montbretia, I think they call it,"

A kettle whistled in a corner. "Would you like a cup of Bovril before you return?" asked the gardener.

David welcomed the warm drink, hugged the mug and walked around the greenhouse as the gardener pointed out different plants to him with the most ridiculous names. "It's like a foreign language to me," said David. "How do you remember them all?"

The gardener doffed his cap as David left and smiled, having really enjoyed some company for a while with a young man who was not abusive but polite and seemed interested in what he was doing.

During the next few days, students returned, and life became what was normal for Cambridge. David was enjoying his lectures, trained with the hockey teams and was good enough to be chosen to play from time to time, played tennis in the summer, went swimming and running to maintain his fitness, became involved organising the college float for the Rag Week, joining his friends to go to London to watch the boat race and just thoroughly enjoying being a student. He would still hover in the background in a new situation, but now he had the confidence to step forward when he had considered what was involved and offer his opinion.

His work ethic was good regarding his studies, he couldn't face John and Jake if he had failed in his first year, and it paid off because his results were very good. He spoke to his tutors towards the end of the academic year, and they had suggested he would do well in research or in the more practical side of medicine. During a visit to a hospital theatre to observe surgery, he was the only student who didn't react by fainting or having to leave to be sick but was in fact keen to take a closer look even though he did feel squeamish at the beginning.

He discussed the matter with John and Jake, as he had done over the Christmas break, and they had been very careful to ensure he understood what would be required in time and dedication, and once into the practical side in a hospital environment, it would be like starting all over again, another three years of study at least.

In the end, he decided to go for it and let his tutors know, so his lectures planned for the following year were appropriate and decided if he had made a mistake in his choice, he would go for plan 'B' and do research.

Once the exams were over, most students went home, but David delayed for a few more days just to avoid the chaos. He sat on a blanket in the grounds by the river with a book, enjoying a packed lunch in the sunshine when he overheard names being shouted at the gardener who was working in a nearby bed of flowers. When he heard the name 'Quasimodo' shouted, he got up and walked towards the group of boys. "That's enough," said David, "you have no right to be so rude to anyone, it's cruel, what would your parents think about you if they could hear you? And in any case, you are wasting your time, the gardener's deaf. Move on and leave him alone." All but one moved on quietly, and he had to turn and two-finger David, who just shook his head and wondered, *what are you doing here, behaving in such a way?*

When the students had gone, the gardener turned and smiled at David. "I never thought of that one," he said. "Perhaps if word gets 'round I'm deaf, they'll leave me alone."

Jake collected David and all his belongings from his room and had to laugh when he saw David had wrapped the ironing board in newspaper and tied it underneath the box with the lock. Likewise, Fay laughed when she helped unload the car when they arrived home, but David was quite smug about the fact that he had been able to conceal it and was not going to be ruffled by their comments.

He spent the rest of the day sorting his things out in his room. Jake had told him to make his course notes available to read before he went back to Cambridge and to just glance at them from time to time to refresh his memory. The holiday was long, and Jake kept his eye on David and spent time with him on the pretext that he was interested in what he had been doing at university, but it was his way of getting David to look at his notes now and again, so he didn't return with a total memory loss. Jake had a gentle way with him, and David would never cross him. They did differ in opinions sometimes, but Jake was clever, he wanted David to realise it was all right not to agree about things all the time, but to be able to put his case thoughtfully and be willing to listen and consider another opinions.

John returned from the surgery and they sat and enjoyed the chicken dinner Fay had cooked.

"I thought I might go along the coast for a walk," David said, after he had cleared away and washed up.

"You need to be careful," said John. "The steps down through the garden are very unsafe. We need to get some mix from the builders and try and secure them."

"Can't one of the builders do the job?" David asked, not realising it was a job they had saved for him to do when he came home.

"We've got someone to do it," replied John, hiding behind the newspaper he was reading. "They call him David."

"I can't ruin my hands if I'm going to be a surgeon," said David, but the comment fell on deaf ears, and the following morning, after breakfast, he wandered up the lane with an empty bucket for some concrete mix from the builders. He stood for a while looking at the new houses being built and noticed that one of them had an occupant already.

"The developer is living there at the moment with his family and dogs. It became necessary to have someone on site, so much stuff was being pinched. If you decide to go and see him, be sure the dogs are in their pen, they are angry beasts, that's why he has them," said the builder.

He asked David why he needed the concrete mix and returned to the house with him and showed him how to go about fixing the steps, and when Jake and John returned home later in the day, the job was done. David had nailed a notice on a piece of wood at the top of the steps which read:

DO NOT USE THESE STEPS FOR 2 DAYS OR YOU WILL SPOIL THE PRISTINE WORK DONE BY A STEP REPAIRER EXTRAORDINAIRE.

Fay confirmed David had been working all day, alone, and it just left Jake and John bemused.

The following morning, David appeared for breakfast like a creaking gate.

"What's the matter with you?" asked John, as David sat down very carefully.

"I don't think I'm cut out for manual labour," replied David, "and I've ruined my hands, just look at them."

He showed the row of blisters on the palms of his hands to John.

"Need some iodine on those," said John. "Come up to the surgery with me. Why didn't I see those last night?"

David shrugged his shoulders and winced as the backs of his upper arms objected to the movement.

"Pride," said Jake, smiling and nodding at David. "However, no pain, no gain, and you have done a really good job. You don't fancy being a builder then?

"I'm not considering a career change at this moment in time," replied David emphatically.

He went to the surgery with John and had the blisters treated and dressed and walked back home wondering what he could do for the following few days, until his hands healed. He managed to slide down the garden and walk along the path to the beach, and he was so happy to be out there. He kicked sand into a mound, leaned against it, and sat for a long time watching a small fishing boat bobbing on the water. The boat came in with the tide, and David ended up with fresh fish to take home from the same fisherman that had given him some before.

"Haven't seen you about for a while," said the fisherman.

"No," said David, "I'm away at university now. It's good, but I do miss this place."

"I hope the bay doesn't get spoilt when the new houses are occupied," said the fisherman, sounding concerned, "I hope the access through your garden isn't available to them."

"I don't know about that," said David. "I'll mention it to my uncle."

During the evening, David did mention the conversation he had with the fisherman, and John reassured him, "Nothing to worry about there, tell him when you see him again."

During the following weeks, David accompanied Jake to the hospital, and was allowed to observe in the theatre, he visited school and stayed for their end-of-year service and had coffee with the masters in the staff room and managed to keep himself occupied before he and John left for their visit to the Gray's home in North Yorkshire, and he was very excited because when they returned, he was to travel back by train with Dora and Bill, who were to have a holiday, travel on a train and visit the coast, all new experiences for them.

These trips were always interesting, there was always something happening at the vet's, or at the farms, or in the village, and as David became more mature, he realised how much John enjoyed this time in a totally different environment, and that Mr Gray was his only close friend. John had been a quiet, reserved man, and being the local GP had distanced him from the people in the village, but he was content in his bubble until David came along and burst it.

David accompanied Mr Gray on some of his call outs to farms and spent some time in the clinic observing. An elderly lady brought her old dog in with a lump on its side, and Mr Gray explained to David that although he was to go in and investigate, his experience told him he would not be able to help, and he was right. He stitched up the wound and moved the dog onto a table in another room, still anesthetised.

"Now David, this will be good experience for you," said Mr Gray. "I want you to go and speak to the lady and explain the situation to her. She will want to come and say 'goodbye' to her dog before I put it to sleep, so you will accompany her and bring her to this room."

"Really," said David, totally unprepared for it. "Will you be here? I don't know the lady."

"I will be here," said Mr Gray, "but this situation will be part of your training in the fullness of time."

David took a few deep breaths and went towards the lady in the waiting room, but he didn't have to say anything before she covered her face with her hands and burst into tears.

"Is she dead?" she gulped out.

"No," replied David, gently, "but Mr Gray needs you to come and see her, I'm afraid there is little he can do."

He helped the lady to her feet and guided her into the room where Mr Gray explained everything to her.

"We will leave you to have a few moments on your own if you wish," said Mr Gray. "You can stay as I put her to sleep so you know she didn't suffer at the end, if you wish, or you can leave before I do it."

They left the lady but could hear her talking quietly to her beloved dog, and then they heard her moving towards the door to speak to Mr Gray. Her eyes were red and swollen, and her voice was shaky. "I knew she would have to leave me today," she said. "It was almost as if she was asking me to let her go this morning."

David asked her about her dog and listened to her story as Mr Gray injected the dog.

"She's gone," he said, "free from pain. She had a wonderful life, better than some children I shouldn't wonder." He took off the dog's collar and handed it to the lady, and David walked her to the gate and asked her if she would have another.

"Not now," she said, "I'm too old to take on another. If I die, what would happen to it?"

He felt her pain as she trudged along the path to her empty home, head down, dabbing her eyes.

David walked back into the surgery. "Didn't like that much," he said to Mr Gray. "She lives alone, she told me, she felt safe with her dog and had someone to talk to."

"The matter is finished with now, David," said Mr Gray. "You have to move on, you have to learn not to let things trouble you, or you'll never be able to do your job. I'm not suggesting you will have to put your patients to sleep," he said smiling, "but dealing with bad news is part of the job. Lesson learnt?"

"Yes," said David, realising why Mr Gray had involved him, "what's next then?"

"Two dogs to be castrated," replied Mr Gray, peering at David over his spectacles with a bemused look, "and that will be it for this morning."

Mrs Gray served lunch outside, it was such a lovely day. The panoramic view was stunning, a patchwork of pastures and hedgerows like a knitted crosspatch blanket over the ground. Tractors were chugging away in some of the fields, turning over the soil or gathering in whatever crops they had grown and just now and again, if something set them off, the geese ripped into the quietness with their squawking.

The telephone rang. "Cow in trouble giving birth, coming David?" asked Mr Gray.

"We need to go and visit Dora and Bill," said John. "I've arranged it for this afternoon."

"Sorry," said David, looking at Mr Gray, but he wasn't really, he preferred to visit Dora and Bill than look at a cow in distress in labour. He'd done that before and wasn't sure what Mr Gray might have had him doing this time, so he was glad to be able to decline.

Dora stood with her arms outstretched for a cuddle as David ran towards her, the dogs came fussing and barking, and Bill stood and shook John's hand and took him to look at his vegetable patch before they all sat down together and made the arrangements for the weekend. John was to collect them and drive them to the station, and David was to accompany Dora and Bill on the train and John return home in his car. There were train changes to be made en route, and having David travel with them made the journey stress free. The landlord had arranged for one of the young farmhands to have the dogs, there were just two days to wait, and Dora was very excited, Bill, it was hard to tell, but David was determined to make it memorable for them.

"Can you pack some sandwiches?" asked David. "We will be travelling a long time. John will take the luggage in the car, but just remember, you will have to carry it when you return."

Dora stood well back on the platform as the train arrived, hissing and scraping to a standstill. She had seen trains gliding along like pencil lines through the countryside from a distance but never been so close before. The steam engine pulled the carriages two stations further along the line, and then everyone had to change and wait for the next train which had a diesel engine and was much more modern inside. Once settled, they all enjoyed the journey. Dora sat enthralled at the window, Bill nodded off, and David read the newspaper for a while. Dora thought it was wonderful that they had a table between them and could eat their lunch from it. Another change of train at another station down the line, and this would take them home to be met by Jake.

John had set off home as soon as he had dropped them off at the station, and as he read the road signs, he decided on a diversion and went to look at the farm which had been Bill and Dora's. He pulled into the lane leading to the farm and drove slowly to a metal gate where two German shepherd dogs were barking furiously. He sat in the car as a man came towards him. "What are you doing here?" he asked.

"I was looking for Bill," said John.

"They are long gone," replied the man.

"Do you know where I can find them?" asked John, feeling sure that would be the next normal question.

"No one knows," replied the man. "Let me move the truck so you can turn 'round."

"Thank you," said John. "Sorry to trouble you."

The man waved and went back through the gate and into his house, and John drove down the lane and decided to go for a snack in the pub where they had all met up before.

He went to the bar to order a sandwich and pot of tea.

"Not from these parts, then?" asked the landlord. "Not by the sound of your accent."

"That's right," said John, "I thought I'd call on old friends on my travels, but they've moved on and the farmer doesn't know where."

"Oh! You mean Bill and Dora? They moved on a long time ago, they sold the farm and did a moonlight."

"I thought the son would have taken over the farm," said John.

"Not him," said the landlord. "A waste of space, he was. Got in with the wrong crowd, I dare say, but he was never going to work hard enough to be a farmer. He did call here a couple of times in the past, but he's in the army now, had to join up to get a roof over his head."

"What a shame," said John. "Good afternoon, I'll be on my way." He had no intention of making the diversion but something in the canyons of his mind drew him back to the farm, and now he felt assured Bill and Dora were truly 'lost'. He never mentioned to them that he'd been, no point in opening old wounds, but should they ever mention their anxieties, he could reassure them.

When he arrived home, everyone was there, wondering where he had been and just relieved he was all right. "Stopped for something to eat," he said. "Should have telephoned, I suppose."

Fay had made a meat and potato pie with mushy peas and a huge rice pudding with a nutmeggy skin in a small enamel washing up bowl. She stayed and had the meal with them as all her children were doing something with their grandma, and it gave her a chance to get to know the guests a little.

David took Dora and Bill to his room, with their suitcase, and took them to the window so they could see the ocean. The house had the same effect on them as it had on David in the beginning, it seemed vast, and of course they had never had a bathroom, just a tin bath.

"Use the wardrobe," said David, "and there are towels there in the corner for you. Come back down when you have unpacked."

Bill enjoyed a glass of port with John and Jake before bedtime, and David made cocoa for him and Dora. They were all tired, but Dora insisted on washing the cups and glasses up before she went to bed and had a good look around the kitchen.

Chapter 27

The rain had fallen heavily during the night, so David decided to wait until the afternoon before he took Dora and Bill to the beach, and then the tide would be out but on the turn. Dora was happy being around Fay, and Bill took himself off into the garden and started to sort out Fay's herb garden.

David was concerned about Dora and Bill negotiating the steep steps down the garden onto the path, but they were fine, and as they walked along the path to the beach, Dora stopped. "I can hear it," she said, like an excited school girl. When they reached the beach, Dora and Bill stopped. "Just look at that," said Bill. "I never imagined anything like it." Dora and Bill stood arm in arm for a long time, taking in the view, whilst David and Jake leaned against the wall and waited until they were ready to move on.

"We can walk on the sand," said David. "You may find some shells to take home for your dresser."

"The tide is on its way in," said Jake, "and it races across the beach, so we had better stay on the path. The time to look for shells is when the tide has gone out."

They walked along the coastal road, and David felt so happy that Dora and Bill were enjoying it so much. They were outdoor people, so the sea breeze and the spray from the waves didn't worry them at all. On their return to the house, they were surprised that the beach had almost disappeared in a short space of time. They stood and watched for a while, and Jake explained about the tides and the power of the ocean that would devour whatever it could. David thought about Ted at that moment, he was never sure whether he had just been careless, or really intended to jump onto the rocks, despite the note he had left David, who had always hoped that if it was intentional, the fall had killed him, and he wasn't floundering about in the water wanting to change his mind. He shuddered and went to talk to Dora.

"What did you think about that, then?" he asked as they climbed back up the steps to the house.

"Wonderful," she replied. "Can we go again before we go home?"

"Every day, if you wish," replied David. "There's no special time, we can always get along the path even when the tide is in."

Jake and Bill sat outside enjoying a beer and talking about the farm.

"I was never sure I was doing the right thing, selling the farm and moving away from our roots as we did," said Bill, "but a month into our new life, I was wishing I had done it years ago. My life is so much easier now, and Dora has a social life, and all this has come at the right time as we get older. We are in a place that is peaceful, as you know, the people are good and solid, and I'm able to pass some skills on to the youngsters, it's a perfect situation. I know Dora would like to know what has happened to our son, and she frets over not being able to see our grandchild, but we don't dwell on it. I can't imagine the women would want to keep a baby, she was too much of a good-time girl and too lazy to be a mother. I hope it was put up for adoption and gone to a good home."

David could hear Dora and Fay laughing. There was no doubt those two would get along. Dora didn't have a fridge, but there was one in the village hall kitchen, so she knew about them, but all the other gadgets were new to her, and she had just covered herself with batter from the electric mixer.

David joined them. "What's going on?" he said, looking at Dora with raised eyebrows.

"I've just been battered," she replied. "I think we need to start again, my way, with a fork."

David walked up to the surgery to meet John, feeling guilty that they were all having a good time and he was having to work. He sat in the waiting room and read a Reader's Digest for the umpteenth time until John had finished.

They walked down the lane together, stopping to look at the progress in the fields. The foreman came across to them and chatted for a while and informed them that in a month's time, they would be laying the pavement and kerbs and putting down a road surface, and John should bear that in mind regarding where he left his car.

"We'll go up to London then, do you think?" he asked David.

"Great," replied David, who enjoyed so much his visits to London.

They had toad in the hole for tea and cabbage from Bill's garden, cleared away and watched Sunday Night at the London Palladium on the television. Dora sat on the edge of her seat all the time, 'oohing; at the costumes of the dancers, the magician, laughing at the game with contestants and just totally enthralled.

"Do they have this on every Sunday?" she asked.

Bill looked at her, he knew what was rattling around in her mind, but she didn't say anything, she saved that conversation for the journey home.

Another first, the following day when they went to see The King and I at the cinema in town, and Bill treated them all to tea and cake before they had a brief walk along the river bank and returned home. Dora hooked up with David and sang what she could remember of 'Getting to Know You' and talked about the costumes and children in the film, pictures that remained in her mind for a long time.

It was windy, and dark clouds were rolling across the sky, and David knew the coastline would be dramatic, so he suggested they might go down and walk along the coastal road if they wished. Of course, Bill and Dora did want to see as much as they could during their visit, so off they went, dressed appropriately for getting wet.

The sea came thundering in and boomed as it hit the rocks and sprayed the air and soaked them as it fell. Dora clung on to Bill and pulled him back, but she still wanted to stay and watch. Sometimes it was difficult to tell what Bill was thinking, he didn't react as openly as Dora, but his expression was one of awe and wonder as he shook his head from side to side. Once they had returned home and had a change of clothes and were sitting round the table having their evening meal, Bill spoke about the experience.

"I never even imagined what the ocean would be like, I never thought I would see it, and I just have to thank you for this whole experience. There's such force in the water, and I know there is because of the water mills used on the rivers that drive machinery, but I never imagined anything like we've just seen. Paintings of the sea shore tell you nothing, you have to experience it, and we certainly did tonight."

"I thought we could have a picnic on the beach tomorrow," said David. "That is, if it's a nice day, but the weather forecast on the radio says it will be."

Jake had given Fay the day off because they were having a picnic. "We can manage here," he had said, so she made a cheese and onion pasty for them before she left, and they just took it with tomatoes, hard boiled eggs, and current and mint pasty and bottles of water, and they were fine. They had taken the folding chairs and David's transistor radio, along with the food, and they spent several hours just relaxing and enjoying each other's company and stories. John joined them after surgery and went a walk with Bill and Jake along the coastal path. David stayed with Dora, for he knew she would be anxious about the tide coming in, and by the time the men returned, it was well on its way. They gathered their belongings and walked on to the path with the little waves snapping at their heels, and Dora turned and looked out at the ocean for the last time before they climbed the steps to the house.

The following day, Bill and Dora had a walk around the village on their own in the morning, bought a bottle of port for John and Jake and packed their suitcase ready to leave the following day. Fay had cooked a ham to have with new potatoes and salad and made an apple pie to have with cream. They all sat outside in the evening until the air cooled and then went inside for Dora to watch television for the last time. David wrote a note for Bill, printing the names of the stations where they had to change trains and the times of the trains.

"There's always someone to ask," said David, to reassure Bill, "and before you get your lift back to the cottage from your station, give us a quick call so we know you've arrived home safely."

The following morning, everyone was up early. Dora made sandwiches for the journey and took shortbread and apples and a bottle of water. She gave Fay a hug. "I've really enjoyed your company," she said, "You've been very kind, and I've enjoyed having my meals made for me, such a treat, thank you so much."

"It's been a pleasure for me too," said Fay. "Have a safe journey."

David had walked up to the station so there was room for everyone else in John's car. Jake and David waited with them for the train to arrive, checked Bill had remembered his list of stations and helped them with their luggage. Dora cried as she hugged David and was still dabbing her eyes with her handkerchief as they waved 'Goodbye' when the train heaved itself out of the station.

"I think they've really enjoyed themselves," David said to Jake.

"I'm sure," said Jake. "Bill assured me that they had, and it's been nice to have him around. We've been friends a good few years, and they were always good to me when I was on the road."

"Do you miss that freedom?" David asked.

"Sometimes," replied Jake, "but not for long, especially when there's a gale blowing, and I'm tucked up in a warm bed. I missed my career, and I'm glad to be back to my normal life."

When they returned home, Fay was working in David's room, changing the bedding, so he helped her turn the mattress and sat by his window and talked to her.

"Need to find something to do until we go up to London," he said.

"Try the hotel," Fay suggested. "They may have something you could do, and you would get paid, but they don't pay much, I can tell you that for sure."

David mentioned it to John, just in case he had something planned that he hadn't mentioned. John approved of him going, but not taking on work behind the bar. He didn't explain why, but David knew by the tone of his voice that he meant it.

Two hours later, he returned, he had secured 3 weeks' work starting at 11 am until 3 pm, serving bar snacks over the lunch period. He kept his fingers crossed John was ok with it, because he was to be in the bar, but not behind it, and it would make him some spending money for his trip to London. Now he was older and had access to his own money, he paid his way and didn't rely on John and Jake so much and took great pleasure in treating them from time to time.

They were sitting having cocoa round the kitchen table before going to bed when the telephone rang. The coin dropped into the box and Dora spoke. "We're here," she said, "safe and sound. We've had a wonderful time and will never forget it. I'm going to meet my dogs now, will call you next week. Bye." And she was gone.

"Thank goodness," said David. "I'm going to bed. I start work tomorrow."

"Tomorrow," said Jake, sounding surprised.

"The regular staff are taking their holidays before business picks up during the school holidays, when families come down to the coast," explained David.

He didn't care for working in a dingy, smoky atmosphere. The kitchen was very clean and run well, and he'd have been happier working in there, but it was not to be. He told John he didn't like it, but John instilled in him he had given his word to work for three weeks, and that he must do. The fact he didn't like it wasn't a good enough reason to let them down, so David persevered, for 21 days, no days off. He could manage to have a run along the coast to clear his lungs in an afternoon or just a walk with Jake.

"I need some fresh air when I've finished," David told him. "I think I'd become deranged if I stayed much longer. Why don't they open the windows and let some light and fresh air in and the smoke out?"

"I think it's supposed to be a cosy, intimate environment," said Jake.

"There's nothing cosy about having to squint to read your menu or see what's on your plate," said David, and then he realised he was having a rant at Jake who could do nothing about it, and they both burst out laughing.

Once he'd finished working at the hotel, he had a few days before he and John went up to London for a whole week. John was working at the hospital for the first three days, and then the time was theirs to do as they pleased. David always went with John to the hospital, managed to find a white coat, and would wander round at will, being careful not to draw attention to himself. John had warned him if he got himself into a tight corner, he would disown him, and whilst David didn't really believe him, he didn't want to be in a situation to find out. He always spent time in the children's ward, reading or playing games unless sister told him it was a 'poorly' ward, when all the children were not up to David's visits. The hospital was vast, a warren of corridors with lifts to operating theatres, lecture rooms, kitchens, laundries, X-ray department and dining rooms where David spent quite a lot of time chatting to people, just picking up little bits of information. If he was asked what he was doing, he told them he was a student making his mind up about his future, and of course, this was true, but he wasn't there officially but never mentioned that. At visiting times, he would look into the wards, and if there was someone who didn't have a visitor, he would sit with them and chat if they wanted to. The elderly ladies who lived alone, widowers perhaps, whose families were unable to visit, were always glad to see him and had a humbug for him. There was a lady called Jenny, she was as yellow as a buttercup and very unwell, but it didn't dampen her spirit and sense of humour. "It's a good job I'm not 60 years younger," she said to the other ladies, "or I'd be giving him a run for his money. Are you married?" she asked David.

"No," replied David, "are you asking?"

They all roared with laughter, even the visitors, and then Jenny spotted a vicar walking towards her. "Oh! God, look who's coming now."

"I'm not ready yet," she said. "I'm not wearing my wooden overcoat, though by the look on the doctor's face this morning, he was surprised I'm still here."

Clearly the vicar was used to Jenny and very fond of her. He held her hand.

"I'd rather hold his hand," she said, nodding towards David.

"I'll come and see you tomorrow," David said, as he left her bed-side, and her veneer slipped briefly in that moment.

"Aye," she said, "if I'm still here, but I've had a good life, remember that."

As he left the ward and turned, she wiggled her fingers at him.

The following day, he visited her ward first thing, but the curtains were drawn, and they were cleaning and re-making the bed. He was wearing his white coat, so he felt able to go and check if she had just been moved to another ward.

"Jenny passed away during the night," the nurse informed him, "she'll be down in the mortuary."

He felt he should go to her but remembered what Mr Gray had been trying to convey to him about disengaging from the sadness the job can bring, so he just went and sat in the garden for a while.

Once John was free from his responsibilities at the hospital, they planned a programme for the rest of the week, and now David was older they could enjoy being out at night time. They sat on the Thames embankment, watching vessels come and go, or went to Covent Garden, and during the day visited The Natural History Museum, had their first visit to St Paul's Cathedral, and as always, went into Westminster Abbey. They enjoyed the throb of Camden Market, and now David was used to the different cultures, he found their stalls fascinating. On their last day, John planned a surprise for David and took him to the Foundling Hospital. David had never heard of it but found the whole experience very moving. It had been founded by a sea captain in 1739, a home and security for the care and education of deserted children, many of whom suffered from smallpox, fevers, consumption and the likes, at that time, and who would have surely died if they had not been in the hospital. They spent a long time there, delving into the history of the hospital, talking to some of the children, who seemed happy in their 'home', cared for and being educated. The man taking them around informed John that there were moves afoot to try and get the children adopted, rather than having them institutionalised. "Changing times and attitudes," he said, "but there will still be a role for us."

On their way back to Mrs Fry's, David had a discussion with John comparing where they had just been to where he had run away from.

"You need to remember the children in the Foundling were homeless, sometimes just abandoned and were very ill. Where you were was for boys who were out of control and had done bad things," said John.

"I know," said David, "it's just the staff were really cruel, no one had a chance of improving, I'm glad I took the risk and ran away, I can't bear to think of where I would be today if I hadn't."

On the journey home, John asked David if he had considered general practice, because he could arrange for him to sit in for the experience with a colleague in the town. It wouldn't be appropriate to sit with John; the people from the village would not approve.

"Well, I will do," responded David, "but I don't think it's something I would want to do long term. Sorry."

"No," said John, "don't apologise. We all have our plans and interests. I wasted time doing what my father had thought I should do, instead of what I wanted to do, but in the end I gritted my teeth and changed course, fell out with my father for a while, but it didn't matter too much because I was away at university, and when I graduated, he turned up."

"So, he was proud of you after all," said David.

"He never told us, ever," said John, "but that was just Father."

When they arrived home, there was a letter from Monique, written in French. She thought David may like to visit them for Christmas, and although it was months away, she knew he didn't have a passport which did take up time to obtain.

"You can send for your passport in a few weeks when you are 21. You have your birth certificate, get a form from the post office."

"I'm not going at Christmas," said David. "Maybe some other time."

"Why not?" asked Jake, knowing full well what David's answer would be.

"I'm not leaving you and John on your own at Christmas," replied David.

"Send for your passport," said Jake. "We'll talk about it later. Do you want to do anything special for your 21st?"

"Not really," said David. "It's not like it used to be when my friends were from the school and they could come for tea, they are scattered far and wide now, and I prefer it to pass unnoticed at Cambridge, it's just an excuse for a booze up, and I'm not having another of those."

"Oh! So you've been on a booze up then?" asked Jake, with a big grin on his face.

David related the episode to Jake, and because it was a long time ago, he didn't feel as awkward about it, and they had a laugh.

"We've all done it," said Jake. "You just have to decide whether it's all worth it. If it impacts on your health and studies and you end up with no money for food, you're in trouble."

When David went down for breakfast on his birthday, there were cards on the table from Fay, Dora and Bill, and inside the envelope with the card from Jake and John was a copy of the highway code and a cheque for driving lessons.

"Oh! Great!" said David, really excited. He had sat with Jake and hiccupped the car down the lane and really wanted to be able to drive but had pushed the idea to the back of his mind, thinking he would have to wait until he had finished university at least.

"I think it would be better for you to have the lessons in Cambridge," said John. "This is a very rural area, the traffic is light; you need to learn where it is busy, so you can cope in heavier traffic."

David wanted to go that minute but realised John was giving him good advice, so he planned to book with a driving instructor on his return to Cambridge.

During the two weeks before his return to university, he spent some time looking through his notes as Jake had suggested and was surprised by how much he couldn't recall. He gathered everything together in his room until it was time to load up the car and return to Cambridge for his second year and was lucky enough to have been allocated the same room. He didn't want to be in a shared house, having visited friends who were, he couldn't live in such a mess and it was noisy, and although he would have a room of his own, he didn't like the idea at all.

He spent most of the day before he left walking along the coast. John and Jake were both working so they could have the day off to take David back to Cambridge, so he just enjoyed his time on his own without the anxieties he had the previous year when he was facing the unknown.

Fay had filled his tins as usual with cake, bread, ginger biscuits and put cheese and onion pasty in the fridge. There was tinned food and porridge oats in his box, which he tied to his ironing board again to conceal what it was as they carried it to his room, his bedding was in one of the suitcases, his clothes in another, and his books in boxes, and he was ready to go and looking forward to it.

The following day they made the familiar journey, and by bedtime, everything was in place in David's room, as it had been the year before.

He spent the next few days socialising with his friends, catching up on what they had done during the summer recess, and detailing his programme of lectures.

He lay in bed the night before the academic year began, and thought, *here we go again*, and he was ready.

Chapter 28

Two months into term, and David was settled in a routine with his lectures and had passed his driving test, having crammed as many lessons in as he could to get it out of the way. John had been right about the volume of traffic, and for his first few lessons, he had worked up a sweat by the end of the hour but gradually got used to it. The day he took his test, he didn't feel over-confident, was lucky enough to have a time for mid-morning when the peak time traffic had eased off, and he passed. He didn't tell John and Jake he was taking his test, but when he returned to his room, he cut up his 'L' plates, put them in an envelope and sent them home.

During the winter months, when the days were short and cold and the rain had an icy sting, he had most of his main meals in the student dining room and enjoyed the cosiness of his room during the evenings, working or listening to his radio. He had a routine where he would go to the call box and telephone home on his way to hockey training, and at weekends would go swimming or to the cinema, spend time with Monique and Jean and from time to time, join his colleagues in the pub, and time raced by up to the Christmas break.

David had thanked Monique for her kind invitation to visit them at Christmas but explained he didn't want to leave John and Jake on their own, which she understood perfectly, but told him she and Jean were to be married next August, and he would be receiving an invitation to that, and she expected him to be there. She and Jean would graduate a year ahead of David, so he realised he would not be having his French conversation sessions anymore and would have to keep in touch by writing letters.

John and Jake would have been fine if David had wanted to go to France with his friends for Christmas, but he was adamant he was not going, so they insisted on collecting him from Cambridge for the holiday.

"I can come on the train," David had said in his conversation with John, who was determined they would collect him.

"You can go back on the train," John had told him. "So remember that, and don't have too much luggage."

Some of his friends who shared a rented house invited him to their Christmas party the evening before Jake and John were collecting him, so he didn't stay long and was quite shocked and amused when some of the guests were finding their way home as he put his luggage in the doorway waiting to be collected the following morning. John and Jake had an early start, and arrived for him around 10:30 am, loaded up the car and went for a coffee and sandwich in a little cafe in Cambridge, away from the university. Nothing was mentioned, but when they returned to the car, John and Jake sat in the back seat and handed David the keys.

"Are you sure about this?" asked David, because he wasn't, he hadn't driven since passing his test. Now he realised why they had insisted on collecting him

"Jake has every confidence in you," said John, "so you'd better get on with it, just start the car and go, don't be hesitating."

Once David was used to the feel of the gears, he was more confident driving the car and drove all the way home, but he was mentally drained and so relieved to turn into the lane to his home.

Fay knew he would be driving back, that was the plan, so she greeted him with a big smile. "How have you gone on?" she asked.

"Phew," said David, flopping into a chair, "that was a task and a half I didn't expect, but I've done it. Getting out of Cambridge was the hardest part because I wasn't used to the car and didn't really know where I was supposed to go; it's a good thing Jake was navigating."

"He did all right," said Jake, smiling as he brought in the suitcase and bag with the dirty washing.

David went back out to the car to collect the other suitcase containing his clothes and presents he had bought in Cambridge, and John patted him on the back but said nothing, so David wasn't sure whether John thought he had done well, was just relieved to get home in one piece or was still traumatised by the whole experience.

It was good to be home; the kitchen was warm and welcoming and smelt of something good cooking in the oven. Fay always made something David really liked on his return, usually stew and dumplings, and that first meal around the table meant so much. When it was almost ready, Jake asked David to take Fay home in the car, and he was glad to because traffic in the village was light.

They sat in the lounge in the evening in front of the fire and chatted for a while, but David was really tired and went up to bed early. He soaked in a bath, a luxury for him now, and sat on his window seat wrapped in a blanket and looked out to sea. The tide was out because he couldn't hear the ocean, but he could see the reflection of the moon bouncing about on the water, and he knew he was home.

The following day, he decorated his new twig with the Christmas decorations which he collected from the turret room. He stood at the window for a while, looking out onto the grey, dank day, not sure but thinking there may be some snow swirling about in the air. As he turned to face the door, he noticed a crack in the wall which he hadn't seen before and thought perhaps he should mention it to John.

Fay kept busy, but she and David had a lovely morning together. He was almost like a son to her, and she loved to hear about what he had been doing at university, a world which she knew nothing about, and he liked to catch up on how her children were doing and the gossip from the village.

After lunch, he dressed for a walk along the coastal road. He had never felt as cold before, and there was an eeriness hovering over the sea which was unusually quiet, despite the tide being in. He came across the fisherman tethering his boat on the small landing.

"Caught anything today?" asked David.

"I haven't been out," replied the fisherman, "just making sure the boat is secure. It's going to be a raw winter, a bad one."

They parted company, and David went back home, he was so cold, cheeks and nose numb and fingers throbbing. He made tea and warmed his hands on the tea pot and read the newspaper for a while.

"It's the school carol service tonight, has John mentioned it?" asked Fay.

"No," said David but was pleased he hadn't missed it, he liked to call at the school every time he was home, and the staff were always pleased to see him to learn how he was progressing at university. He still called the masters 'Sir', and they still called him by his surname, as was the practice at the school, and it kept things on a professional basis in case the students overheard.

"Am I driving?" David asked as they got ready to leave for the school.

"No," said John, "we'll walk, parking will be difficult, and it's dark."

Late evening, returning home was like walking through a grotto in Lapland, everything was white and glistened silver when the moon came from behind the clouds, and it was so cold. It wasn't slippery underfoot; the ground was just white and crunchy.

They put a log on the fire and had toast and cocoa to warm themselves before they went to bed. David's hot water bottles were in Cambridge, and the house was very cold upstairs, so he went to bed in thick socks and a wool hat.

The weather didn't improve, and when David mentioned that the fisherman had said it was going to be a bad winter, Jake said "He'll be right, the fishermen know how to read the climate. I'm concerned about the trains to get you back to Cambridge; I think we should check at the station, you may have to return early if snow is on its way."

Bill and Dora had telephoned on Christmas Eve, and the snow was falling where they lived. On Christmas Day, David got up early, lit the fire in the lounge, the stove in the kitchen and made porridge for breakfast. They opened their presents and were just about to set out to walk to the hotel for Christmas dinner when John got a call out, someone in the village with a suspected stroke. "I'm taking the car," he said. "I'll go steady, but they live at the other end of the village."

"I'll come with you," said David.

"I'll cancel the hotel," said Jake. "Just come back here when you are through."

There was no time to reason or argue, and none of them were bothered about being out and about, so when John and David returned, Jake made lunch, bacon, eggy bread and baked beans, and they had cheese and biscuits to finish with their coffee.

"Well, I don't know about you," said John, "but that was fine for me."

"Me too," said David. "Thank you, chef," he said, using the phrase he had picked up whilst working at the hotel.

"It was a pleasure," said Jake. "Now let's have a look at the camera Santa Claus brought you."

They listened to the Queen's speech, had a game of monopoly and decided to go up into the turret room and look out. "I forgot to tell you there is a crack in the wall up there," said David. "I saw it the other day."

They looked out of the windows across the bay, and watched a cruise liner dotted with lights, sailing across the horizon, but they didn't stay up there long, it was so cold. John slid his hand down the crack in the wall as they left the room but said nothing.

On Boxing Day, David packed up his things to return to Cambridge and decided to take a walk along the coast before he left. He couldn't persuade Jake to accompany him, so he went alone, crunching along the path, taking care in case it was slippery. The tide was in but much quieter than usual; the sea seemed thicker and slower. *Surely it couldn't freeze, being salt water*, thought David, and then thought about icebergs and realised it could, if it were cold enough. He was fascinated by it all but soon returned home with numbed cheeks and lips as snowflakes started to swirl and settle.

Fay had Christmas Day and Boxing Day off, but as usual, she had left plenty of food in the fridge and cupboards for them, so Jake had put some tins into David's luggage, a loaf of bread, some cheese and slices of ham, biscuits and Christmas cake, as it had been decided to just go to the station and hope for the best regarding the train service two days after Boxing Day. The station master confirmed the train would be coming half an hour late but didn't know what the situation would be regarding David's connection when he changed trains for Cambridge.

"I'll risk it," said David. "I'm sure there will be a bus if the trains stop running. There's no need for you to hang around in the cold." He shook hands with John and Jake. "I'll be fine, I'm a big boy now. I want you to go home out of these freezing temperatures."

"Telephone us tonight, it doesn't matter what time it is," said Jake. "We need to know you've made it."

The train journey was slow and timetables in chaos, but he did manage to catch a train to Cambridge which didn't arrive until evening. Even the engine seemed to sigh with relief, and it wasn't going any further. There were no other students on the train, and no taxis outside the station. The trek to St John's was a long one, and he was dreading it with two suitcases and his rucksack to carry. He had not eaten since breakfast, he didn't know there was food in his luggage, and they had forgotten to put sandwiches up. Fay would have remembered, but she didn't arrive until he had left.

He spotted a telephone box outside the station and decided to telephone home from there. "I've made it," he said to Jake. "I'm at the station, actually, but once I get to my room, I can stay there now I've called you. It's snowing heavily, and I'm frozen to the bone. What's it like where you are?"

"Bad," said Jake. "The workmen in the field brought the digger out and cleared a path so John could get back from the surgery. He had to walk, and I think they may have to do it again in the morning. We left the car up at the surgery after we dropped you off, and I think it will be staying there for quite a while by the look of things."

"Keep warm and take care of yourselves if you are out and about," said David. "I'll be in touch. Goodnight."

Someone with a Land Rover had spotted his suitcases outside the telephone box and stopped.

"Are you heading for the university?" the driver shouted.

"Yes," replied David. "St John's."

"Come on, then, we'll squeeze you in," said the driver and got out to help David put his suitcases and himself in the back with a small goat. There was no cover over him, but he didn't care about that, he was just pleased he didn't have to face the walk with his luggage.

"I can't tell you how grateful I am for this lift," said David, when he was dropped off with only a short distance to go to his room. "Thank you so much. How much further have you to go?"

"Not far," said the man. "I'm dreading what's to come according to the forecast. You've come at the right time."

Fourteen hours from leaving home, he unlocked his room door, slid his cases across the floor, took off his rucksack on the landing and brushed off the snow and shook his coat and hat. He lit the fire in his room and went along to the washrooms to put the kettle on to make a warm drink. The water was running very slowly through the tap, and he realised the pipes were freezing up, so he gathered everything he could find that would hold water and filled them. He had three empty lemonade bottles he should have taken back to the shop for a refund, and he was really glad to have them to fill with water. The kettle boiled, and he filled his hot water bottles, and he would re-heat this water and use it again for almost three weeks. He tried the showers, but really knew they wouldn't work, and by the morning, the pipes were frozen solid, and the toilet didn't flush.

As he unpacked his luggage, he came across the food and was so relieved. He didn't feel unwell, just wretched and so very tired. He just took a moment for himself and walked over to the window but couldn't see out for the lacy patterns of thick frost. An hour later, he was unpacked, had eaten and felt settled, wrapped in a blanket in front of the fire, which he left on all night. He stuffed his boots with newspaper to help dry them out and climbed into bed and hugged his hot water bottle. There wasn't a sound from anywhere, so unusually quiet, in fact he realised he hadn't seen anyone else since he arrived, although he knew there would be the foreign students who had stayed, and he would seek them out the following day and find out where to go for a meal, and more importantly, which toilets were still working.

The following morning, his room was warm enough for him to strip off and have a wash, using the minimum amount of water from the kettle after he had made some tea.

He couldn't see out of his window, so he was shocked when he walked down the stairs and outside to see the volume of snow that had fallen during the night. He headed for the dining room and found other students were congregating there, and maintenance staff had managed to keep the pipes thawed and the toilets working. There would be something to eat, but deliveries of fresh food were proving difficult. David sat and chatted with the students and talked about what they were planning for New Year celebrations, which centred around the college bar. Was he bothered, he would see on the night.

The grandeur of the college buildings took on a new vista in the snow, with huge icicles hanging from the colonnade pillars like stalactites, and the River Cam almost frozen over. David used his camera and took many pictures, including the ducks back peddling on the ice, having landed in a search to find water.

A few days later, the river was frozen solid, and people were able to ice skate. There were braziers out on the bank where people were roasting chestnuts, someone had taken a radio out so there was music, and there was a definite need for someone who could do first aid.

David decided to try and walk through the deep snow and see the gardener. The poor man was trying to rescue his plants where the weight of the snow had caused the glass roof of the greenhouse to smash.

"Oh my goodness!" said David. "Is there something I can do to help?"

"Not really," said the gardener, "I've rescued what I could, I think, we can't go into this snow, it's full of shards of glass. Some plants are resilient, but I'm afraid I will have lost a lot for the beds for summer."

"You'll just have to spread out the ones that survive," suggested David.

"A bigger problem is whether the college will replace the greenhouses," said the gardener, and David realised it was not just the loss of the plants he was worried about but his job.

"The beautiful gardens enhance the college," said David. "Surely they will want to maintain that."

"Are you coming to have a warm drink before you go back?" asked the gardener, holding open what was left of the greenhouse door.

"Yes, please," said David, "Don't forget to shut the door."

The gardener looked at him and realised he was joking. They carried four trays of rescued plants back to the cottage which was filled with others he had already taken. There was just a small space on his table where he could eat his meals, and every other surface had a tray of plants on it. Whilst the gardener was making hot drinks, David observed how many books he had on his book shelves, not just about gardening but the classics and art.

"You seem to have a wide range of interests," said David, nodding towards the book shelves.

"I have to read about places. I'll never get to see them," said the gardener. "I was born in this cottage, my father was the gardener here before me and taught me all I know, and I've never been any further than into Cambridge to buy food, books and clothes when I need them."

David left deep in thought about this man, marvelled at his inner strength and contentment with his life. He knew the current situation was a troubling one for him, but he probably didn't realise how valued he was, or that is what David hoped.

David returned to the dining room and stood in line for a plate of what resembled stew and a piece of bread, and 'Oliver Twist' flashed into his mind. The cooks had done well, it tasted good to him, but some of the foreign students were not too happy.

David took his polished, empty plate back. "Thank you," he said, "that was really good. Have you any spare milk for me to buy?"

"Yes," said the server, "the farmer managed to get to the end of the road on his tractor, and the students helped him carry it across from there. I can only let you have a pint; we might have to live off rice pudding tomorrow."

The sky was dark outside as David trudged through the snow back to his room. He thought he would telephone home and tried, but the lines were down from the weight of the snow, apparently, and he couldn't get in touch for two weeks. His room was warm, and he had his radio, so he was quite happy during the evening, glad to be out of the cold. He emptied the cold water out of his hot water bottles into a pan and heated it up again and put them in his bed. He tried all the taps in the kitchen and washroom, but not a drop of water came out, and everywhere in the building apart from his room was below freezing, he thought. Then he had a brainwave, he took a bucket from the kitchen, filled it with snow and took it to his room to melt. *That will do for heating up and washing in*, he thought, *then I can keep the water I saved from the tap for making drinks. Genius.* He punched the air and smiled at himself in the mirror.

There were weather warnings on the radio, and it soon became apparent this freak weather was all over the country, being the coldest month recorded since 1814. What started out being a novelty soon became troublesome. Students and tutors were only trickling back, and the academic year got off to a bad start. He knew Monique and Jean had not arrived, because they would have contacted him. He had heard on his radio that airports were closed, although he didn't know how they travelled between France and England.

The following day, David walked into Cambridge centre where workmen were busy clearing the roads and pavements as best they could, but he didn't see a single bus. He went to the bank to draw some money out and went shopping for food. He bought two loaves, cheese, butter, tins of vegetable soup, tins of spam, pilchards and baked beans and some chocolate. He walked back to his room, off loaded some of his shopping, and set off to the gardener's cottage with a loaf, two cans of soup, one tin of spam and baked beans. He couldn't find the gardener anywhere, but his door was unlocked, so he just left the shopping on the table. The plants seemed to be thriving in the warm room with seed trays now spread on the floor; clearly, the gardener was determined there would be flowers for the beds in the late spring.

The beginning of the term was chaotic, both students and lecturers were missing. Most of the lecturers lived in properties close to the university, but some had gone skiing abroad and couldn't get back, and it was two weeks into the term before everyone was in place, and with so many students with pots on their wrists or arms, it resembled an accident clinic at a hospital. There were others on crutches, and one poor student had two fingers sliced off with an ice skate blade.

When the thaw came, the ground was lethal and became a quagmire on the flat land, taking a long time to drain. It was catch up time with studies, there was not the usual exuberance around the college, not a good start to the New Year, but the ducks were happy.

John and Jake had survived unscathed. The people in the village looked after their doctor and made sure he could get to surgery. The school provided wheelbarrows full of cinders and ash from their boiler, and the labourers working on the interiors of the houses in the field had spread them down the lane so it was easy to walk on.

There had been no contact from Dora and Bill, but Mr Gray said they were all right when he telephoned Jake for a chat.

One evening, David decided to fill the form in and send for his passport. John had signed his photographs for him, and he had put them safely away in the envelope with his birth certificate which was now spread out on the table in front of him. It had been in his possession since Bertha gave it to him after his mother's funeral, but he had never actually read it, but in that moment he realised he had a father. *Of course I have a father*, he thought, *but this man was actually married to my mother. Who was he? I can't even remember ever seeing him.* David, now a mature young man, realised why the men he would call 'uncles' were calling to see his mother and accepted why she did it. Was one of those men his father? Surely, they would have said. In the canyons of his mind, he remembered that his mother had said his father was a sailor, but the birth certificate was blank where his occupation should be listed, he wasn't at her funeral, or was he? And she never mentioned him unless David asked her questions about him. All this time had passed, and he'd never, ever, thought about his father. It was a shock and troubled him for a while, so many questions arose, but he decided not to mention it to Jake and John, and over time, he pushed it to the back of his mind.

Chapter 29

He spent a lot of time with Monique and Jean, once they had arrived and settled into a routine again. It was their 'finals' for their degree this year, so they applied themselves to their studies but took time out for fun as well.

They joined a group going to the boat race and spent a couple of nights in London staying at Mrs Fry's. David took on his role as tour guide and took them to Westminster Abbey, the Foundling Hospital, a boat trip on the River Thames and the Natural History Museum, which they loved. On the train back to Cambridge, they all fell asleep, they were so tired, but Monique and Jean had really appreciated their 'time out' and thought David was wonderful.

"He was going to be a tour guide on a roofless bus, once upon a time," Mrs Fry told them.

"That might have to be plan 'B' if I need one," said David.

David worked hard on his studies for his exams, he was finding that he had to put the time in, and he didn't go into the exam room oozing with confidence, but in the end, his efforts paid off and he achieved good results. Monique and Jean achieved their BA Honours degree, and three weeks later, David met their parents at the graduation ceremony and confirmed the arrangements for him attending their wedding.

Once again, it was time to empty his room and have everything ready for when John and Jake collected him. He had discussed his desire to go to St Thomas's Hospital if he graduated with a satisfactory grade and had asked that his lectures would enhance his chances. He didn't mention his plans to John, he wanted to be able to surprise him, having achieved a place on his own merit if he got one.

David had gone for a walk the day before he was leaving for home to find the gardener. The grounds looked magnificent and no one would know how much dedication had gone into it.

"I'm away tomorrow," said David. "I'll see you in September."

"I'll have a new greenhouse by then," said the gardener, sounding very pleased. "They're starting tomorrow. It's going to have a boiler to heat pipes during the winter."

"That sounds good to me," said David, thinking they should be doing that in the student's rooms. "See you in September, take care."

He'd been allocated the same room again and didn't see why he couldn't leave some of his things in place, but the rooms were cleaned and painted in rotation, so it just wasn't allowed.

He and John loaded up the car and David drove home again, this time with more confidence. As he turned into the lane, he was amazed that the workmen were gone and people were now living in the new houses.

"Has it been ok since people moved in?" asked David.

"Yes," replied John, "they seem to be nice people, and I've got a few more patients on my books now. The shopkeepers and the pubs have benefitted. I know some people had misgivings when they found out about the plans to build in the fields, but now they've seen the quality of the estate and are reaping the benefits in their businesses, they seem to be happy. Also, because of the high standard here, the team have moved on to another project in the next village, so Fay's son is happy to still have work."

Fay was her usual giddy self when David arrived. She took his dirty washing out of the car whilst he carried the cases and boxes upstairs. On his chest of drawers was his passport, which he knew had arrived but had forgotten all about.

After tea, when all was cleared away, they sat outside and talked, enjoying the last of the sunshine.

"What have you planned for the holidays?" John asked David.

"Well, I could go fruit picking for a few weeks with some of the others, and I'm going to the wedding in France the second week in August, for definite, what are your thoughts about that? You know I feel uncomfortable about not being here."

"You should take advantage of all the opportunities that are there," said Jake. "Once you start work, you won't have the time, and you'll regret not doing things then, when you can't. The profession you are planning to go into isn't a nine-to-five job, as we explained to you before."

He spent almost the whole of the following day on the beach. Fay packed up some food for him, and he took a fold-up chair and a book and was content. He didn't dislike the buzz of university, but this beach was what he thought about when he closed his eyes and thought of home when he was away.

The tide was just going out when he arrived, so he sat on his chair near the water's edge and listened to the sea gurgling and bubbling through the row of pebbles. The sand was wet and soft, and the chair kept sinking, so he moved further back up the beach and read his book for a while. He poked about amongst the debris the tide had brought in, and looked for shells, but the sea was cold, so he didn't stay in the water long.

He decided to join some of his friends and go fruit picking, so four days later, Jake dropped him off in town to catch a bus to meet up with them. He took all his old clothes, but no extra socks, some tins of food and a sleeping bag. As David was getting out of the car, Jake handed him a bag with a tin opener, an enamel plate and mug and a knife, fork and spoon. "You might need these," he said, wryly. "Enjoy!"

Five days later, as John was returning from his surgery, he saw David trudging down the lane. He stopped the car, wound the window down, and asked "What happened to you, then?"

David's shirt was splattered in red blotches, his boots and trousers had a coating of mud, he was unshaven and dirty.

"I resigned, I withdrew my services," said David, in a cut-glass accent.

"Get in," said John.

"I stink," said David. "I'll walk down. Ask Fay to bring me an old bath towel."

He flopped onto the bench and kicked off his boots, removed his soggy socks and stretched out.

Fay arrived with a mug of tea and a bath towel, followed by John.

"What has happened to you?" asked Fay.

"As you can see," said David, in a very pedantic way, "the facilities were not good. There were four of us in a tent that was intended for two and no luggage, it leaked, which was not good as it poured down for two days, there was a row of taps under a corrugated sheet, with cold water for washing and drinking, and the toilets, more like a stinking bog, were at the other end of the field, so if you needed a pee during the night, you just found the nearest tree, like a dog, and none of us had thought to take toilet paper. We had to cook on a primus stove at the end of the working day, and because it was pouring down, we tried putting the stove inside the tent and set fire to it, which was surprising, because it was wet through. Luckily, we kept our belongings in our bags, so we just grabbed them and fled without pay for two days' work. The travellers, who did the fruit picking every year, had their caravans and vans to sleep in, and there were others who had obviously done it before and were better equipped than us, but we were just a source of amusement for them all, nobody came to offer help. I'm going to burn my clothes when I've had a bath."

Fay went in the house and upstairs to run the bath, whilst David stripped off outside and wrapped the towel round him. A while later, she went upstairs to ask David if he wanted something to eat, passed the bathroom and realised he had finished in there because the door and window were open, so she crept onto his room and peeped through the door that was ajar. He was fast asleep.

After four hours, they woke him up, and he felt better for the sleep, and hungry. During the evening, one of the friends he had been with telephoned to say he had arrived home and had heard of another farm with much better facilities and would David care to try it out?

The firm reply was, "NO, thank you," from David. He glanced out of the window and saw smoke still swirling from his smouldering clothes in the old dustbin with holes in. Fay had looked at them, wondering if she could make them decent enough for him to wear around the house, but he insisted they were burnt "as a sacrifice to the Gods of hygiene," he said.

The following day, David had spent time in his room, sorting his paper work out from university and intended going into town in the afternoon to buy a suit and new shirt and tie for the wedding, but just as they were about to sit down and have some lunch, they heard a vehicle outside, followed by a knock at the door. David opened it.

"I've come to see how Looby Loo is," they heard someone say.

"It's Dougy," said Jake to John.

David and Dougy had kept in touch but not frequently, so he was amazed when Dougy introduced his wife Jill, who was expecting a baby and quite soon by the look of her.

"Oh my goodness!" said David. "When did you get married?

"A couple of weeks ago," said Dougy. "We're on our honeymoon. Registry office, a quiet do, the in-laws don't like me, but Jill loves me, don't you?"

"I do," she said and kissed his cheek.

"Come and have some soup and bread," said Jake and got up for two more bowls and plates.

"I wasn't sure if you would be home from university, and I didn't have your telephone number with me, so I just thought I'd risk calling on our way home," said Dougy. "I wanted Jill to see how lovely it is down here, to see the sea for the first time and have a holiday before the baby arrives."

"Where have you been staying?" asked David.

"Oh! We've been all round the coast," said Dougy. "We've slept in the van, cooked our breakfast on a little stove and been to a cafe a few times. Jill can't eat late at the moment; she honks up in the morning. We heated water for a wash in the evenings and have been very cosy."

David laughed, he couldn't help but admire Dougy, he was so open about things.

John bid them 'farewell' and returned to the surgery, but they sat and chatted for another two hours before Dougy decided it was time to leave. David was so pleased he was doing well, and Jill seemed ideal to be his wife. Of course, Dougy had always teased Jill about Looby Loo, and she always thought it was a girl until finally the truth came out—she was a toilet. David had forgotten, shamefully, what good company Dougy was and felt it was important to keep in touch.

"I'm so glad you called," said David. "It's important we don't lose touch with each other, and you must let us know when the baby arrives."

"Don't forget your old friends now you have a load of posh ones at university. I have a telephone now, here's the number," Dougy said as he handed a slip of paper to David. "So you can ring me. I do work away from home sometimes, and a few weeks ago, I had a walk along the canal bank. It's over grown, most of the buildings are derelict now. Anyway, our time there was happy, wasn't it?"

The conversation continued with a lot of 'can you remember when', and the memories came flooding back.

When Dougy and Jill were leaving the house, Jake gave Jill a £5 note for the baby, David gave Dougy a hug, and Fay gave them some scones and a jar of her homemade jam, and they were on their way, in the new van.

"Sad news about the canal," said Jake, "but inevitable, I suppose."

"I enjoyed our time there," said David. "I felt safe and, despite all the work involved, there was a serenity about the environment. People were buying the boats to convert for pleasure, so somewhere there will be a canal kept in order for them to travel on, surely."

"Yes," said Jake, "it would be interesting to find out."

David kept himself occupied over the next few weeks. John had arranged for him to be measured for a new suit for the wedding, and hopefully it would still fit him for interviews in the future; surely, he had stopped growing now, at 6'. John visited an old people's residential home on the outskirts of the village and volunteered David's help for a couple of days a week. David had no idea such places existed, so John talked him through why the elderly people were there, the problems they had, what he would have to accept as normal behaviour and above all, to talk to them and listen.

He turned up as arranged and introduced himself to the manageress, and in no time at all, he was doing the rounds with the tea and biscuit trolley, and it was only 9:30 am.

He was introduced to Jenny, who took care of him on his first day, and was there afterwards if he needed guidance, and he found that he looked forward to his next visit. He chatted to the ones who wanted to talk, but so many just slept and did nothing, nor were they encouraged to, which he thought was sad and wrong. He was mortified at the sight of the ulcerated legs, and the screams when the dressings had to be changed and talked to John about it.

"It isn't our place to criticise," said John. "They are all there because they cannot look after themselves any longer, and the carers do the best they can."

"Sorry," said David, "but I don't think they do. The time they spend chatting and smoking in the kitchen, they could be spending engaging with the residents, improving what little quality they have left of their lives. You told me to talk to them and listen, and I do, and I know some of what they say is utter rubbish, and they think I'm their father or son, but they look into my eyes and hold my hand as if they are actually getting something out of that moment. There's a fragile gentleman, Luke, physically weak, but quite lucid and has lead a most interesting life, but he hasn't anyone to talk to, and he asked me if I would go and visit him again; his words were, 'I'm closing down mentally.' I'm going to take him some books and a jigsaw."

"You do realise you can't voice your opinion at the Home," said John.

"Yes, I know," said David, ruefully.

The next time he went, Luke wanted to play the piano, so David wheeled him over only to find it was locked.

"Where's the key for the piano?" David asked Jenny.

"Well, it's up here with all the other keys," she replied, "but I'm not sure it's allowed."

"We'll risk it," said David and winked at her. Ten minutes later, Luke was plinking on the piano, and the people were all joining in the songs, clapping hands and tapping feet. It struck David how strange it was that although most of them had serious memory loss, they could remember all the words of the songs they were singing.

The manageress entered the room looking not too pleased. "What's going on here?" she said. "Who gave them the key for the piano?"

"Me," said David. "Have I broken a rule?" he asked, knowing full well he had.

"Call in my office before you go today," she said as she left the room.

"Good luck with the sergeant major," said Luke as David bid him farewell and left for the office at home time.

"Come and sit down," said the manageress.

"I'm fine," said David. "Do you not want me to come again?

"It isn't that," she said, "but we have someone who comes in on a Sunday afternoon to play for them."

Yes, I'll bet you do, thought David, *because that's when most visitors will call, and it will impress them.*

Words stuck in his throat like dried bread. "I know you have their best interests at heart," David said, "but we were having a good time, I thought that would please you. Didn't you know Luke could play the piano? He could be very useful. Do you want me to come in on Friday or not?"

"Usual time," the manageress replied, and David felt she was only putting up with him because he only had another three visits before he went to France.

Over the evening meal, David related what had happened during the day and wouldn't shut up about it.

"I think each resident should have a journal about their lives if it is possible to get some information from the family and some photographs," said David. "It could be kept in their rooms, and without distractions, a carer could take time out to talk to them for a little while."

"They may not recognise the person in the photograph," said John. "Remember they are very confused sometimes."

"Does it matter if they think it's their mother or sister or Vera Lynn? It gives them something to think about even if it's only for a little while," replied David, impatiently

John looked at David, with a questioning expression.

"No, I didn't say anything out of turn," said David. "I just thought it, so unless she could read my mind, you're safe. Anyway, she's expecting me again on Friday."

David left for a walk to calm down, and John and Jake had a discussion about how he had matured and were impressed at how he was able to see and understand things and reason out how to improve them. It seemed a very long time since they were teasing him as his voice broke, and he had to start shaving. Now he was a mature adult with strong opinions he was able to vocalise.

"Might have to reign him in a bit there," said Jake, "although I've never known him to be so angry or vocal before."

The next visit to the home, David avoided the piano and started Luke off on a jigsaw in his room for a while, and when he returned to the main lounge, there was chaos. One of the ladies had got hold of some make-up, and all of the ladies looked like clowns, sat in a circle passing the lipstick, rouge, bright blue eye shadow and eyebrow pencil round. Some of them had probably never worn make up in their life before, it certainly looked like it, and it didn't help that they didn't have a mirror between them. The squealing and laughter brought Jenny running into the room.

"Oh my God!" said Jenny, and she screamed at them, "Stop it, stop it," and proceeded to take the make-up from them. David helped her, but he wasn't able to help clean up the ladies and wash their hair which took the best part of the day.

"Where were you when all this was happening?" the manageress asked David.

"I was with Luke in his room, but more to the point, where were the staff?" Too late, he'd said it, but there was no reaction.

On his last day at the home, he went and asked the manageress if he could have the key for the piano, so they could have a sing song, and she agreed. "Come and join in," said David. *Let them see you are human*, he thought.

She thought, *Let him get on with it, he isn't coming any more after today.* She was hostile to him, maybe felt threatened in some way, or perhaps hurt because she felt he was implying things were not being done right in the home, which he was, but he could and would have helped her a lot.

The staff were reluctant to engage with him because they knew she thought he was arrogant, and only Jenny was prepared to spend time with him and actually understood what he was trying to do. David thought he was being subtle by just suggesting things quietly, apart from the piano incident when a surge of enthusiasm took over, but he couldn't break through the resentment and, "We've never done that before," or, "We don't do that here."

When it was time to leave, he went to see the manageress to say goodbye.

"I think we got off on the wrong foot, you and I," said David, "which is a pity."

"You young ones think you know it all," said the manageress, hardly glancing up from her paperwork, stubbing out a cigarette in an ash tray full of tab ends. "Is that you finished, then?"

"Yes," replied David and just had to respond to her petulant comment, "I don't think I know it all, but I have learnt some very important things during my visits here, the main one being these homes could be a godsend to people in these situations, but it seems they are just a place to sleep, be fed and die, and bringing any joy and quality to their lives is secondary."

David left her office and stuck his head around the corner of the dining room to say 'goodbye' to the residents. He didn't say he wouldn't be returning, Luke knew, but he hoped the rest would just forget about him. Some did ask Jenny when he was coming, but she just said, "Not today," and as time passed, he was forgotten except by Luke. John took him books and exchanged his jigsaws upon David's request, and a sort of friendship developed there, although John's time was limited, but he called at the home at least once a week, unless there was an emergency.

David never mentioned his parting conversation with the manageress to John, and neither did she, which surprised David.

"You don't fancy running a home then?" said John, as they passed in the car on their way to pick up David's suit for the wedding.

"I want to improve people's lives, not kill them off," replied David, and just at that moment, as if to endorse his comment, a hearse pulled out of the gates.

"Don't say a word," said John. "I think enough has been said already. Remember I visit and try and improve things for them if I can, but you need to realise it is as hard for the carers as it is for the residents."

David didn't speak, he just remembered what he'd seen and was convinced it could be better, rightly or wrongly.

Chapter 30

Jake drove David into town to catch the first of two buses that would take him to Dover for the ferry to Calais. He had a slip of paper in his pocket with the bus and ferry times listed, his passport, ferry tickets bought in advance and a wallet with French francs. His English money was in another pocket.

"Keep your passport and return ticket in a safe place, don't carry them about with you all the time," said Jake, as he dropped him off at the bus station. "Have a wonderful time. I'll be here to meet you on your return."

He had his suitcase and a parcel with a quilt for a wedding present that a lady from the village had made, so he found a place to settle and stayed there and read the newspaper. The sea was lumpy, but he was all right. He'd never been on the sea despite the fact he lived and spent so much time on the coast. He'd watched the cruise liners glide across the horizon from time to time and wondered what it must be like to live on a ship.

He didn't join the surge to disembark, in fact, it took him by surprise, but when he saw the queues to show your passport, he realised what it was all about. As he stood in line, he could see Monique jumping up and down, holding up a card with his name on, cut out in the shape of an iron.

They greeted each other speaking French and were joined by Monique's brother, Louis, who had travelled across on the same ferry and who would make the journey back with David.

"Where is Jean?" David asked.

"He's in Paris, we've booked rooms for tonight, so you can spend some time in Paris," said Monique.

"That sounds great," said David, knuckles white, as he hung on to the door strap as Monique hurled her 2CV Citreon around corners and sped along the lanes to Paris. He glanced at the Eiffel Tower but was more concerned about what was in front of them and was really relieved when he saw Jean sitting on steps waiting for them, and the car stopped.

They left their luggage in their rooms and went straight out and had a walk along the banks of the River Seine and had coffee and cake in a traditional patisserie. David was fascinated by the life taking place on the pavements and in the cobbled squares where there were lovely calming fountains gurgling away amidst the loud conversations, laughter and gesticulating hands. They moved on to a little bar in a higgledy-piggledy street, with tall buildings of apartments with little balconies, the shutters wide open to let in a cooler evening air, the noises of domesticity drifting out. They walked along to a small, dingy, cool cellar bar that smelt of stale smoke and wine where they had the traditional French onion soup. There was a dance floor surrounded by tables for the customers, and as they sat and ate, a man with a violin and another with an accordion started to play music.

"There will be a couple dancing in a moment," explained Monique. "The dance is called the Apache, it's very physical between a man and a woman and originates from Parisian street culture."

It was just as well Monique had explained, because as the couple made their entrance, the man was dragging the woman across the floor as she clung to his leg, and David may have felt compelled to rescue her. *How embarrassing*, he thought and smiled to himself.

The street below their room was noisy, but it had been a long day, and both David and Louis were soon asleep and slept well.

They had a leisurely breakfast with a choice from croissants, fresh warm bread, cheese and meats and fruit, totally different to an English breakfast and very enjoyable.

They decided to move on to La Celle-Saint-Cloud, where Monique lived, before it became too busy in Paris and it seemed only a short journey to her home where her parents were waiting for their guests. The house was cradled in beautiful tiered gardens on a hillside with spectacular views and had huge sliding-glass windows from a dining room where a table was already laid for the evening celebration meal.

David was shown to his room, he unpacked his clothes and re-joined the family. He did his best speaking in French to everyone when he could, but they spoke so quickly he struggled to catch up. Eventually, they realised and made the effort for him and made a joke out of it.

Louis took David for a walk in the town past the 18th-century church of St Peter and St Paul, where the marriage of Monique and Jean would be blessed. It was during this walk that Louis' enthusiasm for buildings became apparent; he was studying to become an architect at the University College of London.

"I'm hoping to get a place at St Thomas's Teaching Hospital when I graduate," said David. "We could meet up from time to time."

"That would be good," said Louis. "It's good to have a change from a studying environment, and Monique says you are a good tour guide. They did enjoy their visit to London with you, they spoke of it to our parents when they visited Cambridge for their graduation." David thought it was strange that Monique had never mentioned her brother was in London or expressed a wish to meet up with him when they were there, but he kept his thoughts to himself.

They walked back to the house and sat in the garden and had a cool drink before dressing for dinner.

The dining room was wonderful, the large, gliding glass windows were wide open, so the room became part of the garden and view, and the dinner, which lasted 3 hours, was a relaxed affair. David wasn't sure what some of the food was, but he definitely had to decline what he did recognise as snails. Jake had told him before he left that the French ate snails as a delicacy, but David didn't believe him, and just watched, agog, as some of the party picked the snails out of their shells with little spikes and chewed them.

Ooh! he thought, *couldn't do that.*

The wine flowed, but there was always water served with it, and Monique's father kept a watchful eye on how much was being consumed. He clearly didn't want anyone with a hangover on the wedding day.

After the meal, everyone sat outside on the terrace appreciating the coolness of the evening, and the smell of the flowers haunting the air, whilst the caterers cleared away. Jean and his parents left for home, and everyone else gradually went to bed.

David lay in bed thinking about the past day. *I wonder what my ma would have made of it all*, he thought. *I have to pinch myself, sometimes.*

He was drifting off to sleep when he felt what he thought was a gentle caress on his cheek, he touched it and turned his head, but there was no one there, or was there?

He awoke early and crept downstairs onto the terrace, surprised to find Monique there, drinking coffee.

"Too excited to sleep?" asked David.

"Today I will belong to Jean, no longer my mother and father. I just realised it, I suppose," replied Monique, thoughtfully.

"They will always be your mother and father," reassured David. "They will always be there for you if you need them."

"What about your parents?" Monique asked. "Where are they? Why do you live with your uncles?"

David, usually very guarded about his past, opened up to Monique. "My mother died at Christmas when I was 10, and I have no idea who my father is, I only know his name from my birth certificate, but my life has been enhanced from the care and generosity of Jake and John. They've invested so much in me in time and expense, so I need to do well and repay them in the same way, and one thing is for sure, when they are old they will not be going into an old people's home for care."

Monique looked at him. "Where did that come from?" she asked, so David related his recent experiences and they had a good laugh, but she could tell the experience had disturbed him.

They had breakfast, and then Monique went to prepare for her wedding and David went back to sit on the terrace and listened to the droning bees and chirping birds flitting about amongst the bushes. *A lot better than screeching gulls,* he thought.

Monique's mother appeared with a cup of coffee and sat beside David, so he took the opportunity to thank her for their hospitality and ran up to his room for a gift of lovely stationery he had brought for her as a thank you.

"That is so kind and thoughtful," she said. "I'm sure we will see you here again. Monique and Jean are going to live here, certainly to begin with, so you can visit us whenever you like. Do you have a girlfriend?"

"No," replied David, "I have not met the right one yet. "

"There will be someone out there for you, and she will be very lucky," said Monique's mother. She patted him on the shoulder and went indoors.

All the guests assembled in the hallway and waited for Monique to come down the staircase decorated with flowers, and when she did appear, looking stunning in her beautiful gown, flowers in her hair, everyone clapped. She held her father's hand as they all walked to the town hall for the mayor to perform the legal side of the marriage. Jean had gathered there with his family and friends, and he walked towards Monique and held out his hands to take hers, and whispered, "You look beautiful, I love you."

Following the ceremony in the town hall, a very basic, unromantic affair, the wedding party left and walked to the church. The children held white ribbons across the road, and it was tradition that the bride cut them on her way. The blessing service

188

in the church was very moving as Monique and Jean pledged their vows to each other, and when they had signed the register, they were showered with rice and flower petals as the party walked to the hall where the reception was to be held.

There were tables set around the room with a circular table in the middle where you went to help yourself from the most wonderful spread of food David had ever seen. Champagne and wine flowed as Monique and Jean mingled amongst their guests before they cut the wedding cake, and at 4 pm, they left to change to leave for their honeymoon. David picked up a little bundle of sugar almonds in a gauze bag tied with a lovely ribbon. "May I take one of these?" he asked Monique's mother.

"Is it for a lady?" she teased.

"My uncle's housekeeper," replied David, "very much a lady."

They all assembled at the station to wave 'goodbye' to Monique and Jean and then returned to Monique's home. David changed into his travelling clothes and packed his suitcase. He was enjoying the company of the family and their guests and would liked to have stayed up longer with them, but he and Louis had an early start for their return journey in the morning.

They had breakfast early with Monique's father, who was heading for the pharmacy in Paris and giving them a lift to the station, so they would be in time for the train to Calais. Having Louis for company on the ferry was good, and the journey seemed much quicker because of it. They went their separate ways in Dover but agreed to keep in touch, even if it was only by telephone or letter initially.

The rest of the journey went to plan, and Jake was waiting for David as promised.

"Had a good time, then?" asked Jake.

"Very much so," replied David, "and you were right, there were snails served during the meal."

"Did you try them?" asked Jake, knowing full well what the answer would be.

"I'd been watching snails slither out of holes in the wall on the terrace before we had our meal," said David, cringing. "Where would they get them from to eat?"

"They are bred on snail farms," said Jake, laughing. "They don't collect them from the garden. It's quite a lucrative business, with minimum effort, it just takes time, as most things do with snails."

The following day, he gave Fay the 'favour' he had brought her, explaining to her what it was about, and she was thrilled and fascinated, and in the evening after the meal, he related all about his trip to France to Jake and John.

For the rest of the holiday, he was content to be around home and decided he would have a try at cooking when Fay wasn't there at weekends, with some success, some disasters, but everything was eaten, that is, everything that John and Jake didn't know he had ruined and thrown away.

As usual, he spent his last day before returning to Cambridge along the coast, almost as if he was re-charging his battery for the year ahead. This was the important year, he had to do well to secure a place at a teaching hospital, hopefully St Thomas's, but he didn't tell John he was going to apply there; he wanted to gain a place on his own merit.

There was the usual buzz at the beginning of the academic year. David stood by his window and watched the new students arriving and thought back to his first day and how he felt when Jake and John drove away and left him to it.

He made up his bed and put everything in familiar places in his room and set off for a walk in the grounds and along the banks of the River Cam, where students were already in the punts having fun. Fresher week was the usual throb of students set free from home and parents, but things settled down when lectures began. He was going to miss Monique and Jean, but of course there were other friends and colleagues to spend time with and socialise, although he knew he had to study and work very hard to get a good degree; he didn't want to have to retake his exams.

He attended all his lectures and took every opportunity to attend a hospital to observe either in the theatre or the laboratory and was becoming unsure of what he really wanted to do for a career.

At Christmas, he was unusually quiet and spent a lot of time browsing through the books in John's study and studying in his room.

Jake had observed David and didn't like what he was seeing so insisted on walking along the coastal path despite the bitter wind blowing in from the grumbling sea and talked to David about being too anxious and steeped in study. "Don't overdo the studying," he advised him. "If you do, you could have a breakdown if you start doubting yourself and could be unfit to sit the exam. I've seen it happen."

"I just need to do well," said David. "In a way, this is my chance to repay all you and John have done for me and the trust you have had in me."

Jake glanced at David and saw the tears in his eyes.

"That's enough," said Jake. "This is exactly what I have just said to you. No more books or studying for the rest of the holiday, give your brain a rest."

When David returned to university after Christmas, he did feel refreshed, and took some time out and went swimming and played hockey, but the looming exams were always at the back of his mind. In the dining room, he listened to some of the students who had just scraped through at the end of their first two years and who were now panicking. *Well,* he thought, *you can't learn and study if you can't attend lectures because you've been out at the pub most nights or in a girl's bed.* He smiled to himself. *How smug am I,* he thought, *people make their choices.*

He had to go to St Thomas's Hospital for an interview which was quite daunting in front of a panel of people who seemed unable to smile. David had a pleasant, relaxed demeanour, so he found the interview in such a tense atmosphere unnerving, and he came away having no inclination as to how well or badly he had done. A few weeks later, he received a letter to say he would be accepted if he had a good result and was given a telephone number to call when he knew what his result was.

It was as if a dark cloud had enveloped the graduates taking their finals, and the colleges became a much quieter place for a few weeks, but at the beginning of June, the exams were over, and as if a volcano had erupted, the partying began. The day the results were posted, David was hesitant and didn't rush to the notice board outside the Senate House, but on his way, he met students either elated or devastated. He looked down the list, 'A FIRST', he gasped, checked he'd read it correctly and hurried to the telephone box to call Jake and John.

"I'm sure this is like waiting for your daughter to have her baby," said Jake, wondering why David was so late in calling them. Finally, the telephone rang.

"Hello," said David, sounding glum.

Jake looked across at John and frowned, indicating all was not well. "How have you done?" he asked.

"Well," replied David, "how does a first sound?"

Jake smiled and nodded at John, "He's done it, he's got a first."

"We'll need to bring your clothes up for your graduation, you didn't take them with you, and you'll have to hire your gown," said Jake and handed the telephone to John.

"Congratulations!" said John. "Well done, my boy, we're very proud of you, we know how hard you have worked, and it has paid off. Are you staying on at Cambridge, or have you other plans?"

"I'll tell you later," said David, who needed to telephone St Thomas's and be sure he had a place there, having obtained a good degree. That was to be his next telephone call, and then he could surprise John if he was successful. He tried several times, but the line was engaged, and he was panicking in case all the places had gone, but finally he was through and assured of a place starting in September. The person he spoke to congratulated him on his first and told him a letter confirming his place and details of what would be required would be sent to him in the post in due course.

He mingled with the other students for a while, interested in how others had done, and then he walked along the river bank and went looking for the gardener in his new greenhouse. He was so pleased to see David and hear his news. "Come and have a cup of tea," he said, "and tell me of your plans."

"I'll be going home straight after graduation," explained David, "and I have a place at St Thomas's teaching hospital in London, starting in September. Write me your name and address down, and I'll keep in touch. Do you realise I don't even know your name?"

"It's Dan," replied the gardener, as he handed David a piece of paper with his name and address on, "and be sure to let me know how you are doing. I will miss our chats; it's been good to have your company."

David shook Dan's hand and left him, feeling sad that he would not see him again, but he was determined to keep his promise and write to him. He didn't see Dan again, but managed to leave a bundle of his woollen cardigans, a hat and gloves and a hot water bottle in the corner of the greenhouse for Dan to find with a little note.

The day before the graduation ceremony, Jake and John arrived in the estate car with David's best clothes. There was a dress code to be observed, which didn't include cardigans with holes darned at the elbows and brown, scuffed boots.

David had spoken to Jake several times and asked that they came in the estate car so he could return home with them after the graduation ceremony, so he was almost packed up when they arrived. He'd been in a numbed zone since his result, pleased he'd put the work in during his time at university, and realising the raggy, undernourished boy who lived in the dark and cold was now on the verge of a wonderful career, and even after all this time, he still had moments when he wondered where he would have been had he not fallen through the roof of Jake's den.

"I'm taking you out for a meal tonight," he announced to Jake and John, "to celebrate and a small thank you to you both."

"You put the work in, David," said John, "and you've managed your finances very well, and we are very proud of you."

They had a wonderful meal in a restaurant in Cambridge where other students were enjoying time with their family members, a happy time, people looking to their future, and it was a lovely evening walking back to the hotel where Jake and John were staying.

David went and sat in the lounge with them and told them of his plans. John had wondered why David had been eager to leave Cambridge and thought he might have stayed on, so he was just taken aback completely, as was Jake.

"You've chosen your path, then?" said John.

"Well, yes," said David, "I didn't see myself doing anything else, it's just a matter of whether I want to be on the research side or the practical side of medicine. I need to go with you and look deeper into it, talk to the right people if it can be arranged."

He bid them 'goodnight' and left to walk back to his room when he encountered a group of students in a huddle and heard debate and crying.

"What's happened?" asked David, joining the group.

A student who David didn't know but apparently had failed his finals had hung himself from the railings on the staircase leading to his room.

"That's tragic," said David. "Couldn't he have taken them again? His parents will be devastated."

"They're here," said a girl, "for his graduation. He lied to them about his result. They asked too much of him, he didn't want to be here, he wanted to go in the navy, he worked as hard as he could," she sobbed.

A couple came out of the building with a member of staff, and the group of students silenced and watched as they were led away.

How sad, how tragic, thought David as he walked back to his room, *the boy must have been so afraid of letting his parents down if what the girl had said was true.* David had experienced the pressure of finals, but it was self-inflicted, there was no pressure from John and Jake, who had been to university themselves. *Perhaps the boy's parents had made great sacrifices to get their son to university, wanting a better life for him.*

David didn't sleep very well, restless with the news about the student who had hung himself and excited about the ceremony the following day.

He was up early, had a shower and ironed his shirt, stripped his bed and packed the bedding up in a suitcase and then went for breakfast to the dining room for the last time. It was noisy, and the conversation was like an icy shower engulfing the students who had not heard the tragic news.

This is not good, thought David, as there were first and second year students there, so he ate and left.

The graduation ceremony was a very formal affair and very long, but the moment David's name and details were announced, he oozed with pleasure and pride at a job well done. He glanced across at John and Jake in the audience, sitting there like two bookends with their white hair and beards, and smiled. Neither had married, so hadn't had the experience of children of their own, but this was a very special moment for them.

There was mingling and introductions after the ceremony, but eventually, the car was loaded up, David handed his key in, had one last glance at the beautiful buildings and gardens of St John's and left.

"Sorry to be leaving?" asked John.

"In a way," said David, "but I'm looking forward to the next chapter."

"You've given up the idea of becoming a tour bus guide in London, then?" asked John.

"That's still plan 'B'," said David, smiling

192

They arrived home at 2 am and just took a warm drink up to bed with them and left the car to unpack the following morning.

As David lay in bed, he could hear the sea, he was home, and he drifted off to sleep.

Chapter 31

David spent the following days, as usual, sorting things out, books packed into boxes and pushed to the back of his wardrobe, dirty washing up to date and clothes he had grown out of piled up in a corner for the next jumble sale at the village hall.

He visited his old school in the village on sports day. There were some new masters from his time there, but the headmaster was still the same and greeted David cordially. He'd heard from John that David had gained a first and said, "Well done, I hope we had a small part to play in your success."

"Indeed, you did," said David. "It all began here."

During the prize presentation, the headmaster made the most of David's success, introducing him to the pupils and parents who were able to attend, and David responded with a short speech.

"There will be times when you all might question the necessity of what is expected of you regarding educational standards, traditions and discipline at this school, but in time, as you further your education, you will understand and be glad of it. Sport plays an important part, learning to work together as a team or striving to win as an individual. I congratulate the prize winners today and wish you all the very best for your future."

He joined the staff for tea and biscuits and asked what the new building was going to be that he noticed was being erected at the back of the original building, almost out of sight.

"The village is growing, and demand for places at the school is high," the headmaster explained, "so we had a decision to make, welcome more students or remain as we were, like when you were here. It seemed senseless that children from the new builds in the village would have to travel an hour's journey at the beginning and end of the day. We have a full register for the beginning of next academic year, the boarders will still be here and 25 new students."

"Good luck with that," said David. "I hope it's a success."

"It has to be," said the headmaster. "We don't fail at this school."

They shook hands, David filled his nostrils with the smell of polish and left for home.

During the evening meal, David told John about his visit to the school. "You never mentioned they were extending; I hope it doesn't spoil the rhythm of the school."

"There's something else we haven't told you," said John. "The timing was completely wrong, so we kept it from you, but sadly, during the middle of your exams, Bill passed away."

David was stunned. "What happened?" he asked.

"Dora was expecting him home, the dogs kept arriving and leaving, and she sensed something was wrong and went after the dogs eventually, and found Bill propped up against a wall on the path. She hoped he was asleep, but he wasn't. He must have felt unwell and sat down to rest, legs crossed, cap in hand. Jake went to the funeral and we sent flowers from you and explained why you couldn't attend, and Dora graciously approved. Jake will be going to the Gray's for a few days, and you should accompany him and visit Dora. They moved her into a cottage nearer the village, and a young farm hand and his wife and baby are in her original cottage. The people have been very kind and helpful and dealt with things quickly, because she was worried she was going to be homeless."

"What was the cause of death?" asked David.

"The death certificate showed the result of death was caused by an aneurysm in the brain," said Jake.

"Would he have suffered? He was alone, he couldn't ask for help," said David, hurting inside

"There are times when people suffer what is commonly known as a stroke and have severe warning pains, but when death is sudden, like it was for Bill, they know nothing about it," said John.

David went to his room and they didn't see him for the rest of the day. He lay on his bed remembering all the things he had done with Bill and Dora, how kind they had been to him as a young boy and was so glad they had been for a visit to his home and enjoyed so many new experiences.

A few days later, John and David set off in the car to North Yorkshire to stay with the Gray's. They had a stop in the countryside and ate the food Fay had packed for them, but David was restless and wanted to get on. He was dreading seeing Dora, he knew what she would be like when she saw him, and he wanted to get it over with.

"We are having dinner with the Gray's tonight," said John, "so please be sociable, and we can visit Dora tomorrow."

There was always a hustle and bustle at the Gray's house. The dogs were barking, the geese were squawking, the billy goat was ramming the gate with his horns trying to get to the nanny goat, there was an argument going on between the youngest son and daughter, and the dog was stuck in the cat flap in the door.

Mr Gray went out to meet David and John and help carry their bags indoors.

Mrs Gray arrived to greet them, "If you want a cup of tea, or something stronger, I suggest you come through to the kitchen where it's quieter. It's bedlam out there at the moment. Can someone get the dog out, please?" she yelled at the children.

David couldn't help laughing, this was so far removed from the dignified Christmas dinner he had at their house so many years ago.

By the time dinner was ready, things had calmed down, and as usual, the family sat round the table and talked about their day, and it was obvious how much they were all enjoying a more relaxed rural life.

"Are you coming with me tomorrow?" Mr Gray asked David.

"I'm going to see Dora tomorrow," David answered. "I only found out about Bill a few days ago."

"Yes, it was a difficult call for John, but the right one, finding out in the middle of your finals wouldn't have changed anything up here but could have changed much for you. Remember Dora will be pleased it helped you, let her know it did," said Mr Gray.

The following morning, David took the car, followed Mrs Gray's instructions where to find Dora, took a deep breath, and knocked on the door. He heard a shuffling from inside the cottage. "Who is it?" Dora asked.

"David," he answered. There was a pause. "Did you hear me? It's David."

The key turned in the lock, the door opened slowly, and this bedraggled old lady with hair awry and needing a wash, clothes stained with food, flung herself into David's arms and sobbed. He held her until she had calmed down and was ready to move inside and close the door. They sat on the couch, and he held her hand until she was able to talk to him.

"I can't cope," she said. "If I sleep, I wake up thinking he's going to be here, so every day is a shock. I can't remember the funeral, where is my son? He doesn't know his father is dead, I don't know where he is. I can't remember much about moving here, I don't know why I had to." She was so distressed, her thoughts in chaos.

David stood up, pulled the curtains back and opened the window to let some fresh air in. "You have been moved here so you are nearer the village to be able to shop or catch a bus and go to the WI or to church. It's too far for you to walk from the other cottage, and you'd be trapped there in winter, remember Bill had the truck," said David.

"I've sold it," said Dora. "The landlord bought it."

Nothing seemed to have been done in the cottage since she moved in, there were small piles of clothes, cardboard boxes stacked in the corners, unwashed crockery in the sink, and a blanket and pillow on the couch which made David think she had been sleeping there. "Right," said David, "I'm just wondering what Bill would think of you if he walked in now. Would he want you to be living like this? Would he recognise you? Have you looked in the mirror?"

"I don't even know where it is," Dora replied, not wanting to have this conversation.

David found it and propped it up on the draining board. "Come and have a look," he said.

Dora didn't want to, he could tell, but he held her hand and helped her up off the couch and stood at the back of her as she looked in the mirror.

"Who is that scruffy woman?" David said, "I came here to visit a very house proud and tidy lady, where is she? Can she make some tea? And I'll help put things away."

He unpacked the boxes and put things away on shelves and in cupboards, and eventually, Dora became interested enough to tell him where she wanted things. He went upstairs and made up the bed that had never been slept in since she moved in and put her clothes that were clean on hangers in the wardrobe.

"Wash the pots," he said, as he left to go into the village to buy bread, butter and ham and was delighted to see Dora had done so on his return.

"Well, that's got your finger nails clean," David said. "I'll make some ham sandwiches."

There was a knock on the door, it opened, and a lady popped her head inside. "Hello Dora, just reminding you it's the WI meeting tomorrow, and I thought you might like some scones," she said, laying them down on a now cleared table.

"Thank you" said Dora. "I'm afraid I won't be there tomorrow."

"I'm sure she will," said David. "Would you be kind enough to call for her?"

David walked to the door to see the lady out. "I'll be here tomorrow, it's a big step for her but it's so important that she doesn't shut herself away," he said.

"We've been trying to get her to do something, but she's resisted us all up to now. Are you David?" asked the lady.

"Yes," David replied. "I was shocked to hear about Bill and shocked to see the state Dora was in, but perhaps we've turned a corner, we'll see tomorrow."

"I'm not going," said Dora petulantly when the lady had gone, but David just ignored her and started to talk about Bill and the time they had spent on the coast and back at their old farm where they had lived for years, when he arrived as a young boy with Jake, and how she had looked after him and kept him from harm.

"I remember," Dora said. "You were a bit of a bedraggled thing then, needed a good wash and feeding up."

"You had a good life with Bill, didn't you?" asked David.

"A very good life, these last few years especially, so much easier for Bill," replied Dora.

"Imagine how you would have coped at the old farm, if you hadn't moved," said David. "Here you have friends and things to do, don't turn your back on them. I'm going now, and I shall be back in the morning, and you need to have put on clean clothes after you have washed your hair and pinned it up as you used to, because we are going shopping together in the village, and then you will be ready for the WI."

Dora just looked at him, stunned. "You're so bossy," she said, "but I'm glad you came." She went for a hug and he picked her up and spun her around, so she didn't cry as he left.

"That was a bit of a challenge," David said to John, as he related his visit to Dora. "I couldn't believe how she was. I can't remember grieving for my ma, so much was happening to me at the time, so I was honestly quite unprepared to see Dora spiralling into such a dark place. I'm hoping to walk through the village with her tomorrow. I was wondering about taking her back with us for a few days."

"No," said John, "it will make it worse for her to return to her home and live alone, she needs to adjust to her life here, and next visit, depending on how she is, we could take her back."

The following day, David knocked on Dora's door and waited. There was no response, so he tentatively opened the door, and there she stood, clean dress and apron, her white hair done in her usual bun. She didn't say anything, just curtsied.

"You are just wonderful," he said. "That's my Dora." He gave her a hug. "Are you ready to go shopping?"

"Not really," she said, "but I know I will have to." She sighed heavily.

She picked up her basket and they set off along the street with the shops, where she was greeted with friendliness, people genuinely pleased to see her. They called in the hardware shop and arranged for someone to set up her television, which apparently needed an aerial fixing, and she bought some groceries, vegetables, and sausages.

David suspected she hadn't cooked a decent meal for herself since Bill died and had relied on others for basic food. Dora held his hand tight as they left the greengrocer's shop. "It's strange buying vegetables," she said. "Bill always grew them," and her eyes filled with tears.

"I know," said David, gently, "these are all stepping stones to get over," and to change the mood, he said, "Can you remember the cabbage he brought down to us when you visited? It was like a football, it lasted four meals."

"Yes," acknowledged Dora, "and it gave us all wind."

David laughed and there was a cheeky grin from Dora.

They returned home and had some lunch, and then he said, "How do you feel about going to the WI?"

"I don't know," replied Dora, sighing deeply. "Although this morning wasn't the ordeal I thought it would be."

"I'll stay until the lady comes for you," said David, "and I'll come for you tomorrow and we can go for a little drive."

"She'll be fine," said the lady as she ushered Dora into her car. "We'll take good care of her. We have a speaker today talking about his travels in China, just imagine that. I'll bring her home and see her settled."

"Thank you," said David, shaking the lady's hand. He stood on the pavement until the car disappeared, waited a while in case it returned, but it didn't, so he went back to his car and drove down to the original cottage where Bill and Dora had lived.

A young lady was standing outside rocking a pram when he arrived. She looked anxious as he approached her, but he introduced himself and asked if it would be all right for him to take Dora for a visit the following day.

"Of course it is," she said. "We've been wondering about her. The people in the village were saying she wasn't doing too well. I'm Jane, by the way, this is Hattie," she said, pointing to the baby, "and my husband is Zac."

David hadn't dared mention the dogs to Dora, he knew they were her 'babies', but he took the opportunity to ask Jane.

"They were very old, struggling to walk far, yet trying to pace up and down looking for Bill, so the vet put them to sleep. Zac buried them in the field and made a little cross, but I'm not sure if it's still there," said Jane.

David wasn't sure it would be a good idea to take Dora back to the cottage, especially as the dogs were buried close by, so instead of making it a surprise, he was going to ask her if she wanted to do it, and otherwise he would have to plan an alternative to be able to keep his promise and take her for a drive out.

He spent the afternoon in the clinic with Mr Gray and later round a table in the garden enjoying a glass of wine.

"Not like you to have a drink so early," commented John.

"I'm exhausted," said David. "Not physically, but mentally, manipulating Dora, I feel as if I'm bullying her almost, but I want to go back home knowing she's in a better place, able to cope. I was going to see if she wanted to go back to the other cottage for a visit tomorrow until I found out the dogs were buried there; now I doubt she'll want to do that, so I'll take her around the countryside."

"Bring her here for a bite of lunch," said Mrs Gray. "I've never met her, but I would be happy to call on her when I'm in the village, shopping, and I could keep you up to date as to how she is coping."

After the evening meal, the adults played monopoly, David ended up broke, and John ended up with a fortune as usual.

The game folded, and David and John went to their room and talked about Dora and their hopes for her.

"I think she may have turned a corner," said David. "I hope so, it will be interesting to see how she coped at the WI today."

"She has a support team here, David," said John. "It's up to her to take advantage of it. I've never known a community spirit like there is here in all my life, it's a good place to live, and I'm sure she will realise it."

The following morning, David called on Dora, and she was tidy and ready to go out.

"Let's have a cup of tea first," she said. "I've never asked you about your exams and your plans."

David explained what he was planning to do next, having passed his exams. Dora had no idea what a first was, she thought he was top of the class, but he didn't offer an explanation, it didn't matter, she was just delighted he had been successful.

"I'd wondered if you might like to go to your old cottage and meet the new tenants," said David.

"I think I would be very sad if I did," she answered, "and I'm trying not to be. I don't ever want to go down the lane again where I found Bill, I couldn't bear it, and the dogs are buried down in the field, and I wouldn't like it if the new people hadn't kept up with the vegetable patch."

"I think that's a no, then," said David. "I called yesterday to check if it would be all right to take you and met Jane and her baby, Hattie, and she said it would be fine if you wished to visit, and I noticed the vegetable patch was in good order. It's in their interest to look after it and continue what Bill had started."

That conversation was ended.

"I saw a man yesterday who had been to China. He brought maps and showed us how far away it is from England," said Dora. "And he had a hat like the ones they wear in the paddy fields gathering rice because the Chinese eat a lot of rice and a beautiful long dress like the ladies wear and lots of photographs," she enthused. "Did you know they bind children's feet to stop them growing too big? We all thought that was very cruel. They eat with chop sticks, they don't have knives and forks, did you know that?"

David sat and listened and smiled and nodded until Dora paused for a moment, looked at him and said, "Are we going out then?"

"If you're ready," said David and stood up and held the door open.

Dora adjusted her hair and followed him out of the cottage, and they had a drive round the country lanes before going to call on the Gray's. David hadn't told Dora they were going to call, or she may have protested, but it turned out to be a very good thing. Mrs Gray, as always, made them very welcome, and as the day progressed, she asked Dora if she would consider helping her two days a week in the house or just cooking in the kitchen.

"Someone will collect you and take you home, so I'd like you to think about it, and I will call and see you next week," said Mrs Gray, "and of course you will be paid."

As David drove Dora home, he asked her how she felt about helping Mrs Gray out, because he knew if she did, Mrs Gray would be able to let him know how Dora was really doing.

"Do you think I should do it?" Dora asked.

"I think you should try it," replied David. "I'm sure Mrs Gray will consider what she asks you to do, but if you feel it is too much you can always stop."

"You're going home tomorrow," said Dora, having overheard a conversation whilst at the Gray's. "I'll miss you," she said tearfully, "but I'm so glad you came, and it was good to see John again, he looks well and content. I wish Jake had come too; he and Bill were such good friends."

"Yes, I know," said David. "He talks about Bill with great affection and will never forget how you both helped him through a difficult time."

"Maybe he'll come next time," said Dora.

"I will write to you," said David, "and when I know which days you are working at the Gray's, if you do, I can telephone you, and you will be able to speak to Jake. I'm going now, need to spend some time with the Gray's, and we have an early start tomorrow."

He gave her a hug. "You take good care of yourself," he said and left quickly.

Dora stood on the pavement and waved until the car turned the corner, turned back into her cottage, hugged the photograph of her and Bill on the beach and sobbed until her chest hurt and her eyes smarted, bathed in salty tears.

It was obvious Dora's situation would be discussed on the journey home, but David hoped she had pulled herself together for her future and not just whilst he was there but was reassured that Mrs Gray was going to be involved.

"Would there be a way of finding Dora's son?" David asked John.

John had never disclosed that on a previous journey he had called at the pub Dora and Bill used to visit near their farm, and learned that the son had joined the army, so he knew it would be possible to trace him if necessary.

"I think you need to respect Bill's decision regarding their son," said John. "It's nothing to do with us, but I don't think it would help Dora in the long run if he landed on her doorstep with a wife and at least one child we know about. Maybe they are long gone, who knows; one thing is certain, Dora doesn't need that sort of turmoil in her life now, she needs calm, routine and peace."

For the rest of the journey, if there was any conversation it was about the changes that were to take place in David's life during the next few weeks, months and years ahead.

Jake had already gone to bed when they arrived home.

"I'm glad I'm doing the late surgery tomorrow," said John, the words mingled in a yawn. "The journey is a lot less tiring by train, and quicker, it's just nice to have the convenience of the car when we are up there."

David lay in bed thinking about the conversation he had with John in the car and realised he would be seeing less and less of John and Jake as he moved on with his own life, and he didn't like the feeling at all; he was quite shocked to be thinking about it. He knew he could talk to them on the telephone and that he would see John when he came up to London, but he wasn't sure how much time he would have to spend at home with them and that troubled him.

I'll work something out, he thought as he drifted off to sleep, but in that moment, he could never have imagined how things would turn out.

Chapter 32

David had been into town to buy new clothes and shoes. As he walked through the village, he saw a tractor coming towards him, pulling a trailer with the fisherman's boat on. The fisherman, sitting inside his boat, doffed his cap and waved at David, who smiled, waved back and never gave it a second thought.

When John arrived home, David and Jake were sitting outside enjoying a glass of homemade ginger beer and had just commented on how noisy the incoming tide sounded.

John appeared in the car.

"Come along, Fay," he said. "Let's get you home before the storm breaks," so she hurriedly finished what she was doing and accepted John's offer of a lift home.

When he returned, Jake and David had walked half way down the garden steps towards the path, and were stood watching the pounding waves, in full swell, the sea exerting its power, tossing foam and debris high into the air.

"Gosh!" gasped David, "I've never seen anything like this before. I bet it's a sight to behold on by the rocks."

"It's a sight you'll have to forgo," said Jake, "this tide will cover the path and swallow anything on it, including you. Look at the sky, I think we need to go indoors."

A darkening sky loomed from the horizon like a velvet blanket, dark blue and purple, and now and again, shards of bright orange light flashed through.

With their backs turned as they climbed the steps up to the house, they missed seeing the lightning far out at sea but heard the rumble of thunder.

"Let's go up to the turret and watch," said David, so they took up the folding chairs and sat in a row and watched the storm getting nearer. When lightning lit up the sky, they could see the vastness of the waves as the sky growled and crackled and flung water at the land.

One almighty crack and bang just above the house, startled them and left them wide eyed and speechless momentarily.

"Phew!" said David, "didn't like that much."

"There will be damage tonight," said Jake. "I can only remember one other storm like this in all my life. A fishing boat was smashed to pieces on the rocks, but somehow the crew of four survived."

The next clap of thunder was inland, so they decided to return to the kitchen and have something to eat. As they walked along the passage past the bedrooms, there was a distant, prolonged boom like a cannon, and the house seemed to shake.

"What on earth was that?" said David, opening the door to the elements, but he could only hear the sound of the waves, and the relentless rain playing tunes on anything solid in the garden.

The telephone rang, and John answered. "Oh dear!" he said. "Oh dear, really, goodness me, we'll make our way over there, but I need to call at the surgery for first aid equipment." He turned to Jake and David. "There's been a landslide and some of the caravans have been swept from the cliff top onto the beach below. We're needed, get your waterproofs."

John's colleague was already at the surgery, and it was agreed that he would stay there in case there were any walking wounded that John couldn't deal with in adverse conditions.

When they arrived at the caravan park, it was mayhem, and there was very little they could do. The people needing help medically were the ones in the fallen caravans, and it was impossible to reach them whilst the tide was still in, and sadly, unlikely that anyone was still alive.

People with caravans now nearing the edge were cranking up the stands and being pulled further back into the field by a tractor, but the land was like a quagmire, making progress slow and difficult.

The groove the falling land, caravans and cars had made as they sunk on to the beach, was now like a waterfall rushing down to meet the tide, and a small touring caravan was being tossed about in the waves like a ball.

There were two ambulances and a fire engine, but the only thing that could be done was set up the generator for lighting. Once this had been done, the light was shone down to the beach below, and they could see a face at the window on the last caravan to fall, balanced precariously on its side. A fireman, secured to a harness, was lowered down, smashed the window, packed towels round the edge so the occupants were not cut, and one by one, timing the waves, assisted to safety was a teenage boy, a younger girl, and an even younger boy clutching his teddy.

The parents of the rescued children were crying and hugging, trying to cope with the emotions of the past hour. They knew their caravan and car had gone, but no one was allowed near the cliff edge, so they had no idea theirs was the last caravan to fall, and feared their children were drowned. They had not been aware of the rescue effort taking place, so to see the children running towards them, soaking wet and mud-splattered was such an emotion-filled joyous relief for them all.

John found Jake and David. "I don't think we can be of any use," he said, "everyone here seems to be all right, apart from being shocked and anxious, I think we should go home. Nothing can be done until the tide has gone out, and hopefully by then it will have stopped raining."

As they walked back to the car, David noticed the fisherman's boat on the trailer in the farmyard. "I saw him earlier today with his boat on the trailer," he said. "Would he know about the storm?"

"If anyone did, it would be him," said John. "He's worked fishing boats since he was a boy and he's in his 70s now, he seems to understand the ocean more than most, but he couldn't have known the cliff edge was going to cave in."

They walked home, their clothes too wet and muddy to be in the car, had soup and toast and rested, wrapped in blankets downstairs until they knew the tide had ebbed, and they returned to the caravan site.

Furthest out, a large caravan tilted on its side, half buried in sand and still in water, was being attended by a lifeboat crew, who returned with the last of the body bags to be put into the undertaker's black van waiting on the jetty. Such a sombre mood hung over the people watching in silence as the van drove away.

Down on the beach, there was much activity. Farmers had brought tractors, there were diggers from the building site, and the farmer from the next village had brought his two shire horses. David stood in awe and watched them using their might, snorting, tugging, working their might together, guided by the farmer and he thought of Biddy. In a moment when they were standing, steaming from their efforts in the damp air, David had to go and stroke them and talk to them. The farmer realised who he was and had a quick word. "You can come down to the farm any time you like if you want to spend time with them," he said.

"Maybe, thank you," said David, but he knew he wouldn't.

"I think we are probably getting in the way of all these people who can really help," said Jake. "I think we should go home, unless you want to stay and watch the horses working for a while." ·

"No, let's go home," said David. "I'm hungry and tired."

Fay made them scrambled eggs and bacon on toast, and they were able to go to bed and sleep until lunch time when John returned from his surgery.

"Been busy?" asked Jake on his return.

"Not really," replied John. "Mostly things were being dealt with on the beach because an ambulance crew and St John's ambulance volunteers were still attending, so the surgery was unusually quiet this morning. Need to go to bed for a couple of hours."

The vicar had opened the church hall and made available clothes that had been given for the next jumble sale, and ladies were making warm drinks and sandwiches for the volunteers.

When the tide had gone out, David decided to go for a walk along his usual route to see what had taken place during the storm. The path and the banking were covered in sand and debris, so he spent the afternoon dragging the worst of it to where the rocks were and throwing it back down into the sea. Jake came to see what he was up to. "The sand will dry out and the wind will take care of it, everything will be back to normal quite soon, even the plants recover," he said.

Within a week, the beach had been totally cleared and the mound of land that had fallen onto the beach had been flattened as much as possible by council workers, tidied up by the ocean, and everything was back to normal, just as Jake had said.

John had persuaded David to stay in the student block at St Thomas's, explaining that if he was there he would not miss out on opportunities that arose quickly in the hospital or a chance to socialise with his colleagues. Jake had told him to resist too much socialising and the importance of keeping up to his work. David smiled to himself. *I'm still their little boy*, he thought, but nothing detracted his determination to work hard and make them proud, as he had done at Cambridge.

Two days before they were to leave for London, David went down for breakfast to find a wooden box on the table where he usually sat.

He looked at John and Jake and opened the box to find a stethoscope and a note which said: *Use me often, I will teach you much. Our best wishes to you for your future. John and Jake.*

Despite his age, David could never hide his emotions, he looked across the table at them, tears rolling down his cheeks. "Can't speak," he spluttered, patted his heart and held his hand out to them. "Thank you."

Both John and Jake left for work, and David and Fay packed up the last few things he was taking with him.

Fay made coffee and went and sat outside with him. "Don't you start getting upset with me," she said, as she handed him a small box, "or you'll set me off."

Inside was a paper weight, clear glass with a swirl of blues and greens in the bottom, releasing blue bubbles.

"Thank you so much," said David, giving her a hug. "So thoughtful of you."

"I thought it would remind you of the sea now that you are leaving home," Fay said. "Do you ever wonder where your career will take you?"

"I'll still be coming home," David replied, "wherever my career takes me." But when Fay had returned to her work, David lay on his bed feeling anxious and uneasy, and when Jake came home, he spoke to him about it.

"This will not be home for any of us, soon. Have you seen the crack in the turret wall? Come and have a look," said Jake, determined to divert David from his misery.

They went up to the turret room and David was shocked to see how much longer and wider the crack had become.

"The house isn't about to fall down," said Jake. "I'm just saying that this will not be our home for the rest of our lives, but wherever we are will be your home, and that's the last I want to hear on the subject."

There was a telephone call from Dora who was at the Gray's house, and David was pleased to hear from Mrs Gray that Dora was doing well. He had spoken to her almost every week, as promised, and could tell and was happy that she had come out of the doldrums of grief.

Dougy telephoned to wish him well and made him laugh relating things that had happened at work, and Louis telephoned with good wishes and hoping to be able to meet up with David more often when he was in London. Monique and Jean and the family sent their good wishes, and even Dan wrote to wish him well.

No one wanted to drive into London, so all three of them went by train, loaded with luggage for David's student accommodation, which he had located during one of his previous visits to the hospital. They left the luggage in his room, and David put on his white coat and hung his stethoscope round his neck, did a twirl, a bow, and said, "Come on then, let's go and have something to eat."

"What will you miss about Cambridge?" Jake asked as they sat having their meal.

David thought for a moment before he replied, "The buildings, the beautiful grounds, the music wafting from choir rehearsals, punting on the river, and of course, friends, and one last thing, the ironing board."

"Well, you'll certainly have the buildings in London," said John, "but I think the music will be replaced by the drone of traffic, and I wouldn't try a punt on this river."

John and Jake stayed overnight at Mrs Fry's guest house. "Has he settled?" she asked.

"No idea," said John, sighing and shaking his head. "We left him to unpack and put things where he wants them. He's been very uptight, he needs something to do to occupy him until the lectures begin, and then he'll be all right. He'll be calling to visit you, I'm sure."

Three days later, David was hurtled into the routine of the hospital, quite stunned by the pace of life compared to being at Cambridge. There were many lectures, the occasional visit to a theatre or ward and many notes to write up. There was one exam that counted at the end of the three years, so it was imperative to have good notes to refer back to. The River Thames' embankment took the place of the coastal path when he needed a walk to clear his head and have some fresh air. Even as autumn turned to winter and the evenings were dark, the life on the river continued and fascinated him. He'd managed to meet up with Louis and some of his friends on one occasion and spend a lively evening at a Greek restaurant, but apart from that, he'd done very little socially, preferring to go swimming if he found he had some spare time when the pool was open.

John was able to make his visit coincide with David's leave for Christmas, so they could travel home together. Although they had spoken on the telephone, John had avoided meeting David on his visits, preferring to leave him to get on with what he was supposed to be doing, so there was much to talk about on their journey home.

"I wasn't ready for the pace of life in the hospital," said David. "I'm just getting used to it, but I was exhausted after the first few weeks. It's noisy in the student block, and I'm pretty sure some students are not keeping up, they can't be, out on the town so much. I'm certain someone got into my room and copied some notes from my clip file."

"How are you sure?" asked John.

"Because the notes in the ring file were not in the right order," replied David. "I think I know who it is, because he was answering questions in the lecture with details from my notes, I'm sure of it, because some of the detail came from one of your books from your office at home."

"What do you intend on doing about it? No one should have access to your room," said John.

"Nothing at the moment," replied David. "I've brought some work home with me, and the rest is locked in the box under the bed, out of view. How useful has that box been? "

"Things will settle down," said John. "They throw you in at the deep end so you realise from the very beginning what is involved. Remember you have spent time in London, but some students will have never been until now and go a bit wild in the beginning. Some will just want the white coat and to fraternise with the nurses, but they will soon be gone, the end of the first year sorts the wheat from the chaff."

It felt wonderful to be home and walk into the cosy kitchen that seemed so big after living in his small room. There was the homecoming stew in the oven and dumplings in a dish covered with a damp cloth for them to add to the stew when they arrived home.

In the lounge, Fay had decorated David's twig, which made him smile, and there was holly on the window sills, an acknowledgement to the festive season. London was festooned with Christmas lights, the shop windows were decorated, restaurants were filled with partygoers, people were scurrying about carrying parcels, and always, somewhere, there was Christmas music. Even the hospital had several Christmas trees, and Father Christmas was due to visit the children's ward, so in comparison, the village seemed very quiet.

The following morning, he dropped John off at the surgery and drove into town to do some shopping. He had a good look around, did his shopping, and on his way back across the square by the Christmas tree, he stopped to listen to the Salvation Army members singing carols, and his thoughts went back to when he was a boy, cold, in a doorway, holding a bag of scraps he had retrieved from the market traders. He put some money into the collection box.

"Thank you. God bless you," said the lady holding the box.

David smiled. "He surely has," he said as he walked away.

Christmas was celebrated as usual, lunch at the hotel in the village, and New Year watching TV and it all seemed to pass very quickly, leave being much less than at university. On the 2nd of January, David was on the train back to London and found himself looking forward to it.

The rest of the academic year was more settled, David realising he didn't have to have his head in his books and notes all the time. The tutors set tests without warning, and he did enough to satisfy them, so he became more relaxed and became a law unto himself as regards where he should really not be in the hospital. He would visit the children's ward, and spend time playing games or reading stories as he had done in the past, but because he was more aware of their illnesses now, he became curious, and when blood had been taken from the children for testing, he would take it up to the laboratory and stay and ask questions. Glandular fever and leukaemia had very similar symptoms, and sister had explained it took a long time for the correct diagnosis, during which time the children's health diminished. He'd also been observed sitting in at lectures on certain research for cancer. Even though he shouldn't have been there, no one questioned it, he would always slip in when the lecture had started, and slip out before the finish, and from time to time, he did question whether he was on the right course being on the medical side of things rather than research.

He managed to keep his promise to Dora and contacted her at the telephone box in the village or at the Gray's and was in regular contact with John and Jake at home, but John mostly avoided him at St Thomas's, just now and again they would have their evening meal at Mrs Fry's.

Returning from a lecture one afternoon, he found a note pushed under his door from John.

Dora unwell, ring Mrs Gray earliest possible. John.

David gathered as much loose change as he could find and went to the pay phone.

Mrs Gray answered, "Oh! David, I'm so glad you've called, Dora has pneumonia and is very ill. She's staying with us but has been troubled because she hasn't been at the telephone box if you've tried to call her." The Gray's had been away in Scotland for two weeks, and so they had all lost track of each other, during which time Dora had become ill. When Mrs Gray had caught up with her, she was in a very distressed state in hospital and just wanted to go home, so Mrs Gray took it upon herself to take her home where she could look after her. She handed Dora the telephone. "It's David," she said.

"Ooh! David," gasped Dora, "I'm not well."

"So I gather," said David, "but you're in good hands."

"I wanted to talk to you one more time before I go. I've loved you since the day you came as a scraggy lad to the farm, I'm so proud of you now, and I want you to promise me that you won't break off your studies to come all the way to my funeral. I will not know whether you are there or not, will I? What's important is what we have shared together in our lives, not me in a wooden box in a cold church. Promise me!"

"I promise, if that's what you wish," said David, "but I have to thank you for all your kindness to me as a scraggy lad. We've much to look back on, and I'm glad we kept in touch."

"Yes," replied Dora, who paused for a searing, rattly cough. "I think about the seaside when I close my eyes, that was very special for us. Bill is waiting for me, I know it won't be long, and I'm ready now."

Mrs Gray spoke next, "She's closed her eyes, she's resting now."

"I couldn't say 'Goodbye'," said David, unable to hide his emotions as he spoke. "I just couldn't. I'll telephone tomorrow."

He returned to his room and lay on his bed, thinking back, a reality check on his past, when there was a knock on the door and John walked in.

David made tea and they talked about Dora, who had also insisted that John and Jake didn't make the journey for her funeral.

"As far as I know," said John, "there has been no mention of her son, and as far as we are concerned, we will leave it that way. Do you understand what I'm saying?"

"Yes," replied David, and the conversation was ended, but he did wonder if that was the right thing to do.

John left, and David went into Westminster Abbey and sat for a while, took a walk along the embankment, returned to his room with a sandwich and listened to his radio.

David telephoned Mrs Gray the following morning to learn Dora had passed away during the night.

"The doctor and I were with her, and she's now at the Chapel of Rest," she said. "I can't tell you when the funeral is, but don't send flowers, she wants there to be a collection at the church, so if you wish you can send me a cheque and I will cash it and put the money in the collection which is for the church hall and community centre. I took her to the solicitor a few months ago so there is a will, leaving any money remaining in her bank account to you and anything you want from her home. She told me you had a memory box, so think about what you would like, and the rest of her things are to be distributed amongst the needy in the village. Nothing will be touched until after the funeral, but I need to know because the landlord has someone waiting to move in. David, are you still there?"

"Yes," he replied, "I was just thinking. I'd like the little bedside table Bill made for them if you will keep it for me, and the photograph of us on the beach. I feel a bit uncomfortable about it all, she's only just passed away and we are talking about getting rid of her treasures. They will be gone in a week and it took her and Bill a lifetime of hard work to get most of them."

"I know," said Mrs Gray, fully understanding his point of view, "but her treasures are no good to her now, she had the pleasure of them when she was alive, and they will help many in the village, and that's what she wanted."

He bid 'farewell' to Mrs Gray, and went along to a lecture, but he was in a sombre mood and not really listening.

"What's wrong?" asked Mandy, a colleague whom he went to many lectures with.

"I had bad news this morning," replied David. "A lovely lady whom I cared for very much passed away during the night."

"I'm sorry to hear that," said Mandy, gently. "I'll type up my notes and run a copy for you if that will help."

"Thank you," said David, "that's very kind. I'll treat you to lunch, but not today, it would be one of those times when conversation is awkward, and I'd prefer it to be fun."

"I know," said Mandy, "that is fine, I'll catch up with you later." And they parted company.

Time passed, and when the cheque arrived from the solicitor's for David, Jake recommended that half of it went into a new bank account and was left there for five years, just in case Dora's son appeared on the scene.

Arrangements had been made for David to pay for a headstone for the grave at the appropriate time, and that would be the last chapter in the life story of Dora and Bill, logged into his memory to recall many times during his own life.

When he closed his eyes and thought about them, he saw Bill standing in their farmyard with the dogs, Dora collecting eggs in her basket amongst the strutting, pecking hens, and the smell of fresh baking bread wafting from the kitchen.

Chapter 33

Now, well into his second year of study at St Thomas's, David was experiencing visits to different wards and theatres in the hospital and still visiting the research laboratories when he could.

Sitting having his lunch one day in the hospital restaurant, he was approached by a very colourful presence of a man wearing a tweed suit of large checks, a bright green waistcoat, green and white striped shirt with a red bow tie. His spectacles were half-way down his nose, flat on the top so he could peer over them and he was sporting a moustache that was turned up and waxed at the end.

"May I?" he asked, indicating he wanted to sit in the empty seat opposite David.

"Please," said David, moving his teapot to make room on the table.

David became aware the conversational noise had quietened in the restaurant and people were staring or glancing across at him.

"Am I missing something here?" he asked, looking puzzled.

"Probably," said the man, "I'm Professor Bouvais."

David knew then who he was from his reputation as the renowned and respected surgeon who worked in St Thomas's and Guys hospitals and occasionally further afield.

"Did you get lost?" asked David.

"Get lost," the professor repeated, with a questioning expression on his face.

"Did you take the wrong turning to end up in our dining room?" David said mischievously.

"No," replied the professor, "I just like to stir things up sometimes."

He peered at David over his spectacles with a wry smile on his face.

From then on, the conversation was comfortable and good humoured, the professor wanting to know all about David, his education, what he had been working on recently and his plans for the future.

"How are you coping with the gore in theatre?" asked the professor.

"The gore doesn't bother me," replied David. "The actual plumbing in the body fascinates me, but the smell gets to me, it's eye-watering sometimes."

The professor laughed, wiped his moustache with his serviette and stood to leave.

David stood and shook his hand. "I'm pleased to have met you," he said.

"Likewise," said the professor and left.

As soon as he'd left the dining room, there was a clatter of chairs and David was surrounded by students wanting to know what the professor had said.

"Just chatting about student life," said David, who wasn't prepared to disclose details of their conversation, even though it had been on a very general basis.

"Did he invite you to go with him on his visit to Yorkshire?" asked one of the students.

"Never mentioned it," answered David. "I don't know anything about that."

"He takes four students with him each year to shadow him at the teaching hospital in Leeds for four weeks," explained the student. "That's an opportunity most of us would like."

"It was never mentioned, and this is the first time I've heard about it from you. Actually, I've never been to observe any of his work, I've just heard about him and how skilled he is," David informed the students.

The following week, David was scheduled to observe the professor in surgery with another student. By coincidence or intentionally, he never knew, he just was glad of the opportunity and was totally absorbed in surgery he had never experienced before. The professor talked through what he was doing, and why, and invited David and the other student attending to look and ask questions.

After surgery, the two students were invited to the professor's office where the operation was discussed, the professor wanting to see what the students had taken from the experience. "Any problems?" he asked.

"Well," replied David, "I realised I didn't know many of the names of the instruments that were needed."

"If you get a good senior theatre nurse, she will help you along, and you learn all the time, and of course the instruments change and improve over time, but you do need to familiarise yourself with them. How do you both feel about accompanying me to Yorkshire for a four-week period?"

"Absolutely," said David, enthusiastically, smiling like the cat that got the cream, and the other student gave a similar response.

David telephoned home that evening full of energetic enthusiasm, and Jake and John were so proud and happy for him.

"You may have chance to go to the village," said Jake, "if you feel inclined and have the time."

"Maybe," said David. "That could be interesting."

The four students selected were given a list of surgeries that the professor would be covering where they would observe and possibly participate, so they had chance to read up on the subjects, and a list of what was expected of them professionally. They had to be appropriately dressed at all times, know the patients' name, age and history of illness, and he had a saying, "It is more important to aim to be safe than brilliant." David had managed to spend some time with a theatre nurse and make a few notes on instruments, and a month later, they were in student accommodation at the Leeds Teaching Hospital with a timetable to adhere to.

On one of the days, the students were to be collected early morning and travel out of Leeds to another hospital, and as they drove into the hospital grounds, David realised it was where his mother had died. He recognised the ornate arched doorway, and as they walked down the corridor, the shiny green tiles he had run his fingers on as a boy, that were above his head, were now waist high. He remembered the tinkling of the Christmas decorations as the draught caught them from the open door, and the eeriness of that moment crept over him.

"I'll catch you up," he said to the other students. "I just need to do something."

He remembered his way to the tiny ward his mother had been in, which could have been changed into anything by now, but as he turned the corner, it was still there, unoccupied. He pushed the door open and stood looking across at the bed and felt cold, there was a presence, a voice whispering, "Well done son, I'm so proud of you." He felt a rustle behind him and he jumped and turned to see a very round lady with rosy cheeks, wearing a navy-blue dress with a white collar and an ornate head piece, clearly matron.

"Can I help you?" she said, in a voice as starchy as her white collar.

"I'm here to work with Professor Bouvais in theatre G," said David.

"So why are you here?" she asked. "This is nowhere near the theatres."

"My mother died in this ward at Christmas when I was 11," said David. "I just felt compelled to come here."

Matron's tone changed. "I'll give you a few moments," she said, "and I'll accompany you to the lifts for the theatres."

"It's fine," said David, "I'm ready now." He was glad she was there.

He spent the entire morning in theatre with the professor explaining about the surgery he was undertaking in a quiet but pedantic manner. The senior theatre nurse had worked with him before, and it was clear she had drilled her team, because everything ran smoothly, and at the end of the session, the professor thanked them. "Good teamwork today, people," he said. "Thank you very much."

The afternoon was free, so whilst the others returned to Leeds, David caught a bus to the village where he was born, had lived and gone to school in and finally run away from. He walked around for a while, some things had changed, houses had been built on the land where the station used to be, but little else had changed.

He walked up the hill towards where Rebecca used to live, and saw a lady rocking a pram in the garden of Bertha's house, which told him Bertha had probably passed away.

"Hello," said David, "does Mr Brown still live here?

"Yes," said the lady, "just knock, but he takes a while to get to the door."

David knocked and waited. The door opened, and Mr Brown, now smaller than David, looked up and said, "Yes?"

"I wonder if you remember me?" said David, "My name is David."

"My God!" said Mr Brown. "Just look at you, come in, come in, I'll put the kettle on."

"We talk about you every Christmas," said Mr Brown, "and I was glad when Hobo told me you were safe, but that's all he said. You must stay for tea, Rebecca will be here in half an hour, she's been on early shift this week."

"How is Mrs Brown?" David asked, having forgotten Jake had told him she had left.

"She left us, a long time ago. Rebecca grew up very fast, she had to. Bertha helped her a lot but eventually, Rebecca became her carer too. I had to retire, the company I worked for moved away, and I couldn't cope with the travelling due to arthritis. Couldn't afford a car, so the job stopped."

The door burst open. "Hello, Dad. Oh! Sorry, I didn't know you had company," said Rebecca.

"Very special company," said Mr Brown, as David stood up to greet her. "It's David."

David smiled at her and she just flung herself at him and hugged him. "Where have you been?" she asked.

David suddenly became aware that there was a man standing in the kitchen, watching.

"This is Ben," said Rebecca, pulling herself together, "this is David."

211

The two men shook hands

Mr Brown saw Ben looking at the table set for three, so quickly said, "I've asked David to stay for tea, so you can catch up."

"Don't forget we are going out," said Ben to Rebecca.

"Can we go another night?" asked Rebecca. "It would be very rude of me not to stay when our guest has come all this way."

She had no idea where David had come from or where he was going, but he was there now, and she needed to spend time with him and find out what had happened to him.

Ben left, not happy, glowering at David.

Of course, David had noticed Rebecca was wearing a nurse's uniform when she arrived, but it was later when they were talking that he learned she worked in the same hospital he had been in earlier with the professor.

When she went upstairs to change, David spoke to Mr Brown. "I hope I've not caused a problem for her with her boyfriend," he said.

"Don't worry about him," said Mr Brown. "He turns up when he wants and messes Rebecca about, I don't understand why she puts up with him."

"I take it you don't care for him," said David, smiling.

"I think you might be right about that," said Mr Brown, "but I'll only interfere if I have to. Rebecca knows how I feel about him, and I think he does too. There's a dark side to him which I can't fathom out. Sometimes we don't hear from him for weeks, not even at weekends, he says he's a travelling salesman and has to be away from home, and she believes him, but I'm not sure I do. When I ask him where he's been, I can almost hear the cogs spinning in his head, and his knowledge of the geography of this country is questionable. Maybe that's why it takes him three weeks to do what I did in one." Mr Brown giggled as Rebecca entered the room, so the conversation ended.

They spent a wonderful evening together, and when Rebecca walked down to the bus stop with David in time to catch the last bus to Leeds, she didn't say anything, just hoped she would see him again.

"Can I telephone you sometime?" David asked.

David wrote her number down in the small notebook he always carried in his pocket, usually for bus or train timetables, or any other trivia he might want to remember from his travels.

She sat on the wall beside him and stared. "What?" he said looking back at her.

"I can't believe how you have turned out from such humble beginnings, that puny scrap of a boy. You have much to thank Hobo and his brother for, but you must have worked very hard to get where you are today, and I just feel so glad for you."

The bus arrived, he patted her on her head and said, "I'll call you," and was gone.

David waited a few days and telephoned in the afternoon and spoke to Mr Brown. "Will it be all right for me to call Rebecca this evening? I don't want to complicate things with her and Ben."

"It will be fine," said Mr Brown, "don't worry about him, he's on his travels."

At the middle of the third week in Leeds, the professor and his students returned to the hospital where Rebecca worked. There was a young widow with two small children awaiting surgery for stomach cancer that the professor was to undertake, and it was David who had been assigned to go into the history of her case and the diagnosis and what was anticipated regarding the surgery. He spoke to the lady at length and learnt she was a widow of 32 with two young children, an ailing mother and no other family. When he visited her with the professor and the residing consultant, he was able to answer the questions put to him and was prepared for the theatre an hour later, but she died, unable to cope with the extensive surgery.

David had gasped when the team gave up on her, so the professor pointed out how the cancer had migrated to other organs, and her frail body had no chance of surviving.

David was uneasy with the matter of fact way the rest of the team had accepted it, and the professor noticed this, so asked David to accompany him and the ward sister to give the news to her mother. "She will know why we have called her in," said the professor, "but I always think it is important to go through things with the family, to explain fully, so they are not left wondering all kinds of weird things."

David stood and listened to the professor explaining to the mother why they had been unable to save her daughter's life. His words drifted over her numbness, and David just stood and felt her pain, and just managed to mumble, "I'm very sorry," as he left the room.

David couldn't manage lunch but felt the need for a strong coffee, so he called into the dining room and spotted Rebecca sitting at a table with three other nurses. He drank his coffee, his mind still reeling from the earlier events, and then as he was leaving, he walked over to Rebecca and said, "I'll call you tonight."

"Who is that?" asked one of the nurses. "Very dishy!"

"Oh!" replied Rebecca, closing her eyes and holding up the palms of her hands. "Just a figment of my imagination."

The nurses tried to prise more information out of Rebecca, but they didn't get any, and it was time to return to the ward.

David left the hospital and walked the mile into town to catch his train back to base, needing to settle his mind and enjoying the sunshine. There was time to call in The Huntsman for a shandy before his train was due, and he was sitting on a bar stool when he became aware of the laughter from a group of people around the corner from him.

"Someone is having a good time," David said to the barman.

"Yes," said the bar man, "they've just got married, and not before time, by the look of her. She's ready to drop anytime, I'd say."

As the group broke up and were leaving, David observed them through the mirrored wall at the back of shelves holding miniature bottles of liqueurs and was utterly shocked. The very pregnant bride was holding hands with her new groom as they waved 'Goodbye' to their family and friends and left. It was Ben.

David sat, unnoticed by the group, finished his drink and walked to the station to catch his train, his mind racing. He felt angry now knowing that this man had lied and manipulated Rebecca, and she was bound to be humiliated.

When he arrived at his accommodation, he telephoned Mr Brown straightaway and related what he had seen.

"Well," said Mr Brown, "I always felt there was something not right about his excuses for being away, and now we know. You are absolutely sure it was him?"

"I am," said David. "The guests spoke his name several times."

"Well," said Mr Brown, "It's going to be a jolly old evening here. I think I'll wait until after tea before I tell Rebecca, or we might not get any tea and lose a few dishes. I'm really glad you telephoned me, he could have continued turning up here, he may do even now he is married, but we will be ready for him, and he'll only come once. I've never really known just how Rebecca felt about him, she never said much, but I hope she didn't know he was in another relationship."

"You'll soon know by her reaction," said David. "I'll be thinking about you tonight."

During the evening, David took himself off onto the surgical ward and spoke to sister on duty, gleaning information that wasn't sinking in altogether, but he just wanted to take his mind off the events of earlier in the day. He went to talk to a man whose operation David had observed and was glad to see him looking much better than before the surgery. The professor was doing his rounds, having been absent for two days and was surprised to see David on the ward.

"How long has he been here?" he asked the sister.

"Not long," she said, "he hasn't interfered with anything, just looked at the patient's notes and talked to him. This young man wears his heart on his sleeve."

David waved at sister as he walked passed her office, and didn't know the professor was there, sitting on a seat in the corner reading through his notes.

Returning to his accommodation, he collected an envelope addressed to him that was pinned to the notice board, an invitation for him plus one to a garden party at the professor's home on the Saturday before he was due to return to London on the Sunday. This, he learned, was a tradition each year, just 20 people were invited with their partners of choice.

He smiled. *This could be just what the doctor ordered*, he thought. *I could invite Rebecca, but I need to speak to Mr Brown first, I need to check how Rebecca is coping.*

The following day, the professor sent for him and told him to spend the day in the research department of the hospital. A man was introduced to him, who would accompany him for the day, and once they had left the office and were walking towards the new building, he quizzed David as to what his interests were in research.

"Well, it all fascinates me," replied David, "but cancer research has drawn me."

During the day, he was shown many aspects of the research they were covering in the huge, sterile laboratories. He asked many questions, making the most of the opportunity, and took notes as usual, because he knew there would be tests on his return to London. He was reluctant to leave when the time came, he was so engrossed in it all and thanked everyone very sincerely as he left. He went back to the dining room and had his meal, and returned to his room, extended his notes whilst he could remember things and decided to telephone Rebecca.

She answered the telephone. "Hello!" she said.

"Hello," said David, "are you ok?"

"What do you think?" she said, "I'm bloody furious. How could he?"

"Well," said David softly, "it's better, you know. Did you think the relationship was going somewhere in the future?"

"I don't think I did," replied Rebecca. "I think he was just a bad habit I had. Should have listened to Dad, I suppose, but it isn't over until I've seen him, I think he could turn up one day, and he won't know I know he's married, so I'll let him run with it to see what sort of rubbish he comes out with and then I'll give him a proper tongue lashing. If I see him with his wife, I'll just ignore him, it wouldn't be fair to upset her. Anyway, that's enough about him, how have you been?"

"I've been fine," said David, "and I'm really calling to see if you would like to accompany me to a garden party at the professor's home next Saturday? You will need to be in Leeds by 1 pm to catch the coach to his home, the party finishes at 6 pm so there will be plenty time for people to return home without it being too late."

"I'd love to," she said. "I really would, and I'm not due into work, so that would be great."

"I gather it's quite formal, so don't turn up in slacks and a sloppy jumper," said David.

"Can't come then," replied Rebecca, teasing. "I've only got slacks and sloppy jumpers and clogs."

Mr Brown was so pleased Rebecca's spirits had lifted after the telephone call, and they discussed the conversation.

"What shall I wear?" she asked.

"I'd get something new," said Mr Brown. "It's ages since you bought new clothes, and remember the company you are going to be in, you'll be at David's side, so just put some thought into what you buy. Take some money from what Bertha gave you and call in town tomorrow after your shift."

When Rebecca left home to meet David, Mr Brown stood on the doorstep until she waved and disappeared. He closed the door, sat in his chair and sighed. *How like her mother she looks*, he thought, and memories came flooding back until he fell asleep.

David was standing on the platform when he caught sight of Rebecca. She looked stunning in a floral skirt swaying on top of just visible frilly petticoats and a white gypsy style blouse with puffed sleeves, white handbag, shoes and gloves. He had only seen her with her hair scraped back from her face in a bun for her work, but now her long brown curly hair was bouncing off her shoulders as she walked towards him. She smiled when she saw him. His stomach did something unfamiliar, his heart seemed to leap into his mouth, and he could hardly speak.

"Hello," he said, "you look wonderful."

"Don't sound so surprised," she said, playfully, but was glad he approved.

He took her hand and they walked through the station to the awaiting coach where there were some familiar faces to David, and Rebecca recognised two nurses from her hospital who had clearly managed to persuade the visiting students to take them along.

She was enjoying the scenery as the coach drove through villages she had never heard of, but now and again, she glanced across the aisle at two couples who presented themselves very differently to the rest of the group. The ladies were demure, in smart suits with pencil-slim skirts and fitted jackets, and blouses with big bows at the neck and hats. The men had cream coloured trousers, tweed jackets and bow ties.

"Who are they?" she whispered to David.

"No idea," David replied, "but if they wanted to stand out in the crowd, they've certainly succeeded." He didn't say it, just wondered if there was a hint of Professor Bouvais in the men's attire.

David held Rebecca's hand as they walked up the long drive to the house to be greeted by the professor and his wife. Tables were arranged around the edge of the huge lawn, and in a corner, there was a small group of musicians playing songs from the musicals. Two waiters were walking round with trays of drinks, and Rebecca had her first taste of champagne.

"Ooh! This is nice," she said and quickly emptied her glass and reached for another.

"Steady on," said David, "it's not pop, just take little sips or you'll get drunk."

She did manage to get another when David went in to the bathroom and was feeling very frivolous and light headed, so decided that was enough. However, she had been to the band and asked them to play music for the Paul Jones dance and managed to get everyone but the 'demure couples' up on their feet and dancing. They looked startled, as if they couldn't believe what was actually happening, and couldn't be persuaded to join in. All the other ladies had taken their shoes off, the men were in a circle on the outside, the ladies in a circle on the inside moving the opposite way, and when the music stopped and changed, they danced with whoever was opposite them, to whatever the band played, maybe gay Gordons or the barn dance, or just waltzing round. When David returned to the outside, he stopped dead in his tracks when he saw Rebecca in the centre of the circle twirling round, clapping her hands, and encouraging everyone to dance.

"Come on," she said, "join in," and she joined the circle of ladies.

Everyone was having a good time, laughing and singing to the music until the band stopped playing and it was time to go and have some food. David caught up with Rebecca and stood at the back of her as they approached the table of food.

"Behave yourself," he whispered.

Rebecca had never been to a buffet with so much food, the likes of which she had never seen before, and although she was tempted to try everything, she took small portions of what she recognised, and carried it outside to a table, accompanied by David who had grabbed a glass of water for her. He didn't tell her to drink it, just nodded at it, and she got the message. Another two couples joined them and said how much fun they had had during the dancing, so Rebecca was hoping that would lessen the telling off she expected from David.

When it was almost time to leave, Rebecca was sitting on the steps, shoes still in her hand, gloves in her handbag, when the professor's wife, Stella, sat down beside her.

"Oh, gosh," said Rebecca, "have I blown it for David?"

"Not at all," replied Stella. "This may be the last time we have a garden party, and it will certainly be memorable. These occasions can be very stuffy, today has been fun, and I'm pleased to have met you. Are you and David engaged?"

"No," replied Rebecca, "we grew up together and just met recently having not been in touch for many years."

"Better snap him up then," said Stella, "before someone else does. He's quite a catch."

David joined them and thanked Stella. Rebecca put on her shoes, and they joined the others walking towards the coach, Rebecca remaining very quiet. When they climbed the steps into the coach, everyone apart from the 'demure' couples clapped and cheered. "Nice one, Rebecca," shouted someone from the back of the coach, "we needed someone to jolly things along, it was really good fun." The 'demure' ladies looked positively sour, but one of the men winked at her, unnoticed by his partner.

Rebecca snuggled up to David on the coach, and they held hands as they walked towards the platform to wait for Rebecca's train.

"Are you all right?" David asked.

"I think I might be getting a headache," Rebecca replied.

David smiled and shook his head, put his finger under her chin to lift her head to kiss her 'goodnight', and blew her a kiss as the train left the station.

The other two nurses who worked at the same hospital joined Rebecca and chatted and giggled on the journey home. She got off a station earlier than the girls and had a half-mile walk now they had closed the station in the village, so by the time she reached home, she was bursting to tell her father all about the day. He could tell she was happy and more like her old self.

"He kissed me, Dad," she said.

Mr Brown was surprised she mentioned it. He knew it wasn't the first time she had been kissed, but it seemed to mean something quite special to her.

She stretched out on the sofa and closed her eyes for a few moments before she stood up and said, "I think I'll just float off to bed."

Mr Brown laughed at her as she kissed him 'goodnight'.

"Rebecca." He asked, "Why are your feet green?"

She just gave him a cheeky smile and said nothing.

David had walked back to his accommodation and packed his case, ready for an early start the following morning, had a shower and lay on his bed reflecting on the day. The feelings he had towards Rebecca were new to him, she was energetic and good fun, and he was taken aback by her looks and presence, he wanted to spend time with her, get to know her better and take care of her, but he knew he had to return to his studies in London and be realistic about when he could see her again.

Chapter 34

On his return to St Thomas's, David was back into the routine of shifts on the wards, days in theatre, or attending lectures, and stuck to his routine of keeping up to date with his notes, hoping he had done enough when the exams came around. A sister on the men's surgical ward had told him it would be advantageous to engage with the nurses and ask for their help, and by doing this, he gleaned further information which was not in the textbooks or passed on at lectures, and he hoped this information would enhance his chances of good results in the exams. He respected the nurses, which meant they were always willing to explain things to him and have some fun when work was done. Whenever he could, he would take himself up to the research laboratories, his interest stimulated more and more, especially when a senior member of staff took time out to show and explain to him what they were doing.

At the end of a busy day, David had taken a walk along the embankment to clear his head, and as he walked back towards his accommodation, he noticed the glow in the sky where bonfires had been lit on spare ground. He could hear the whizz of the occasional rocket and noticed the pathetic effort as they shed a few stars before the stick fell to the ground. As a child in the village, he never had any fireworks of his own, and he just hung around in the background and watched, hoping someone would offer him a piece of plot toffee, sometimes targeted by boys throwing bangers. When he lived with John, there was a bonfire on the spare ground in the village, but he was always more interested in the pie and peas and parkin available in the village hall, and whilst at university, he never attended any bonfire. He did notice that the fireworks had become louder and some more vibrant and colourful than he remembered, but he just wasn't interested.

As he approached the hospital, he became aware of the many ambulances announcing their arrival and walked towards Casualty, curious to see what was happening.

"Are you free?" a sister shouted, recognising him. "Get a white coat from my office and follow me."

He did just that and followed her down the corridor into the Casualty area. He was stunned, he'd heard screams and crying as he walked down the corridor but was not prepared for what he was seeing. There were many children with burns on their hands from grabbing hold of the wires from sparklers, one teenager had her hair set on fire, her neck was burnt, and her scarf had welded itself to her skin, a little boy had bad burns on his legs, and the more David looked around, the more horrified he was. He shadowed the sister for three hours; all evening long, patients were coming and going, but he just did what he was asked. He noticed even Professor Bouvais was in a corner of the room assisting with patients being admitted with heart attacks, suspected strokes and abdominal problems, the more usual cases to arrive in Casualty.

"Come with me," sister said and led him to a side ward where a man lay on a stretcher, waiting to be transferred to a burns unit, his face, hands and arms covered in gauze dressings. Sister removed the dressing from his face, took a shiny spoon from her pocket and held it over his mouth for a moment to see if breath clouded it and shook her head. "He's gone, his body would never have recovered from the severity of these burns."

David was frozen to the spot, hardly able to bear to look at the man. One eye socket was just a charred black hole, the other eye was a huge red blister like his ears and lips, and the whole of the rest of his face and neck was covered in blisters as if someone had spread strawberry jam over him. His hands and shins were the same. David gasped and put his hands to his mouth, feeling sick and faint.

"Sit down," said sister, as she soaked gauze dressings in sterile cold water and covered the man's burns again, still compelled to care for him until they took him to the mortuary.

"What happened to him?" asked David.

"He was putting petrol from a can around a bonfire to light it, and someone threw a firework in. He has a wife and three children. His wife came with him, so she will have that memory with her for the rest of her life. A terrible accident, so many lives changed in seconds, and of course, the person who threw the firework will have to live with that memory too."

David left the room, sat on the bench in the corridor and closed his eyes as tears scalded his cheeks. *This isn't good, what's happening to me?* he thought. He became aware that someone was there with him, and when he looked, it was the professor.

"Whew!" sighed David deeply, unable to hide his emotions. "Have you seen the state of the man in there? What's going to happen to his family? It's been like a war zone in there tonight, don't people think about what they are doing? A moment's carelessness or wilfulness, and lives are changed forever."

The professor went into the side ward, had a look at the deceased man, and even he was horrified at the sight of him. "The worst I've ever seen," said the professor when he returned to David, "but Florence Nightingale would have to deal with much worse."

Two staff from the canteen were pushing a trolley along the corridor that contained everything for making mugs of tea and jugs of hot milk for making cocoa or a malted drink. They stopped when they reached the two men. "Cup of tea?" one of the staff asked.

"Thank you, yes, please," replied the professor. "One sugar I think."

"And for you, sir?" David was asked.

"No, thank you," David replied.

"Yes, he will have a tea," said the professor.

They sat together and sipped their tea, and the professor enquired how David's studies were going.

"I've done my best to keep up, and only time will tell now," said David, "but I think I need a break. I'm thinking of going home for a few days."

"A good idea," said the professor, "but I would like to speak to you before you go. Make an appointment with my secretary. Now I need to check on someone I admitted earlier this evening before I leave; I suggest you go home as things have quietened down."

The air was cold and smoky as David walked back to his room. He had a shower and lay in bed thinking over the events of the evening and was unable to sleep. He squirmed and sighed, got up and made a drink, and eventually went back to bed and to sleep. When he woke up, he was already an hour late for his shift, so he decided to call in to see the professor's secretary and make an appointment to see him.

The following day at 8 am, David was sitting opposite the professor wondering what was to come out of the meeting, why was he there at all?

"Right," said the professor peering at David over the top of his glasses, "let's get down to it. I don't want you to think I have any doubts regarding your commitment or ability regarding what you are doing now. I know you will do well in your exams, both practical and theory."

"Then why am I here?" asked David.

The professor continued "It's inevitable that there are failures in our work despite all our best efforts. People die, mothers, fathers, children, old and young alike. I know you understand that this can happen and why but having observed you over a period of time, I have concluded that it takes a lot out of you and am concerned that over time you may find it hard to cope, and I have seen what can happen to people working under this pressure. Patient's personal circumstances are not our concern, there are other people in the hospital trained to deal with all that. How do you feel about what I am saying to you?"

There was a pause, David sighed deeply and said quietly, "I think you are right, I'll just have to find a way of coping."

The professor continued, "In answer to your question, you are here because I wondered how you felt about going into research. How do you feel about visiting Leeds with me after the exams and spending four days in the laboratories where you spent time before? There will be an opening there next year if you make the grade. I've procured this opportunity for you; the rest is up to you. You said you were going to have a break, I think you should, and don't take any work home with you, clear your head, and let me know of your decision on your return."

The professor could see David was becoming emotional, so he changed the subject.

"How's your young lady, Rebecca, isn't it?" he asked.

"We're still in touch," said David, "but I have not seen her for a long time. It's difficult, she's a nurse working shifts, she looks after her arthritic father and runs the home. We talk on the telephone once a week as long as our shifts don't collide, and that's it, at the moment."

The professor winked at David. "You'd be able to see a lot more of her if you were in Leeds," he said. "Just understand I am trying to help you here with your career, nothing more. See me when you get back from your leave."

David shook the professor's hand and left his office, thoughts reeling from the conversation.

The following day, he was on his way home. He hadn't telephoned to let John and Jake know he was coming so as not to disrupt any plans they had, so he had to walk from the station home. It was a dark, clear November evening, and as he neared home, he could hear the sea and was breathing in the salty air and loving the moment and feeling glad to be home.

He opened the door gently and walked into the kitchen to find Jake eating his dinner and Fay by the sink, washing up. She ran across the room and hugged him. "Oh my gosh," she said, "are you all right?" Jake was clearly just as pleased to see him but was taken aback that David hadn't let them know he was coming. David looked at Jake and realised he was waiting for an explanation.

"I'm just frazzled with it all at the moment," David said. "I just needed to get away and clear my head."

Jake understood perfectly, having gone through the same pressures many years before under the watchful, strict eye of his father.

Fay fussed about and filled four hot water bottles to air David's bed.

"I won't need four," David said, laughing at her.

"Oh, yes, you will!" she said and disappeared upstairs. When she returned, she put on her coat to leave.

"John has the car," said Jake. "Perhaps you would care to see Fay home."

"Sure," replied David, and they set off arm in arm up the lane.

"We turn right here now," said Fay. "I've moved house."

They walked along the road where council houses were being built, and at the very far end of a row of finished properties, Fay walked up the path and took a key out of her pocket and smiled proudly. "Come in and have a look," she said, excitedly. "It's got two bedrooms, which is enough because the chickens have left the nest apart from my youngest, a bathroom so I have an indoor toilet, and outside I have a little garden to sit in." Everything was tidy, she had made curtains and cushion covers to match from a pretty floral fabric, the floor was covered in a light grey vinyl with a shaggy red rug in front of the fire.

"This is wonderful," David said. "I'm so pleased for you. I could never fathom out how you all managed in the tiny cottage, especially when the four children were growing up."

"It's all we knew," said Fay, laughingly. "But we were never cold at bed time. I'm pretty sure John helped me to get one of these houses, our cottage was so damp it was a case of dying from pneumonia or being flattened under a pile of slates, because just a week after I moved, the chimney stack fell through the roof. We think someone had been stealing lead. He got me a job in the kitchen at the school, too, so I only go to the house three afternoons a week now, but it seems to work very well.

David returned home and made himself beans and egg on toast and went to sit with John and Jake in the lounge. The rooms in the house seemed huge and cold after living in student accommodation, but the fire in the lounge was piled high with glowing logs and this room was warm as he cosied himself into an armchair. He knew they were waiting to hear why he had turned up out of the blue, so he settled and related his conversation with the professor.

"How do you feel about Bouvais' suggestion?" asked John. "He's a very clever and well-respected man. If he's prepared to help you, he will certainly think you are worth it, students clamour for his attention."

"I know," said David. "I appreciate all the time and effort and opportunities he's given me, but I'll be wasting the work and effort I have put in over the past three years; in fact, is there any point in taking the exams if I'm moving into research?"

"Of course there is," said Jake, emphatically. "You'll have that qualification behind you and will have gleaned so much knowledge along the way that it is bound to help in research. Your experience over the past three years will be invaluable.

"Jake, did you never fret over losing a patient?" David asked.

"My surgery is involved with diseases and injuries of the musculoskeletal system. I'm working with fractures, spine disorders, dislocations and the like," said Jake "There can be disappointments and setbacks, but my surgery is not a high risk. Although it does happen sometimes after a bad accident, it is usually from other injuries to the brain or internal bleeds."

"Maybe that's a route I could go down," said David.

"Maybe it is," said John. "That's why it's important to do well in your exams. A good result is there forever to back you up if you try research and don't take to it."

"That's enough to go to bed on," said Jake. "We'll talk tomorrow, there is much to discuss."

Jake accompanied David up to his room, using a torch to light the way.

"Has the light bulb gone?" David asked.

"More than that," said Jake, shining the torch on to a large crack that was working its way down the outer wall. "We've had to stuff it with rags to keep the draught out."

"Am I safe in here?" David asked.

"You'll be fine" said Jake, chuckling. "You've slept in worse places than this in the past. See you in the morning."

Early the following morning, David took the torch and found his way down the steps onto the coastal path. The tide was just turning and quiet, the little waves just slushing and turning, finding their way back into the sea, yellowing as the sun rose. He didn't stay long, it was so cold, but before he turned to go back to the house, he threw his arms into the air and shouted out loud, "I'm back."

Jake had lit the stove, and compared to being outside, it felt comforting and warm in the kitchen. In the past, Fay had always seen to the stove as soon as she arrived if it had gone out during the night and was there most days to do breakfast, which left David wondering why John had got her the job at the school. Perhaps she needed extra money for her rent, he reasoned, and the school was half a mile nearer to her new house.

When John and Jake had left for work, David went up to the turret to investigate the crack in the wall. He knew there was a crack appearing from way back, and he could see it from the outside on his way back from the beach, but was shocked when he entered the room tentatively, at the size of the zig-zag gaping gap, which had now migrated down through the floor into his bedroom below. Wind and rain had dislodged rags that had been squeezed in to keep out the elements, so he pulled them all out, squeezed the water out, rolled them tightly and pushed them back in securely. The plaster surrounding the gap was flaking off the wall ready to drop onto the soaking floorboards.

Oh dear, he thought as he returned to the kitchen, *what a shame. I couldn't possible leave John and Jake to cope with all this and go to live in Leeds. I wonder why they never mentioned it when we spoke on the telephone or when I met with John in London?* Of course he knew why, they wouldn't want to worry or distract him.

He stoked up the stove and wandered up the lane and had a walk through the ever-changing village before going to the surgery to meet John.

"Hello," said the receptionist, sounding surprised to see him. "It's been a long time since you called, but I was hoping to see you again before I finished working here."

"Are you retiring?" asked David.

"Yes," she replied, "at the same time as Doctor John, at the end of the year."

Before David had time to comment, a stranger came out of the consulting room, put files down on the desk, nodded at David and asked, "Can I help you?"

"This is Dr John's nephew, David," said the receptionist.

The stranger shook hands with David. "I'm Dr Lang, very pleased to meet you," he said. "Must be off, calls to make." And he was gone.

David looked at the receptionist with a questioning expression.

"He's one of the new doctors," she explained. "When John's partner retired, Dr Lang came as a locum to begin with, now he is staying, and there is another doctor coming to share the practice, shortly. They need a more up-to-date model for a receptionist, so I made it easy for them and decided to retire."

"I'm sure they would value your knowledge regarding the history of the patients," said David.

The receptionist smiled. "They don't seem interested," she said, "and the population in the village is growing. They have their own ideas about how they want the practice run. It's called progress, I'm told."

John appeared from his consulting room. "Oh! Hello," he said, "I was hoping to catch up with you whilst it's daylight. Get in the car, I'll drive."

David gave the receptionist a hug. "All the very best," he said. "I'm sure you will be missed by many."

She bit her lip and couldn't speak, so David just blew her a kiss as he walked out of the door.

John drove through the village and stopped in a lay-by overlooking fields, two ploughed, two meadows with grazing sheep.

"These fields are part of our estate," said John.

"I thought they belonged to the farmer," said David, sounding surprised.

"No," replied John, "he rents two fields from us, and we've let him use the two meadows to graze his sheep. He's taking up a vacancy as a tenant farmer in Wales next summer, so we've decided to sell the land. Our house is falling down, and the cost of restoring it is a ridiculous amount of money, so we've decided to move. The contractor who bought and developed our other land, down the lane from our home, is interested, along with two other business-men. They are intending to use the stone from our house that can be saved and re-dressed, on cottages for holiday homes or even permanent homes. At the moment, all this is subject to the price being offered following an independent valuation, and planning permission being granted, although I am informed that there will not be a problem with that."

"Are you planning to live in one of the cottages?" David asked.

"We've no plans to do that," said John, "we want a complete change, a house with smaller rooms that is warm without having to light fires all the time, away from the damp air from the ocean, and the rattling, rotting window frames that welcome the draughts in."

"Won't you miss the ocean and the beach?" asked David.

"Yes! It will be wonderful," said John, taking David completely by surprise.

That evening, David telephoned Rebecca but disclosed none of his news to her, feeling the need to wait until everything was clear in his own mind. They chatted, and he picked up on the fact that she would be working over the Christmas period.

"Being single," she explained, "I always have done. Staff with small children need to be at home with them on Christmas Day. Dad and I manage, we're ok with it, and I get a week off over New Year."

"Are your feelings serious towards Rebecca?" asked Jake.

"I'd like them to be," replied David. "I just can't see a way forward at the moment."

"What's the problem?" asked Jake.

"She will have to be near her father whatever happens, she wouldn't leave him on his own, and I can't leave you two with too much distance between us."

"You need to be carving out your own life now," said John. "We'll cope, we always have."

"Not without me," said David, "don't even consider it. I will be there for you as you have been for me."

This conversation triggered thoughts and ideas in Jake and John's heads, and in a private conversation between them, Jake had said, "Let's wait and see what David decides about working in Leeds and then we can think about where we might live. Clearly, all this is leaving David in a quandary, the timing is not good, he needs to get on with his exams and look forward to his visit to Leeds."

The day before he returned to London, Jake had walked along the coast with him.

"If you decide on working in Leeds, then maybe John and I could look for somewhere nearby. That's all I can say, because it has to be a mutual agreement between John and I, and it must not influence your decision regarding your career. I'm saying this to you now so that your mind is on what you should be doing, and not what we might be doing in the future. I hope you can settle down when you get back, have you made your mind up about going to Leeds for a trial run?"

"I'm going to go, I feel more positive about it now," said David. "Looking forward to it. Not sure when it will be, I just remember the professor saying it would be after the exams."

Fay was busy in the kitchen when they returned to the house, making a meat pie for the evening meal and ginger buns and currant and mint pasty squares for David to take back with him to London.

Fay stayed and had her evening meal with them, and when she and David had washed up and tidied, he ran her home. Wind was blowing hail horizontal.

"Don't get out of the car," said Fay. "Good luck to you; whatever you decide, you'll make it work I'm sure." She pecked him on the cheek and waved at him from her window before he drove away.

That night in bed, he lay listening to the hail pelting the windows, the wind howling and a choking sound gurgling from where the rags had been pushed into the crack in the wall.

The old house is sighing, telling us it has had enough of the elements, thought David just before he fell asleep.

Chapter 35

When David returned to London, the first thing he did was to confirm with the professor's secretary that he did want to travel to Leeds and spend time in the research laboratories.

When he telephoned Rebecca, he felt tempted to tell her he would be in Leeds, and able to visit her, but he decided against it in case things didn't work out. They chatted about work, and David asked her what she was doing for New Year.

"Not sure," Rebecca replied, "could party if I wanted, had plenty of offers, just not sure."

They bid each other 'goodnight' and David returned to his room.

Rebecca put the telephone down and slumped onto the couch, put her head back and closed her eyes.

"Are you tired?" her father asked.

"No," she replied, "just feeling a bit lost."

"What do you mean?" asked her father. "You need to go out partying with your friends on New Year's Eve, that will cheer you up. I hope you are not turning things down because of me."

"No," Rebecca replied. "There's a nice man at work who keeps asking me out, and I do like him, and he's not married," she added emphatically, "but I know if I accept, he'll want it to be serious."

"And why would that be a problem?" asked her father.

Rebecca sat up and looked at her father, tears rolling down her cheeks.

"Because in my mind and in my heart, I'm clinging on to David, but he never says anything to make me feel that he feels the same."

"He's still studying, Rebecca," said her father. "He has to focus on exams and where his future lies, where his career will take him, and then, perhaps, that will be the time to talk to him, let him know of your feelings, and at the same time be prepared for an answer you don't want to hear." He peered at her over his spectacles with a look that said, "That's enough!"

They snuggled up and shared a bowl of peanuts and watched TV.

There were only two weeks left before part one of David's exams, so it was working and studying and no socialising until it was over. There was a real sense of panic amongst some students, who were frantically flicking through tattered notebooks whilst they waited in line to enter the exam room. When the announcement came, "10 minutes left," there was a sigh of relief from those who had finished and had been sitting for a long time, flicking through their papers and frantic scribbling from those who had not finished.

David telephoned Jake, as promised, as soon as the exam was over.

"How did it go?" asked Jake.

"Tough," replied David. "I could answer the questions, but whether there was enough content in my answers remains to be seen. Anyway, it's done, and I'm going to join the others in the pub."

Jake laughed. "Just be careful," he said, "and before you go, the Gray's have invited us up for Christmas."

"I'm going to be working over Christmas," said David. "It's not worth the journey up to the Dales in the unpredictable weather for four days. They have been appealing for staff and I have volunteered; however, I was going to ask if it would be all right to invite Rebecca and her father down for New Year if they feel they can make it."

"I don't see why not," replied Jake, "as long as you explain about the state of the house. Do you think Mr Brown will manage it?"

"I'll meet them in London and travel down with them, but I had wondered if John could borrow a wheelchair from the nursing home."

"I'm sure we can manage that," reassured Jake. "Off you go and join your colleagues.

The conversation amongst his colleagues was going to be about the exam, but there was much laughter during a conversation about the outcome of removing the wrong piece of anatomy, and David soon realised that one of his colleagues had actually answered a question wrongly.

"Can't believe I did that," said the man, putting his hands over his face.

"It's a good job it was only on paper and not in theatre," came another comment, followed by more sarcasm and laughter.

They finally parted company, and David went to his room and decided to have a couple of hours sleep but in actual fact, slept for 10. He'd been burning the midnight oil studying as well as working, and it was just as if his body and brain had sighed with relief and relaxed.

Because it was 5 am when he woke up, he had a cup of tea and decided to take a walk along the embankment, and although the streets were quiet, apart from the odd warning from an ambulance, the Thames was still busy, and because there was little noise from traffic he could hear the sucking sound as the water slapped against the walls.

So much history here, he thought. *I'd like to know about people who lived and worked here over hundreds of years past.*

He knew the original hospital was the Thomas Becket Hospital built in the late 1100, and that the site had been moved, and it became a medical school in 1550, but whenever he thought about it, he couldn't absorb the timescale in his mind.

He sat in the cold November air and tried to imagine what it must have been like in the eerie morning mist when Viking long ships, galleons, warships, and men in small boats up to no good were up and down the river.

He suddenly realised London had woken up and traffic was flying about like demented flies, and it was time for breakfast and work in the here and now.

John came down the following week and they had dinner together and discussed Christmas and the New Year.

"Are you ok about Rebecca and her father joining us for New Year?" asked David, "I have not asked them yet."

"If you think Mr Brown can manage, it's fine," said John. "It's time I met Rebecca. Fay has the sleeping arrangements worked out already, and she's very excited."

That evening, David telephoned and spoke to Mr Brown because Rebecca was out, and he was pleased in a way because he wanted Mr Brown to have time to think it through. He explained he would meet them at King's Cross station to change trains, and everything would be taken care of at home, and they had a wheelchair in place.

"I'll telephone in a couple of days to arrange the dates and train times if you feel you can manage it," said David. "It would be good if you feel you can, I know Rebecca will not leave you, so I'll leave you to deal with it, I don't want to create a problem."

Mr Brown was quite taken aback but remembering how upset Rebecca had been, he was determined to go.

"That's very kind of you," he said. "I just need to think it through, as you say, and will speak to you in a couple of days."

When David telephoned as promised two days later, Rebecca answered. "We're coming," she said. "I've got paper and pencil, tell me the train times."

David pretended to be someone else to begin with, but in the middle of her apology, she realised he was teasing her because she could hear him laughing.

She confirmed dates, so she could book her holiday time off and was so excited. "Dad's friend will run us to the station and pick us up when we return," she said. "Something to look forward to, I can't wait."

"I need to explain to you about the house we live in," said David. "It's falling down around us, but it is safe to live in."

Rebecca didn't believe him; she thought he was teasing again. They chatted for a while, David had a word with Mr Brown to ensure he was happy with the plans and walked away from the telephone feeling great, looking forward to the New Year. He'd been stressed more than he realised being galvanised to his studies and considering his future, and he felt Rebecca was feeling down, so it was good to hear her bubbly self and to have a relaxed, chatty conversation again.

Christmas Eve was busy in the hospital despite as many patients as possible being discharged or sent home to spend Christmas with their families. Babies were born, broken bones needed attention, gashes needed to be stitched mostly on heads as people hit the pavement from the effects of too much alcohol, and there were the normal admissions of people suffering heart attacks or strokes and the usual abdominal problems.

David was stitching a gash on a lady's head who had clearly had a wonderful time. She had wandered into Casualty with blood dripping down her face, smelling of alcohol and slurring her words. David's thoughts went back to the memory of his mother bleeding on the stone floor of their home, so many years ago. He had paused for a moment.

"Are you all right?" asked the nurse in attendance. She said it again. "Are you all right?"

David heard her the second time and continued with his task.

"Yes, I'm fine," he said quietly and smiled, "just having a moment, a memory."

He turned to the patient as the nurse helped her off the bed.

David looked at her as she gave him a watery smile. "You may have a headache in the morning," he said. "Take the painkillers, keep the dressing dry, and have a Merry Christmas."

"I think I've had one already," she said, "need to get a turkey and a pie and go home now." She waved a zig-zag, blew them a kiss, and tottered off down the corridor carrying her shoes.

David and the nurse laughed, couldn't help it.

"I don't know where she thinks she will get a turkey at this time of night," said the nurse. "It's 8 'o' clock, I can see they will be having a tin of corned beef with their sprouts tomorrow."

When David left, he could hear the nurses singing carols somewhere in the hospital, and as he left the building, he could hear the Salvation Army band playing nearby, amidst the crowd of party goers. He'd never been in the city before at Christmas, nothing seemed to slow down, so different from being at home.

Before he returned to his room, he telephoned the Gray's to make sure Jake and John had arrived safely and to wish them all a Merry Christmas. Mr Gray was out at a remote farm dealing with a difficult delivery of a calf saying, "Don't wait up," as he left.

David hung up. *It's all going on*, he thought, *all around us.*

The following morning, he was dressed in a long red coat, a red hat with white fur trim and beard attached, a white curly wig and shiny black boots.

"Ho! Ho! Ho!" he growled as he wheeled the sack of toys into the children's ward, to be greeted by screams and cheers. Most of the children were keen to receive and open their presents, but David noticed one small boy who had smiled when given his gifts but had pushed them to one side and closed his eyes. David looked at the notes at the bottom of the bed and was saddened because he could see the boy was very ill and unlikely to recover.

Sister had known David many years, from being a young boy who came on to the ward to read to the children and play games, to the man he had become, and she was always pleased to see him and followed his progress with interest, and she knew only too well that he would be struggling and feeling the pain at the loss of such a young life.

"We can't save them all, David," she said quietly. "There needs to be work done, the drugs we have rarely work, maybe one day, I hope so, before I retire."

David told her in confidence that he was considering going into research, and she whole-heartedly approved.

David spoke to all the children before he left the ward and had many laughs with them. A boy with both legs in plaster asked him to sign them for him.

"Ain't it time you went 'ome?" said the boy. "You've 'ad a long shift."

"I'll soon be gone," David replied, but before he left, he went to talk to the quiet boy who had turned his head and was watching as David prepared to leave.

"Do you like your present?" David asked.

"Yes, thank you," the boy replied, "but I can't play with it."

"Well, maybe not today," said David, "but when you are feeling better, you can."

"I'm going to heaven," said the boy, in such a matter of fact way it took David by surprise.

"Why do you think that?" asked David.

"I heard the doctor tell me mam, and she cried," replied the boy. "How long does it take to go to heaven? Every time I wake up, I'm still here. It's a nice place, everyone is good there, and I might get to see God."

The nurse rescued David. "It's nearly time for Christmas dinner," she said to the boy. "Are you going to try some?"

"No," replied the boy, frowning, "it makes me belly 'urt. Can I just have some jelly and custard?"

"I'm sure I can find some," said the nurse. "Say 'goodbye' to Father Christmas, he has to go now."

All the children shouted 'goodbye' as David left the ward and went to change into his own clothes.

The nurse went in search of jelly and custard, and David stood gazing out of the window pondering over what had just happened, and realised what the professor had said was right in his observations, for he was feeling the sorrow and pain of the boy's family, and he knew he would think about it for a long time.

A colleague popped his head round the door, "Coming for Christmas dinner?" he asked.

"Sure," replied David, shaking himself from his sombre thoughts and joined the group going to the restaurant where they had a happy hour and a good meal.

By 2 pm, the hospital was buzzing with visitors, the staff sought out and spent time with patients who had no visitor, and by tea time were settling patients in who were returning having been allowed to go home to spend the day with their family.

When David's shift had ended, walking along the corridor towards the main entrance, he could smell pine from the Christmas tree, and hear the sound of chimes as they moved gently in the draught from the doorway, and it reminded him of the Christmas when he went to visit his mother as a young boy, not knowing it would be the last time he would see or speak to her. He always remembered his mother at Christmas but being in the hospital with the rows of shiny tiles on the walls and the smell of antiseptics made the memories more vivid.

Two days later, he was in a cafe in the station waiting for Rebecca and her father to arrive, feeling excited and impatient. As the train pulled into the station, he summoned a porter to assist with the luggage and finally caught sight of Rebecca tugging her suitcase out of the way to help her father. Mr Brown had enjoyed the journey down and transferring on to the other train was not a problem with David's help.

Jake was waiting for them with the car, and by this time, Mr Brown was feeling jaded from the day's travelling and was relieved to have reached their destination.

Fay was busy in the kitchen, but as soon as she heard the door open, she ran across to hug David and covered his jacket in flour from where she had been rolling dumplings into balls, ready to top up the huge pan of stew. She was introduced to Rebecca and her father and then went back to her culinary skills. David's old school, where Fay now worked, now closed over Christmas and the New Year, re-opening on 2nd January, so she was able to be there to look after them, which is where she wanted to be, having spent Christmas with her family.

The table was set for five, so David set another place, tapped Fay on the shoulder, pointed to it, said nothing, just gave her a look, and when she was about to protest, he made a gesture to zip up her lip, indicating 'matter closed'. She was pleased to stay, having looked forward so much to meeting Rebecca. She was well aware she was not David's mother, although she had felt like it sometimes, but loved him and felt close enough to him to care about his future happiness, as she had done with all her children. He once called her 'his mother hen' and she loved it.

Rebecca helped Fay to wash up and clear away before David took Fay home, and when he returned, Rebecca was with her father, settling him in for the night. David was sitting in the lounge with John and Jake when she came running down the stairs, stopped and called, "Hello."

David went to her. "Are you lost?" he asked, smiling.

"There are so many doors," she replied. "The kitchen is as big as our entire house, it's like a museum."

The lounge door was open, so both John and Jake had heard what she said and burst out laughing.

"Oh, gosh," she said and could feel herself blushing as she covered her mouth with her hands. She peeped round the door, "I only meant the size of the building," she said meekly.

"Not the contents and the people living here, then?" teased Jake.

She sensed they were not offended, so quickly changed the subject.

"Is it all right if I warm some milk for my dad?" she asked. "And I think I'll go to bed too, it's been a long day, and I was on late shift yesterday." She looked at David. "Do you mind?"

David nodded. "See you in the morning. Goodnight," he said and blew her a kiss.

The following morning, Fay took Rebecca a cup of tea up to her room. "Good morning, sleepy head," she said, as she opened the heavy, faded velvet curtains, hoping they wouldn't come off the rails again.

"What time is it?" asked Rebecca, pulling her cardigan round her shoulders as she drank her tea.

"9:30," replied Fay. "What about breakfast? Can I make you anything?"

"I'll just have some toast and jam," replied Rebecca, "and I'll make it. Is Dad up?"

"Yes," replied Fay, "he's up and out with David somewhere."

This was not a house for drifting around in pyjamas; it was so intensely cold upstairs, so Rebecca was soon washed and dressed and munching toast in the warm kitchen and chatting to Fay when Jake joined them.

"You had a good sleep," he said. "You must have needed it."

"I think I must," Rebecca replied, thinking how cosy and warm she had been in the huge bed. "Shift work plays havoc with your sleeping pattern."

Jake nodded in agreement, said nothing, but was thinking how hard it must be for Rebecca to be working full time, taking care of her father and running the home. Rebecca looked at Jake for a moment. "What?" he asked her, realising she was wanting to say something but hesitating.

"I just wanted to say that I think what you risked and did for David was wonderful," she said.

"He told you?" asked Jake.

"He told me that when he ran away from the home, you had hidden him until you could send him safely to live here with your brother. I never thought you were a real tramp, you know, you were too clean and gently spoken. I always said that to my dad."

She wanted to ask why he had chosen to live as he did in the village but felt it was up to him to offer that information, or maybe David would tell her one day.

She helped Fay prepare for the evening meal and chatted about her childhood and where she was in her career as a nurse. When David returned with her father, it was time for lunch, the usual homemade soup, bread and butter and a slice of ginger cake.

David had taken Mr Brown for a drive through the village, pointing places out to him, his school and the new builds, and then along road to the car park above where the land slide had been. They sat looking out to sea with their own thoughts for a while, and then David turned and looked at Mr Brown. "How would you feel if I asked Rebecca to marry me?" he asked.

There was a moment of silence, the question was so unexpected, but the reply came genuinely. "Delighted," said Mr Brown, "truly delighted. All I could ever wish for is that she is happy and cherished."

"How do you think Rebecca will feel?" David asked.

"Rebecca," replied Mr Brown, "will probably do cartwheels along the village street. Seriously, I think it's what she has been hoping for. She made a mistake with someone, as you know because you were involved in making her aware of it, but she has had her chances since with nice young men but always found an excuse for not accepting their invitations. I used to think it was because she didn't want to leave me to cope on my own, but we had a conversation recently when I realised it was not just that, although I do feel I hold her back."

"I have exams in March and July," said David, "so it will be when they are over. Things are changing with my career and much is happening here, so all this needs to be settled so I can explain what our future will hold for us when I propose. It would be helpful if you could draw around one of her rings and send it to me; I'll let you have the address secretly before you leave."

After lunch, Mr Brown took his book and had a lie down. There had been an anxiety within him he hadn't realised totally, but it had dissolved, and he felt calm and happy.

David and Rebecca wrapped up against the cold, and he took her down to the beach and along the coastal path. The tide was coming in like heavy sighs as the waves hit the shore. They hurried off the beach and stood leaning against the wall at the back of the path, looking out to sea.

"I bet it was wonderful living here as a child," Rebecca said. "How lucky were you?"

"Very," said David. "I spent hours on this path. I used to have a little place I curled up in where I used to read or study or just close my eyes and listen. Every day is different, the sea is moody and powerful, changes its colour, and even when you think it is gentle, it can lure you into the little waves and have you sinking in the sand and losing your balance. You realise its might when you see the huge cruise ships on the horizon."

They walked further along the path to where the waves were crashing into the rocks, booming, echoing, spurting foam into the air.

"Gosh!" said Rebecca. "This is a dangerous place to be."

She clung to David and watched in awe as the ground shook from the pounding.

"My friend took his life here," said David, "whilst we were still at school."

231

"Oh my God!" said Rebecca, trying to imagine what he must have felt like moments before he jumped. "Why would he do that?" David explained,

"All he wanted was his father to be proud of him and to be able to spend some time with him, but it didn't happen, just a lot of broken promises. His father was in the air force and lived abroad a lot, but he always kept their daughter with them, and Ted was sent to boarding school here. His life became complicated, his father's parents didn't want anything to do with him, and he knew and talked about that, but no one could have known how desolate he had become. He was a clever boy and great fun to be with and spent a lot of time at our house. He was a good liar and able to hide his pain and disappointment well, so no one really knew how much he was hurting."

"You don't think he just fell in?" asked Rebecca.

"No," said David, "he left me a message in a little tin in my place where he knew I would find it. We let the police have it, but eventually they gave it back, it's in my memory box."

Rebecca wiped a tear from David's cheek with the end of his scarf.

"Let's go back," she said. "I'm really cold."

David pulled her to him and looked down at her tenderly.

"Don't kiss me now," said Rebecca, "my lips are numb, I really do want to feel it when it happens."

She turned and ran away, laughing, until they reached the bottom of the steps up to the house, silhouetted against the bronze and dark blue sky.

"Gosh," said Rebecca, as she looked up, "that's one foreboding place, it's massive." She thought, *it's like Dracula's castle*, but she didn't say it.

"It's falling apart," said David. "I wasn't joking, didn't you see the big crack in the wall in your room?"

"No," Rebecca replied, frowning at him, not really knowing if he was joking.

David didn't know Fay had covered the crack with a tapestry type rug.

Chapter 36

On New Year's Eve, David collected Fay from the village with groceries, vegetables and a chicken to prepare a meal for the evening. She left mid-afternoon to be at her son's home for the New Year celebrations, having gone through everything with Rebecca as to what was left to do regarding the dinner.

"Is David the one, then?" Fay asked Rebecca as they sat having a cup of tea.

Rebecca looked Fay in the eyes and replied quietly, but so full of meaning, "I'm hoping so, but I just can't tell what he's thinking or feeling. Has this been a test for me with John and Jake?"

"Possibly," said Fay, "but I think you will have passed that one ok." She smiled and patted Rebecca on her hand. "David needs to get through his exams and do well, he's driven and works hard, he couldn't bear it if he didn't do well or worse still, failed, because he has always felt he couldn't let John and Jake down. They never put pressure on him, he loves and respects them and just feels compelled to do well. I believe his last exam is in July, so just let the year flow by, and by this time next year, things may be so different; I hope they work out for you. Let's do the apple pies, and then I'll be away to my sons."

As Fay was leaving, she shook Mr Brown by the hand. "I'm very pleased to have met you," she said, and glancing at David, continued, "and I do hope we shall meet again."

The dinner went well, a happy, chatty meal. Rebecca had been determined to get it right and was pleased when John complimented her on her efforts.

"Yes," agreed David, "that was very nice. Well done."

"Don't sound so surprised," said Rebecca. "We don't live off fish and chips at home."

Mr Brown sensed Rebecca was rattled by David's comment, so he intervened. "I do most of the cooking," he said. "It's about the only thing I can do these days."

"David can make pancakes," John said and related the story, well remembered from the experience of being splattered with batter and having to clean windows, worktops and the floor.

It was a relaxed, happy evening. There was common ground for conversation from the medical professions and funny stories from the past. Rebecca was fascinated as to how different her and her father's life had been in comparison to that of John and Jake, and yet they still had their struggles living with a strict father, no mother from a young age, just each other for companionship, and something had happened to Jake for him to move away from his home and become Hobo, but that was a question for another time.

Rebecca helped her father to bed way before midnight, and John went shortly afterwards, which just left the three of them to see in the New Year on television and make plans for a long walk the following day.

The day before Rebecca and her father were to return home and David to London, they had planned for Jake to stay with Mr Brown whilst the rest of them were to have a long walk, but when they awoke, their world was grey outside, all of it, and very cold. Almost black clouds, spitting sleet horizontally, hung over a grey, silver-streaked ocean, even the land was wet and grey, and the wind bitterly cold, so they had an early lunch and went to see Dr Zhivago at the cinema. Rebecca was bereft when it finished and couldn't stop sobbing. David took her to one side and cuddled her tight.

"Oh my gosh," she said, "I'll never forget that. Their love took them through so much, and just for a matter of moments, he could have died in her arms, and at least she would have known what had happened to him."

"It's only a film, a story," said David, wishing he could think of something better to say, as he handed Rebecca his handkerchief.

"Well, it's a dammed good one," blurted Rebecca. "It's ripped my feelings into shreds."

She took a few deep breaths, blew her nose, gave David his handkerchief back and walked to the car to join the others.

"We are going to the pub for tea," said David.

Rebecca glanced at her father.

The film had been long, and she wondered if he could manage going to the pub. He nodded at her that he was all right, so off they went, had chicken and chips in baskets and were settled back at home early evening.

The telephone rang, and even though John had officially retired, he put his coat and cap on and picked up his bag.

"Coming with me?" he asked Rebecca.

She wasn't to ask twice even though she had no idea where they were going, off she went, just to observe or maybe help, she didn't care.

John explained he was visiting an old friend, a fisherman, born in the house he was still living in, alone for many years. He had caught his calf and shin with fish hooks and left it too long before he sought medical help.

"He should be in hospital," said John, "But he's very vocal in refusing to go, even though he's never been in hospital in his life."

"That's probably the problem," reasoned Rebecca. "He'll be imagining what it will be like. If he fought in the war, he would have seen some terrible things to influence his thinking."

John was impressed with Rebecca's reasoning, didn't say anything, but thought how right she could be.

When they arrived, the man was laid on the bed now in the living room, clearly in pain, and the smell from the infected leg was strong and signified gangrene to Rebecca, although she said nothing, it was not her place.

The neighbour left, and John removed the dressings whilst Rebecca held the man's hand and talked to him as he screwed up his face and winced in pain.

"Who are you? I haven't seen you before," said the man.

"I'm a guest staying at the doctor's house with my father, my name is Rebecca, and I am a nurse and work in a big hospital," Rebecca replied, "and I think that is the best place for you to be now, you really do need that extra care. They have better drugs to help you than Doctor John. Trust me, you will be looked after well."

"What will happen to my home whilst I'm away?" the man asked.

"Nothing," said John. "Leave your key with your neighbour, and I'll keep an eye on things."

"Can't you fix it?" the man pleaded softly to John.

"I've tried all I could, but I'm afraid it's not working," said John. "I'm going next door to telephone for an ambulance. Nurse, could you please freshen him up and find him some clean pyjamas or something? I'll be back shortly."

Rebecca talked to the man as she gently washed him, maintaining his dignity as she had been trained, careful not to move his leg, just covering the wounds with sterile gauze for the journey in the ambulance, so he wouldn't have to endure the pain of having them fully dressed and the dressings removed in a short space of time at the hospital.

The man gave John a tin from a cupboard for safekeeping, and too weak to argue any more, went reluctantly to hospital, and John and Rebecca were on their way home.

"We need to disinfect when we get home," said John, who was driving in a clean pair of surgical gloves.

"I think he'll lose his leg," said Rebecca. "Do you?"

"If they discuss it with him, he'll refuse surgery. He's a tough old nut, can't remember without looking at records just how old he is, his neighbour says he has a daughter and her family living in Australia, so when I get the fuller picture I'll write to them. I'll visit him tomorrow morning. What time are you leaving tomorrow?"

"No idea," replied Rebecca. "David said it was an early start but didn't actually say how early."

"Thank you for your help tonight," said John. "It's easy to see you are in the right job."

Back at the house, David had made sandwiches for the journey the following day for Rebecca and her father and put them in the fridge and set about making warm drinks whilst Rebecca and John washed with disinfectant in the water.

"Can't believe he agreed to go to hospital," said Jake.

"There was no choice tonight," said John, "but Rebecca soothed him and made him calmer about going. He was very weak, very little fight left in him, but we did stay until the ambulance had left because there was every chance he'd change his mind. Poor old chap was thinking he would have to pay and wouldn't have enough money, he hadn't heard of the NHS. A gentle private man."

"Just imagine," said David, "tomorrow at this time I'll be back in London, you and your father will be back home, and John and Jake will be here on their own, so quiet they will think they've gone deaf."

And that's just how it was.

Rebecca settled into her routine, loving her work as a nurse, the different challenges each day could bring, taking time out with her friends from time to time, and always caring for her father. She remembered what Fay had said regarding letting the year flow, but it was dragging, and sometimes her mood was low. She didn't know what her father knew, she was just impatient to see David again, and even though they talked on the telephone regularly, there was no discussion regarding seeing each other.

David too settled into his routine, and the day he was sitting at a desk reading through the questions for his second exam seemed to come very quickly. "Settle down," he told himself as he re-read the first question, having to search the canyons of his mind, not fully understanding what was required. Glancing around, he was not the only one, but eventually he thought things through and progressed.

"That was a hard paper, really hard," he emphasised as he spoke to Jake after the exam. "I need to look at my notes."

Jake didn't ask any more, he could tell David was anxious and wanted to look through his notes. "Ring tomorrow," said Jake and hung up. Away David went to his room and flicked through his folders until he found the subject matter he wasn't sure of and gasped with relief, realising he'd got it right. Whether he had done enough to get a good result was always the question after an exam; all he could do now was wait.

He took a few deep sighs to calm down and went to join the others in the library. Panic had set in, because the first question led into the second and then on into the third. He slipped into the library and sat down quickly and froze as their tutor rendered a lacerating rant at the students who had got it wrong. Not all had, of course, but the situation was not good. A student interrupted, "I couldn't understand the question, sir."

"It's going to be tricky for you if you don't understand the notes presented to you before surgery," remarked the tutor, who couldn't hide his impatience and disappointment. He nodded at David, "Well?" he asked.

David nodded 'ok' but didn't speak, still caught up in the emotion of it all.

There was no going to the pub this time to celebrate 'exam over'. Just a few went to drown their sorrows, but David didn't join them, he had a long walk along the embankment, met up with Louis and enjoyed a meal together in a new Chinese restaurant. His thoughts were diverted from the exam, Louis was always good company, and he brought news that Monique and Jean were expecting their first child. He had not written to them for a while, waiting for their new address after they had moved nearer to Paris, and was looking forward to meeting up with them later in the year when they were to visit Louis.

Two days later, he called to see Professor Bouvais' secretary to see if there was any news regarding the visit to Leeds, and two weeks later, they were on a train. David was browsing through notes he had made on his previous visit to the research centre, and the professor read his paper for a while, then he folded it, pushed it to one side, looked at David and said, "I need to speak to you."

David put his exercise book down on the table and waited for the professor to speak.

"Do you understand exactly what will happen this week?" he asked.

"Not really," replied David. "I know why I'm going, I need to know if I really do want to move into research, and to prove I'm worthy of a position if I do."

"Based on what happens this week," said the professor, pointedly, "you will be given the option of a formal interview later in the year, when you will really have to convince them you're the man they should choose. These interviews are stringent. They will require records of all your qualifications through school, university and St Thomas's, and if your final exam results have not come through, they will wait for them before making a decision, but that will be the same for all applicants. I'm sure you will be fine, but always remember to consider your answers and lean towards their guidance. There is just one other thing, when you go for that interview, I will have taken up a position at The University Hospital in Zurich."

"Really!" gasped David, totally shocked at the news.

The professor continued, "I've bought a cottage near Ilkley, handy for the airport, because Stella loves that part of the country, and it's near family. This visit is to finalise things and to spend a few days with my brother."

"You're not working in the hospital, then?" asked David.

"No," replied the professor, "and when you return to London, I will just have another few days until the month end when I leave. I don't want this discussing on your return, the people who need to know do, and that's all that is necessary, there is to be no fuss."

When they arrived in Leeds, a man came towards them wearing a kippah, and was introduced to David as Asha, the professor's brother, followed closely behind by Stella, who gave David a hug.

"Let's go and have a coffee before we part company," she said. "I want to know all about David and Rebecca."

"Nosey woman," muttered the professor, peering at her over the top of his glasses and shaking his head, but Stella just smiled and led them to the coffee bar.

They're Jewish, thought David, *and the professor is going to Switzerland, there must be some history there.* He'd have loved to have asked but knew better.

Stella just wanted to know about the situation between him and Rebecca, so he explained, and she was genuinely delighted that they were almost together.

"Have you got a ring yet?" she asked.

"Still saving up," said David, smiling. "I've got her size on a piece of paper from her father."

"You should speak to Asha," said Stella. "He's a jeweller."

As they parted to go their separate ways, Asha gave David his business card for future contact, Stella hugged David, and the professor shook David's hand tightly, holding on and looking David in the eyes and said, "Continue to work hard, opportunities will present themselves, seize them. I wish you well."

"Thank you for everything," said David and could say no more for the emotional lump in his throat, he just picked up his bag and walked away and sat on a wall outside the station to gather his thoughts.

Although no words had ever been passed between them to indicate preferences, David had always felt the professor had helped him, subtly, in so many ways, and he had much to thank him for. He felt numbed by the knowledge he wouldn't be around anymore, but his feelings were slightly flawed, because if he were to work in Leeds, the professor wouldn't be there anyway, apart from the occasional visit. Despite his reasoning, David felt crestfallen as he made his way to his accommodation for the week. Having settled in, he decided to take a walk and telephone Rebecca, who had no idea he was in Leeds. She chatted on in her usual happy manner, and by the time the money ran out, his spirits were lifted. As evening approached, the shops closed, but people were starting out to enjoy themselves, heading for the restaurants or theatres, and David realised Leeds was a vibrant city to be in. He walked through the back streets and bought fish and chips, found a quiet place to eat them and let vinegar soak through the paper and stain his trousers.

"Oh! Damn it," he said, and made the stain worse by trying to rub it off with the handkerchief he had in his pocket. Fortunately, he did have another pair with him, and when he asked the landlady where the nearest launderette was she laughed at him, shook her head and offered to wash them for him.

The following day was Sunday, so he spent his day familiarising himself with the city and made a point of locating the National Swimming Pool. He loved to swim and kept up with it as much as he could in London, visiting the Lancaster Baths in Kensington whenever he could but always once a week. He was both relaxed and invigorated after a good swim, and he felt it was important to keep fit. He had played hockey at Cambridge, as well as swimming, but because of his work pattern could not commit himself to being reliable at a club, so swimming was all he could do on an as and when basis.

The following five days, he was totally absorbed, mentored by the same person all the time. He was taken to an office at 8 am on his first day to be introduced to Professor Renouf. David shook his hand, "Good morning, sir," he said.

"I am not sir," said the professor. "I am professor and that is what you call me to my face, what I'm called behind my back is varied, you will be able to choose."

David beamed a smile, but the professor did not, so that moment taught David no messing about, no joking, no familiarity, just work. The professor handed him a timetable because he was to be in a different section each day, and David made sure he was where he should be and on time every day, having realised very quickly that aggravating Renouf would not be good.

One day, he was taken into the hospital to visit two patients who were on a new drug trial. When they arrived at the ward, the staff were waiting, standing to attention, even the patients were sitting up straight and in silence.

"Good morning, Professor Renouf," said sister.

He didn't speak, just nodded and led the way down the ward, in silence, followed by the patients' consultant, sister, staff nurse, David, two other men who David had not met before, and two other nurses whose sole purpose was, as far as David could tell, to pull the curtains round the patient's bed. A glance passed between sister and David, who was having to suck his cheeks in to prevent him from smiling, thinking they resembled a flight of geese wafting down the ward. After Renouf had spoken to the patients, and he had examined their medical record, notes were passed to David and the other two men to look at briefly, and when the retinue had returned to sister's office, accompanied by a few two-fingered salutes from patients as they passed, the professor asked, "Well, do you think the results show promise or not?"

The two men gave their opinions, and then he looked at David for his.

One thing Professor Bouvais had instilled in his students was never to make rapid diagnosis if there was time to consider and think about it, especially with something you had little or no experience in, so David's answer was, "I don't know."

"You don't know," said Renouf with a hint of sarcasm, and raised eyebrows. "Why don't you know?"

"I don't know," replied David, quietly and calmly, "because I don't know enough about the patient's history or the trial drug. I will need time to research both before I can form an opinion. All I can say is I hope it's working. Is it?"

Sister, standing behind Renouf, pursed her lips and closed her eyes, waiting for the tirade which quite often accompanied the visits to her ward, but it didn't happen, he just closed the folder, flicked the elastic band round to secure it, turned and said, "Right then, back to the lab."

David never saw the two men again, and the situation was never mentioned, and when he was left to work and learn from people he could be working with in the future, the atmosphere was friendly and relaxed.

He was expecting Renouf to speak to him before he left on the Friday lunch time, but he was nowhere to be found, so David bid 'farewell' to the others he had been with all week, collected his bag from the locker, bought a bunch of flowers and caught the bus to the village to see Rebecca.

As he walked past the spare ground where they used to play when he was a child, he came across a group of children trying to decide what to play.

"Play kick the can," said David. "That can be fun."

"What's kick the can, mister?" asked a gruff little voice.

David explained and sent the children scurrying off to rummage in dust bins to find a can and left them when the children had dispersed to hide.

"This could go on a long time," he remembered and smiled to himself as he walked to Mr Brown's.

David slumped in an armchair and sipped at the cup of tea Mr Brown had made, having put the flowers in a vase.

"How do you think it's gone, then?" asked Mr Brown.

"I've absolutely no idea," sighed David, heavily. "Professor Renouf, who was monitoring me, was the strangest man I have ever met. There was no reaction or feedback from him at all, ever, during the week. There was no conversation regarding my education and training, which I did expect. Nothing. No personality to endear him to his staff, to whom he was quite abrasive, although I do believe he is a very clever man."

"Personality is good," said Mr Brown. "Clever is better if he's doing good work in his field of research."

The conversation about Leeds ceased as Rebecca shouted, "Hello Dad," from the kitchen. "Who are the flowers from?"

She walked into the room and flung herself at David who, fortunately, was now standing up. "What are you doing here?" she asked. "Why didn't you tell me you were coming?"

It had been agreed with Mr Brown that Rebecca was not to know that David could be working in Leeds in case things didn't work out, so he said, "I came up with the professor, but I'm going back on Sunday, so we just have tomorrow, are you working?"

"Yes," replied Rebecca, "early shift, I'll finish at 2pm."

"We'll go out for dinner tomorrow evening then," said David, "wherever you would like to go."

Mr Brown had cooked bacon chops, cauliflower cheese and mashed potatoes for tea, and afterwards, when they had washed and cleared up, David and Rebecca went for a walk through the village where David noticed a billboard advertising a plot of land for sale. He memorised the name of the agents and looked the telephone number up in the directory when Rebecca was busy upstairs. He didn't know why he had done it, he just folded the piece of paper up and put it in his wallet.

They were not late to bed, Rebecca had to be ready to be collected at 5:30 am so she slept on the couch, and David slept in her bed. He snuggled into the pillow that smelt of her hair and perfume and had a deep contented sleep, and by the time he awoke, Rebecca had been gone two hours. When her shift was over, she hurried to the locker room to collect her belongings.

"Are we going for a coffee?" asked one of her colleagues, because that was what they often did at the end of a week of early shifts.

"Not today," said Rebecca, "I've got something on," and she was gone, racing to catch her bus home, in so much of a hurry she ran straight past David waiting at the gate for her. He grabbed her by her coat belt to stop her, she spun round and thumped him before she realised who it was, and then they walked hand in hand to the bus stop, laughing.

They got off the bus two stops early and walked through the woodland where they had spent time playing as children.

"Can you remember?" said Rebecca. "This was our playground in the holidays. We used to build dens, and have picnics, two slices of jam and bread and a bottle of water, and we'd be out all day and go home black bright."

"If you remember," said David, "I was rarely included, but I remember sledging one Christmas."

Rebecca had momentarily been insensitive, forgetting how sad and lonely David had been when all the rest were having fun. "I'm so sorry," she said, taking hold of his hand. "I didn't think. I just see you now as you are, strong, educated, with a successful career. I wasn't remembering the other stuff."

"I coped with a lot, more than anyone knew," said David, "but I do believe I developed a coping mechanism that made me strong, and here we are, back in the playground so many years later, and nothing much has changed here, it even smells as I remember it."

"Smells? What of?" said Rebecca.

"Wood," replied David teasingly and ran up the hill ahead of her.

Once home, they sat and chatted to Mr Brown until it was time to get ready and go out for the evening. Rebecca wore the same clothes she had worn for the garden party, she was happy and glowing, and David couldn't take his eyes off her, consumed with feelings he'd never experienced before. He wanted to hug her and whisper in her ear, "Marry me." Because of what Mr Brown had told David about Rebecca's feelings, he sensed she could be hoping for his proposal, so he avoided any conversation about the future, apart from mentioning he needed to work hard and concentrate on his next exam in July.

Chapter 37

On the train journey back to London, he flicked through the notes he had taken in the research laboratories. He had found it so interesting, so many challenges ahead, and by now he knew this was what he would really like to do as a career, but his mind was muddled. He could apply to work in research in London, in St Thomas's or one of the other hospitals, and be nearer to John and Jake, although he didn't know where they were intending to move to, and he knew Rebecca wouldn't move far from her father. Before he married he would have to get a mortgage to provide a home and furnish it. He wanted to work in Leeds to be nearer to Rebecca, but he felt a responsibility to John and Jake as they grew older, and he would not abandon them.

David, normally a calm person, didn't like this feeling of uncertainty, and it left him restless. Whilst he was living with John, his life had been mapped out for him, uncomplicated, but now there were so many facets to his life, decisions he had to make for his future.

Having checked his schedule, he found he was not on duty until the following day, so he took himself off to the Old Lancaster swimming baths where he swam for an hour and left calmer and invigorated.

"No point in wallowing in uncertainties," he decided. "Just get on with the job in hand, day by day."

That is just what he did.

When the month end drew near. David called to see Professor Bouvais' secretary and left a parcel and a letter of thanks for the professor. He'd bought a set of table mats and coasters with pictures of the Yorkshire Dales on them, thinking they would be useful at the cottage. The professor was in theatre, so David stayed and chatted for a while to his secretary.

"I'll miss him," said David. "What made him decide to go to Switzerland?"

"I don't know," replied the secretary, "a challenge, perhaps, an opportunity he couldn't turn down. He's a very private person, he only discusses hospital business with me, but I do know he was approached from Switzerland. He'll be missed here, very few know he's going, he doesn't want a fuss."

"What will you do?" David asked.

"Oh! There's always someone ready to move into that office," she replied. "I've seen several come and go. I'm here for the duration of the next one, that has been agreed already, so please come and see me."

"Yes, for sure," said David, but thinking, *I may be moving on myself quite soon.*

Eventually, back into his recognisable routine, weeks passed by and his final exam date became nearer and nearer. He'd put the work in, studying, cutting back on his theatre visits and nights out with colleagues. He'd used his birthday money to put towards a new suit to wear at his interview and bought himself a pair of black brogues, something he'd promised himself all his adult life, and when he'd paid for them, hoped they would last him the rest of his life.

Prior to his last exam, he had spent a few days at home with John and Jake and found it beneficial, so he decided to do the same. It was nice to lie in the big bed and listen to the sea and the wind howling through all the cracks and the house creaking and settling for the night as he remembered it. Having got used to living in his small bed sit, the house felt huge and cold, as it had done when he first arrived and thought he was going to live in a castle.

The three of them walked along the coastal path and stood looking out to sea which was calm, the waves curling into the sand, sunrays fanning out over the horizon from behind clouds.

"Surely you'll miss this," said David. "I do. The ocean has so many mood swings, powerful, frivolous, angry, noisy, threatening, never the same."

"It's all right waxing lyrical about the ocean," interrupted John, "but it's very wet and very cold, and although the sea air is bracing, the damp air from the sea fret is not good for ageing bones. You are right to say it's threatening because that is exactly what it is doing to our coast line."

David had often thought how little time John spent along the coast compared to Jake, but only just realised he didn't much care for it at all.

"Any thoughts on where you want to live when you move?" asked David.

"Nowhere near the sea and not in a bungalow," replied John, "Jake thinks I'd like it in the village where you grew up. Let's see what happens regarding Leeds for you. Have you heard anything yet?"

"No," replied David, "but I'm not expecting to until after my exam."

David's stomach churned with excitement at the possibility that everything could dovetail into place, it would be perfect if they moved to the village, he just needed to be accepted in Leeds, but at that moment, he didn't even know if he had been accepted for an interview.

John continued, as they walked back to the house, "The best plan is for Jake and I to travel up when you go to Leeds for your interview, then we can all look around together. If we can't find a house, we'll have to have one built."

Clearly there was no doubt in John's mind that David would get an interview.

"Gosh!" said David. "That's a big step. If you do that, my friend Louis is an architect earning a good reputation for his work, and I have a telephone number for a company that had land for sale. I noted it down when I was up there visiting Rebecca. Don't ask me why, I just did."

Jake felt this obsession with Leeds and Rebecca was overriding what lay ahead in the next few weeks. "Concentrate on your exam," he said. "It still matters that you do well. You've gleaned knowledge and skills over the past three years, but you still need the diploma at the end, and if you have to continue as you are, you may have to consider an opportunity to specialise in something you are interested in." Jake didn't want the final exam to slip out of focus, because although he and John wanted very much that David was successful in his application to work in Leeds, it was possible he would not succeed because they knew these positions were very much sought after.

Three days later, back in London, David telephoned Leeds to be told that letters for interviews had not been sent out yet, so he contented himself with the fact that he hadn't missed out and was still in with a chance.

The final exam seemed easier than the second one, and after the shock and controversy over that exam, it seemed all his colleagues seemed to have realised they needed to study harder, and conversations after the exam were of relief and promise of better results.

Another week passed before David received a letter with a Leeds postmark. He took it to his room and put it on the table until he had made a cup of tea. He could feel his heart pounding in his chest as he slit open the envelope with a knife and unfolded the letter which said, "We are pleased to be able to invite you for an interview…"

"Whew," sighed David. He clenched his fists and looking at himself in the mirror said, "Now all I have to do is convince them I am the man for the job."

He hurried to the telephone and spoke to Jake, who was as relieved as David. Arrangements were made to meet up just outside London and travel up to Leeds together in the car, so David made arrangements for them to stay at the B&B he had used before. He also arranged to meet up with Asha to discuss buying an engagement ring for Rebecca and planned to visit her if he could but refrained from saying so when he spoke to her on the telephone. Leeds was still to remain a secret until he knew for sure that he would be there permanently.

They enjoyed a meal at a pub local to the B&B. Afterwards, John and Jake returned to their room whilst David set out to find exactly where he should be for his interview at 9 am the following morning.

A group of noisy youths were gathered, so David crossed over the road to avoid them, but he was spotted, and they ran across the road and blocked his way. He could see the building where he needed to be, and that should have been enough, he should have turned around and gone back, but he didn't, and as he tried to pass them, they started pushing him from one to another.

"Come on boys," said David, "let's be sensible."

"Oooo, la di dah, let's be sensible," mimicked one of the boys.

At this point, David tried to defend himself, but things got out of hand and he took a beating and was abandoned on the pavement, unconscious, bleeding. When he came around in an ambulance, all he could remember, apart from the fracas, was the red flash in his head as he hit the pavement, and the pain in his side as they kicked into him.

The staff in Casualty looked after him very well. He had his head, ribs and hand X-rayed, and he felt very lucky that he had not fractured his skull, or had any broken fingers, and although he had four broken ribs, they were in line and would not cause any problems and would heal in time.

He explained to the attending consultant that he had just taken his final exam to become a junior doctor and the reason he was in Leeds at that time.

"I need to get back to my lodgings," he said to the sister in charge. He had been stripped of his clothes on admission, they were in a paper sack somewhere, and she was not going to let him have them. "You will have to stay here overnight," she explained. "You have had a head injury, you will be under observation." David understood this, said nothing, but thought, *I've got to get out of here,* and sister was thinking, *he's not having his clothes back yet, or he'll be off out of here.* When her shift ended, she arranged for a male nurse to return David's clothes and to accompany him to the interview room.

David had no idea what state his clothes were in, he hadn't seen them, and being in a paper bag overnight hadn't helped.

"Oh dear," said the nurse as he unravelled them out of the bag, "you can't go in these."

"I can," said David, defiantly. "I've got to go, my future is at stake here. It's a hospital, they will have seen worse. What's my face like?"

"Not good," replied the nurse, hoping David would not go into the bathroom where the mirrors were, but he did and was truly shocked as he peered at himself through swollen eye sockets.

"What are you going to do?" asked the nurse.

Ten minutes later, a lady opened the door from inside the interview room, called his name, and David stepped inside. There was a stunned silence at the sight of him. He stood in his bare feet because his socks were missing and he'd lost a shoe, his crumpled trousers had scuff marks and blood stains on the knees, his shirt was covered in blood stains, he had stitches over one eyebrow, and under his chin, his eyes were red and swollen like two plums, one hand was heavily bandaged, and he needed a shave.

"Good morning," David said.

"It doesn't much look like it," said one of the men.

There were four males and one lady sitting behind a highly polished oak table, and after a few moments of silence one of the men indicated to David to sit down.

"I prefer to stand, sir, if you don't mind," said David. "Sitting at the moment is uncomfortable."

"What happened to you?" asked Professor Renouf, the only person David recognised.

David explained and made sure the panel knew sister had insisted on him staying in overnight and taken his clothes.

Another man on the panel asked about the injury to his hand.

"No broken fingers," David replied, "just cuts from being stamped on with a boot that had segs on the heel."

"Right," said the professor. "Let's get on with it."

Despite the headache, the smarting and the pain, David was fired up and did well. He expressed his desire to work in research with conviction, emphasising his understanding that Leeds was the place to be, and related in detail, when asked, what he had found interesting during the week's visit earlier in the year.

As he was leaving, David turned and apologised for the state he was in. "I couldn't miss this opportunity, it's very important to me, and I do scrub up well, usually."

"Thank you," said the professor, mentally pushing David out of the room, but as soon as the door was closed, whilst the others were discussing the very unusual situation, the professor was thinking, *he's on my team.*

Sitting outside the interview room were three men and a woman waiting to be interviewed, all pristine, in suits, looking as if they had come out of a tailor's shop window. They looked aghast as David walked past them, and none of them realised this person had just had an interview for the same position as them, more that he'd lost his way from Casualty.

As he turned the corner, wondering how he was going to get back to the B&B, he came across John and Jake, complete with his suit in the protective bag, and his shoes, shirt and tie in a holdall. They both stood up together when they saw him, as if someone had pressed a button to activate them.

"What in God's name happened to you?" asked John, as he looked at David's face in the professional way he was used to doing. "The landlady knocked on our room door at 7 am to say there was a call for me from the hospital. We were not aware you had not returned to the B&B yesterday evening. The hospital assured us you were all right and were insisting on going for your interview, so we just turned up with your clothes, but clearly not soon enough."

As they walked to the car, Jake shook his head and laughed, "Whatever the outcome, they'll never forget your interview, and at least they can't deny your determination."

As they were driving back to the B&B, David was looking out of the car window to see exactly where the attack had taken place. "Stop, stop," he said, "my shoe is on the wall."

Jake went to get it, and said, "Thank goodness for that, I was dreading taking you into a shoe shop, you'd have terrified the staff."

"Don't make me laugh," said David, "it hurts."

When they arrived back at the B&B, Jake telephoned Asha to explain why David couldn't meet him at lunch time.

"Tell me where you are," said Asha, "and I'll call after I've closed the shop. Is 5:30 all right?"

That was agreed, and Jake went to David's room to inform him and helped John to wash David and settle him in bed, with pillows down either side so he didn't roll over in his sleep. By this time, everything was hurting, and he was exhausted, but having sucked some milk through a straw and taken pain killers, he did fall asleep, and slept for several hours with John at his side most of the time, reading his book.

The landlady had washed David's shirt and trousers, but couldn't get the stains out, so Jake cut out the size labels from them and went to buy new ones, also socks, drinking straws and a pair of dark spectacles.

Later in the day, whilst John and Jake had gone out for their evening meal, the landlady had prepared something soft for David, because she knew he couldn't chew very well, because his jaw was sore.

"Come and join us in the kitchen," she said. "I've made you some soup, and there's some rice pudding too." She introduced the youth sitting at the table. "This is Peter, my son. Peter, this is the man I told you about who was attacked last night. Senseless thugs. Why would they do such a thing? They didn't even know him." She turned to David, "Did they steal anything?"

"My wallet," said David, "there was only a 10/- note in money, but there was the only photograph I had of my mother, who died when I was 11 and a photograph of my girlfriend, but I can get another of those." He remembered that the piece of paper with Rebecca's ring size was also tucked inside the wallet, so he would have to obtain another.

David looked at Peter and knew he was one of the youths that attacked him, and Peter knew that David knew, and was wondering, dreading what was going to be said next.

"No point in trying to understand these people," David said. "I'm a doctor driven by a desire to heal people, not break them, but of course what these senseless thugs don't realise is that they could end up in prison for most, if not all of their lives, living in a small room with bars at the window. From last night's attack, I could have ended up with a fractured skull, blind, brain damaged, my broken ribs could have pierced my lungs, they could have killed me."

Asha arrived, so when the landlady went to answer the door David said to Peter, "Is that how you want to end up? Is that how you think your mother will want to know you? Will she be proud of you? Choose your friends wisely, don't let them impact on your future."

David stood up to leave, exaggerating the pain from his effort, to make a point, and left to go to his room with Asha, whilst Peter hung his head and continued hiding his bruised knuckles under the table.

Asha was appalled when he saw David. "Are you going to be all right to do this just now?" he asked.

David closed the door behind him, so their conversation could not be overheard, he didn't want any harm to come to Asha as he left.

Asha had brought rings and diamonds for David to look at and spoke of clarity, colour, carat, settings, all of which meant nothing to David.

"Write down how much you want to spend," said Asha, "and I'll show you what comes into that category."

"All I'm bothered about is that Rebecca will like it," said David. "I want it to be a surprise, I don't want to take her shopping for a ring. I want the occasion to be romantic."

"David," said Asha, emphatically, "all ladies love diamonds, as much as the meaning behind the gift. If Rebecca doesn't like it, we can change it, but I know I can make you a beautiful ring with confidence."

David promised to let Asha have the size as soon as he possibly could. Asha wrapped a diamond in tissue and put it in a tiny box and wrote Rebecca on it, packed up and left, wishing David a speedy recovery.

When John and Jake returned, David had made his mind up to return to London the following day. He wasn't up to looking for a house, and he certainly didn't want Rebecca to see him as he was, so after breakfast, John and Jake moved on from Leeds to the village, dropping David off at the station to catch a train back to London.

He carefully wedged himself into his seat, sometimes closing his eyes, listening to the throb of the engine, or watching the raindrops picking up the hues of autumn and sliding down the windows of the carriage. Even though he fell asleep for a while, the journey seemed endless, so he took a taxi from the station to the hospital, checked to see if he had any post on the way to his room, dropped his holdall and went to Casualty to have fresh dressings on his hand.

The sister, whom he had worked alongside before, walked up to him. "You're in a bit of a mess," she said. "What's the other guy like?"

"Better than me," replied David. "Please don't make me laugh, I've some broken ribs."

"You will have to go to admin," said sister. "You will not be able to work until your hand has healed and you've had the stitches removed from your face."

David returned to his room and started to unpack his holdall where he found his wallet, obviously put there by Peter. The 10/- note had gone, but the photographs and piece of paper with the size of ring were still there, so he was able to send it to Asha.

In the two weeks David was unable to work, he spent a lot of time with Louis. They went to the National War Museum to look through records, and then went to visit places that had been bombed during the 57 consecutive nights of attack by the Germans to see how they had been re-developed. Louis hated the high-rise council developments but realised they had to be built to accommodate so many people made homeless. They visited the East End, targeted because of the docks, and the Aldwych tube station used by so many as an air raid shelter.

"Did you know they had concerts down here during the air raids?" said Louis. "And the Salvation Army and Red Cross provided warm drinks and sometimes treats for the children."

"No," said David, and wondered where he had been when all this was happening, and so glad he'd missed it. He also realised that he would miss living in London, he liked the throb of the city and there were so many places to visit, so many different things going on.

Louis pointed out architecture that David had totally missed even though he passed by it often.

"People look on the ground, or ahead," said Louis, "and there is so much more if they were to stop for a moment and look up."

"When I came to London as a boy with John, I used to lie on the pavement and look up. I'm going to miss all this," David said pensively.

"What do you mean?" asked Louis.

David realised his unguarded comment had aroused Louis' interest, so he told him of his plans. "I'm just waiting to see if I get the position in Leeds; if I don't, there will have to be a re-think," he said. When David told Louis about his interview, Louis couldn't stop laughing, and he reiterated what Jake had said, "They won't forget that in a hurry, I just hope it works out for you."

They parted company and David returned to his room, checking enroute to see if there was any post for him, but frustratingly, there was not.

During the evening, he telephoned home, as he had done over the past few days, but there was no reply, so clearly John and Jake were still somewhere in Yorkshire. When he telephoned Rebecca, he had to be so careful with his conversation and made an excuse for cutting it short, but he knew she hadn't seen John and Jake or she would have most definitely mentioned it.

Where are they? he wondered. *I'm in limbo at the moment, the only thing I can be sure of is that I will be at work on Monday.*

Chapter 38

A month later, he was sitting in the corridor near the interview room in Leeds, waiting to be seen by Professor Renouf. This time he was wearing his new suit, shirt and tie and his shiny new brogues.

"Good morning," David said, in his usual pleasant manner. He'd decided before he entered the room that he wouldn't let the professor's bullish manner throw him or make him nervous, and he remained very calm.

"You've recovered well, then?" asked the professor.

"Yes, thank you, but it took a while," replied David.

They discussed the working hours, so David understood he may have to work some weekends, that he was expected to keep his notes on his research up to date, and this would be checked on without notice and his salary.

"The starting date of your contract is 3rd January," confirmed the professor, to David's delight. "The contract is for a probationary one year, when your work will be assessed, but I shouldn't worry too much about that. If there's nothing else, you can go up and see your team before you leave, otherwise we'll see you on 3rd January. Well done on your final exam results, by the way. I'll have copies of your contract sent to you which will need signing and returning," concluded the professor, as he stuffed a fan of untidy papers into a battered brief case with a broken handle.

He's an unusual character, thought David, *he runs a tight ship, but is he worthy of the respect of his staff, or are they just frightened of him? Time will tell.*

David went upstairs and tapped on the window of the lab, and two of the team came out to greet him.

"Who got you ready this morning?" jibed one of the men, called Keith. "How have you gone on?"

"I'm starting here on 3rd January," replied David.

"Have you sorted out some accommodation?" asked Keith.

"Never even thought about it," replied David. "No point until I knew for sure I was moving to Leeds."

"The man who is leaving shares a house with me, and his room will be available. He's moving down to London. If you want to have a look, get in touch, here's my number," said Keith.

"Thank you," said David. "I'm up here for a few days, I'll be in touch."

He left the hospital and went to find Asha in his shop.

"Ah! David," he said, "come in. See what I have for you."

He removed the magnifying lens that was strapped to his head and went to the safe in the back room, returning with a small black leather box which he opened.

"I've put the diamond in a four-claw setting," said Asha, "so more light shows through the diamond."

"I don't know much about these things," said David, "but to my eyes, that is a beautiful ring."

Asha looked pleased and shone a light over the ring to show how the diamond picked up the light and glistened.

David wrote his cheque and didn't linger long because Asha was busy when he arrived.

"I'm glad to see you looking well," said Asha as he shook David's hand. "I hope Rebecca is happy with the ring, and maybe you'll be back for a wedding band."

David then took the bus to meet up with John and Jake at their B&B. They had already been to view the site they were interested in with Louis and his colleague, a surveyor, as they were travelling back from the North East, very conveniently.

"What happens now?" asked David.

"Well," said John, "that is a good question, and one we need to answer quickly, so that Louis can proceed with plans. Are we to build a house that accommodates us all, possibly including Mr Brown, or do you and Rebecca want a place of your own?"

"I think I need to speak to Rebecca and see what she thinks, but just remember we are not engaged yet. I think it would be perfect, able to care for each other as long as we have our own space," said David. "If it's urgent, perhaps you could speak to Mr Brown, he may be able to get her opinion on the matter without her realising it's a definite question. I'm going to telephone her tomorrow to tell her I am going to be moving to Leeds, so give it a few days."

"Well, when are you likely to propose to her?" asked John, impatiently.

"Do you still feel the same about her?" asked Jake.

"Of course I do," said David. "It's been difficult keeping my whereabouts and plans a secret from her."

"It was with good intentions," said Jake, "and she didn't have to see you in such a mess when you were attacked."

David showed them the ring and said the next time he was in the village he would pop the question.

"Let's hope she doesn't turn you down," said John. "Just get on with it, and then we will all know what we are doing. Why can't you go and ask her now?"

David laughed. "It has to be a romantic moment, not when she's washing up or ironing."

"What's the difference?" said John. "The question is just the same."

David replied, tongue in cheek, "Because when we are as old as you, the memory of that occasion has to be special, where we were when we agreed to spend the rest of our lives together, maybe a place we can go back and visit with fond memories."

"Right," said John, "this is what is going to happen, we hope. If the planning situation goes ahead, and whether it does or not, Jake and I are planning to rent a house up here. The long journey is tiresome, and we need to be near to keep our eye on the new build if it goes ahead. We have told Louis we will let him know if we want a house designed for all of us, or just Jake and I. Obviously, if we go for the bigger house for us all, you will need to speak to Louis, but there is certainly room on the land to build a splendid house, but not two houses, according to him. He was certainly keen on the challenge. Just putting you in the picture so you have time to think about it."

David was totally taken aback by John's surge of enthusiasm, as he sat at a dining room table surrounded by pamphlets and brochures on tiles, glass, stone, floor coverings and windows which Louis had left.

"Wait a minute," said David. "I don't have any funds for such a project."

"You'll need to get a mortgage for an amount that can be agreed on between us and the Building Society," said John. "We are not bothered, but we know you will be, so that's the way to go about it. Land up here is a lot cheaper than at home, we've made good with the sale of our land and the stone from the house, and if we hit broke we'll have to get a paper round, and you'll have to keep us."

Jake was sitting reading his newspaper when he sensed David was looking at him.

"I'm in his wake," Jake said, "he seems to have migrated into the building trade."

If John had heard the comment, he didn't react. David had worried about how John would adjust to being retired, so he was pleased to see him wallowing in his new project and was quite surprised that so much had been thought out already.

He stayed with John and Jake for the night and arranged to meet Keith, the following day being a Saturday, to view the house. The room, still occupied, looked like a cyclone had swept through, but David was assured it would be cleaned when the present occupier had gone, so he accepted the offer thinking if it didn't work out, at least he had somewhere to start off with.

He caught the train back to London, with so much to think about his mind was spinning like a top from one situation to another, but that evening he was to telephone Rebecca and tell her about his new job in Leeds. The conversation didn't go well, Rebecca was furious that he hadn't been to see her when he visited Leeds, and no matter how he tried to explain his reasoning, she wasn't listening and slammed the telephone down on him. Her father was listening, he couldn't help it, she was shouting so loud.

"What's all that about?" he asked.

Rebecca was indignant in her explanation.

"Perhaps," said Mr Brown, "David was thinking that if he didn't get the job you both would be very disappointed. Perhaps his schedule didn't allow him time or your shifts clashed, and how could he have explained why he was here without telling you about the job. Perhaps he was thinking he wanted to be nearer to you. I think congratulations would have been more in order than a tantrum. How old are you? You didn't have tantrums like that when you were five."

Rebecca ran up to her room and slammed the door, and her father knew she would be crying and feeling ashamed, but he also knew how much it meant to her to spend time with David.

That went well, thought David, feeling crestfallen. *I'll give it a couple of days, and try again.*

He had decided that if John and Jake were going to move, he had to leave St Thomas's and give himself a month to be with them and help, but none of their plans had a date to them, so he just continued in his normal routine, waiting for someone to indicate what was happening,

Two days later, he telephoned Rebecca. "Hello," she greeted him, "I'm so sorry about the other night."

"So you should be," said David teasingly, "after all I went through to get the job."

"I don't know why I behaved so badly," she said quietly. "It was so selfish."

"I bet your dad had something to say to you, if he heard you," said David.

"He certainly did, and made me feel very ashamed," said Rebecca.

They chatted for a while, and David explained that he didn't know when he would be up to visit again, but he was able to explain John and Jake's intentions of trying to find somewhere in the village to rent until they could find somewhere to live permanently, careful not to mention the new build, that was a conversation for another time.

John and Jake were keen to give as much of the work to the local community as they could but had to be convinced they were the right team for such an expensive project. They had been approached by a building contractor when they were looking at the land that was for sale, so John had asked to be taken to see work in progress if possible, and that is where they went on the Monday morning. As they arrived, a row of men were sitting on a wall eating sandwiches from dirty hands and drinking from flask cups. As their boss, John and Jake approached, they all stood up and took off their caps.

"As you were," said John as he passed, sounding like a sergeant major. *Can't believe I just said that*, he thought.

Jake just grinned at the men as he walked by.

The house they were looking at was already built, most of the work being done was inside, but the contractor took them around the whole house, going into detail, so they understood what was involved, and why some of the work undertaken took much longer to perfect. When they were ready to leave, John asked to meet the men. As each man was introduced, he wiped his hand on his shirt before shaking hands, said his name and what his skill was and how long he had been doing it. One of the men stood forward. "Sir," he said, "We're a good team, we are reliable and work hard and need the work. It's so much better than the red brick council stuff, and we'd build you a house to be proud of."

"I can see that," said John, nodding approvingly, but he was not giving anything away at that moment regarding a decision, it would not be appropriate to do so in front of the labourers, there was much to be discussed with their boss. Louis had advised him not to be too eager. "Quotes invariably come down rather than lose the business," he had said, "get everything in writing, even from me, and be sure to study the small print because that can be where any snags are. "

"Nothing more to be done here," said John to Jake, "let's get off to the Gray's. I've arranged to meet Dougy on our way home next week, if we have a new build, I want him involved, on site, if possible. We'll get a small caravan for him to live in, and we'll have to pay him a wage, but he's the man to have supervising on our behalf. When the plumbing comes into play, there will be two men on the job, which should speed things up, and he may get some work in the village when his skills are not required in the house."

"Has anyone said how long all this is going to take?" asked Jake.

"Two years was the estimate from Louis, but a lot depends on how long it takes to get planning permission to build in the first place, that is why Louis thought it best that the local men took care of that, someone they knew, and then he'll design the house when he knows what we want," replied John. "Our buyer is wanting to get on with the job, he will not wait two years, so we have to find a place to rent up here, the sooner the better."

David had given his notice at St Thomas's to leave on 30th November, which was just as well, because eventually it was established John and Jake were moving up to the village on 10th December, so everyone would be where they needed to be by Christmas.

On his last day, he took a bunch of flowers for Professor Bouvais' secretary, but she wasn't in her office.

"She's just gone into the little kitchen," he was informed, so he set off to look for her, leaving the flowers behind in case he couldn't find her. He opened the door to find the kitchen full of people he had worked with, a cheer went up and people clapped.

A colleague stepped forward. "We'll miss you, but wish you well, and would like you to accept a small gift from us," he said, and presented David with a huge card with many signatures and personal comments, and a Parker fountain pen, engraved with his name, in a gift box.

"I'm overwhelmed," said David. "I didn't realise any of you knew I was leaving. I'll think of you all when I'm writing my notes. Thank you so very much."

He shook hands with the male colleagues as they left, and gave the ladies a hug and made his way back to his room where everything was packed up in cardboard cartons and suitcases. The significance of putting his stethoscope back into its box stirred his emotions and he became emotional just as Jake arrived. David couldn't speak; he just pointed to the box.

"I know," said Jake, gently, "it's just another milestone. Our lives are not just one long journey, there are many to take us to where we want to be, and sometimes where we don't want to be if you remember."

They carried David's possessions out to the car. "We are taking this, then?" asked Jake, picking up the ironing board.

David just raised his eyebrows, gave him a look that said, "Why ever not," and walked past him with two suitcases and waited for Jake to put it in the car first, before everything else. He went and had one last look around his rooms, and they were on their way home.

Home was not as David remembered it, dealers had been in and put their marks on what they were to take, the fireplace in the lounge had already been chipped out and taken, leaving a draughty, black sooty hole in the wall, the four-poster bed had gone, which meant he would be sleeping on a mattress on the floor, the iron fireplaces in the bedrooms had gone, the oak book cases were empty and there were wooden crates everywhere. At least the cooker, fridge and washer were still there, and the kitchen table, which meant they could cook, eat and wash their clothes.

John had been sorting and packing books until he got fed up and was glad to see them and help off load David's things from the car, before he went for fish and chips.

They sat and had a glass of port together after tea and talked of the future.

"I should imagine this is what a squat is like?" commented John.

"We've lived in worse, haven't we?" said Jake, looking at David.

Things became easier and more organised with David being there. The things going into storage were in one room to go into the removal van first, things to go with them to the rented property to go in second were in another room, and David's things were to go in last.

They hadn't been to look at the house they were renting in the village; they had relied on Rebecca and Mr Brown to deal with it for them. Rebecca had checked the house had been cleaned, and with money John had sent, had been and bought two double divan beds and bedding for them.

Jake was taking his time emptying his desk and chest of drawers, and then he decided to wax them, which irritated John for no reason David could see, so he decided to take himself off along the coastal path. The wind was chasing the clouds across the sky on this cold December afternoon, and he could hear the boom of the waves hitting the rocks much further on. The tide was in right up to the path, so there was no beach to walk along. He reached the jagged rocks, and was covered in the salty, foaming spray, so he moved along and sat on a wall gazing out to sea. He remembered how he felt the first time he saw the ocean as a young boy, he was afraid of it then, now he respected it. He closed his eyes and inhaled the salty air before he walked back slowly, remembering his birthday parties and picnics, and taking Bill and Dora to see the ocean for the first time in their lives. The old fisherman had died, the old house would be gone, new houses were to be built, so much was changing. He felt in a few years the place would be unrecognisable, and he just hoped it wouldn't lose its charm.

He stood at the bottom of the steps and looked up at the house, silhouetted black, against a darkening sky.

I can't imagine the skyline without it, he thought, *but soon it will be gone.*

He climbed the steps to the house but didn't look back, and he never walked the path again.

Two days later, Dougy arrived. He was to stay until the dealers had been to collect their purchases.

David was so pleased to see Dougy, who was accompanied by a beautiful black dog with a wavy coat.

"How long have you had him?" asked David.

"About 6 months," said Dougy. "He was only a pup, ambling along in the middle of the road in a remote part of the countryside. I've no idea how he came to be there, but I stopped and gave him a drink of water; he snuggled up to me and whimpered. I couldn't leave him, so I put him in the passenger seat and he's been with me ever since."

"What's his name," asked David.

"Bat," replied Dougy.

"Bat," echoed David, in a disbelieving tone, not sure if Dougy was teasing.

"What?" said Dougy. "He's black all over, and he did have pointed ears before the curls grew."

Jake had been to Fay's to collect a chicken casserole for their meal, and David, Dougy and the dog walked to her house in the evening to return the dish and spent an hour with her. As they left, she became tearful. "Will I ever see you again?" she asked David.

"You'll be coming to the wedding, I hope," he replied.

"Ooh!" said Fay, "When is it?"

"I haven't even proposed yet," replied David, "but it's going to be a couple of years probably, plenty of time to save up for a posh frock and hat."

"The children are paying for me to have a telephone installed as a Christmas present," said Fay, "so I'll be able to talk to you from time to time."

"That will be perfect," said David, blew her a kiss as he walked down the path and waited until she had gone inside and locked the door.

"She's been like a mother to me," he said, "and although I went away to university and London, she knew I would always be coming home, but this time it's different for both of us."

Dougy chose to sleep in the van with Bat. "I think it's more comfortable than in the house," he said. "It's like being in an echo chamber, and it's no warmer. I'll see you in the morning."

The following day, the removal van arrived early and was loaded in good time because there was order in the way things had been prepared, and they left the village ahead of John, Jake and David. They packed their personal files and brief cases and some bedding into the car, John spoke to Dougy, Jake had a last look round the house, whilst David sat in the car with the engine running.

This must be gut wrenching for them leaving the home they were born in, thought David. *It's bad enough for me.*

The two brothers got into the car. "Right," said John, "off we go." Jake said nothing.

David drove slowly up the lane, glancing briefly where he used to meet Ted, past the school and out of the village. No one spoke for a long time, lost in their own thoughts and memories. Eventually, when they pulled in at a roadside cafe for something to eat, David let John or Jake lead the conversation and was surprised it focused on the future with no mention of the past.

Far more pragmatic than me, thought David.

When they had left, Dougy busied himself and removed the stained-glass windows from the front and back doors, chipped away and removed a one-piece stone archway from over the door that led to the back garden, some stone from the garden wall, and the 'looby loo' toilet door. His plan was to incorporate these in the new build if it was possible. He made himself something to eat, fed Bat, and then wandered round the house checking the list that John had given him, making sure he knew where everything was, who was collecting it and who needed to pay. He settled down for the night on the mattress in the kitchen where he would hear if anyone was about up to no good, but the night was uneventful, and he was up and about when the first people came. Some dealers seemed to know each other, and money was already changing hands for the beautiful carved bed heads. They joked amongst themselves, helped each other out lifting and securing their purchases, and even the contractor who had purchased the house was helping Dougy out and watching to make sure nothing was taken that shouldn't have been.

"When are you actually leaving?" he asked Dougy.

"As soon as they've been to read the electric meter and cut off the electricity and the telephone," replied Dougy, "and I hope it's sooner than later; it should be today."

"This is my number," said the contractor, "ring me before they cut off the phone, and then I can come down with my men; we need to get as much lead away as possible before somebody decides to help themselves."

Dougy agreed but used the telephone in the village on his way out, so the contractor didn't see what he'd put in his trailer and was well on his way when the men arrived at the house.

A week later, John and Jake were settled in their rented house but found it very strange. The whole ground floor, which was a kitchen and living room was not as big as the kitchen they had left, and it didn't help that David's things were scattered about in boxes. John was very excited about the gas fire and how quickly the room heated up.

"No grate to clear out, no ashes, no wood to chop, no need to keep an eye on the coal situation, wonderful!" he said to Jake.

They took themselves off to the Gray's home for Christmas, so David had the house to himself and could sleep in a bed instead of on the sofa.

On Christmas Eve, Rebecca was working, so David took Mr Brown into town to do the shopping. He wheeled him around the market to buy vegetables and fruit, and they stood and listened to the Salvation Army band playing carols by the Christmas tree in the square.

"I used to come here and pick up the scraps from the stalls," said David.

"I remember," said Mr Brown. "We gave you a lift home once, if you remember."

"I do," said David. "That was the year my ma died, and they took me away."

"You've done all right, despite all that," said Mr Brown. "Let's go and have a coffee."

At home, they unpacked the shopping, wrapped last minute presents before Rebecca came home and decided to go to the pub.

A man, sitting on a stool at the bar, unshaven, his stomach hanging over his belt from consuming too much of something, kept glancing across at David, so he asked Mr Brown who he was.

"You'll remember him," said Mr Brown. "It's Tom, and he's still got attitude problems. He's been in prison for grievous assault, but it didn't make a blind bit of difference. It's the drink, sometimes he's black and blue from falling over."

David went to the bar for drinks intending to ignore Tom, but he tapped David on the shoulder.

"Are you that David," he asked, "thi mother wor a tart?"

There was a flash of red in David's head, and for the first time in his life, he wanted to punch someone, but he took a deep breath and stayed calm.

"Sorry," said David, "who are you?"

"Tha knows who I am," replied Tom, "don't pretend tha doesn't know me. Don't you want to talk to me, does tha think thi summat special?"

David turned away to walk back to Mr Brown with the drinks, but Tom grabbed his arm, so David put the drinks back on the bar, looked Tom in the face, and asked, "What do you want to say to me?"

"I just said," replied Tom, "does tha think thi summat special?"

The landlord, used to Tom, realised he was firing up, and intervened. "He is special," he said. "He's made good, he's a doctor."

Tom sat upright, blinked a few times until he could pull the words out of his frazzled brain and pulled up his trouser leg to reveal a festering ulcer on his shin. "Fix that, then," he said. "Let's see 'ow good ya are."

David was horrified, the ulcer was not dressed and was in contact with congealed blood and pus on the inside of Tom's dirty trousers, and the smell was too familiar to David.

"You need to go to hospital with that," said David. "You need to go home, clean yourself up, have a shave, put on some clean clothes, and see if someone will take you."

"Are you sayin' I'm mucky?" responded Tom, clearly not understanding the point David was trying to make, so he tried again, saying every word slowly and emphatically. "If you don't have that seen to immediately, you could lose your leg, or worse. Do you understand what I'm saying?"

"I'll take him," said a man listening to the conversation.

David quietly said to the landlord, "Don't let him have another drink, this is serious."

The following day, David called at the pub to see if Tom had actually gone to hospital.

"I'm afraid not," said the landlord, "unless he took himself off, which I doubt. I'm expecting him to turn up here within the hour. The gentleman who offered to take him ran him home, so he could get washed and changed, but he sat outside in the car waiting. Half an hour later, he peered through the letter box and Tom was there, still in his outdoor clothes, spark out, snoring his head off. The man couldn't rouse him, so he called in here to let me know and went home."

"I can't get involved," said David. "I leave the village in a few days, and in any case, he needs to see his GP. If I could suggest that the best time to discuss it is before he starts drinking, but that's hardly the thing to be saying to a landlord."

The landlord smiled. "It's fine," he said. "We should look out for each other, but Tom is a law unto himself. He's never been the same since his parents passed away within a month of each other."

He'll be joining them, David thought but didn't say it and felt quite sorry for Tom. He remembered Tom's father hitting him with his belt, and now, as an adult, David was able to reason that Tom became a bully because that was all he knew.

Rebecca was working over Christmas as she had done in the past, having committed herself before she realised David would be around, but he and Mr Brown made a roast chicken dinner and steamed Christmas pudding to have with brandy butter. David and Rebecca washed up and cleared away and snuggled up on the sofa and watched TV whilst Mr Brown fell asleep. Eventually, he woke up and reminded Rebecca she needed to be up at 5 am to be ready for the car that collected her for work when there were no buses, so David took the hint and went back to John and Jake's house.

Rebecca worked Boxing Day and came home and made one of her favourite meals, bubble and squeak, and used up the chicken that was left. She had leave from work until 3rd of January and was looking forward to spending time with David, who had been at home most of the day getting his things together to take to Leeds, and prepared a meal for John and Jake, who were on their way back from the Gray's.

Chapter 39

David and Rebecca packed David's belongings into the car and set off for Keith's house. As promised, the room had been cleaned and smelt of fresh paint. Rebecca made the bed up, hospital fashion, whilst David carried everything else up to the room, including his painted jugs from the boat and his little table from Dora.

"Did you need to bring these?" asked Rebecca. "Where do you want them?" She remembered seeing them in David's room when they had stayed at the old house.

"I like them near me," he said, "and John will not be tempted to throw them out. These are precious, given to me by people I cared for and who cared for me."

"What about this tin?" Rebecca asked, rattling his memory box.

"Be careful," David said. "Bring it here."

They sat on the bed and he opened it. Rebecca was curious. There was a shell, one he'd picked up the first time he went on the beach, a car from his first Christmas cracker, a spoon he'd found at the cottage, a piece of blue john rock from his visit to the caves with the Gray's, a black plastic Scottie dog brooch that was his mother's, photographs of horses, Ted's note, various other bits and pieces, and right at the bottom was the toothbrush Rebecca had given him.

"Remember that?" he asked her.

She sat and thought for a while. "Surely that isn't the one I gave you when we were at school."

"It surely is," he replied. "That's why it's in my memory box."

Rebecca's mind flashed back, remembering the undernourished little boy who had nothing, and she had understood why these things in his box meant so much to him. She had another look before she closed the lid and put it in a drawer.

When they left, the room was ready for David to move in to. He drove into Leeds and took Rebecca to see where he would be working and to have a walk around the city for she had never been to Leeds apart from when she went on the train to meet David for the garden party.

Might have made a mistake here, he thought as Rebecca became very enthusiastic with the shops and department stores.

During the days prior to New Year's Eve, they spent time together walking and calling on Rebecca's friends and were invited to several New Year's Eve parties.

"How are you going to choose which one to go to?" asked David. "It's tricky." He was prepared to do whatever Rebecca wanted; she knew these people, he didn't.

"Better not go to any," she said. "Can't just you and I do something?"

"I doubt we will be able to book a table anywhere decent for a meal at this late hour," said David, "but I'll try."

He'd no intention of trying, he had something else in mind if they were not going partying and were going to be alone.

On New Year's Eve, he had tea with John and Jake and sat and chatted with them about what the new year would bring.

"Have you managed to approach the subject regarding you and Rebecca living in the new build with us? Louis needs to know what he's doing regarding the plans," said John, urging David to deal with it.

"I'm going to propose tonight, all being well," said David.

"Thank goodness," said John. "Are you taking her somewhere romantic?" he asked, with a hint of sarcasm in his tone.

David just laughed and wagged his finger at John.

David had a look at the ring before he left for Rebecca's. He sat and talked to Mr Brown for a while and whispered his intention when Rebecca went upstairs.

"Fancy a walk?" David asked her when she returned. "It's cold, but it's clear. We can call in the pub on the way if you wish."

"A walk is fine," she said, "we can hardly go to the pub, there will be people there who are going on to the parties we've declined to go to. We'll see the New Year in with Dad on TV when we come back."

There was no frost, but the sky was cloudless, jet black, there was a huge moon and thousands of stars.

"We'll go on the wood top," said David, "there's less light pollution up there. Louis said to me not long ago that people should look up more and see what's above them."

"That's when you trip up because you are not looking where you are going or bump into things," said Rebecca. It's going to be very dark up there."

"We'll see," said David. "I've brought a torch."

They stood looking at the moon, which seemed so much closer now.

"It feels like I could almost touch it," said Rebecca. "It is beautiful. I wonder if there is any life out there? It's so quiet here. I used to come up here with my dad and the dog, and we would sit and watch the farmer in the valley below, and I knew every type of tree in the wood. The stinging cold air was making Rebecca shiver. "Shall we make a move? I'm feeling cold."

David stood at the back of her and wrapped his arms around her and whispered in her ear, "Marry me."

There was a pause when nothing was said, and then Rebecca moved away from him. "You took your time," she said. "I really need to think about it."

David knew she was teasing, and a moment later, she flung herself at him. "I thought it was never going to happen," she said, "I've been waiting so long. Come on, let's go home and tell Dad."

David produced the ring box, opened it and shone the torch on it. "Oh my goodness!" Rebecca said, as he slipped it on her finger. "It fits too."

They kissed, hugged each other tight, and stood looking at each other. "Are you happy?" asked David.

"You've no idea how much I've longed for this moment," said Rebecca.

By the time they had reached home, she had planned the wedding. David just smiled as she bounced on happy clouds and let her roll on with her plans. This was not the time to be realistic.

She bounded into the house, where John and Jake were sitting enjoying a glass of port with Mr Brown.

Rebecca took off her gloves and wiggled her finger, so they could see the ring

Hugs and kisses and congratulations all around, and eventually Mr Brown said, "Make a cup of tea for us."

Rebecca put the kettle on and went to the fridge for the milk and found a bottle of champagne with a white ribbon round it.

"You knew," she said and just went all giddy. "I like champagne."

"Yes, I remember," said David. "Shall we open it at midnight?"

"No, open it now," said Rebecca, "it's three hours to midnight."

"I'll be in bed by then," said Mr Brown.

"So will we," said John, "and it will be the first time for many years I'll not be called out."

Rebecca and David stayed up and watched the New Year celebrations on TV and stood on the doorstep and listened to the church bells chiming and the laughter and chatter of revellers.

"The moon is behind the clouds now," said David, looking up.

"But it came out for us," said Rebecca. "I think I will always think of tonight when I see the full moon."

"We'll go out and celebrate, have a nice meal somewhere, the first Saturday you are not working," promised David, as he kissed her goodnight and left.

Rebecca sat on her bed and looked at her ring, pondering whether to wear it in bed or not. She put it back in the box and put it under her pillow.

The following day, David called with the car to pick her up. "Get in," he said, "I need to show you something."

They drove through the village, David stopped the car on the main road, and they stood and looked upon the plot of land that could become their home. Unusually, Rebecca didn't say anything, she didn't know why they were there.

When they were back in the car, David said, "There are two important things to discuss now. The plot of land we have just looked at is where John and Jake are hoping to build their new home. Before Louis designs the house, he needs to know if he is designing a house for just John and Jake, or for us to be included so we all live together. From what I gathered from Louis, he would ensure we all had our own space, and I trust him with that, and if we don't agree with what he has done, we can object when we see the plans. I want you to think about it, but you must let John know as soon as possible so he can contact Louis."

"Gosh!" said Rebecca, taken aback, sitting quiet for a while deep in thought, then asked David, "How do you feel about it?"

"It's to be our home, Rebecca, we have to agree whatever we decide," he replied.

"But we don't have any money, David," she reasoned.

"The question is, would you like us all to live in the same house?" said David. "But since you asked, I think it's a good idea."

"Well, so do I," said Rebecca. "Who wouldn't want to live in a new house? And I would be near enough to look after dad."

David was aware that John had suggested that Mr Brown may want to move in with them, and that was to be considered in the instruction for the plans, but it was not for David to mention, things could work out differently.

"You said there were two things to discuss," said Rebecca, "so what's the other?"

"You are not going to be happy about this," said David, "but it's going to be 18 months to two years before we can get married."

Rebecca groaned and put her head in her hands. "WHY?" she asked.

"Because we've nowhere to live, and we need to save up to buy furniture," David replied.

"Can't we live at my house?" she asked.

"Hardly," said David. "Think about it. I'm going to drop you off at home now, so you can discuss things with your father, but it's imperative that you let John know of your decision as soon as possible."

Rebecca was returning to work after her break for the 2 pm shift, so David would not see her again until the following morning when they all got together and had a detailed discussion before it was agreed that they should share the house.

Mr Brown had already told Rebecca she should not turn down this opportunity. "You'll be near enough to me," he said, "and I know I'm the reason you may hesitate. Most children fly the nest one day, it's something we have to accept as parents."

David walked Rebecca to the bus stop as she went to work, and then took the rest of his belongings to Leeds to settle in and prepare to start his new job the following day.

Rebecca chatted to her friends about the festive season but kept her news secret. The only jewellery they were allowed to wear when working were wedding rings, so she kept her secret until they all went out for a meal, then she wore her engagement ring, said nothing, and wondered how long it would take for someone to notice it. Not long. Rebecca's friends were all nurses who had started their training together, they were always supportive of each other and were thrilled for her. She was the last of the group to have a relationship, some were married with children already.

"He's quite a catch," said one of the girls. "How have you managed to net him in?"

"Because I'm irresistible," responded Rebecca, happy to engage in all the banter, sarcasm and innuendo hurled at her. She kissed her ring and smiled.

Mid-April brought the big excavator trundling through the village like a big yellow dinosaur to begin the process of digging out the trenches and moving and levelling earth for foundations and pipes to be laid. John, Jake, the contractor and all the workmen were there, waiting, watching the beast as it made easy work of its task, and there was a palpable sigh of relief that the project was beginning. The wall which ran along the pavement had been knocked down and the stone stacked to be used for the dividing wall to the adjoining property.

Flags had been laid to accommodate the caravan that Dougy was to live in, so it was stable and didn't sink when the ground became softened and was ready for when he turned up later in the day.

Jake had walked round the cul-de-sac and posted letters to each house apologising for the disturbance and noise inflicted on them during the work. Mr Connor, who was to be their next-door neighbour, screwed his letter up and threw it back into the field. He had been the only person to object to the plans, and he was there all the time, complaining, sending for the building inspector, who had to follow up on each complaint. There was never anything untoward, but he dutifully turned up with his clipboard, inspected whatever the complaint was about and sent a follow up letter to Mr Connor.

"Time waster," he commented one day to Dougy. "He'll go mental when you are working inside and he can't see what you are doing."

The summer was kind to them as they progressed, and work only had to be laid off because of snow for a few days during the first winter, and they were working inside when the second winter approached.

Dougy had put a sign in the newsagent's window offering his services as a plumber and was kept quite busy as word passed around the village, but when he was required in the house, it took priority, always.

Jill came every other weekend, leaving the children with her family, bringing clean clothes, towels and bedding, arriving Friday lunch time and returning Sunday afternoon, and occasionally one of the men would stand in for Dougy, so he could go home and see his children.

If there was a social evening or concert in the church hall, they would go with other members of the construction team, maybe invited back for supper and liked the feeling of being in the village.

David was enjoying his work and took every opportunity to do extra hours for extra money. Rebecca stuck to her usual routine of shifts, running the home and looking after her father, and while she was looking forward to living in the new house, she fretted about her father being on his own. She was given the task of choosing things for the kitchen and drew a plan with one of the joiners to ensure the fridge was not fitted against the cooker, and there was plenty of cupboard space. She knew the big kitchen table from the old house would be coming out of storage and wondered how it would fit in with modern formica units. She had insisted on only one shelf, her take on it was that things on shelves get greasy and need cleaning all the time, far better off in cupboards. The floor was to be covered in a product she hadn't heard of called vinyl, and she was able to match it to the colour of the worktops.

"I hope I've got it right," she said to her father. "What if they don't like it?"

"Compared to what their kitchen was like in the old house, they can't not like it," replied her father, "they asked you to do it because they had confidence in you. John and Jake wouldn't have known where to begin."

"The joiner sat with me, and we worked through it, he was very nice and patient," said Rebecca.

The arch over the front door was placed having been engraved by the mason with the name WILLOW. John wasn't too fussy about having a name at all, so Jake chose it because it was the name of Jed and Betty's boat. He'd always liked the name. *It's a good name for a house to spend the rest of your life in,* he thought. The door had been made to incorporate the stained glass that Dougy had saved from their old house, and the stone arch he had saved was built over the gate that led down the side of the house into the garden. All this was done whilst John and Jake were away visiting the Gray's, so Dougy was excited when he knew they were back in the village and would be visiting the project. He stood back, out of view, watching for their reaction. It was good. John and Jake were overwhelmed that Dougy had thought about doing it. "I just thought you had spent all your life in that old house, this would be a link to it for you," explained Dougy. "I'm glad you're happy about it."

"Indeed, we are," said John, feeling quite emotional. At the beginning of the project, John had a surge of enthusiasm and involvement, but now he was feeling jaded by it all and just wanted Willow to be finished and to be settled in. Jake was calmer and took every day in his stride. David and Rebecca talked about their wedding plans but couldn't name a date yet. Mr Brown just carried on as normal, but was enjoying the company of the brothers, and he had not thought too much about how his life was going to change when he was living alone.

The single-storey part of the building had almost been completed when Jake decided to take Mr Brown inside the house. The entrance door, the doors to the three large rooms off to the right, and to the bathroom at the bottom of the passage were all wider than normal. Louis, aware that they were considering asking Mr Brown to move in with them, drew his plans to accommodate a wheelchair and have all the doors in the passage the same, to maintain a uniform look.

The rooms had been plastered and were drying out. There were boxes of tiles on the bathroom floor waiting to be stuck on the walls when the plaster had dried, timber was cut and laid out for wardrobes to be fitted, with strips of skirting board alongside the walls cut to size, there was the luxury of a radiator in each room beneath the window, and in one corner a toilet and washbasin to be concealed by a cubicle.

"What a splendid idea to have a toilet in the room," said Mr Brown.

"Louis got an award for his design for a care home," explained Jake, "and I think some of it rubbed off here, but he says it will be much better for us as we get older. Better to have it done in the original build than have to make alterations later."

The rooms were large so John and Jake could have their own space, not only as bedrooms, but with their desks and armchairs and personal things.

"Sanctuary," John would say when talking about them.

They went into the third room, identical to the other two.

"Is this to be Rebecca and David's room?" asked Mr Brown.

"No. No," explained Jake, "if you remember the plans, next door is the kitchen, then the lounge, and their accommodation is over the garage and up another level."

Back home, the two men sat and had a cup of tea and talked about Willow.

"It's certainly been a massive undertaking, and it's kept the village enthralled," said Mr Brown. "I think you should have an open day when it's finished," he joked.

"I'm going shortly," said Jake, "but before I do, there is something I want to say to you. The third room is for you if you feel you could come and live with us all. You've seen that you can manage there, and I think you should consider it seriously. We know it would make Rebecca happy, but we have not discussed it with her, the decision has to be yours."

"It would be wonderful," said Mr Brown, "but I don't have the funds to engage in such a project. I'll have to decline."

Jake knew he was a proud man, he had discussed this situation with David, and they came up with a plan.

"How about if you moved in," said Jake, "and paid rent for your room like you do here? That would help with the running of the house. You need to think it over, and discuss it with Rebecca now, but I think we both know what she will say without hesitation."

He was right, the minute her father mentioned it, she was planning the move. She had been so worried about leaving her father on his own, she didn't want him to be lonely and was anxious about his health, although since John had looked into things and had him put on a different medication, he had been much better.

"By the way," said Mr Brown, much later in the evening," I almost forgot, your mother telephoned to invite you and David to dinner next Saturday."

"That's not going to happen," came the expected reply, and as far as Rebecca was concerned, that was the end of the conversation.

It was not.

"Rebecca," said Mr Brown, in a stern tone, "she's still your mother, she wants to meet her future son-in-law, she will be his mother-in-law, and if you have any children, she will be their grandmother, and you WILL invite them to the wedding when it happens. A mother dreams of going with her daughter to choose her wedding dress, and she will be denied that I've no doubt."

Too true, Rebecca thought, but knew better than to say it.

"Well, I'm working next Saturday," said Rebecca, "and in any case, I need to see what David has to say on the matter."

To Rebecca's annoyance, David was fine about it.

"Your mother was kind to me," he reminded her. "You have a mother, mine will not be at my wedding, she died knowing she was leaving me in a sorry state, I'd give anything for her to be here with me now."

Rebecca's heart melted, and they arranged to go.

Three weeks later, Rebecca was in her bedroom getting ready to go to her mother's house for the first time ever for dinner.

"Tonight will be challenging," said Mr Brown quietly to David.

"Yes, I've realised that," David replied, "but at least it's happening."

Mr Brown smiled. "She's capable of changing her mind even when you've rung the door bell," he said.

David smiled back and thought, *I hope he's joking.*

Rebecca's mother was standing by the window when they arrived, she went to the door to welcome them, and although she longed to give Rebecca a hug, she resisted, knowing Rebecca would recoil from her, and she wasn't going to give her the opportunity.

Mr Wade came to greet them, took their coats and invited them to join him in the lounge until the meal was ready. He shook David's hand and just said, "Hello," gently to Rebecca. "Congratulations!" he said. "Belated, I know, but we are very happy for you and have champagne to toast your good health and happiness."

Whilst Mr Wade poured the champagne, David gave Rebecca a sly nod, knowing she was capable of refusing, so she accepted the glass and said, "Thank you."

David chatted to Mr Wade, and Rebecca sat and listened and had a good look around the room until her mother appeared to tell them dinner was ready. She could have set the table in the splendid dining room and used the best dinner service and cutlery, but she didn't, instead she set the table in the kitchen and served a chicken dinner and rice pudding with a nutmeg skin. Over the years, she had become very good at giving dinner parties to entertain Mr Wade's colleagues and their circle of friends, but this was not the night to show off, she knew it would irritate Rebecca.

Since she had left Rebecca and her father, she had only seen Rebecca by chance, in passing, never by arrangement, but she had never missed sending presents and cards for Christmas and birthdays, and when Rebecca was 21, she sent a generous cheque, but it had never been cashed. She telephoned Mr Brown now and again to see how they were doing and was genuinely saddened to learn he was in poor health and had to give up work.

Rebecca sat and watched and listened to Mr Wade, and he was not the man she had made him to be in her mind, he was good-humoured, quietly-spoken and although he didn't approve of the way Rebecca had behaved with her mother, he tried to engage her in conversation. He saw her looking at a photograph. "That's

Dorothy," he said, "with her husband and our 4-year-old grandchild, Rosie, and we will have another one shortly."

"I need the bathroom," said Rebecca, "and then I think we had better make a move."

Her mother took her upstairs and asked her to join her in the bedroom when she had finished in the bathroom. Rebecca didn't want a mother-daughter conversation, but she did want to see the bedroom so she went in. Her mother walked towards her with a tiny box in her hand. Rebecca stared at her and put her hands behind her back, her mother ignored her and held the box out for Rebecca to take.

"Your father gave me this on our wedding day," she said. "I think it's right that you should have it."

Rebecca opened the box to find a single pearl pendant on a silver chain, and she recalled her mother wearing it from time to time. She accepted it and said, "Thank you" meekly. Her mother looked at her, hoping, but the hug didn't happen.

On the way home, David spoke to Rebecca about her behaviour. "There's a side to you I have not seen before," he said. "Why are you so brittle with them?" Your dad has forgiven her, why can't you? Life is never just black or white, there are many shades of grey in there too."

"Has dad forgiven her?" Rebecca flared back. "Or did he just get used to it?"

"I'm leaving you at the door," David said. "I have no wish for this conversation to continue, it will turn into a quarrel over something that really has nothing to do with me."

He kissed her 'good night' and walked away, turning to blow her a kiss, but she'd gone.

Little madam, he thought.

Chapter 40

David was enjoying his work, the spot checks on his work and notes were approved, and a year down the line, his contract was renewed, and he became a permanent member of staff. He'd worked hard and thought he was doing all right, but it still came as a relief when it was confirmed.

He and two other colleagues would accompany Professor Renouf on to the ward where patients were having treatment on trial drugs, purely out of interest, just noting success or failure, always accompanied by the patient's consultant. It was his way of teaching them to always question why they thought the drug worked or failed, and to speak to patients to glean first-hand information was very useful. They attended post mortems to observe the effects illnesses had on the human body, and because David had worked in theatre, he was not distressed by what he saw and just found it very interesting, whilst one of his colleagues passed out and never attended another.

David couldn't help comparing Bouvais with Renouf. Everyone wanted a chance to work with Bouvais, but people backed off from Renouf. David just wanted to learn, so he decided to ignore Renouf's acerbic manner and impatience and always dealt with him in a quiet, calm manner. It didn't go unnoticed. *He's taking me on,* thought Renouf, quietly amused. David always remembered to call him Professor, or that would have lit the blue touch paper.

When Rebecca was working the night shift over the weekends, David stayed in Leeds and went swimming or to the cinema or sometimes spend the whole day, if the weather was good, walking along the canal towpath. Keith now had a girlfriend and David felt she preferred him not to be in the house when she was, which was often. Out of ear shot of Keith, she had asked how much longer he would be staying, so he was never comfortable with her and tried to stay out of their way as much as possible.

Two months later, the ground level part of Willow was completed, John and Jake moved in, and everything was delivered from storage. The big kitchen table had to be delivered through the kitchen window before the glass went in, and it did look strange amidst all the new units, but John insisted. "Too much history there, it stays."

Rebecca and David were out for a walk and called to see how John and Jake were coping. Rebecca showed them how to use the new oven and wrote some notes down for them to follow.

"Where's Rebecca?" asked Jake, having made cups of tea for them all.

"Being nosey, I expect," said David.

She reappeared. "I've had a brilliant idea," she said, excitedly. "Why don't we go and buy our bed? You can use what will be dad's room until our side is finished. We can collect your stuff in one trip if two cars go, and you can get away from that awful girl. Dad will not move in here until we are married. You will have to get up earlier than you do now for work, but that's how it will be when we live here, so you will be used to it by then."

The three men looked at each other in silence, knowing full well that was exactly what would happen, and it did.

When the bed was being delivered, Jake and Rebecca were stood in the doorway directing the delivery men, when there was an almighty clatter from the other side of the wall, a horrendous piercing scream and panic moaning.

"Oh my God, woman, what have you done?" they heard Mr Connor yell.

Jake and Rebecca hurried round to assist.

"Send for an ambulance," Jake instructed Mr Connor, glancing down at the bone sticking out of his wife's leg.

Rebecca went straight into the house. "Where are the clean towels?" she asked.

"Excuse me," said Mr Connor, "I can't remember inviting you in the house."

"Oh, shut up!" said Rebecca impatiently. "Clean towels, where are they? Do you want your wife to bleed out?"

The bone in her leg had snapped and pierced through the flesh, and her elbow was injured. Jake covered her leg with towels to soak up the blood and stem the bleed, and he manipulated her arm as gently as he could to try and ease the pain from her damaged elbow.

"What were you doing?" asked Jake.

"That stupid fool had me standing on the ledge to see what you were doing," she said tearfully.

"You'll need to pack a bag for her," Rebecca said turning to Mr Connor.

"What do you mean?" he asked.

"Nighties, dressing gown, underwear and toiletries, she will not be coming home for a while," Rebecca informed him.

When the ambulance arrived, Jake stood and explained Mrs Connor had, what he suspected was an avulsion fracture of the elbow and a compound fracture of the tibial shaft.

"I want a professional opinion," said Mr Connor in his usual belligerent manner but was totally ignored by the men attending to his wife, for it was clear Jake knew what he was talking about.

Connor hadn't packed a bag for his wife, so the ambulance left him standing on the doorstep wondering what to do, but eventually he left to go to the hospital, and when he had gone, Jake was about to throw some buckets of water over the wall to wash away the blood.

"Don't," shouted Rebecca, "he needs to see that, he needs to realise what he caused."

When Rebecca was working, she visited Mrs Connor and soon realised what an intimidated, lonely little lady she was and felt sad that her husband was her only visitor.

"My mother made me marry him," she confided. "He pulled the wool over her eyes and mine too, but he changed his act very quickly once we were married. I wasn't allowed to see my friends or go anywhere alone again, and he wouldn't consider having children, so I've had no company at all.

"We'll be secret friends," said Rebecca. "I'll pop 'round when the blunderbuss is out."

Mrs Connor laughed. "That's a good name for him," she said.

Rebecca had never met Jess, Keith's girlfriend, but had taken a dislike to her because of the way she had treated David, so it was an uncomfortable meeting which became much worse.

David had spent the night with John and Jake, so he was able to drive the small car over to Leeds with Jake driving the estate car, and during David's absence Jess had been into his room, stripped the bed, taken all his clothes out of the wardrobe and drawers and laid them on the bed.

"Did you do all this before you left for work yesterday morning?" Rebecca asked David, knowing full well that he hadn't.

"No," replied David, sensing an eruption, "but it's ok."

"No, it's not," said Rebecca and turned to Jess. "You did it, didn't you? You had no right to come into this room. Who gave you the key?"

"I just thought it would help," Jess said as Keith appeared to see what the raised voices were about.

"That isn't answering my question," persisted Rebecca. "Who gave you the key to David's room?" She then turned to Keith, "Was it you?"

"No," Keith replied, taken aback. He looked at Jess.

"Well, I just thought it would help," said Jess in a voice like butter through a hot crumpet, blinking her doe eyes at him.

They continued loading up the cars, with Jess still lingering, totally undaunted by the previous confrontation.

"Where are the canal boat jugs?" David asked.

Rebecca knew she hadn't seen them either, so she turned to Jess, "Where are they?"

"Oh! I didn't realise they were yours," came back the reply. "They are in the garage, I'll get them."

Rebecca followed her, retrieved the jugs and David's reading lamp. She noticed other things were packed in boxes and covered over, and as Jess walked out in front of her she had a sneaky peep under one of the covers. Keith's house had been his mother's, and from a very brief glimpse, Rebecca felt these boxes held what had probably been her treasures, possibly some of value.

When it was time to leave, Jess was first out of the door to see them off. Rebecca hung back and grabbed Keith's arm to delay him.

"Do you go into your garage?" she whispered hastily.

"Not really," replied Keith. "I don't have a car, and actually, I can't find the key."

"She's got it," said Rebecca. "Honestly, you need to keep your eye on her."

On the way back home, Rebecca spoke of her suspicions that Jess was up to no good, and that David should have a word with Keith about what she was up to in the garage.

"You're like a little terrier when you get going," jibed David. "I'm glad you were not snapping at my heels."

Rebecca wagged her finger at him. "Lesson to be learnt," she said. "Don't mess with me."

When David moved into Willow, he was able to spend more time with everyone, including Dougy. They arranged to take the girls to the ballroom in town for a special night out. There was a live band and singers in a steamy room full of young people enjoying themselves, and it would have been wonderful for them if any of them could dance, but neither David or Dougy had been to a dance before, and Rebecca and Jill were not much better, but they shuffled around, had a laugh and decided to have lessons after the wedding.

During the journey home on the last bus, Jill told Rebecca that Dougy was not looking forward to the completion of Willow. "He's liking life here in the village," she said, "and I quite like it too, but all our family are close to where our home is now."

"Why don't you move up here permanently?" asked Rebecca.

"We'd need somewhere to rent," replied Jill. "I honestly don't know if Dougy is looking."

"I could ask dad to have a word with our landlord," said Rebecca. "You could move into our house after our wedding. Mention it to Dougy. It needs a fresh coat of paint everywhere, I haven't been able to keep up with that, but the house is clean."

"How many bedrooms has it?" asked Jill.

"Two," replied Rebecca, "and you can get a double bed in both, with some drawers and a wardrobe, and we have a bathroom."

"We'll need three bedrooms" said Jill.

"The two girls could share," reasoned Rebecca.

"No, we'll definitely need three," said Jill, making a gesture over her tummy. "I haven't told him yet."

"You had better do," said Rebecca, "or he may rent the wrong house."

Jill and Dougy left David to see Rebecca home, collected Bat and took him for a romp in the little park nearby. Jill decided to tell Dougy her news as they sat on the swings, realising what Rebecca had just said to her was important. Dougy was elated, never daunted by the prospect of a big family, and it seemed that was the moment when they decided to find a place in the village.

When Dougy realised who the landlord was, he approached him, having done some work on his properties in the past. A landlord knows the benefit of having a skilled tradesman in his house, and two months later, Dougy was offered a house.

In all his spare time, he worked in the house, improving the plumbing, re-arranging the lay out, replacing the two splintered sash windows, remembered to have the chimney swept before the plastering was done, and painting all the woodwork inside. Six weeks later, with a great deal of voluntary help from various people he had worked with on Willow, it was ready for the family to move into, and although he still stayed in the caravan until Willow was completed, he felt happy and settled.

David was pleased Dougy had made the move, there was such a strong bond between them, he was near to hand, and Rebecca and Jill had become friends. David had joined the local hockey club and there was a social side to that which he and Rebecca enjoyed, and although he got on well with his work colleagues, Leeds was difficult to get home from after a night out, so they avoided it usually.

Time passed, and David became aware that there was a clear up operation taking place around the house. When he returned from work that evening, the contractor and Rebecca were waiting for him in the kitchen, along with John and Jake.

Rebecca ran towards him. "It's finished," she said excitedly. "We are going to have a look."

She had chosen the bathroom suite and tiles, carpets, colours for the walls, units and worktop for the small kitchenette and wall lights for the lounge. She and David had decided not to keep checking on the progress, and although there had been moments when they were tempted to take a peep, they did not, so this moment was very special to them as they followed the contractor and walked slowly through what was to be their home. Rebecca held David's hand and burst into tears.

"What's wrong?" he asked.

"I can't believe how lucky we are," she said. "It's just perfect, and we can plan our wedding now."

They returned to the kitchen and she ran and hugged John and Jake and gave them a kiss.

John noticed she had been crying. "Is everything all right?" he asked.

Tears started to roll down Rebecca's cheeks as she gulped out, "I can't find the words to describe how I feel right now." She turned to the contractor as he picked up his hat to leave. "It's wonderful, I'm so happy," she said.

David walked him to the door and shook his hand. "Thank you so much," he said. "You should feel very proud of your team, it's an amazing house."

"I do," said the contractor. "Your uncles put their trust in us, and I think we have honoured it. It was not only guaranteed work for the men, but it gave them the opportunity to fully use their skills and has generated a lot of work for us, and yes, we are all very proud with the finished house. Just the flags and the turf to be laid at the back and we are done."

Rebecca was off the starting blocks, she had planned every detail of their wedding, written it all down in her 'planner', and proceeded to work her way through it.

They had a meeting with the vicar, who was slightly taken aback because they wanted to get married at 9:30am, but David explained they would have to be leaving at noon for the honeymoon, so it was necessary to have the early service.

One of Jake's hobbies was calligraphy, so Rebecca had been with him to choose some unusual paper, given him a list of guests to be invited to the wedding and left him to it.

She had seen a wedding dress in the window of a shop in town and hoped it had not been sold when the sale came around, because although she had money from Bertha which she had saved 'for that something special' she was not going to pay full price for a dress to be worn for just a few hours. On the morning of the sale, she went into town early and sat in a chair in the corner of the shop whilst 2 other brides-to-be were choosing their gowns. She watched as the girls interacted with their mothers, who were emotional every time they came out of the changing rooms, and just for a moment felt a pang of something, remembering what her father had said about mothers and daughters choosing their wedding dresses, and just for a moment, she questioned her behaviour. The girls seemed to be trying every dress in the shop on, and when the assistant went towards the one she liked, she stood up and said, "Is it possible there is somewhere I could go and just try this on? I have to be somewhere."

She struggled in a small cubicle, with the assistant's help, and it fit perfect, and within half an hour, it was wrapped in tissue, with a bouffant veil, and she left the shop, leaving the two girls still floating about making their minds up.

David soon realised that their wedding was not going to conform to what was considered normal, and apart from insisting on the early service, he left Rebecca to it.

269

As time passed, working full time, organising the wedding and getting their home ready was beginning to take its toll, Rebecca was bickering over very little, and when David tried to calm her down, it made her become awkward or tearful, so Jake intervened eventually.

"I believe you have a long weekend coming," he said, "Stella has telephoned to say the professor will be over, and she wondered if you would like to visit them and have lunch. I think you should go, have a break from all this and have a nice day out."

The day Rebecca and David visited Stella and the professor, they first called to collect their wedding rings from Aysha. "We're on our way to see your brother," David informed him.

Aysha paused for a moment, "Oh! Bouvais you mean, he's actually not my blood brother. We lived next door to each other as children and have remained friends ever since. His mother died when he was young, and his father died just before he went to university, so we took him in, and sold his house to friends of ours. Lots of people think we are brothers, but we don't mind that."

David smiled to himself. He had assumed Bouvais was also Jewish and had been puzzled as he had often seen him enjoying a pork pie and pickle in the hospital restaurant. Puzzle solved.

Bouvais was relieved to hear David was enjoying his work so much, they discussed what he had been working on and, of course, pending married life.

Rebecca and Stella were talking weddings. "We're really looking forward to it," said Stella. "Bouvais has been working long hours with hardly a break, and he's tired, that's why I insisted on having this cottage, a place to come and re-charge his batteries, well away from Zurich."

Mid-afternoon the air became oppressive, dark clouds were gathering on the horizon, and the cattle in the field had gathered in a corner and were lying down.

"There's a storm brewing," said Stella. "That's why the cows are lying down."

"You've become very rural and knowledgeable," said the professor, teasing her.

David and Rebecca decided to leave for home as the rain threatened.

"See you in church," said the professor as he opened the car door for Rebecca and handed her an envelope containing a cheque as a wedding gift. "It's a cheque, better you buy something you really need." He stood at the gate with his arm around Stella's shoulder as they drove away, a completely different persona to his professional one.

Heavy drops of rain started to splat and ping around them, so Stella hurriedly took the tray of crockery and glasses through to the kitchen and washed up, and by that time the rain was pounding down.

"Where are you, darling?" she called, turning into the passage towards the door. "For goodness' sake, you've left the door open, everything is getting soaked." She ran towards the door to close it, and could see Bouvais still sitting in the wicker chair, and she was consumed in a cold, ominous feeling, her heart racing, and although she knew at that moment he had left her, she ran to him and checked his vital signs, but there was nothing in response, she knew she couldn't move him, so she covered him in the plastic tablecloth, went into the cottage, dialled 999 and returned with his golfing umbrella. When the ambulance arrived, accompanied by a police car because it was an unexplained death, Stella was sitting at Bouvais' side, soaking wet, shivering, holding his hand and leaning on his shoulder, beneath the umbrella.

The policewoman walked towards Stella, fighting her own emotions when she saw the pair huddled beneath the umbrella. "Let the medics deal with things," she said gently, "and we'll go inside and get you dry and a change of clothes." She led Stella into the house and made a cup of tea whilst Stella changed her clothes. "I'm afraid I have to ask you some questions," she said, "and there will have to be an autopsy."

"It's so sad," said Stella. "He saved so many people's lives, but he couldn't save his own."

The police woman looked puzzled.

"He was a surgeon," continued Stella. "Our home is in Zurich. What am I to do?"

"Is there someone I can call for you?" asked the police woman.

"Not today," said Stella. "I'll do it tomorrow, today I need to think about what has just happened here, I need to scream and cry and beat my fists against the wall and sleep and wake, hoping it has just been a bad dream."

The following day, she telephoned and spoke to John knowing David would be at work. She arranged to send a letter to David written in green ink to identify it but addressed to John and asked him not to give it to David until he had returned from honeymoon. "I will be returning to Zurich," she explained, "and will not be attending the wedding, and I will leave it up to you when you tell them."

"Had he been ill?" asked John.

"Not that I know of, just very tired lately. I'm thinking pulmonary embolism to take him so quickly, we'll just have to wait for the result of the autopsy," replied Stella.

"Give yourself time to grieve," said John, "don't compress it, and remember we are here for you if you need us. Please let us know when the funeral is."

"I want to live here and have him buried in the local church yard, so I can take flowers and talk to him, so it may be some time before it can be arranged, and I'll have to go back to Zurich to sort everything out. So much to do, I'm totally drained. I'll just have to deal with it all, there's nothing anyone else can do."

John sensed the panic in Stella's voice.

"Are you alone there?" he asked.

"Asha's wife is on her way over and will stay until I go to Zurich. Sorry to start your day with bad news. Goodbye."

Chapter 41

The week before the wedding was hectic. Both Rebecca and David finished work on the Wednesday when David collected Fay from the station in Leeds. She was so happy and giddy to see everyone and be shown round the house, but she hadn't been in the house long before she put on her apron and asked, "What's for tea?"

"We're going to the pub," said David. "You're going on my stag night with me," he joked. Fay was to bake ten apple pies the following day, and she had been travelling all day, so they were not having her cooking dinner but instead had a wonderful time at the pub catching up on the news from where they used to live.

Mid-morning the following day, Monique, Jean and Louis arrived. After lunch, the men went for a walk and Monique and Rebecca sat peeling and coring apples for Fay and helping where they could. They made jellies in red, orange and green, in little round wax dishes for the children and put them in the garage to set.

When the men returned, John chose to have a word with David. "Stella has telephoned from Zurich, regrettably they will not be able to attend the wedding," he said.

"Something important must have cropped up for them to have to go back, it's such a shame, they were so looking forward to it," said David. "Rebecca will be so disappointed."

John chose his moment whilst there was a room full of people chatting, so David was distracted from the conversation, thus avoiding questioning John further.

Whilst David was trying to have a conversation with Monique in French, Rebecca took Fay up to her room and showed her three boxes with letters attached to them for John, Jake and her father, and asked her to put them in their rooms when she and David had left for their honeymoon.

"There's a bedside lamp for each of them, and we've both written our own letters to all of them," explained Rebecca, "and this is our thank you to you," she continued as she gave Fay a tiny box, containing a brooch with two blue and turquoise glass dolphins rising out of a silver hoop.

"I think David thought of you as a mother figure," said Rebecca. "I know he loves and respects you. He told me how hard you worked to keep your family together, doing the best you could for them when you lost your husband. We hope you like it and will wear it, not just keep it in the box. Also, remind Jake to take my posy to David's mum's grave. I have not said anything to him, but I feel that is where it should go."

"I will," said Fay, moved by Rebecca's thoughtfulness, "and thank you so much for the brooch, I don't know what to say."

"Saying nothing is good," said Rebecca, "as long as you are happy."

"I am happy, just seeing you and David and John and Jake settled," said Fay. "I did have concerns about John and Jake when they left for a new start somewhere else, especially for John because he had spent his entire life in the village, whereas Jake had travelled away from home for a few years, but now I see them in their lovely new home, and it makes me very happy. The brooch is beautiful, I will wear it, and the sentiment behind it is deeply appreciated."

They returned to join the others, and Rebecca whispered to David, "Can you take me home now and bring my suitcase back for taking away with us?"

"What's wrong with tomorrow?" David asked.

"I'm spending tomorrow with Dad," Rebecca replied, "I need to make sure he has enough food in to last until Dougy moves him across to Willow on Wednesday, and help him pack up, although he has done very well so far."

Mr Brown was sitting in his chair watching television, wearing his new shoes, his new suit and ironed shirt hanging from the cupboard door handles, the contents of his wardrobe draped over the sideboard, surrounded by cardboard boxes containing the contents of his cupboards.

David sat on the sofa waiting for Rebecca to get her suitcase from upstairs. "Been tidying up?" said David, grinning at Mr Brown.

"I'm amazed at what I've found," said Mr Brown. "It's all in the boxes for Rebecca to sort out when she has time."

"Are you feeling ok about the move?" David asked.

"I'm deeply grateful to John and Jake," said Mr Brown. "They ooze human kindness; I cannot thank them enough for opening their home to me, and I know Rebecca is happy about us all living together."

"I think it will be a happy home," said David. "We all have our own space when we need it. I owe John and Jake so much, the only way I can start to repay them is by caring for them as they get older, and I will. I think Louis had that in mind when he made the doors wider for their rooms—it will be like 'care in the community' if you all end up in wheelchairs. Dodgems!"

Mr Brown laughed. "It's a possibility," he said, peering at David over his glasses.

Rebecca appeared with her suitcase. "Time to go," she said to David. "I'm getting married in the morning, I'll have you know, and I hope he realises what a lucky man he is having me for a wife."

"I'm sure you'll remind him constantly," said David as he got into the car. He wound the window down, blew her a kiss and winked. "See you in church," he said and drove away.

When he returned to Willow, everyone was busy doing their own thing in preparation for the wedding. Monique couldn't believe she was pressing her dress on David's old ironing board that she used when they were at Cambridge. He sat and chatted with her as he polished his brogues.

Fay cooked a special meal for them of roast pork, apple sauce, stuffing balls, mashed and roasted potatoes, cabbage and carrots and a thick onion gravy and Yorkshire pudding especially for Monique to try.

Rebecca and her father had fish and chips out of the paper they were wrapped in and shared what was left in the packet of fig biscuits, washed the two forks and beakers up and sat together on the sofa.

"I've just been thinking," said Rebecca, "that when I leave for church in the morning, I will be leaving the house where I was born and have lived in for all of my life for the last time."

"That's true," said her father, "and it will be the same for me when I move out on Wednesday. It's all about looking forward and not back. I can't say I'll be sorry to leave, but I never ever thought I would."

They spent a while blowing up pink and white balloons and tying them with ribbon for the children after the ceremony.

Rebecca snuggled up to her dad and they chatted away until bed time, remembering so much of their time in their home. There were good times and bad times, but she and her father had dealt with all the challenges after her mother had left.

"I wish Bertha was here," said Rebecca, pondering on how much she had relied on her and how patient and understanding she had been. *She'll be here in spirit,* she thought, *she paid for my dress.*

Mr Brown had hoped the day would come when Rebecca married and was happy in her own home, but although he never spoke of it, he dreaded the time when she wouldn't be bouncing into the house, chatty, enthusiastic, grumpy, moody, but mostly full of fun. It was no longer a worry.

At last, thought Rebecca as she went downstairs to make some toast and tea the following morning, *it's my wedding day.* She looked out of the window to check the weather, the sky was clear and blue, and she was praying it would stay that way because she had organised the reception to be outside at Willow.

Everyone staying at Willow walked to the church, posed for photographs and took their places inside. Still outside, David and Dougy stood shaking hands with John and Jake at either side of them when David noticed a man standing in the shop doorway opposite, watching them. He wore a brown suit and waistcoat, a brown trilby and a red neckerchief. In a strange way, David felt his presence unnerving, but his thoughts were soon diverted as Dougy ushered him into the church.

A wedding in the village was always a special event, and despite the early hour, the church was full of people in their finery. Rebecca had lived her whole life in the village, and by now, almost everyone knew who David was and were fascinated. Those who knew him well knew he was emotional. He sat waiting for Rebecca telling himself, "Don't cry, don't cry, smile."

Mr Brown had seen Rebecca's dress, but he hadn't seen her in it, so he was quite overwhelmed when she walked down the stairs into the room. She looked stunning in her guipure lace dress and bouffant veil, her hair draped over her shoulders. "Will I do?" she asked, trying to avoid a tearful encounter. Her father hugged her, "No one could have had a better daughter, I'm so very proud of you," he said.

"And no one could have had a better father, we're a team, Dad, and I love you," she said.

Mr Brown's friend arrived to take Rebecca and her father to church in his pristine Triumph Herald car, bedecked with white and pink ribbons to match the flowers in her posy, looking very dapper in his suit and wearing a chauffeur's cap he had borrowed for fun. The box with the balloons went into the boot to be given to the children after the ceremony.

Jake and Mr Brown's friend helped him up the steps and took their places in the church and left Rebecca and her father having their photographs taken. If Mr Brown was in any pain, he didn't show it, no one was to deprive him of this proudest moment as he walked slowly down the aisle with his daughter on his arm.

David turned and smiled at Rebecca and stunned with emotion, tears trickled down his cheeks. Dougy nudged him and handed him a handkerchief. Rebecca's mother was crying also, so Dougy looked at David and whispered, "Is this a wedding or a funeral?"

The vicar heard and laughed, David took a deep breath to calm himself, turned and held his hand out to Rebecca. From then onwards, they were lost in the moment, exchanging their vows as if there were just the two of them. After the register was signed, they made their way out of the church for the photographs. During this time, David glanced across to the shop doorway and made eye contact with the man still standing there, watching, raising his hat in acknowledgment. *It can't be*, thought David, *it just can't be.* He decided to walk across and have a word with the man when there was a moment, but the next time he looked, the man was gone.

A pretty little girl ran to Rebecca with a silver horseshoe with some lucky white heather on it. Rebecca crouched down. "Thank you," she said, "that's lovely. What's your name?"

The little girl looked coy. "Rosie," she said and turned to run towards her mother. When Rebecca stood up straight, she came face to face with Rosie's mother, it was Dorothy Wade.

"Hello, Rebecca," she said. You look stunning. Congratulations, I wish you a long and happy life together."

"Come on to the house with mum and your dad," said Rebecca, "we may have a moment to catch up." They didn't, but Rebecca's mother was pleased they had been included with the guests.

When it was time to leave the church, the photographer having finished, Monique gave out the balloons to the children, and everyone set off walking along the high street like a carnival procession, towards Willow, and as they neared the house, they could see smoke rising from beneath an awning and smell bacon cooking.

This was a risk Rebecca had taken considering the time of day they would be eating, so she had decided to have a wedding breakfast in real terms.

Tables and chairs had been set out in the garden, and the caterers were cooking bacon and sausages and had trays of eggs to cook for anyone who wanted one. Fresh bread rolls and tea cakes had been delivered by the bakery, and on each table were serviettes, cutlery and bottles of brown and red sauce.

Fay's apple pies were warming in the oven, and there were two glass jugs full of cream to serve with them.

Rebecca was so relieved to see everyone enjoying their food and having a good time chatting and laughing, but she suddenly realised the children were missing so went to look for them. As she approached the house, she could hear laughing and couldn't believe her eyes when she walked into the kitchen. An unfamiliar John was there, with his shirt sleeves rolled up, twanging his braces, telling a story as the children sat and ate their bread rolls with a sausage smothered in red sauce. He had lined the jellies up in rows like traffic lights, fairy cakes were piled onto a three-tier cake stand, and each child was wearing a hat made out of serviettes. Rebecca clapped, blew John a kiss and left him to it, realising his agenda, 'to stop them running riot with so much red sauce about'.

She made a point of mingling with David's work colleagues, noticing Keith had come on his own, and she felt pleased about that. At one point, she came across Jill wiping dripped egg yolk off Dougy's shirt. "He's worse than the children," she said. Dougy, ignoring the remark, reassured Rebecca they would take good care of her dad on Wednesday, and that she was not to worry. He covered the drip mark with his tie and walked away, whilst Jill just shook her head.

David had walked up to the top of the garden, sat on a step and watched his guests. He felt as if someone was close to him stroking his head, even though he knew there was no one there, and he closed his eyes until Fay joined him. "Are you all right, David?" she asked.

"Just having a moment," he replied, not wanting it to stop.

"Everything is packed up in the car now," said Fay.

"Thank you so much for all your help. When are you going home?" David asked, putting his arm around her.

"Tuesday," she replied. "John and Jake are taking me to Howarth to the Bronte Museum tomorrow. I became fascinated with the Bronte sisters when the children were studying their works at school, but I never thought I would actually visit Howarth. I need to thank you for the lovely brooch, it means a lot to me and I will wear it."

The caterers brought out the wedding cake to be cut, so David tapped a glass to quieten the guests.

"There is only to be one short speech," he said. "My wife and I (whistles, cheers and clapping,) want to thank you all for joining us to celebrate our marriage. Everyone here is special to us for so many different reasons, and now I'd like you to raise your glasses in a toast to my beautiful wife, Rebecca," who grinned and blushed as they did.

Mr Brown stood and said, "To the happy couple, with love from us all."

"To the happy couple," the guests echoed and clapped.

Dougy read a carefully worded telegram from Zurich.

David tapped his watch when he caught Rebecca's eye.

"I'll just be 5 minutes," she said, and she took two pieces of wedding cake and walked round to the Connor's house, knowing they were sitting outside. They had been invited but declined, and as soon as Rebecca turned into their drive, Mr Connor got up and went into his house, but his wife stayed put and held out her hand to Rebecca. "You look beautiful," she said. "I love your dress. I hope you have a happy life together," and Rebecca knew the depth of feeling in her wish. She whispered, "I'll come and see you when I get back, it will be easier now I'm living next door." She said farewell and left, and as soon as she had turned the corner at the bottom of their drive, Mr Connor threw the cake onto the floor, stamped on it and threw it in the dustbin. His wife was hurt but not surprised that he should be so petulant, but she didn't give him the satisfaction of a reaction, she had a secret, a friend, Rebecca.

Dougy brought the car round from the garage, a row of tin cans clattering and scraping on the road, and a JUST MARRIED sign fastened to the back bumper. After a lot of handshakes and hugs, they were on their way, disposing of the cans and sign once they were out of the village.

"Are you going to tell me where we are going now?" Rebecca asked.

"No," replied David, "just sit and be quiet, wife, you'll have to wait and see."

Rebecca had no idea where they were when David turned into a country lane and took a sharp left turn into a gravel yard with wooden buildings, and then she saw the canal boats as David stopped the car.

"Stay here, I won't be long," he said.

It's not Paris, then, she thought. *Crikey! If we are going on one of these it's going to be interesting.*

David returned with a bunch of keys and drove down the narrow lane to a boat called 'Happy Days'.

"Here we are," he said, holding the car door open for Rebecca.

"It's a big boat," she said. "Can you drive one of these?"

"I hope so," he teased. "Climb on board and I'll pass you the luggage."

She stood in the middle of it all until David returned from parking the car, just looking at the canal stretching like a black ribbon ahead of her.

David had walked along the canal towpath in Leeds and had the opportunity of being invited on to a refurbished boat, so he knew what to expect when they went below, but Rebecca had no idea, so was very surprised to find it was like a little house with a kitchen, a shower room, two bedrooms and an area with padded seats fastened to the wall and a small dining table. David took the luggage and cool box with food in that Fay had packed below.

"Can you manage to unpack?" he asked. "We need to get going. I've booked a table for us at the Barge Inn for this evening. The blue case has the bedding and towels in. If you need a hand with the bed, leave it until later."

"I think I've made up enough beds in my time to be able to manage, thank you," retorted Rebecca, in a brittle manner. She was anxious that they were responsible for such a big boat, and when it started to move, she gasped, but David seemed fine with it, and he'd arranged the trip, so she said nothing more and just got on with the job at hand, unpacking. After a while, she heard David calling her. They were just about to arrive at the first lock, so he felt it was important for her to understand the process. This lock had a keeper, probably because it was the first lock to be encountered by boats from the hire company. She listened and watched, startled as the big oak gates groaned opened and the water rushed in to raise them to a higher level, and as soon as they were on their way, she returned below, said nothing, just wondered.

David got the impression Rebecca wasn't impressed by his choice for their honeymoon but decided to give it a few days before he asked her what she thought.

They enjoyed a lovely meal at the inn. Prawn cocktail, steak with onion rings, chips and vegetables, and death by chocolate pudding.

They took their time walking back to the boat, and although neither spoke of it, both were feeling a little nervous as they climbed into bed. David held Rebecca close and whispered, "This is our time, I love you so much."

Rebecca closed her eyes and whispered back, "I love you too."

They lay together learning about each other with respect and tenderness, a special time they would never forget.

The following morning, Rebecca was awakened by what sounded like a xylophone, but when she sat up, bleary eyed, realised it was David stirring the coffee he had made. He popped his head round the door. "Come up," he said, "and be very quiet and still."

She put on her dressing gown and joined him. He pointed to his eye, and then to a bush a short distance away. Suddenly there was a flash of blue and orange as a kingfisher dived into the water for its breakfast. Rebecca didn't say anything, just pursed her lips into an "Ooh!" and mouthed 'beautiful'. The silence was broken by a flight of ducks and Canadian geese deciding to hold parliament by the boat, darting, quacking, splashing, such a racket, and then they left as quickly as they had appeared.

As the days passed, they saw herons and dragonflies, there were water hens scuttling about below the banking, and one day, two swans were gliding by with six grey, fluffy cygnets chirping away, and Rebecca was overwhelmed by their size and grace.

"They mate for life," David informed her, "and can live a long life, 20 years or so. A pen, flapping her wings to protect her nest, could break a human limb. It's said that when one of the pair dies, the other one dies soon after of a broken heart."

Rebecca was so impressed by how much David knew about the canals and the wildlife. He pointed out the marks made by the stone masons that had built the canal and talked about the industries using the network of canals for trade, tea from India, fruit from the Mediterranean, and even timber from America.

After a few days, Rebecca was enjoying the tranquillity and the different interesting aspects of the holiday, and when they telephoned home on the Wednesday to make sure her father had moved into Willow as planned, David was pleased to hear her say, "Loving it, Dad, absolutely loving it. I didn't think I would when I saw what we were doing, but it's peaceful and beautiful, David has been amazing handling the boat and the locks, and the weather has been wonderful."

David smiled but said nothing.

Spoke too soon about the weather, she thought, as they were awakened during the night with the rain pounding on the roof of the cabin.

David found two hooded waterproofs in a locker, and they proceeded into the grey world, along the canal that was no longer smooth but dimpled by heavy rain drops. The wildlife was hidden and silent, the only sounds were the drip, drip, dripping and splashing of rain from the trees, and the gurgling of little streams running from the embankment into the canal. Occasionally, a duck would appear, quack and flap, and retreat to its shelter again. The rain was unrelenting, so they were both glad to have reached their mooring for the night, have a hot meal and a shower and were soon snuggled up in bed.

The following morning, the landscape was eerie, a moody mist hovered until mid-morning when the sun came out and shafts of sunlight found their way through the tall silver birch trees again, making silver patterns on the water. The weeping willow trees were wonderful to observe, raindrops reflecting like gems, glistening as the sun caught their tears dropping to the ground, and the cool air smelt of wet grass, a totally different ambience to previous days.

David and Rebecca had been into the town to buy groceries and were on their way back when David noticed a familiar stack on a boat moored further along the canal, and before he could say anything, Rebecca said excitedly, "Look, a boat called Willow."

The man, standing on his boat looked round. "Good afternoon," he said.

"Is this your boat?" David asked.

"Yes," replied the man, "we hired it for many years, but the owner died last year, his family didn't want it and offered it to us. We live in it most of the summer, we love the life. Did you used to hire it?"

"No," replied David, "when I was a small boy I lived on it, it was my home for a while, a working boat."

"Really," said the man, keenly interested, and he and David chatted about the routes and cargo and business closures as the road and rail took over. David declined the offer to have a look round, he wanted to remember it as it used to be with Jed and Betty, but glad it was still afloat, maintained and loved by someone.

They bid 'farewell' and David braced himself, anticipating the barrage of questions that were to ensue, and they came thick and fast.

Although Rebecca was taken aback, she didn't speak until they were out of earshot of the man, then she pushed David. "You cheat," she said. "There was I, thinking how clever you were managing to handle the boat, and your knowledge of the wildlife and the history of your surroundings, and you've done it all before. I didn't even know you had been on a canal boat before, why didn't you tell me?" She fired questions at him one after the other.

"Stop," said David, "no tantrums. I was going to confess when the holiday was over. Tonight, when we have eaten, I'll tell you all about it. Now we will get under way and find some bulrushes for my jugs which came off Willow when Jed sold it."

"So that's where they came from," said Rebecca. "I understand now why you would want to keep them."

Having eaten, they went outside to enjoy the evening with a bottle of wine and two glasses, but within minutes, they were back inside, having realised they were on the menu for the midges' dinner.

David propped himself up in a corner and Rebecca lay with her head on his knee as he related all the details of his adventures to her and explained why he had never spoken of it. Every now and again, Rebecca would sit up, wide eyed, and ask a question, or comment, "Really," or "Goodness me."

David finished his story by saying, "Then I met a girl who was kind to me when I was young, she gave me half her orange or her apple core at school, gave me cream to put on my chapped legs and bought me a toothbrush one Christmas, and I fell in love with her and married her." He stroked Rebecca's hair. "It's turned midnight, time for bed," he said.

Rebecca went to the shower room and returned brushing her hair and smelling of toothpaste. David held his arms out to her. She walked towards him, pinched his cheeks between her fingers and thumbs, kissed him and said, "You should write a book, David, you really should."

The End